Bluebird Rising

Also by John DeCure

Reef Dance

Bluebird Rising

John DeCure

 ST. MARTIN'S MINOTAUR ♋ NEW YORK

www.minotaurbooks.com

Library of Congress Cataloging-in-Publication Data

DeCure, John.
    Bluebird rising / John DeCure.—1st ed.
        p.   cm.
    ISBN 0-312-27308-8
    1. Public prosecutors—Fiction.   2. California—Fiction.   3. Surfers—Fiction.   I. Title.

PS3604.E49B58 2003
813'.6—dc21

                                                    2002191968

First Edition: December 2003

10   9   8   7   6   5   4   3   2   1

Acknowledgments

Thanks to Paul S. Levine for his continued professional guidance, to Benjamin Sevier for his patience and expertise in editing this book, and to my wife, Cynthia, for her unwavering belief and support.

Thanks also to the Honorable Gail Andler for helping steer me past a bureaucratic roadblock and into the State Bar's Office of Enforcement for a terrific five-and-a-half-year ride; Gail, your wise handling of a sticky hiring situation helped make this book possible. In an opposite vein, a hearty, extra-special no-thanks to former Governor Pete Wilson for ending that ride in such hollow fashion; you put the lame in "lame duck," Mr. Wilson. (Although I suppose you unintentionally helped make this book possible too.)

Bluebird Rising

One

The lawyer who represents himself has a fool for a client.

This old saying is something of a proverb for the state bar prosecutors in my office, we attorneys who make a living cracking down on our own fallen brethren for their acts of professional misconduct. It has to do with ego, when you're talking about those who defend themselves on their very own, a kind of arrogance you develop from being so close to the problem for such a long time that you no longer realize that *you* are the goddamned problem. Now, a few of these do-it-yourselfers I run up against are just hard-luck broke and have no choice but to go it alone. Another small contingent is of the pragmatic skinflint variety, the guy trying to save a few grand on a trip down the regulatory rapids that he just knows is going to result in a good soaking anyway—and if you think about this for a minute, it makes some sense, especially if, like me, you're the prosecutor sending the poor bastard over the falls headfirst. But the saying best fits the swell-headed fool who simply thinks he knows better than anyone else how to lawyer a case because, hell, he is a lawyer.

I believed I was looking upon just such a fool.

His name was Eugene Podette, and it was Thursday afternoon. February 1994. The city of Los Angeles was still recovering from the big Northridge shaker that had hit in January. As everyone knows by now, earthquakes are a part of life here, something you learn to deal with, or at least tolerate, over time, like the seasons of drought and canyon wildfires, the crime, and the constant influx of new arrivals to California, all of them hungry for a piece of something that may no longer even exist. But this quake had been a bad one even by L.A. standards, flattening freeway overpasses and tossing homes off their foundations like a bored kid swiping at his toys. What with the riots—I mean, the social unrest—of '92 still fresh in the city's collective consciousness, these days folks were not just talking about packing up and getting out, as some invariably do after every major disaster. People were actually leaving.

But bailing never crossed my mind—Southern California is home to me.

On that particular Thursday afternoon I was standing before Judge Herbert Renaldo in state bar court, just finished with my closing argument. Thanking the judge, I stepped away from the wooden podium as my red-faced opponent shuffled in, eyes bulging, probably wondering what he would have to say to convince the judge that the state bar had entirely the wrong picture of him. That he was not, as the bar's young prosecutor alleged, a Bible-thumping law boy who'd bilked his congregation out of close to four hundred thousand bucks in a phony fund-raising scam for the guarantee of a heavenly new church he had no intention of ever building. Eugene Podette glanced behind him to the gallery, where his wife, Trixie, sat alone. Trixie was wrapped in a soft pink sweater, her lip quivering under a pile of permed curls, but she held her chin up like a prizefighter at a weigh-in, showing the judge that her solidarity with Eugene could never be in doubt. Eugene gave Trixie the nod, but he lingered and seemed to study the space behind her, a row of vacant gallery seats. I saw in his sweaty white face a look of longing as he stared into that emptiness, too, the look of an astronaut floating helplessly into deep space when his lifeline has been cut. He was probably wishing he had a string section back there right now, I figured, anything to help him as he made his final plea for leniency in the *Matter of the State Bar of California versus Eugene Vern Podette, Respondent.* But he was on his own.

With some cases, you just don't know how the judge is going to call it, but this one felt solid. The trial had glided along swimmingly thus far. I'd offered into evidence the forged title documents for the proposed building site, the letter of intent from a make-believe millionaire donor pledging to match dollar for dollar every last greenback raised for the project, and the bank records showing Podette's methodical embezzlement by way of sizable "project expense" withdrawals at carefully timed intervals. Three hundred and ninety grand of the half million raised, all gone. My handwriting expert had nailed all the document issues shut—thank you, no further questions.

And how about the testimony of the Reverend Jimmy Joe Kavner, the good preacher who'd had the guts to finally start asking questions about Eugene's scam? In a word: sweet. My best move, perhaps, for Reverend Jimmy Joe, in his shiny green suit a size too small but plenty big in the lapels, had dusted the short brown bangs off his short, worry-rutted forehead and offered a teary-eyed display that put a human face on Podette's misdeeds. Nobody's fool, Jimmy Joe had queried Eugene about the shrinking bank balance and inexplicable delays in starting the construction. The Lord works in mysterious ways, Eugene told him. "Well, c'mon, he's not *that* mysterious," Jimmy Joe had retorted. Renaldo clucked appreciatively at that one, and I could've kissed the good reverend for leveling the judge with a stink-eye that said, What, you think this is funny?

I sat down and poured myself an ice water from the beaded pitcher on the table like I was pouring it straight into my veins, enjoying a tingly, self-satisfied little minirush. On the bench, the old judge ran his hand across his mouth to conceal an escaping yawn, but hell, he wasn't going to worry me with an absent gesture or two. Judge Renaldo had gotten the message. Eugene Podette had earned himself a permanent vacation from the practice of law.

The podium stood directly between the two tables for the opposing lawyers, so I had to look straight left to see my adversary. I usually don't give them the satisfaction when they're talking, and Eugene was no exception, but the skin at the base of my neck prickled the way it does when something inside me senses an encroachment. So I risked giving the bastard the satisfaction and turned my head. Podette's meaty lips were parted in hungry anticipation, as if he knew what he was about to say would get a rise out of me. But his cue-ball dome and witless frown reminded me of Curly from the Three Stooges. If this was a stab at intimidation, it had fallen short. Should have got yourself a lawyer, Eugene, I wanted to tell him. You might have had a chance.

Then Eugene Podette straightened his tie a little, cleared his throat, and made his move. "Your Honor," he said in that droopy fashion of his that mirrors his posture, "beggin' your pardon, but I've got a . . . rather special request." The judge nodded. "As you know, I'm here representing myself. Well, I'm doing my best and all, and it hasn't been easy, to say the very least. Mr. Shepard here, he is a worthy adversary"—a nice hand gesture floated my way— "but, Your Honor, I am a humble man, and I am finding it harder and harder to discuss the case, you know . . . this whole . . . terrible misunderstanding, without getting all . . ." He sniffled like he was holding back the flood.

"Go on," the judge told him more gravely than I would have liked. "Unless you would like to take a break."

A break—from that transparent act? I wanted to say, Christ, Judge, give *me* a flipping break.

No thanks, Podette told Renaldo, he would boldly shoulder on. "But I do have one request, Your Honor. I would like for my wife to have the honor and privilege of addressing the court, that is, on my behalf." He sighed with deep feeling. I felt like I was locked in a B movie.

"Very well," Judge Renaldo quickly agreed. I didn't like that he had not even asked me if the bar had an objection. Typically, only the lawyer of record may speak, which in this case was Eugene alone. But, I wondered, what was the harm? Renaldo knew he would be giving this guy his walking papers soon enough. Maybe the judge was just humoring him in the meantime. Under the circumstances, this was not so unreasonable. I eased back in my chair and sipped my ice water, for lack of anything better to do, then made a mental note that sometimes I have to remind myself to be a more gracious winner.

Trixie Podette, Eugene's wife, rose and took her husband's place at the podium, but before she began, the courtroom door moaned and cracked open and a tall, slightly disheveled-looking man in a rumpled suit stepped in. The man shared a brief, puzzled glance with me, the way an old, unfriendly acquaintance will look at you with surprise and regret at the same time if your paths should cross by happenstance. Then he took a seat near the door.

"Good afternoon," Judge Renaldo said with some anticipation. "Are you related?" Eugene Podette craned toward the back with what-the-hell befuddlement.

"No, Your Honor," the disheveled man said. "I'm here to . . ." He stopped as if to rethink what he was saying. "I'm just watching."

"I see," Renaldo said. "The public is always welcome to view our proceedings." He flashed his big, crooked yellow teeth in a big, crooked smile. "Welcome, sir, welcome."

I wanted to laugh, what with the judge acting like a millionaire showing off his private art collection to the little people. Must be the Jurist of the Year Award, I thought, the one Renaldo got last fall from a dubious so-called legal ethics foundation run by a well-known congressional swindler, an outfit that handed out awards to earnest types like Renaldo to help bolster its credibility and had got some unwanted attention last month from the IRS for misusing its nonprofit status. Christ, the *Times* had had its fun marveling at the irony of that unfolding saga. But that damn award, it must have gone straight to the old judge's head.

I recognized the man in the gallery, and he looked like he'd gone to hell and back since the last time I'd seen him, ten years ago by now. His name was Dale Bleeker. He was a former deputy district attorney, a once brilliant trial lawyer whose courtroom skills had made a huge impression on me at precisely the time when my life lacked any sort of a game plan for the future. Subtly I watched him as he hunched his lanky frame over and eased into a seat in the gallery like a guy who'd slept on a hard floor or maybe a park bench the night before, and it struck me that the man had done more than just influence my decision to follow the path of the Law. No, he hadn't just made me want to be a lawyer. He'd made me want to be a lawyer like him.

Dale Bleeker was a legal role model to me—even though we'd never actually met. I'd been stunned when I heard he had recently been convicted on a one-count misdemeanor for lewd and lascivious conduct, a wienie-wagging incident that had landed him a low-level discipline from the bar with a year of probation. Something had obviously gone wrong in the man's life. I wanted to find out what it was, so last week I'd volunteered with the Probation Unit to be his monitor.

Lawyers on probation with the bar are supposed to get a monitor, another attorney who can help keep them in line for the length of the term. For years, the Probation Unit passed out lots of continuing-legal-education credits to lawyers who volunteered to monitor, and since easy credits are tough to come by, plenty answered the call of duty. The monitoring program worked well, so well that by the early nineties, probation violations had dropped to a historic low. Then some bar gadfly with nothing but time on his hands—and a lawyer at that—criticized the program for being unfair to other lawyers who had to study legal course work to earn their lousy credits, and the bar had to drop its CLE offer. The endless supply of opportunistic legal altruists dried up overnight, and the volunteer monitor program withered and died. When I offered to monitor Dale Bleeker's probation, the probation supervisor said fine, but her eyebrows pricked, and she also wanted to know, rather cynically, what was in it for me. I pricked my eyebrows back at her and said I wanted to make sure the man got through probation okay and left it at that. The super sighed like a punctured inner tube, rolled her eyes back, and said okay, fine, then sent Bleeker an appointment notice for later today in my office. Bleeker was way early, which I didn't like because it signified that he probably had all day. For lawyers on disciplinary probation, having hours to kill isn't much of a positive. It just means there's more time to backslide. I fixed my eyes on the judge again. He must be early, I thought and turned back to the bench.

The case at hand was still to be decided. Trixie Podette made a point of holding her composure together just enough to say, "Good afternoon to you, Your Honor." Then she wept and blew into her hankie and slowly but assuredly invited the judge to wallow in the melodrama of her husband's predicament, confiding in the court, beseeching the good judge to show mercy.

"Your Honor, my Eugene—I mean, Mr. Podette—he is indeed a man with his share of failings." Trixie paused to cast a loving glance toward her chastened mate. "He is a man whose deep love of the Lord is true, I know. Yes, sir, Your Honor, it is a love so profound as to . . . temporarily blind him to the fact that he just isn't much of a businessman." She tittered at the notion of her bumbling hubby, a false little laugh that rattled the air and died a quick, deserved death. "And that's a fact," she went on. "But that is all there is to this"—looking right at me when she said that. "My husband did not intend to cause any *misunderstandings.*"

Christ, there was that word again. I stared right back at the respondent's unflappable woman, getting a taste now for the thing that had probably made them a pair in the first place. Trixie Podette was putting an accomplished spin on the facts, doing as good a job as her husband could have managed. No, probably better. I felt myself sliding lower in my chair, as if sucked down by the force of my own foolish complacency.

"He just harbored a deep desire to build a special place of worship," Trixie said, "a church like no other for the good folks of the Henefer Church of Christ. Yes, mistakes were certainly made, Your Honor, serious miscalculations that the good Lord himself will surely scrutinize on Judgment Day, we can all rest assured. But my Eugene, he is a fine man, a devoted husband and the father of three fine children, Winnie, Paul, and little Davey."

Trixie paused, gripping the podium like she was expecting an aftershock from the Northridge rumbler. Eugene sniffled at the counsel table opposite me, his shiny head bowed penitently. I checked Renaldo for a response to all this, hoping to see him hiding another yawn. What I saw I did not like.

"Please continue, Mrs. Podette."

Fuck me, the voice in my head said, he's buying it.

Trixie held up a finger, inciting a wordless pause to the proceedings. Then she slid back to the courtroom door and opened it. "Children?" she called into the hallway exactly like Maria Von Trapp does in *The Sound of Music.*

My heart nearly gave out at the sight of Winnie, Paul, and little Davey Podette, three of the cutest school-age mopheads I'd ever laid eyes on. Renaldo was biting, and hard at that, his eyes misting up and his ruddy nose twitching as the kids draped their adorable little selves all over dear old Dad.

A fool for a client? Yeah, right. I just sat there, grinding my teeth as I pondered the utter uselessness of overused sayings.

Standing stiff-legged in my office window, framed by the downtown L.A. skyline, Dale Bleeker looked nothing like the confident deputy district attorney who had so impressed me ten years ago.

His dark suit looked dusty, the jacket a decent fit for his tall frame but badly creased in back and rumpled at the elbows. Somehow, the pinstripes had been robbed of their power, making Bleeker appear more like an overdressed hick or a second-rate mortician than an experienced litigator. He shifted his weight so he could see his reflection better, tightening the knot of his tie, an out-of-fashion foulard in an electric teal with a grease spot shaped like the Big Island of Hawaii. His black wing tips were standard-issue patent leather but had needed a shine sometime around last summer. He seemed to have dropped some pounds over the years, but his face and cheeks looked veined and swollen. The slicked brown hair of the assured counselor had given way to strands of gray comb-over that kept falling onto his spotted forehead.

Dale Bleeker had been a hot prosecutor the last time I'd seen him, a tiger prowling the courtroom, marking his territory. But that was then. This day, he reminded me more of a big cat I once saw in a cheesy, second-rate circus on a wind-lashed night in Santa Monica. I remembered the night, watching a bare-chested young tamer in tights whip the poor tiger as if it were some kind of fearsome man-eater, the old beast so haggard he could scarcely roll off his stool. My date that evening had been a wispy, animal-loving vegetarian moonchild, and she'd hidden her eyes from the sorry spectacle. Depressing.

I walked over and stood before the glass next to Dale. The view from nine stories up was a good one. The storm front was headed east and the sunlight was hopscotching its way through breezing thunderclouds. Below us, the scene at Eleventh and Hill Street looked almost frozen. Traffic was scant and steam rose from wet, deserted crosswalks. The Mayan Theater, with its ornate multicolored facade, was tucked behind a few old shade trees whose roots tilted the sidewalk out front. A Persian restaurant stood on the corner, its empty tables hiding beneath half-drawn blinds. Get there at noon, you might wait twenty minutes before the guy with the big gut and silver teeth can seat you. But lunch was over and the place resembled a waterless aquarium from where we stood.

Next to the Persian restaurant stood an abandoned old revival hall, its bricks painted a faded, frosty green. High up, a triangular sign hung over the side, a neon cross and fat block lettering speaking a message of hope: PRAYER CHANGES THINGS.

"Prayer changes things, huh?" Dale Bleeker said, reading the sign aloud.

I shrugged. "I'd like to think so." I mean, why not?

He looked away. "Nice closing argument by the little lady, huh."

"Peachy." I caught his smirk in the reflection. "I'd rather not talk about it, if you don't mind."

"Fine." He seemed unsure of himself, and I could almost hear the gears grinding inside his head. "So why am I here?" he said a minute later.

I gestured toward a chair but he stayed at the window. "I told you, I'm your monitor. I'm going to help you get in compliance and stay there until your probation is up."

The rain had gone for now and we both watched the checkers of light. The sparrows were fluttering back to their spot on the gray metal ledge outside my windows. Bleeker rubbed at his beard, which sounded like sandpaper. "Right. You state bar guys are all the same, just looking out for the brethren."

The attitude was tiresome, a cliché, something you had to learn to endure if your business, like mine, was disciplining bad lawyers. "Good thing you called Probation when you did, Mr. Bleeker."

"Yeah, lucky me."

"You're already four weeks late for your intake interview. Apparently you aren't getting the mail the Probation Unit has been—"

"Apparently."

"I looked up your membership-records address. It's a residence. Is there a problem with your mail delivery?"

"Problem is, it's none of your damn business." He turned his back on the view and his eyelids narrowed. I figured he was working up the sack to make for the door. "Look, I've made a decision," he said.

I rested a hand on the back of one of the chairs facing my desk. "Good. Sit down." I wanted him to stay.

Bleeker stayed put by the window. "No offense, but I've decided I don't want a state bar prosecutor as my probation monitor. It was bad enough getting dinged by you guys following the conviction."

He shook his head. "But I'm not letting you set me up for another fall. No way." Licking his lips as if his throat was dry.

My objective had been to ease into the past with him so as not to cause him undue embarrassment about his ragged present state of affairs. But this wasn't going according to plan. I had to tell him. "All right, but wait . . ."

"All I've been doing my whole life is waiting." He sounded defeated when he said it.

"I know you," I said. He stared back, befuddled. "I mean, I knew you. From a while back."

He absently gnawed at a fingernail, then rubbed the side of his neck, which was red and chafed like a bad sunburn. I could hear those gears grinding again. "You do look a little familiar," he said, squinting a little. "Hair used to be longer?"

I nodded. "Let me make it easy for you. Does the name Thelma Ruffo jog your memory?"

He smiled for the first time since I'd seen him perusing the rack of how-not-to-get-shafted-by-your-attorney brochures the bar displays down in reception, a little while before my trial with Renaldo was to resume this afternoon. I hadn't recognized him at all as I'd brushed past his shoulder then, not two hours ago, the old Dale Bleeker still alive and thriving in my memory. It's funny how the better part of a man can outlive the reality of who and what he has become. Still, I wasn't ready to abandon my belief in the man, and standing there, trying to jockey him into a chair in my little government lawyer's office, I figured that this would be the shape of our dichotomy.

"I'll be damned," he said, "juror number four, am I right?" I nodded. "You were the big blond kid, college student." He sized up my upper body. "Still got those guns, that barrel chest. You lift?"

"I surf," I said. I got this way from paddling a board through lines of white water for the last twenty-five years or so. "That is, when I can find the time." It hadn't been easy lately.

Dale Bleeker looked tickled to have made the connection. "You were a tough nut. Gave me zero visual feedback, didn't crack a smile. Youngest foreman I'd seen in a lotta years, too."

"That was what you call leadership by default," I said. "No one else wanted it."

Dale kept grinning. "Hell, I thought I'd lost you before I even rested my case."

He was right. Thelma Ruffo, a dowdy baby-sitter with a big black purse and these round, sad eyes, really had the Aunt Bea aura going for her. She sat there, hands folded, looking like she'd just finished baking a pie from scratch, and I couldn't see it. The woman just didn't look capable of heisting six pieces of fine jewelry from the well-to-do family she'd worked for, and in all honesty, my fellow jurors and I were straining for a way to believe her. The pawnbroker could only say he was reasonably certain it was she, the receipt had another name on it, and her prints weren't on the stones. She denied it all indignantly, invoking God as her witness more than a few times. But Dale Bleeker took his time, his cross-examination so low-key it seemed more like a friendly chat. Thelma Ruffo did the rest. We deliberated for forty minutes, convicting her on every count.

"She almost had me," I said.

"Burned you but good, didn't she? I could see it in your face when the verdict was read."

"You were very good. It was like you understood something no one else did."

He shrugged. "Not really. I knew the evidence. Knew the truth. That can be a powerful weapon."

"It made a difference, the whole experience." I stopped, mulling my next words. "I mean, it made a difference for me. Made me want to be a lawyer."

He'd lost the grin as if a raft of bad memories had come calling for him. "Yeah, well, whatever." Then he read the nameplate on my desk, the one my fiancée, Carmen, had surprised me with when the state bar hired me a few years back: "J. Shepard."

From where he stood he couldn't see the photo of Carmen on my desk, her straight black hair that, when it swishes, reveals a fine layer of rust-colored strands that twinkle in the sun like the strings on a harp. Her eyes in the photo appear to be black, but they are actually a rich cocoa brown that can either pull a man in or turn him away, depending upon her mood, and they are many. The beauty mark above her mouth adds an imperfection to the marvelous symmetry of her face that I can describe only as perfect, and her smile is so natural, it makes you believe she is humble about her physical gifts—which in fact, she is. I keep that shot at an angle only I can see from my chair. You could say I'm hoarding Carmen's smile for myself alone.

I'd offered my probationer a perfunctory handshake downstairs, which he'd rejected. I tried him again.

"My pleasure, Mr. Bleeker."

"Never mind that, call me Dale." We shook. He was apparently through with the bar bashing for now, and he slowly took a seat in that hunched-over way, guiding the creaking frame in for a landing. "Let's get this over with, shall we?"

I went behind my desk, a huge L-shaped cherry job that looks a tad elaborate for a government lawyer's digs. Where to begin? I was still a little jarred by Dale Bleeker's general state of decline—but curious, too. His lewd and lascivious conviction certainly didn't fit the picture I'd preserved in my memory through law school and five years of practice. I wanted to ask him what had happened, but it seemed too soon.

He crossed his legs and waited. I wasn't quite ready yet for a dry discussion of terms and conditions of probation, either, but I found his file and opened it.

Someone rolled a set of knuckles across my office door. Eloise Horton, my manager, poked her head in. "Excuse me," she said, nodding toward Dale Bleeker as if he were the one who needed an excuse for being here. Eloise is not too keen on good manners, and she doesn't mind letting you know they aren't a priority. "J., you didn't turn in your F-due report yet for this month." Ever the bureaucrat, Eloise is passionately in love with all manner and form of state bar reportage.

F-due stands for filings due, which means cases assigned to a trial attorney that have not yet been filed. The idea is the fewer F-dues on your report, the better—that is, if you don't mind filing a lot of cases that aren't yet ready for prosecution, and a few more that will never be. Management also constantly squeezes our investigators to keep their numbers up and backlog down, which means that a lot of half-baked cases get forwarded for filing. If you slow down to prep the cases that need prepping, you'll have cases busting out of your credenza in no time.

I haven't even got a credenza, just a floor-to-ceiling wall of file boxes.

"You know me, boss, I'm the Paul Masson of F-dues—I'll file no case before its time," I said in an attempt at levity, which Eloise deflected with a glacial stare.

Eyeing Dale, she leaned against the door frame and sighed. "Do it now, if you don't mind, J."

Eloise is about my height, a few inches over six feet. She wears her hair in a short Afro and always wears these flats that look like slippers because she's got legs like a gazelle's and I suppose she doesn't want to look any taller. I've heard some bar people say she was once a track star, a sprinter. Apparently she won a medal once in an international meet and caused a big controversy by slouching her way through the national anthem, her right hand balled into a fist over her heart. She later claimed she wasn't making any kind of black power statement, her feet were just tired. Sure, whatever. That sounded about right for the Eloise I knew. A complex, headstrong pain in the ass.

I found my half-finished report. "Is handwriting okay?" I asked Eloise.

"Not a problem." She looked at her watch. "Reggie's meeting with the board of governors tomorrow morning. He'll need our unit's numbers."

"Right," I said, scribbling the names of a half dozen case files I'd not yet even opened. Describing their status took only three words: reviewing for filing.

Eloise was talking about our chief trial counsel, Reginald Hewitt, the only other African-American manager in the bar's discipline operation and the man who'd brought Eloise in as an assistant chief, sans job interview. They were reputedly close, had to be for her to get hired the way she did, but then, I'd never seen them get together for anything but management meetings. A lot of my colleagues don't think much of Eloise, because she had little trial experience when the chief hired her, yet here she was managing a unit of trial lawyers. I didn't much care; she'd watched me do a few trials, decided I knew what I was doing, and had the good sense to leave me alone. Except, that is, for the constant numbers game she forced on me weekly.

But in fairness to management, I know what the numbers are intended for. They keep us in business.

The State Bar of California is a strange political being, a pseudo–state agency that's actually a private organization financed solely by the mandatory dues it charges the lawyers of this state for the privilege of practicing law. Although the bar is essentially in the consumer-protection business, it taps not a single taxpayer dollar. Yet, because the bar was created by the state in its constitution, its yearly dues rate and overall operations budget must be approved by the state legislature and signed into law by the governor. This means that any politician in Sacramento who is less than enthralled with the concept of regulating the legal profession can stand in the way of the dues budget, disparage the bar for sloth and wastefulness, howl for reform, even call for its abolition. This he can do every time that bill comes around again for a vote. Most politicians are lawyers, so you can imagine how popular bar bashing is with the capitol crew—it has become something of a blood sport. The numbers we crank out are to show both our supporters and our detractors that we're winning the game.

I finished up my report. Dale Bleeker shifted in his chair as if he could feel the bad vibe between my boss and me and wanted to shake it off. I handed the F-due to her and waited.

"You're still behind," Eloise said, "but a good month will cure that."

She looked at me as if that were my call to kiss some managerial ass, but I knew that was not going to happen, the way I knew the sun would be setting tonight and rising again tomorrow. She was out of line to be talking productivity with me in mixed company.

"You know I've got complex cases," I said, which was true. Most of my caseload involved white-collar fraud, major misappropriations, forgery, and embezzlement. Lots of tricky paper trails to uncover. These cases take a bit longer to prepare than your common one-count failure-to-perform case, where some poor boob misread his calendar and filed suit after the statute of limitations had expired.

But when it comes to F-due reports, a case is a case. This makes no sense, yet around here the management is not exactly clamoring for my opinion on how to produce more meaningful statistics.

"Just make an effort," she said, her lips tight.

I was tired of her pissy mood. "I'm in a meeting," I said. "I will have to speak with you later."

Her high forehead wrinkled the way it does when she gets peeved, which is frequent when she's around me. "Looking forward to it already." Eloise turned and walked out, perusing my report with a tiny shake of her head.

"My," Dale Bleeker said, cracking a smile. "Lotta love floating around this place."

"Who was it that said bosses are like diapers?"

"Full of shit and always on your ass? I don't know. A very wise person."

"Amen." His teeth were discolored but straight. Despite his broken-down appearance, I rather liked Dale Bleeker's company.

The sun was making a move on the clouds outside my window, and the room brightened. At the moment I was glad I'd taken a chance and volunteered to be Bleeker's probation monitor. He'd obviously been through hard times of late, fired from his job because of his conviction, professionally humiliated and forced to start over. His other problems I could only guess at, but the man had been an example of good lawyering to me once, exploding my own studied indifference to matters of serious long-term employment. Dale Bleeker had inspired me at just the right time, and it had always seemed a most unexpected gift in my life. I was still hoping to somehow return the favor.

"How about yourself, you working right now?" I asked.

He got a funny look in his eyes, the kind of look a witness gets when you catch him in a lie. "Well, yeah. I am."

"So, what are you doing?"

He drew a tired breath and stared at the loose papers on my desk. "Good question," he said. "I've had the job three weeks now." Then he stood, straightened his back like he was testing a rusty hinge that needed oiling, went back to the window and resumed his gaze at the streets below. "Thing is, I still don't know when the work part gets under way. I keep waiting for a phone call but nothing's happened, haven't heard a word since I got hired. Got my first paycheck, though. Last week."

I didn't get it. Here was a disgraced criminal prosecutor with no real job prospects—except, perhaps, a shot at starting a solo criminal-defense practice, which took time, patience, and a little capital to establish. But Dale Bleeker hadn't started his own office; apparently he didn't even have enough change in his pocket to get his shoes shined. You could almost smell the desperation on his clothes.

"How's the pay?" I asked.

"Pretty good." He blushed. "Actually, darned good."

"What are we talking about?"

"Sixty-five hundred a month."

"Nice. And you haven't done a thing?"

"Like I said, I'm still waiting." But Dale seemed more concerned now. "Funny, isn't it?"

"You haven't met a single client yet?"

"Nope."

"Haven't actually been to court, or filed anything?"

"No, I haven't."

This was starting to sound familiar, and I didn't like it. "Maybe I'm wrong, but I think they might be using your license, Mr. Bleeker."

His face seemed to tighten, as if he was taking on a new level of pain. "Oh, that's just great. And please, you can call me Dale."

"If they are, it's illegal, for them and for you. They could wreck your career in a hurry."

"You mean what's left of it."

I was glad my windows didn't open to a balcony, because Dale Bleeker probably would've been tuning up for a swan dive by now. A bank of rain clouds momentarily blocked the sun, their shadows riding up the downtown high-rises like a rolling blackout.

"Shoulda known," he said. "Never been out of work before . . . I mean, not until lately. It just felt . . . felt so good to get employed. Damn! What was I even . . . Ah, damn it to hell!"

Damn right he should have known. Dale Bleeker had been a prosecutor for over twenty years. Hadn't he ever heard of the unauthorized practice of law? It is a crime. Or maybe he knew what kind of job he was taking and just didn't care anymore. Maybe he was jerking my chain just now. I thought of Trixie Podette doing her *Sound of Music* routine on Judge Renaldo a little while ago. Careful, I told myself. Don't let this thing get out of hand.

His hazel eyes searched my face for a reaction. "So, what do we do now?"

"We may have to get you unemployed. Fast."

"What if it's too late already? They could have used my name on a hundred cases by now."

I didn't have an answer for that. "We'll go out there, see how deeply you're . . ." That didn't sound so good, so I started over. "We'll check it out."

Dale stared at his feet. "Yeah, sure. When?"

I checked my wristwatch: almost 3 P.M. "We go now, we'll beat the rush hour."

He stood very still before the glass. "Hell of a streak I'm on right now. Sometimes I wonder, what is it going to take?"

We watched the sparrows hop and flutter in a window-ledge puddle, Dale silent, probably mulling his regrets. Shadows ghosted across the sluggish street scene on Hill Street. I was mulling a few things myself, hoping I'd done the right thing by taking on the problems of Dale Bleeker, hoping a plan of action would begin to take shape—posthaste. Hoping the preacher who commissioned the PRAYER CHANGES THINGS sign knew what he was talking about, if it came to that.

Two

We walked outside to the crosswalk at Twelfth and Olive, squinting into a field of golden glare on wet asphalt. Dale was looking pretty freaked.

"Been out of work going on a year," he mumbled. "You don't know what that'll do to you."

"Must have been rough."

"How could I have missed this one?"

I avoided eye contact. "Don't worry about it. They say hindsight's twenty-twenty."

Dale snorted. "Not if you're blind."

He had once been a gifted trial lawyer. During the years I was sweating through law school I followed his career through newspaper clippings that often read like movie scripts. I remembered a socialite's double murder of her husband and his lover, and Dale shredding the woman's self-defense motive with testimony from a shooting-range employee who'd seen her taking target practice the day before the killings. He'd handled a city hall bribery scandal involving rigged contract-bidding, and sent the mayor to prison when he linked the politician's down payment on a new yacht dollar for dollar to a hefty "consulting fee" simultaneously noted in a local contractor's books. There was the prominent surgeon who killed his student intern—and his own unborn child whom the intern was carrying—by staging her accidental death by drowning; Dale nailed the pompous ass by bringing in the best forensic expert in the nation to testify that, based on his examination of the fetus, the intern had been strangled first. Just now, I could not recall ever reading about Dale Bleeker losing a case.

Appearances aside, this was a lawyer of significant experience and savvy—perhaps too smart to play the well-paid dupe in a UPL scheme. UPL means the unauthorized practice of law, a confidence game that involves nonattorneys doing routine legal work at cut-rate prices, often using an absentee lawyer's bar identification number to give their dealings legitimacy. UPL predictably leads to late filings and blown deadlines, nonappearances at scheduled hearings, disappearing retainer fees, and worse. People who run the scam typically stick around just long enough to burn a lot of unwitting clients before disappearing—only to pop up later, in some other community, under a snappy new name that promises some form of shortcut or another. UPL is a criminal misdemeanor, a felony if fraud can be proven, and DA's offices do prosecute UPL cases, which meant that Dale Bleeker, a former prosecutor of criminals, should at least have been aware enough to pick up the signs. Then again, the man appeared to have taken the news I'd given him like a rib shot. He'd endured a run of bad luck, made some faulty decisions, maybe hit a patch of alcoholic excess that further blurred his perspective. Enough distraction to explain his latest professional misstep. Perhaps.

The signal changed a few feet ahead of us, but Dale headed into the crosswalk as if he didn't see the commuter bus roaring up Olive and through the red. I clamped a hand on his shoulder a second before the bus tore past and shot a wave of chocolate-colored gutter water up over the curb.

"Jesus!" Dale yelped. His big hands were held open like Moses demanding that Nature provide an explanation. "That light was red! You see that?" A particle cloud swept through behind the bus, the scent of diesel and dust settling into our lungs. I let go of his shoulder and let him straighten his jacket. His hazel eyes had gone dark and were rattling in his skull as if the hardwiring behind them had frayed. "Jesus, doesn't anyone obey the law anymore?"

I looked away, for his remark had brought the wienie-wagging conviction to mind. I could taste my disappointment, as bitter as the exhaust fumes stinging the edge of my nostrils. Dale Bleeker had been a senior prosecutor who made a living putting criminals away, an ace trial lawyer, a role model—my fucking role model. I wanted to say one thing to him now: What happened? Don't you realize that I used to want to be like you, to control a courtroom like you did? One true voice, one clear-eyed vision. To coolly reason my way through anything, reducing, deducing, analogizing, hypothesizing, trusting my instincts and intellect. Jesus, doesn't anyone obey the law anymore, indeed.

But the probation monitoring had been my idea, not his, and now he was probably in some form of trouble. I decided this wasn't the time to voice my personal disappointment.

"You're driving," I told him. "Where's your ride?"

He pointed across the street to the only machine at the far curb, a faded gold Buick Regal the size of a Rose Parade float. A wire-wheel hubcap was missing from the left rear tire. Bird shit riddled the hood and roof, a thousand little bull's-eyes that instantly got me thinking about the last-stand shoot-out in *Bonnie and Clyde*. The front end had minor damage, the chrome bumper rippled on one side like aluminum foil, streaks of candy-apple green paint from the other car mingling with fresh rust at the point of impact.

We headed over. "Why am I driving?" Dale said as we left the crosswalk.

"I'm having car trouble."

Dale slowed a bit on his final approach to the Buick. "Not too regal anymore, I guess." Embarrassed. I suppose he saw me checking the crapped-up roof, because he said, "Damn birds. Public menace."

"So, how's it run?"

My question sounded like pleasant conversation, but I was already calculating survival odds, picturing myself trapped in this ratty yacht on the freeway. I envisioned the motor sputtering and stalling at an inopportune moment, Dale frozen behind the wheel, a speeding big rig roaring forth to wipe all traces of my sorry ass from the planet.

"Strong. It's an eighty-one, but low miles, fifty-three-K original. I never had much of a commute."

"You live in Long Beach, up in Belmont Heights," I said.

"Right."

"I'm nearby, in Christianitos."

He smiled. "Nice little town. Like the Beach Boys said, if everybody had an ocean . . ."

I thought of the body jam that tramples my tiny hometown every summer, the bumper-to-bumper traffic on Main, the cars illegally parked across the back of my garage in the alley, the fast-food wrappers blowing down the street like tumbleweeds in the afternoon sea breeze.

"Sometimes I wish they had their own ocean," I said. "That way they could just stay home." I know it's a crappy attitude, but when you live at a place as nice as the beach, there are times when it's hard to remember to share.

He fished for his car keys, frowning as if he was turning something over in his mind. Fast-moving clouds skirted over our heads and took the sun, sending a chill through me. "Got 'em," Dale said. His empty pants pocket flapped open like a dirty tongue, a cigarette butt stuck to the tip. "So how'd you get to work?"

"Blue Line." The Blue Line is one of the tiny handful of commuter trains that constitute L.A.'s pathetic mass-transit system. It goes from the downtown financial district through the industrial blight of Vernon, making stops in such South Central garden spots as Watts, Lynwood, and Compton, neighborhoods that blond white boys like me would never, ever visit alone after hours without an absolute death wish. But the train keeps chugging south, eventually running out of tracks a half hour later just shy of Ocean Boulevard and the *Queen Mary* in seaside Long Beach.

"That must be interesting," Dale said.

"I had no choice. My car wouldn't go this morning."

Dale stuck a key in the passenger door and jerked it open; when he did, an empty Coors can fell into the gutter. "Whoops." Acting surprised. "What have we here?"

I stuck out my hand. "An open container. Here, I'll find a trash can."

Christ, what a shame if he was just another drunk. A good many low-level bar cases involving otherwise fine lawyers in trouble for the first time are rooted in drugs and booze.

"It's not what you might be thinking, J." Dale said it as if he'd read my thoughts. "I recycle." He popped open the rear trunk and pulled out a huge clear plastic bag stuffed with smashed aluminum beer cans. "See?"

I was unconvinced. Dale stuffed the bag back into the trunk and slammed the top. We both stood straight and still behind his boat of a car, without a twitch, like gunmen in a standoff.

"Just trust me, okay?" he said. "I'm trusting you."

I said to myself, Shit, he's right. This was my idea. You take on a probationer, really intend to see him through his term, well, you do it together.

"Fifty-three-K original," I said, sliding up to the passenger door. "Bet you've never even had it in the fast lane."

Dale shook his head and grinned. "What you don't know."

I got in, dead set on locating a working seat belt before we swung into traffic.

We drove north on the Harbor Freeway toward Interstate 5 and the city of Glendale, the lines of rain-spotted cars before us slowing to a stop-and-start, lane-jumping turtle race as we curved past Dodger Stadium and into the Elysian Park tunnels. Dale told me about the help-wanted ad he'd spotted in the *Around-Town News,* a free rag that always sports a front-page piece or two on some new restaurant or art exhibit but does its real business with the legal-notice listings in the back.

It seemed like an odd place to find a help-wanted ad. Before coming to the state bar, I'd spent a few years working in juvenile dependency court, representing parents who abused or neglected their children using every method imaginable—and a few more ways you would not care to imagine. Some cases took years to resolve, and sometimes my clients would lose interest and drift outside the county's viewfinder before reclaiming custody of their kids. The Department of Child Welfare used to send those wanderers statutory Dear John letters in the *Around-Town News,* giving sufficient legal notice in small print by announcing the imminent termination of so-and-so's parental rights at an upcoming hearing. In three years not a single parent I represented had ever even heard of the *Around-Town News,* let alone responded to a notice in time to do something about it. This made the little fish-wrap a pretty effective tool for notice-giving county prosecutors. No appearance, no contest—no problem.

But most people wouldn't go looking for a professional position using the *Around-Town News* classifieds. I wondered if Dale knew this. Maybe he actually was as desperate as he looked.

We crawled through the freeway tunnels, our windows down to

keep them from fogging, the damp air pungent with the scent of wet rubber and carbon monoxide, impatient drivers leaning on their horns as if that would part the sea of vehicles before them. Dale told me an answering service had patched him through to a guy on a cell phone on the Ventura Freeway, a hollow voice yammering at Dale like he was using a tin can and string. Mr. Julian, the guy called himself, withholding his first name as if he were a man of the world.

"Sounds like a hairdresser," I said.

"Looked more like a wealthy goombah, except he was a kid."

Dale had summed up his work experience in a phrase: twenty-two years and five hundred–plus jury trials. Julian's response was equally terse: That'll do. Then he gave Dale directions to a place on Broadway down in Chinatown, leaning on his horn at some truck that had swerved into his lane, bitching about the traffic as if no one else in L.A. had noticed it before. Dale knew he didn't like the guy, but he needed the work.

They met the next afternoon, Julian in an Italian suit, black shirt, and gold jewelry, the tin-can-and-string cell glued to his ear, looking like a Hollywood wannabe.

"An employment interview in a Chinese dim sum palace—the hell is that?" Dale said.

"You have to wonder."

"Potstickers, the guy whispering how they're simply other-worldly, man, chin dripping with that sweet ginger sauce, barely even glancing at my résumé. He was too busy stuffing his face with potstickers."

"Must have been rough. I mean, for a professional of your experience."

"It was, but I was thinking a job is a job, that's all."

I could respect that. "So how was the food, anyway?"

He glared at me. "When those steel carts wheeled up to our table, I didn't even look."

Over lunch, Julian told Dale he ran a small law office in Glendale purportedly staffed by a cadre of crack paralegals who handled both the client contacts and the paperwork. Simple, low-cost stuff: Chapter 13 bankruptcy filings, wills, living trusts, burial instruc-

tions, name changes. Applications for green cards, amnesty, political asylum. Services that could be performed more economically by nonlawyers—that was the angle. A volume business, and those numbers piled up quick.

" 'Filthy lucre, pal'—that was the term Julian used," Dale said. "The opportunity of a lifetime."

Dale's job—if you could call it that—was to review and sign off on an occasional document or two that required an attorney for filing with a court, nothing more. For this he would collect $6,500 a month.

"Knew it sounded too good to be true," Dale told me, those hangdog eyes of his radiating grief, his shoulders hunched over as if he was already doing penance. "Too good to be true, no doubt."

But his employment prospects were a joke that wasn't funny anymore.

"You figured you couldn't afford to say no," I said.

"Exactly."

"And in your three weeks on the job thus far, you haven't been asked to review a single case, meet a client, peruse a file."

"Nope." A red Ford Mustang cut into our lane without signaling and Dale leaned on his horn. Then he waited, and said, "This is bad, isn't it?"

It was classic UPL, I thought. No doubt about it.

"We'll see."

We finally caught the Interstate 5 northbound and a little relief from the commuter derby. The hills behind Glendale were dark and grainy from the rain, like giant piles of used-up coffee grounds. I leaned my head out the window, a rush of clean air shooting up my nose. A storm drain running parallel to the freeway frothed and bubbled like a real live river, which around here qualified as a spectacle of nature. Somewhere along these concrete banks right now, a street kid from a run-down inner-city neighborhood without a single swimming pool was spellbound by the same view, goofing and tossing rocks at a tattooed buddy, his pant legs rolled up as he waded in knee-deep to snag a bobbing TV set for some target practice. A half hour later he'd be floating eight miles downriver, gulping muddy water, hypothermia setting in, his eyes blinded by

the white light coming as a rescue crew tried to save his life by casting ropes from an overpass. For a supposedly laid-back city, L.A. has its unforgiving moments. Thousands of them.

"Hell," Dale said, "they didn't even invite me to the office, not once. I called the number a week ago—concerned, you know. Julian phoned me back, discouraged the idea, saying you wouldn't want to get in the way of a smooth operation for no good reason, would you?"

"We've got good reason," I said. "Considering the fee you're getting monthly for services not actually performed."

Dale's cheeks had lost their color. "Think so?"

"They probably have a stamp of your signature in heavy use, since a lot of those filings require an attorney."

We drove on, Dale death-gripping the wheel of the big Buick, the blood returning to his face now, filling in beneath the shadow of beard. The color of rage, I suppose.

"Don't take it personally," I told him. "A city this size, so many people moving around all the time, coming and going, UPL is a pretty common game."

"UPL," he said. Then he sped up for no apparent reason, changing lanes without signaling.

I waited, figuring he should know what it was. "The unauthorized practice of law," I finally said. Could a former DA be this obtuse? Or was he playing dumb? We were approaching the Los Feliz off-ramp. "Get off here," I told him.

"So how's it work?" His apparent earnestness made me puzzle even harder.

"Easy. You take a nonlawyer, a Mr. Julian type looking for a quick buck. Hire a paralegal or two to do the grunt work, a down-and-out lawyer to lend his bar number—" I realized what I'd said. "Sorry. I didn't—"

Dale waved a hand. "No offense taken. Continue."

"Then you spread the word. Let me tell you, it's quite a hook."

"Let's hear it."

We got off on Los Feliz, turning right just across from a three-par pitch-and-putt course sprinkled with retirees.

"You tell people you can deliver low-cost legal services without the lawyer," I explained, "because who needs the greedy bastards

anyway, am I right? See, you're working the average Joe's mistrust of lawyers against him."

"Then what?"

"That's it. You sit back and watch the line stretch around the block."

I briefly considered telling him about how hardcore certain UPL practitioners can be about making money and how quickly they will destroy a lawyer's professional standing in the process. How, just last summer, an unwitting lawyer hired into a San Jose UPL operation had turned himself in to the bar and exposed his employer when he realized what was going on. The next morning he was shot twice in the head, execution-style, in a supermarket parking lot. But I said no more. Dale knew all he needed to about UPL for now. I didn't want him falling apart on me before the situation even unfolded.

We came to Brand Boulevard, one of the major drags in Glendale, made a left, and quickly spotted the place a few signals up. A white Glendale Lo-Cost Law Center sign that looked new was settled in among a block-long row of businesses, a nail salon to one side and a Cuban bakery on the other, slanted parking spaces along the curb. Dale swung across the double yellow and glided into an open spot in front of the bakery. My window was down, and I could smell the pork sandwiches through the open door.

The law center looked sleepy—no line around the block today. A girl in skintight fake leopard pants and a low-cut copper halter top was standing on the sidewalk not far from the law center's entrance, conducting a major search through the contents of her purse.

"We might want to talk to her," I said, "see if she was a client."

The girl finally found a stick of gum, popped it into her mouth, and strolled to a vintage cherry red Porsche roadster parked next to us. She caught me checking her out through my open window but didn't seem to mind.

"Hi."

"Hi," I said. "I'm J."

"Gina."

"How you doing?" I privately winced. How unoriginal can you get?

"All right, considering I'm heading in to work." She leaned against her roadster. "Bummer on a nice afternoon like this, but oh well."

"What are you doing here?"

She laughed as if to say Wouldn't you like to know? Then she said "Leaving" with a perfectly straight face.

So much for my skills as an investigator. But when she gunned her motor, Gina handed me a business card through her window before she zoomed off, the Porsche sustaining a low roar that was a pure triumph of German engineering, all the way down the block. I gave the card to Dale for inspection.

He smiled. "Our Cups Runneth Over," he announced. It was a topless juice bar on Ventura Boulevard, apparently specializing in busty help and wheat grass shooters. He handed the card back to me. "What'll they think of next, huh?"

"I'm all for good health."

"I'll bet," he said, grinning like a wolf. I thought of my fiancée, Carmen, how gratified she'd be if she knew I was following up on a "lead" that wore leopard-skin pants. Better to focus on what we could ascertain inside the center, for now.

We got out and stepped onto the wide sidewalk. Through the front windows I could see a short row of desks and an Asian-looking man in armpit-stained short sleeves typing at a computer terminal, a cigarette dangling from his lips—the center's lone paralegal for today.

"High-class operation," Dale observed. I glanced at the towering glass bank buildings up the road a quarter mile, the place where people bought and sold investments over the phone and real attorneys charged real-attorney prices for their services. Another world.

"Let's get this over with," I said.

Dale tried to straighten up, cinching up the knot in his tie and sliding his thumbs along his collar to smooth out the wrinkles. He seemed to be suffering from a case of nerves, his breathing labored. I tried to be patient, watched him pull a state bar visitor badge out of his jacket pocket and inspect it.

"When we left your office, we went a different way than when we came up," he said.

"I'll take care of it tomorrow." I reached for the badge and pocketed it.

"That was the back elevator we used, wasn't it?" His observation was correct but I said nothing. "I was wondering . . . are you embarrassed to be seen with me? Because . . ." His voice was wavering. "If you are, just . . . let's just end this probation monitoring arrangement right here and now."

I stared into the law center, not knowing what to tell Dale. Inside, cigarette smoke floated in a fluorescent haze. A paint-by-numbers seascape hung on the wall above the lone paralegal, two-dimensional breakers battering a cardboard-brown beach, a cartoon rendering. The place was cut-rate all the way and didn't appear to be inhabited by an attorney—a bad indicator for a business calling itself a law center, what I had expected. If UPL was involved, I had to investigate; I could tell Dale as much and leave it at that. But I would be lying. He had inspired me once, stoked my ambition at exactly the right time. Now he was on a slide, and I wanted to stop it. I was reasonably certain Eloise Horton would say I was wasting my time—time better spent filing new cases—if she knew. Well fuck it, I decided, there's more to being a lawyer than filing cases. She didn't have to know, at least for now.

"I was trying to avoid my boss," I told him.

"How come?"

I caught a glimpse of my reflection in the bakery window. In my dark blue suit, brittle sunlight flooding the sidewalk behind me, I looked as thick as a bodyguard and not very tan anymore. My blond hair used to glow with youthful streaks, but it looked flat and thick with dark roots. This winter the surf hadn't been much, and the crowds at the pier were worse than ever. I'd been passing on surfing a lot this season.

"I wasn't really supposed to be your monitor," I said. "It's generally not done. You screw up probation, your monitor can wind up testifying against you about the violation. It wouldn't look so hot to have a bar prosecutor doing that." I looked away. "But I didn't think it would come to that. I felt like I knew you, from before. I wanted to help you, give you an inside track."

Dale seemed to soften with that bit of information. "I'm not

30 ⩤ John DeCure

concerned about your being a prosecutor," he said. "That was my gig too. If there's a problem, I believe you'll be fair."

I thought of Eloise Horton, whose general distaste for "respondent rabble" no doubt informed her opinion that probation—and the overriding goal of rehabilitation—was mostly a waste of time and bar resources. She'd write me up, or worse, if Dale got in trouble and I was involved.

"Something bugging you?" he asked.

"My manager's pretty tight-assed."

"Certainly looked that way. She doesn't know about our arrangement?"

"No."

I glanced through the window into the center again, but saw no movement. Still, I felt like we'd been standing out here too long. Sooner or later someone would spy two men in suits and see trouble coming.

"Look," I said, "you're in a spot, and probably I am too if we can't extract you from it. Let's go in, see what we can do."

"I'm game," he said, but not too gamely.

The northern sky was dense with gathering storm clouds. Rain in the high desert, I thought. The prairie meth labs and skinhead kids and tacky chain discount warehouses east of the mountains are probably getting a soaking—a cleansing, actually. Damn straight. Whatever was in store for us, it felt good to be out of the office for a change, away from the wall of file boxes in my office, beyond Eloise's scrutiny. We always needed more rain in L.A. I suddenly felt thirsty—not for a shot of wheat grass, but for what, I wasn't sure. It was the same thirst I'd had the first time I'd met Dale Bleeker, when he stood at a podium and chatted with me about the information on my juror's questionnaire. A thirst for direction, or change, or maybe answers to why no change seemed imminent, or why true changes of the personal kind seemed so damned difficult to come by.

The northern storm hung there beyond the law center's roofline like an omen. I found myself buttoning my suit coat, which by some miracle always helps me feel a tiny bit more like a lawyer. How silly that is, but what the hell; as I get older and more set in my ways, I find that I don't really question some things anymore, not the little things, at least.

You do whatever works.

The man at the computer looked Filipino, and when his wrinkled face broke into a smile, I saw chunks of gold and silver in his mouth. Behind him was an identical desk and terminal that looked dusty and unused. The place was pretty much four walls, the back one wood paneled with an open door to a rear space full of file boxes. No attorney's name on the door, no private office—just as I had suspected. Coffee-shop artwork of the same caliber as the cartoon beach scene assaulted the eyeballs from all angles.

"Help you?" the man at the computer said with a quick grin, catching us temporarily speechless.

We'd stepped into a postage-stamp-sized reception area consisting of a mismatched chair and orange vinyl love seat, a tilting plastic plant, and a coffee table laden with dog-eared magazines.

Dale nodded at me. "Your call," he said.

"Hi there, gentlemen, come on in," a small brunette of about twenty called to us as she emerged from the back room, an empty glass coffeepot in hand. She glided up past the smoker and smiled as if she thought we were customers. Her black skirt was a size too small, and the paralegal had quit his typing to take in the view.

"Is Mr. Julian in?" I said.

She stared at us. "Mr. Julian?" As if no one had ever come calling for him before.

Dale introduced himself, to further mild puzzlement from the girl. "Mr. Julian hired me three weeks ago," he explained.

"Oh, right, right," she said, the empty coffeepot stuck like a bowling ball to her hand. "Thought I recognized your name. I'm Nichelle."

"So where's Mr. Julian?" I asked her, but before she could answer, the glass door opened behind us. A black-haired girl about Nichelle's age who looked Chinese walked in, gripping the hand of a happy-looking old man as if she was afraid he might wander off. A thick young Hispanic guy in his twenties with a black beret pushed in behind the old man, blocking the door.

"You the lawyer?" the Chinese girl asked me.

"I don't work here," I said.

"I do," Dale blurted, "and I'm a lawyer." Nichelle the receptionist looked like she wasn't expecting this, not at all. But she said nothing.

"Cool," the Chinese girl said. "Julian said you'd know what to do. I'm Angie, this is my husband, Rudy." She ignored the thick who came in behind them. "We're kinda in a hurry. We need, um, a powerful attorney." She checked her watch, a neon pink plastic job. "Like right this minute, you don't mind."

The old gent was breathing a little hard beneath a Glendale Rotary Club ball cap that was pulled down so far I had to strain to see his face. Husband Rudy, my ass, I was thinking, Angie had to be fifty years the man's junior. The glaring young dude with the beret watched Dale and me now as we took in Angie's plump lips, the perfectly round little mole dotting her right cheek, her tight curves, tanned tummy, and pierced, diamond-studded navel. I'd seen that proprietary stare in a hundred nightclubs, the one worn by the leering, antisocial guy who doesn't dance but came along for the ride with his heat-seeking lady. The tough guy had to be Angie's boyfriend.

"A powerful attorney?" Dale said.

Angie shrugged. "That's what Mr. Julian said we needed. Right, honey-bunny?" she said to the old man, snuggling at his neck. The old man giggled as if she was tickling him. The spectacle struck me as both strange and pathetic, and instantly, I felt sorry for the guy. Somehow he seemed like a more dignified sort than to keep this kind of company.

Nichelle introduced herself as the office manager, and by now she looked none too pleased to have Dale and me taking up space. "Uh, I don't really think this gentleman," she said, gesturing toward Dale, "is not, um, he's not—"

Dale appeared to take instant offense. "Not what? I'm a lawyer, and I work here." That seemed to temporarily stump Nichelle. Then he asked Angie what he could do for her.

"You mind?" Angie said to me. "This is confidential."

"Not at all."

I went back outside, took a few steps toward the battered Regal, but thought better of waiting in that old boat. Waves of gorgeous bakery smells rippled over the empty sidewalk. Aah, that tender Cuban-style pork. My stomach tightened at the thought of some real food. The pea soup and limp salad I'd lunched on in the cafeteria had barely registered. A *medianoche* sandwich would make a nice snack while I waited for Dale. I was still picturing those thin-sliced pickles, the hot white bread lathered in spicy mustard, when another line of thought took over. We'd come here to look around, have Dale review any files with his name and bar number committed to them, do any necessary follow-through, tender his resignation from the center. Then in walked Angie and Rudy, the happy couple looking for a powerful attorney, Angie's boyfriend in tow. Asking for a "powerful attorney"—that's what she'd said— an invitation a man in Dale's straits, with his proud background, couldn't pass on. But an invite to what kind of trouble? This looked like a bogus marriage between an old man lacking capacity and a girl probably fifty years his junior, her real man hovering like hired muscle. I turned toward the law center's door and almost started back, but caught myself. Dale was a long-time prosecutor, he knew the lowdown on UPL—at least from what I'd told him. I decided that he could assess the situation on his own.

I strolled to the bakery door and stepped through just as a tubby old bald man inside fed himself half a guava pastry in a single bite.

Powerful attorney.

The words suddenly made sense to me. I let go of the door, watched the bald guy disappear as he inhaled the rest of his pastry. Damn, the Cuban sandwich would have to wait.

They were ripping off the old man Rudy, and I knew what they'd come for.

I started back just as a mud-splashed black Cadillac Fleetwood swung into an open spot next to the law center. A bulb-nosed, potbellied man in funky brown slacks, a sky blue dress shirt, and a string tie bounded onto the sidewalk, pulling on his suit jacket as he went. I felt sure I'd seen him somewhere before but couldn't quite process the memory. He stared back at me like he knew me too, then seemed to decide he didn't and powered into the law center. My first thought was of Julian, but the man didn't fit Dale's description at all—nothing Hollywood wannabe about this guy. I followed him, trying to place the W. C. Fields nose. Something to do with a state bar case, maybe, but not one of mine.

I know all my cases, all the lawyers currently in my sights. They're not easy to forget. I recently prosecuted a bankruptcy attorney who secretly put himself at the front of the creditor line by taking a deed in trust on his client's vacation home as his "fee," then quietly forced a sale and collected his money, ruining the client's hope of reorganizing. Last fall I pursued a tanned, handsome estate planner from Palm Springs who wrote himself into the wills of ten deathbed "clients" in a six-month span, working on tips from his girlfriend, an ER nurse at the region's finest hospital. Just before Christmas I clipped the wings of a high-dollar attorney and TV executive who siphoned a half million to a partner in crime by paying out "finder" fees to a fictitious company, then kiting checks at the end of each month to keep the depleted account falsely balanced. Every one of these lawyers was a virtuosic rationalizer; all were innocent, of course, their well-funded defense counsels decrying the state bar's investigative zeal and intrusive reach whenever the bald facts betrayed them. No one seemingly hampered by a conscience or sullied by a whiff of doubt during trial, everybody leaping onto the religious bandwagon during the discipline phases. Hallelujah, what's it to ya?

Inside the law center Dale's voice was already raised in argument with the man who'd just arrived, Angie cursing loudly over them both. I thought about what I would say to lend support, but before I even got there the glass door burst open and out spilled the potbellied man in the funky suit, pulling Angie and Rudy with him, hand in hand like a human daisy chain.

"Never mind that idiot, let's roll," the funky-suited man said over his shoulder. I was right in their path, and I had an instinct about the man who'd just arrived.

"Afternoon, Counselor," I said.

He stopped dead, as if he'd been called out by a ghost from his past.

"Don't you go gettin' in my way." Sounding southern, maybe from Texas. "You guys got no business followin' me around."

You guys. I *did* know him from the bar, though I still couldn't place him.

"Free country," I said.

Angie's boyfriend stepped into view. "Move aside, asshole."

I didn't flinch, but I had no cause to stop him. He brushed past me, smiling as if he owned me before he hopped into the backseat with Rudy and Angie. The southern lawyer backed the Caddy out hard, and a delivery truck coming down Brand had to swerve into another lane, the driver honking and shouting. Just before they roared off, Rudy raised a palm from the backseat and waved at me like a child going out for ice cream.

Dale was on the sidewalk with me and I asked him for a rundown.

"Christ if I know," he said. "The southern guy just burst in, took a look around, and realized the girl had been consulting with me. I tried to introduce myself and he started shouting at me, threatening me with a lawsuit for stealing his client. I said like hell, then bam! Out the door." He massaged his temple, breathing hard. "I think they're up to something, J. Powerful attorney? I don't think so."

"Exactly. It's not powerful attorney, it's *power of* attorney."

We jumped into the Regal and Dale threw it into reverse, the engine chugging in halfhearted compliance. "They want the old man's assets," he said.

I nodded. "Whatever he's got. The wife Angie must want the full access that being his legal representative would bring her." I pointed through the windshield. "There they are." The Caddy had swung a U-turn and was headed back up Brand, toward us.

Dale faded toward the curb and cut it hard across the double yellow as they passed.

"Where you think they're headed?"

The glass high-rises loomed ahead like a shining Emerald City.

"My guess, to get the money straightaway."

The light ahead had turned yellow and I thought we weren't going to make it, but Dale jammed on the gas and shot us by a grimacing bus driver waiting to make a left. "What do we do next?" he asked.

For the second time in an hour I had no plan, but whatever I did have that had gotten me here, I wanted to keep it moving forward.

Three

The big Caddy glided to a stop in a red zone in front of a two-story brick structure that housed a savings and loan. From down the block we watched the girl named Angie pop out and rush inside, tugging the old man's arm like a dog on a leash past the Colonial pillars and phony white shutters. Dale and I drove past the bank to the next street, found parking in a liquor store lot, and hoofed it back without speaking. Not too long ago, he had been a great observer, as all fine trial attorneys must be. He must also have known by now that I was improvising heavily, this probation-monitoring thing heading south on both of us. As the matter stood, he could already have violated probation with what he had done, and I could be presently witnessing the event. But he hustled to match my stride without further comment or inquiry, and I welcomed the silence.

I had a sick, sinking feeling about that old man Rudy, though, with this little snuggle-bunny wife angling so openly for the privileges that power of attorney would bring her. It made Dale's situation seem all the worse as well. The old man's exploiters had come to Dale's place of employment, which probably was no coincidence because the law center most likely had a shady reputation among shady characters such as these. I wanted to believe that Dale was being used, just like the old man, but that yearning did nothing to lift my spirits. Instead I was left with the sad inkling that Darwin was right, and the wolf ravages the lamb, and the world, well, maybe it keeps spinning along not in spite of these truths, but because they are so.

The savings and loan was set up inside like your standard bank, with ropes and metal standards for herding customers toward the row of teller windows on the right. A loose conglomeration of desks and low-slung cubicles filled the wide-open spaces. A single teller was open for business, waiting on a white-haired guy in a wheelchair with a money pouch in his lap. No lines to see the teller, maroon carpet everywhere, the quiet hum of bank employees at work. No one looked up from the afternoon's business at Dale and me.

Angie was getting after a wispy man in a dark gray suit who looked like management, his forehead rippling as he shook his head. I could read his lips as he said no, ma'am, no, ma'am, to whatever proposition she had for him. The lawyer with the Caddy must have found quick parking outside, for he was already on the scene, barking into the manager's other ear. When the lawyer turned toward us, I saw his western belt buckle rubbing the sag in his beer gut, which triggered a memory.

"The tubby guy, the one who rushed you at the law center," I said to Dale.

"The concrete cowboy?"

"I think his name is Robert Silver." I'd come across him at work, but I couldn't remember how or when. I felt certain he was some form of legal douche bag.

The wheelchair-bound customer was buzzing through on motor power and we stopped to let him pass. The money pouch in his lap looked bulky. I gave him a friendly nod but he clenched the pouch tighter with a hairy forearm and shot me the stink-eye from under his Dodger ball cap. Probably thought I was patronizing him, but I told the guy to have a nice day anyway.

"Let me guess, you disciplined Silver before," Dale said.

The memory was coming into focus. "Not me. But I think he was in our office a couple months ago. One of our lawyers took his deposition." That lawyer was a recent hire named Therese Rozypal, young and smart and politically conservative, I guessed, based on the autographed photo of Richard Nixon she kept on her desk.

"She got a case against him?"

"Not exactly. I think he had his ticket pulled a while back and is seeking reinstatement now. It's his case to prove."

Lawyers who are disbarred or resign with disciplinary charges pending can wait five years to petition the bar for reinstatement of their licenses, but it isn't easy. The reinstatement petition is a lengthy document calling for a detailed employment and financial history, a narrative describing what the attorney has been up to during his years spent in professional exile, and personal income tax returns for the past three years. A trial is automatically set with the filing of each new reinstatement petition, and the hopeful lawyer must prove by clear and convincing evidence that he has been rehabilitated from his former bad behavior, has paid restitution to any clients he ripped off back before he lost his license, and is current with changes in the law and therefore fit to practice again.

I've done a half dozen reinstatements in my time as a bar prosecutor, and have come away from the experience with the rather cynical view that it is hard to buck human nature—particularly when that nature runs toward the procurement of ill-gotten gains through fraudulent means. Put another way: Once a legal douche bag, always a legal douche bag.

"Don't look now," Dale said. Angie's boyfriend was also in on the meeting, guarding Rudy. He'd spotted us and was headed over.

"He can't touch us," I said, sizing up my advancing opponent. One sixty or seventy, not in bad shape, maybe he lifted. He was probably ten years my junior and no real match for me in the push-to-shove department. His bad ass glare could be broken down into equal parts of "Fuck you" and "Boy, I'm stupid," and it didn't rattle me, not here at least, in a well-lit bank full of employees. I felt my fingers twitching at my sides.

The boyfriend stepped into our path with his arms folded like Mr. Clean. "Better split, gen-tle-men. Now."

He had the black eyes of a mongrel and his teeth were small and tightly packed. The face was brown and smooth and far too handsome to have had much experience tearing ass on people. The little shit was so close he was looking up at me, and that smirk was beginning to grate.

"Thanks," I said, "but you don't own the bank."

I proceeded to step around the guy, but he took exception and clamped a hand on my right shoulder, harder than I anticipated.

"I said split, you stupid fuck."

He'd gone over the line, putting his hands on me, and I felt that sweet burst of anger that helps me temporarily override my initial chickenshit instincts when it comes to confrontations. Meeting his stare, I quickly snatched his wrist at my collarbone and twisted it,

corkscrewing his arm inward as my free hand swung up from behind, the butt of my palm nestling under his exposed elbow joint.
He was bent over badly and panting already.

"You're about to hear a large pop," I said.

"Followed by a lot of girlish screaming, I'm guessing," Dale
added. Dale looked pale, but he hadn't backed away any, which I
appreciated.

The boyfriend strained, thoroughly off balance. I tightened my
corkscrew twist, hunching him over until his black beret flopped
onto the floor.

"Okay," he whispered. "Leggo."

"You first," I said. He released his shoulder grab on me and I
let him loose in turn. Dale scooped up the beret and handed it to
the guy.

"This isn't over, man," the guy said, fixing his beret onto his
head as if he was replacing a bird's nest laden with fragile eggs.

My heart was banging a double-time beat, but I wanted to deny
him any edge of intimidation he might think he still had.

"Wearing a beanie doesn't make you a Guardian Angel, pal.
Next time, I'll put you down and you'll get no warning. Now do
something smart for a change and bail." I leaned into his space,
almost daring him to take a swipe.

Just then, I recognized something in me that I didn't much care
for: I only fight when I'm attacked, or sure to be attacked, that's
my rule. But lately I've caught myself taking chances, as if I'm
coaxing that rule into play—bending it, even. Like giving this character a clean shot right after I'd humiliated him. I knew I should
pull back, but the adrenaline buzz I was getting was too sublime
to cut short. Shit, I knew full well what I was fighting against.

In a word: boredom. Monitoring a has-been lawyer's probation,
saving the free world from the unauthorized practice of law, twisting the arm off a dumbshit bully. I was extemporizing heavily, no
doubt, but I was alive and alert and free from the usual routine,
avoiding another tedious, ass-numbing, clock-watching afternoon
at a computer screen. Were I not here now with Dale Bleeker, I'd
be ten floors up and inside those four walls, zoning at the keyboard,
drafting charges against another schmuck lawyer who couldn't resist
skimming his clients' settlement funds, a coke addict who missed

the first day of his client's murder trial, an overstressed divorce attorney who mailed opposing counsel a used tampon with a simple note that said "Thinking of you." Filing, filing, filing, keeping the damned assembly line rolling, only to come up for air to see a scowling Eloise Horton in my door, seeking more of her precious stats.

I pulled back to a safer distance and told Angie's boyfriend to stay the hell out of my face. He pointed a finger at me. "You're dead."

"You talk a lot," I replied. I walked on, intent on showing no further emotion.

"My," Dale said, regarding me as if I'd been halfway brave and halfway foolish. "That was . . . interesting."

We walked by a few startled-looking women at their desks, one who was dabbing at a puddle of spilled coffee. They probably weren't used to seeing a man in a suit square off for action inside their bank.

"Yeah, interesting," I said.

"These guys are serious," Dale added.

I wanted to ask him what that was supposed to mean. He'd seen his share of lowlifes as a prosecutor. The one thing you never do is carry on as if their shtick impresses you. Otherwise, you give them an edge.

"So are we," I said.

Dale looked at me slightly askance. "I mean, they're *serious.*"

Had he lost his nerve?

"That should come as no surprise. One thing I've learned from this job is that money brings out the worst in people." I stopped to face him. "You know that."

Of course a guy like Dale knew.

We continued across the lobby and were not twenty feet from the young bride and her ancient husband when Dale said, "So, what's your take on this? You really think they're jobbing him?"

Christ, he *had* lost his sack.

"I do."

As we approached the manager, I saw the old man Rudy's ball cap pulled down too low again for decent visibility, saw him standing there on the margins of a conversation about his own fucking stake, no doubt, and felt something else breaking loose in me. I'd seen that wrinkled, timid face piling into the Caddy back at the law center, that strange quality of looking lost and carefree at the same time, the kid going out for ice cream but with a blind, sorely misplaced trust in his companions. And I knew I'd been wrong about feeling bored. Whatever was going down, this was not about a few cheap thrills away from the office.

Dale stopped before we reached the others. "What's our tack, J.?"

"Maybe this is a stretch, but technically, you're still the old guy's lawyer. I think he needs you to step in for him, Dale."

Dale seemed to teeter a bit beneath the weight of the responsibility I'd hoisted onto him. "I dunno. It's a big stretch, don't you think?"

I didn't answer him.

"I mean, I only met with him for a few minutes, and the girl did most of the talking."

"Listen," I said, "think about all the files back at that center with your name on them. That Julian character wasn't going to pay you that fat salary out of the goodness of his heart. Remember, they came down there to meet with a lawyer, and for better or worse, right now you're that lawyer."

"Right," he said. "I know."

We pushed past a final cluster of white-faced bank employees. Angie was privately scolding old man Rudy when she saw us coming.

"We don't need you no more, lawyer," she said to Dale with a hint of Chinese accent. "So get lost, huh?" A peach of a girl. Behind her, the sad-eyed bank manager silently beseeched us to do something.

Dale caught Rudy's eye and smiled widely. "Hi, Rudy, I came by to discuss your affairs with you some more."

"This is his lawyer," I said to the manager, nodding at Dale. "Is there somewhere they can talk in private?"

"Hell no, he ain't his lawyer!" the cowboy lawyer snapped. "I am."

The bank manager looked thoroughly confused. "Somebody please help me out here."

I introduced myself, then Dale. I also managed to vouch for Dale without mentioning the probation aspect of our affiliation.

"The question is, who is this guy?" I told the manager, nodding at the cowboy lawyer.

The lawyer sneered, rubbing his protruding gut. "That is none o' your damn business."

"Nice," I said. "An attorney who won't give his name."

"The name's Sawyer, for your information." He winked at the manager. "Now I'd like to get back to what we were discussing before Mr.—"

"Sawyer," the manager said, chewing on the name. "Just a minute. When you came, I thought you said your name was Silver."

"Now just hold on a minute, aah think you're mistaken. What aah said was—"

"No," the manager said, "I'm sure of it."

Angie huffed. "Fuck, Bobby, that was smart."

"Bobby Silver," I said. "How could I forget. You came in to my office to have your deposition taken, remember? So, you still trying to get your law license back?"

"I don't know you, sir, but you can kindly go to hell just the same."

"Mr. Silver is not currently licensed to practice law in this state," I told the manager.

Silver's face reddened and his eyes got rounder. "That's a damn lie!"

"Which means he can't represent anybody."

"Aah am still this man's lawyer!"

"We can sort this out with one quick phone call to my employer," I told the manager. "Do you have an office?"

He looked over his shoulder. "Right over here."

"Let's."

Angie turned to look for her boyfriend's backup, which wasn't there, and in that instant, Dale Bleeker found a way to really help his new client. In a flash he snatched Rudy by the hand, yanking him out of Angie's reach as he led him away.

"Come on," Dale told the old man, "we need to talk about some things in private." Rudy didn't appear to know what was happening, and offered Dale a smile and no resistance.

Angie was hot. "Hey, fucker!" she snarled at Dale. Then she whirled to find her boyfriend. "Carlito!" But Carlito was still rubbing his elbow where I'd tweaked it. "Hey, you, hold on!" she shouted as we headed in full-tilt-boogie mode for the manager's office. "Stop 'em, Bobby!"

We made it to the office door, but Bobby Silver and Carlito had come up fast on Dale and the slow-footed Rudy. Then, just as Angie made a stab at Rudy's free hand, a wide-bodied uniformed security guard stepped into the action and addressed the manager.

"Mr. Dobbs?" he said, reporting for duty with one hand on his black leather gun holster.

"These three are causing trouble," Mr. Dobbs told the guard, nodding at Angie and her merry band of idiots. "Please escort them out."

Silver and Carlito went rather quietly, but not Angie. "He's my fucking husband, goddamn you! No!" The guard waltzed her by the elbow toward the glass doors. "You're making a big mistake! My husband got one big-ass account! We'll take our business right out of here!"

Christ, I thought, where is this poor man's family? And where were they when the girl got her hooks in him? I felt disgusted with the whole spectacle, the blatant money grab.

Angie's final threat had apparently resonated with Dobbs the manager. "She'll be back," he said, watching her go. Then he turned to us. "Mr. Kirkmeyer," he said to Rudy, "these men and I are going to try to help you."

Rudy tugged at the bill of his Rotary Club ball cap. "Hi there." His memory was obviously coming and going like a breeze through an open side window.

I glanced across the lobby, where Bobby Silver, Carlito, and Rudy's new wife, Angie, were getting the royal sendoff. For the first time since Eugene Podette's wife, Trixie, had stepped to the podium in state bar court and so convincingly stolen my thunder, I sensed that I was in charge again, controlling the play.

Or maybe I was deluding myself again.

Mr. Dobbs led us into a square office with two big burgundy leather chairs facing a no-nonsense oak desk with a gold nameplate that read "World's Greatest Dad." He was fair-skinned, with round

Howdy Doody ears and brown hair as fine as peach fuzz on a smallish head, like a boy who didn't quite fit in an adult's body. I watched him close his office door rather mechanically, like a blind man following directions, and I realized that he had been seriously shaken up and was having trouble concentrating. I had Dale and Rudy sit down and told Dobbs I wouldn't need a chair, but another employee was knocking at the door with one for me already. People at this bank apparently aimed to please.

"Anything I can get you?" Dobbs asked. I thought of Carlito adjusting his beret out there on the sidewalk, waiting for me, and almost made a joke about taking that security guard on loan. Dale wanted coffee, black, and I wondered again if he'd been drinking earlier. Shit, what an afternoon.

I called Honey Chavez, my secretary at the state bar, and had her look up Bobby Silver on her computer. Robert E. Silver. The E stood for Earnest. He'd been disbarred six years ago on multiple counts of misappropriation of client funds, charging unconscionably high fees, client abandonment, and various acts of moral turpitude involving the proffer of false documents and perjured statements. Not exactly living up to his middle name.

His petition for reinstatement had been filed nine months ago, Honey went on, trial date set for February 22—shit, that was next Monday. I'd guessed right a minute ago that Bobby Silver was ineligible to practice law, yet here he was "representing" a dubious wife and her rather out-of-it husband in an inside fleece job.

"Thanks, Honey," I said, which always sounds sexist, but what am I supposed to say?

By the time I handed the phone back to the manager, I was already certain I would testify against Silver on Monday. He would pay a price for the crap he'd tried to pull today.

I told Dobbs and Dale about Silver's history. "But forgetting Mr. Silver for a moment, what do you think this means?" Dobbs said. He shoved a sheet of paper stamped "confidential" at me. It was a marriage certificate: Rudolph John Kirkmeyer and Angelina Ho. Two days old. "I've never dealt with a situation quite like this," Dobbs added.

"I don't know if you can marry someone if you lack capacity," I said.

"Even if it's valid, the marriage doesn't entitle her to Rudy's assets," Dale said.

"She's not worried about legal entitlement," I said. "All she needs is the authority to get at his property, and that will be that."

"You won't let that happen, though," Dale told Mr. Dobbs, but the manager just shrugged.

"I'll forestall any access or withdrawals as long as I can, but if she produces legal authority, I'm not sure there's much I can do."

Dale and I stared at each other. I guessed that he, too, knew that this little saga was going to end very badly unless we could show the marriage was invalid.

"Just buy us a little time," Dale told the manager.

Dobbs's eyes darted between us. "I'll try."

"Rudy," I said, "do you know that lady who just left, Angelina?"

"Sure do," he said, the ball cap still riding way too low. "She's . . . she's my friend." Not exactly the answer I was hoping for.

"She's very pretty too," Dale said. "Is she nice to you?"

"Yeah." Rudy smiled, his teeth small and gray, but his sun-spotted face tightened like withered fruit and his blue eyes began to blink hard. It was as if he was fighting something inside but didn't know what it was or when it would strike next.

"What's the matter?" Dale asked in a gentle voice. I remembered what a marvelous questioner he was—that is, had been—back when he had a career.

"Who, me? Oh . . . sometimes she gets mad."

"Like when?" I asked.

"Oh . . . I dunno." His eyes slipped into a fog.

"When, Rudy?" I said. "Tell us."

"Oh, you know? . . . Well, it was last night. They were going out. *Again.*" As if he was offended.

"You wanted to go too?" Dale said.

"*Yes,* I wanted to *go too.* I don't want to be alone every night, watching the tube. *Jeopardy* was already over."

"What did she do to you when she got mad?" Dale said.

Rudy smiled. "Alex Tre-bek!" he said the way Johnny Morton does when he kicks off the show. Then he looked at Dobbs. "I like watching *Jeopardy.* Literary liftoffs for four hundred, Alex. It was the best of times, it was the worst of times."

I couldn't tell if this was part of his dementia or he was throwing up a wall against an unpleasant memory. "What is *A Tale of Two Cities,*" I said.

"Correct! Select again."

"All right," I said. "Right after a word from these sponsors." Rudy's gaze was affixed to the maroon carpet, still shutting us out. "Why don't you tell us what happened last night?" I suggested a moment later.

His lower lip was jittery, and I noticed one of his white tennis shoes had come untied. I bent over to tie it. When I looked up, he was staring at me with something approaching anger.

"They locked the door when they left. I couldn't open it! I . . . got hungry." His voice trailed off in a whimper.

"They do that a lot?" Dale said. "Lock the door on you when they go?"

"You gotta know, it's for your own good, daddy-o," Rudy said, mimicking Angie's street accent.

"What about last night?" I asked him.

He nodded. "Last night? That room got *dark* last night! No windows. No TV! I have three suits . . ." Suddenly he was shaking a little through the shoulders. "But I haven't worn them in ages. Out with the old, in with the new, daddy-o."

Dale put a hand on his shoulder. "You're okay now, pal."

No one spoke. Rudy broke the spell with, "Potent potables for two hundred, Alex!"

Dale took me aside and asked for my assessment. "Sounds like they stuck him in a closet," I said.

"This British novelist created the protagonist who prefers his martinis 'shaken, not stirred,' " Rudy asked me.

"Who is Ian Fleming."

"Correct! He created the dashing James Bond. Select again."

It was like Rudy had memorized a sizable tract of TV trivia and was escaping back into it at will.

"They came in yesterday morning," Mr. Dobbs told us. "She had a key to his safe-deposit box. Left with stocks, some cash and jewels, I think. Cleaned it out."

Dale nearly came out of his chair. "What? That's terrible. Why didn't you stop her?"

"I couldn't, not legally. I hadn't seen Mr. Kirkmeyer in eight, nine months at least. His current condition . . . was a bit of a surprise to us."

"This is recent?" I asked.

"Very. I sensed something right away yesterday. When she asked for access to Rudy's portfolio I tried to chat with him, as I always will with longtime customers. I noticed the change immediately."

"Apparently not soon enough," Dale said.

"No, I did hold her off," Dobbs said, his tone defensive. "Only Mr. Kirkmeyer himself can access his portfolio, and I made that clear. She tried to feed him directives to pass on to me, but I put a stop to it."

"But if she has power of attorney, she won't need Rudy," I said.

Dobbs's upper lip twitched, and he dabbed a few tiny beads of sweat from it with a handkerchief he pulled from his pants pocket. "That's right, but that's not all. She showed me that certificate to prove the marriage was legal. Says he married her of his own free will."

"Rudy," I said. "I want to ask you an important question."

"Select a category."

"We'll be right back with Final Jeopardy after these messages. Rudy, are you married?"

"Oh yes, I am," he said without hesitation. Dale slumped with disappointment at that answer.

But I wasn't convinced. "What is your wife's name?" I asked. "Tell us that."

Rudy gave it some thought. "Thirty-nine years of bliss."

"Thirty-nine years, you were married that long?" I said.

He rubbed his wrinkled chin, grating the gray stubble. "I think so? . . . I think that I would like to go home now."

"Jesus," Dale said. The poor old man was fading in and out on us like a searchlight in fog.

"Rudy," I said, "who can we talk to that's a friend, a really good friend, or a relative of yours?"

Rudy smiled at Dale. "Are you my friend?"

Dale smiled. "Yeah, buddy." He seemed touched by the old guy's sincerity.

"He's got a daughter in Seattle," Dobbs said. "I called her yesterday. Haven't heard back." He saw the look on my face and picked up the phone. "But I think I'll try her again."

Her name was Kimberly Kirkmeyer-Munson, and this time she was in. Dobbs filled her in on what was happening—the confidential marriage, the emptied safe-deposit box, her father's present "difficulty," the assistance Dale and I had provided of late. Then he put her on with Dale. I wasn't up for another round of imaginary *Jeopardy* with Rudy while we waited, so I tried talking about his daughter, but Rudy clammed up, acting put out. I figured he must be tired out from all the running around and backed off. Then Dale hung up the phone and stood over it without speaking, as if he was deciding whether what he'd heard was good or bad. I asked him what was up.

"Nice lady," he said. "Pretty upset about what's happening. Says she had no idea."

"She coming down?" I said.

He frowned. "Not right away. Next week."

Shit. "That won't do," I said. "He can't take care of himself like this." I picked up the phone to call her back and asked Dobbs for the number.

"She can't get here any sooner, J.," Dale said.

I replaced the receiver. "Yeah, well, we can't let those three get hold of him."

"She asked me to look after him," Dale said. "Just until she can get here."

"What do you have in mind?"

He shrugged. "Don't know yet. Take him home. Or we could put him up. His daughter has money, said she'd pay our expenses."

"I can't take him in," I said. "My fiancée and her brother just moved in with me temporarily this morning. I don't have room."

Which was true. My house sits on a small beach lot and is pretty modest in the square-footage department. Three bedrooms, one for me, the others for Carmen and Albert, or so the plan had been as of this morning. Though Carmen and I have been together a few years, she didn't want Albert, who is in his late twenties and mentally handicapped, to recognize that we were sleeping together yet. Carmen is his big sister, his only sibling and primary caretaker for the last ten years or so, and he's attached to her in a major way.

They'd both been out of sorts since January, when their mother's doctor recommended that she be put in a nursing home for full-time care following surgery to remove a brain tumor. The surgeon got the tumor, but the operation left their mother weak and without speech, probably six months from the end of her life.

The nursing home would cost a lot, and Carmen wasn't going to be able to make it for long on her social worker's salary. I'd suggested they look into selling their mother's house, and though Carmen hated the idea, she'd reluctantly agreed. The title search was a shocker: the house was in the name of Carmen's father, a sour, violent, beaten-down old dog she hadn't laid eyes on in something like twenty years. He was still living in East L.A., as far as she knew, but he was a dedicated boozer and might be dead by now. The drinking had started a long time ago, when Albert was tiny and not developing normally and Carmen's dad began pitying himself on an operatic scale. His apparent excuse was that he couldn't accept the fact that his only son was retarded, and the family name would die off. He felt that God had spited him.

The beatings had started when Albert was about six, just a slap on the hand or buttocks at first for an ill-timed cry or a wet bed. The slaps turned to spanks, and slowly, the fingers closed into a fist, with a gangly preteen Carmen intervening for all she was worth because her mother wouldn't take a stand. Eventually the old man lost his job at the Firestone tire factory, started drinking full-time out in front of the neighborhood bodega, and quit coming home at night. Carmen was pleased about that development, though her mother remained loyal and refused to toss out his possessions.

The title search I'd so helpfully suggested had been like taking a crowbar to a fucking Pandora's box. There had been no divorce. Carmen's parents had a common-law marriage, which meant there was no official record of their union. Carmen's mother had made every house payment for twelve years until the mortgage was paid off, but the deed was nowhere in her records. For now, at least, the house was in the name of Ricardo Manriquez. This fact creeped Carmen so badly that she could no longer drift off to sleep under the same roof—"his roof!"—that had sheltered her for every one of her thirty years. Legally, he could blow back in at any time, and every time the doorbell rang, his daughter fairly jumped.

A couple nights ago I'd tried to breathe some hope into the situation by explaining to Carmen a little about the research I was doing on community property law in California. The look she leveled on me was enough to make me swallow my helpful little breath on the spot. Another time, I said timidly.

"You okay, J.?" Dale Bleeker's tone was beseeching. I must have looked pretty glazed, because Mr. Dobbs was handing me an ice water.

"I'm fine."

I chugged the cup of water, picturing the look on my fiancée's face when I told her I was taking an incompetent old man in for a few days, greatly complicating what should have been an easy-does-it period of adjustment for Carmen and Albert. Carmen is an accommodating woman, so she would tolerate the disruption; yet I knew what she would think of me, without her even voicing it.

There you go again, J., trying to do too much. Taking care of others to the exclusion of yourself—and your own.

I remembered the beer-can collection in Dale's Regal. What did I know? Maybe the guy truly did recycle. Yeah, right, what I knew was that I was stroking myself with the recycling excuse. I'd seen too many lawyers like Dale Bleeker to believe that convenient little story.

But I had nothing to lose by trying Dale.

"Think you can watch him full-time until she gets here?" I asked him.

"I don't see why not. Ms. Kirkmeyer-Munson basically hired me to look after him."

Mr. Dobbs nodded, studying something in Dale's expression. "She told you what's at stake, didn't she?" Dobbs asked him. Dale just swallowed. Dobbs cracked a thin smile. "I would certainly hope you know."

I asked Dobbs what he meant. He took up a fancy gold quill from a slanted holder on his desk, scratched something on a slip of paper, and handed it to me. Some nice-looking numbers, trailed by a whole lot of zeros. "Whoa," I said. "Are you sure?"

"That's what careful planning and several decades of compounding interest can do," Dobbs said.

Dale opened the door to Dobbs's office and peered toward the bank entrance. "The guard's still out there, but I don't see the others," he said over his shoulder.

I asked Dobbs if the place had a rear exit. He said it did but that it was rigged to an alarm. He got on the phone again, got a code from an off-site security outfit, and wrote it down. Then he regarded his client with a campaigner's smile that made me begin to see Mr. Dobbs in a less than flattering light.

"We'll continue to take good care of you, Mr. Kirkmeyer, yes we will."

"Heartwarming," I muttered to Dale.

Dobbs turned his nose up at my remark. "I hope you know what you're doing." It was as close as he could come to saying Don't blow this for my bank without actually saying as much.

"You just hold off the wife for a few days," I told the manager.

"What if I can't?"

"Be creative. We'll do our part."

"I certainly hope so."

Rudy just stood off to the side, eyeing a British line drawing of horses and a barn that hung a little sideways on the far wall. Poor guy. Nobody really gave a shit about him, at least not first in order of priority.

We slipped out of the manager's office and into an employee break room in the back with a single metal door that looked formidable. Near the doorknob was a keypad with illuminated red numbers. Dobbs checked his slip of paper and began tapping in a code. "Just a minute," he told us without looking up. "Haven't done this since the last fire drill."

I noticed that my hands were shaking. I suppose I was anticipating violence again. Dale just stood there like a statue, his face a whiter shade of pale. Anticipating God knows what, I supposed. But he caught my eye and nodded affirmatively. I'd seen that look once before, a long time ago in a county courtroom, sitting sore-assed in a jury-box chair as Deputy District Attorney Dale Bleeker wrapped up his closing argument against the jewel-thief baby-sitter, Thelma Ruffo. I remembered the vibe I had gotten when the confident prosecutor gave me that nod, as if he were saying, Hey, whatever the outcome, there's a job to be done and we're in this together. And it made me believe in myself, which, at the time, was something.

Still is.

I nodded back at my probationer.

Rudy's soft-focus gaze had an observant quality I hadn't noticed until now, and I could be wrong, but I thought I saw him wink at me. Suddenly, he didn't seem so out of it after all, and I wondered if he was even sizing me up for what I was worth. Hell, that would be tit for tat, since everyone else had done the same to the old boy repeatedly this afternoon. Behind him, the bank manager persisted with his tapping and fiddling until a red light popped off and a green light popped on atop the keypad on the door, followed by a persistent beeping tone.

"Got it!"

"Players, get ready for Final Jeopardy," Rudy said, his smile so blank that I instinctively reached out to take his hand. Dale's breath was on my collar, he was so close behind.

Then Mr. Dobbs sighed like he knew what awaited us out there, gave a sharp all-or-nothing yank, and wrenched open the door.

Four

Bobby Silver, Rudy's kid wife, Angie, and the sore-armed boyfriend hadn't anticipated our back-door exit, for the alley was empty. We hustled Rudy to Dale's Buick, explaining that we were taking him to meet his daughter, which was a sizable stretch, since she was out of state at the moment. But Rudy didn't protest; my guess was that he'd become used to being shuffled about without apparent reason. He stopped flat when we arrived at the Buick, as if some obscure chord of memory had been struck without notice and was resonating within. I looked at Dale and he at me, and I knew that the unspoken question between us was the same: Is the fogbank lifting? And if it is, shouldn't we ask Rudy the question on both our minds: Is the little spitfire Angie really your wife?

The moment seemed to crawl to a halt. I suppose I was expecting something of true portent to issue forth from those rather thin, cracked lips of his, such was his poise as he stood there, the blue eyes blaring now, the smallish mouth twitching on the brink of a revelation, like an oyster harvested by the low tide and slowly splitting in the afternoon sun, offering a peek at a pearl whose beauty had, until now, lain hidden at the bottom of the sea. I was waiting for him to utter a word like "Rosebud," maybe, to offer us the key to a riddle beyond our grasp, a thoughtful rumination on the nature of growing old or time passages. But that's not how it went.

"Eighty-one Regal," Rudy said. "Four-door, vinyl top, walnut interior, power seats, cruise control, straight eight." Apparently, the Bonnie and Clyde bird-shit-spatter special didn't rate a mention. He winked at Dale. "A very smooth ride."

Dale beamed. "Quite right. This baby just needs a little attention." He ran a finger across the roof; I had to suppress a grin when it came up sooty black.

"Still got the owner's manual?" Rudy asked. I nodded at Dale as if to say, Christ, this guy is sounding pretty good.

Dale hadn't moved yet to unlock the car. "In the glove, Rudy," he said. "Want to see it?"

I was growing tense at the passage of time and began checking over my shoulder. Any second now the concrete cowboy, the kid wife, and the boyfriend would figure things out and be circling back here. "Let's see that key go in the ignition," I told Dale. "We can show him the manual in the fast lane."

"Right."

Dale frowned, but I could tell he was done with his automotive reverie. Rudy went quiet again as I helped him into the backseat and buckled him up. His manner was helpless and distant, that fog rolling right back in already. I decided to hold off on any more tough questions about his latest entanglements.

We cut through residential streets beneath a canopy of mature elms, then traversed an empty restaurant parking lot, bouncing through a big dip in a shower of front-end sparks and flattening a row of rubber cones like bowling pins as a valet pumped his fist at us in the rearview mirror. I knew we'd shaken them when we hit the freeway on-ramp at about seventy-five, not a pursuer in sight.

"Where to?" Dale said. We were currently headed inland, due east, toward Pasadena.

Good question. "What day did the daughter say she'd be flying down?" I said.

"Not really sure."

I shot him the stink-eye across the big front seat. "Say what?"

"Thing is, she didn't exactly say. Really soon, I think."

I thought of the bag of empty Coors cans in Dale's trunk, considered again his claim that he was recycling, and the possibility that what he was recycling was actually the evidence of his own inevitable demise. Was he reliable? The question made me wince, for if he wasn't, I could get stuck housing a semicoherent elderly man for days on end. Carmen was going through something of a grinding transition, facing the imminent passing of her mother, the problem of finding a caretaker for Albert—maybe even caring for him herself—and as of today, adjusting to living in Christianitos, in my own home, and with me. If she and I were ever going to cut it together, helping make her and Albert feel at home had to be my first priority. So why hadn't I gotten on the phone with Rudy's daughter, ironed out the plans myself? Because I'd felt obligated to defer to the Dale Bleeker Redemption and Rehabilitation Project currently under way, and because, more important, Rudy was Dale's client. I needed to give Dale a little room to work, at least for now.

I thought of Eloise Horton, her tight-ass sneer cocked in my direction, shaking her head at me like it was pointed, hands on those high, high hips. Hissing: Told you so, Shepard. Writing me up or demoting me or pounding me with whatever bureaucratic hammer was within her reach at the moment she got wind of this reclamation project gone awry. Hissing: Reaching out to a probationer has its price, Shepard. Should've considered that before you galloped off to save the world. Should've stayed home and done your stats, like I told you.

I didn't even want to think what Carmen would have said right now, yet I could see those round, brown eyes going even rounder and fixing steadily on me as she listened, not blinking, as if to hold back the hurt from another sadly inevitable disappointment. Well, what else is new? she might ask me if she were the cynical type— which she is not. But you don't need a weatherman to tell you it's raining when the drops are spattering on your goddamned forehead. I didn't need to hear her say that something was always getting in the way of real togetherness for us. I knew this much by now.

I waited until Dale guided the big Buick into the carpool lane before I hit him up for more details. Behind us, I saw no signs that the shyster lawyer with the Cadillac was following, which was encouraging. "You talked to her about coming to get her dad," I said. "I heard you."

We hit a relatively open stretch of highway and Dale opened it up, his window half down.

"Mind if I smoke?" he said. He took out a pack of Lucky Strikes from the glove box, handing them to me so I could light one for him. Then he toked with the left hand, flicking the ashes into the breeze as the Buick roared forth and found its groove at a steady seventy-eight miles per hour. Dale was looking a tad too nonplussed for my liking, considering the task at hand, and I frowned. But he didn't look away from the highway to catch my expression, which was a mild reassurance that I might yet live.

"Like I told you," he said, "she didn't exactly say what day. Wasn't sure on such short notice and all." He dragged hard and flicked his butt onto the roadway. This time he caught me looking. "What?" he asked.

"Nice touch," I said. "Next rain, that butt goes in a storm drain and washes into the ocean, right where I'm surfing."

That seemed to pop Dale's little comfort bubble.

"Sorry, my mistake."

A cool, clean breeze shot through the car's interior like an electrical charge. Without notice, Rudy began to sing in a rumbling baritone.

"Won't you come home, Bill Bailey, won't you come home? . . ." Dale and I eyed each other across the front seat. Rudy was slipping again, with that child's smile shining through the wrinkles.

"So, he'll stay with you then," I said. When Dale nodded yes, I felt relieved enough to sit back and enjoy the ride. This Buick still looked like it had a date awaiting at a demolition derby in a mud-caked arena on some clear, wind-whipped, moonless late-winter Saturday night in Bakersfield or Fresno or wherever they still wreck cars for sport on weekends, but the machine did undergo a bit of a transformation at seventy-eight miles per hour, I must admit, shedding its familiar pings and shimmies like a rattlesnake slipping out of its old skin.

"So what about you, J.?" Dale said.

"I guess you can take me home for now. Just go six-oh-five south until you hit Christianitos Boulevard." I sat back, beaten down from the day's events, but a loose spring in the vinyl seats rose up and scratched at my shoulder until I couldn't take it and had to straighten up. I sat there, arms folded stiffly around my knee, no longer wishing to hear about what the top end was for this rig, for it was simply a royal piece of shit.

And try as I might to assimilate this information with my precious vision of Dale, none of it would fit. Not the wienie-wagging rap, or the disheveled suit, or the hundreds of empty beer cans in the trunk, not the bad judgment required to get hooked up with a shady office of nonlawyers, and certainly not the hungry seat springs in the piece-of-shit ride. I sat up straighter still, the seat gnawing at my ass this time as I shifted my weight forward, and I felt like a child confronted with a simple interactive toy I had no hope of mastering, shoving a square peg into a smooth round hole again and again, clinging to the vain hope that the hard edges might somehow wear down enough to make a fit.

"Righty-o," Dale said. He seemed content, as if full up with a sense of hope that had been but a dark cavity inside him an hour ago. Perhaps finding himself to be of use to someone again was the shot he needed.

In the backseat the saints were marching in.

Dale swiveled his head and caught Rudy with a grin. "Oh, when the stars—oh, when the stars! Refuse to shine—refuse to shine!"

An out-of-service commuter bus in front of us finally slowed our pace. Traffic was loading up in every lane, the red lights blinking on in a chain reaction. A billboard plastered across the back of the bus screamed *"Abogados!"* and *"Accidentes!"* in bold neon pink letters, a bigger-than-life Hispanic dude with a pencil mustache and an unhinged grin bearing down on us.

"You'll call me when his daughter gets here?" I said to Dale. But he and Rudy kept bellowing, trading their creaky end-of-the-world verses, and the Hispanic dude kept eyeballing me from the billboard as if he somehow knew an accident would befall me of all people and soon I would be sorely in need of aggressive legal representation, and I gave up. Dale was a licensed practitioner, an experienced former prosecutor. The discipline against his license was minor, unrelated to his professional competence. He could handle the care of an incompetent old man for a few hours without my assistance, couldn't he? Well, he would have to try.

I remembered what Carmen had said that morning, when I tried to carry four bags at once and tripped on the front walk, pulling a nice three-point header into the roses. Don't try to help too much, J. No need to overdo it. Then she'd looked at me, those round eyes going rounder, as if to say: Remember why I'm even here, displaced and forced to move in like this, unable to sleep another night in what I thought was my own home.

Because you had to help.

I wish I could say how it got to be this way, my lending a hand where no other has reached out to take it, offering an answer when no question is pending. Doing more at times when to do less would be advisable, maybe even a virtue. Looking back on my personal history, the view seems somehow oversimplified, like a bad painting, a doctor's-office landscape with spring grass, trees, a fence and a barn dashed into the foreground in bold, easy colors and a swift brown line of rolling hilltops in back connoting the horizon, all of it rendered in a pleasing fashion that, upon closer inspection, reveals itself as a rank counterfeit of any scene you would ever stumble upon in real life. I suppose this is one of my many shortcomings, having a limited view of my history, but I will offer you the best counterfeit vista of my past that I can manage.

I used to think my problem was that I didn't know what I wanted to do with myself, and that until I did, my life would proceed from one diversion to the next, offering plenty of distractions and titillation, but little substance. That suspicion probably arose from my tireless pursuit of the surfing life, particularly during the year after my graduation from college. I was twenty-one, without a girlfriend, wife, or parents to please, my degree in English guaranteeing little more than a low-paying gig as a teacher, or maybe an entry-level sales job with a corporate giant looking for fresh bodies. I had yet to return the rented cap and gown when the phone rang late one night, a lawyer from Chile on the line, telling me in broken English that my mother's aunt Miluca had died a few months earlier, bless her soul, and by the way, I was in the will.

A week later a Banco Pacifico money order for roughly ten grand arrived, made out to me. For three days I propped it up on my kitchen table, leaning it against the salt and pepper shakers, repositioning the thing like a skewed picture on a wall every time I had to season my food, thinking about what it meant to me, almost listening for an answer to that question as if the small instrument of commerce might actually pipe up with a helpful sug-

gestion at an opportune moment. The money order did not speak
to me, but on the fourth day, a travel agent did. The following
Monday, on one of those solemn gray days in June on the coast
when you know the sun will be a miserable no-show, I split for
South Africa, aiming to catch up with my best friend, Jackie Pace,
hoping to just surf and travel and live and put off all the big questions in hopes that, in Zen-like fashion, the answers would come
precisely because I hadn't done any asking. I figured the trip—and
my money—would last for maybe a month or two. I'd packed
relatively light, bringing three new surfboards, two wetsuits, a pair
of trunks, a ding-repair kit, my Walkman, roughly five K in trav-
elers' checks, and not much else. In the surf world, Jackie was a
legend, a former competitive great and short-board innovator who
had refined the noble quest (at least among surfers) for uncrowded,
perfect surf into something of an art form. Perhaps teaming up
with such a veteran seeker would help me locate some new personal
signposts. Perhaps eight thousand miles of separation from home
would shed a new perspective on my aimless situation.

A month or two turned into a year. I remember surfing deserted,
sharky point breaks in the South African Transkei wilderness.
Sleeping all day in hammocks on the beach in Mozambique, drinking cheap East African rum and playing chess with the old men in
town outside the same little restaurant that served nothing but slabs
of fresh sea bass that the half blind chef would incinerate nightly.
Riding huge, perfect lefts in Mauritius, Jackie blowing minds while
I took the wipeout of my life, broke my big-wave gun, and fought
the seagoing rip for an hour. Camping in a wild animal park in
Kenya with a twitching yellow-toothed diamond smuggler who
wanted us to carry for him, Jackie enthused, me repeating the
words "No fucking way" like a chant. Moroccan dust storms,
empty Portuguese reefs, Spain looking as green as Austria in the
winter. A slow thaw in southern France and a long flat spell made
tolerable by a side trip to an ancient spa high in the Pyrenees. A
lot of a certain shy Basque local girl who spoke no English but
managed to cut my heart from my breast like a surgeon, and a lot
of absinthe, not necessarily in that order. Hurricane surf, a stolen
rent-a-car, and a bout of roadside sunstroke in the West Indies.

Through it all, not a single question answered about myself, my personal inventory uncounted and undisturbed, nothing Zen-like to report. Except that, in spite of the hell of a good time I had, I sensed a hollowness metastasizing in me, not creeping like a cancer often does but fairly busting around, like a stray helium balloon at some kid's birthday party bouncing along the ceiling, well out of reach and groping for the sky. One night Jackie and I were in a popular local seafood spot, playing pinball and slamming rum and Cokes after dinner. I guess the competition got hot, because when we finally ran out of coins, we looked up and found ourselves alone, a storm siren sounding off an unseen hilltop. The next two days we spent hunkered down in a one-room cinder-block apartment, playing penny poker, go fish, and old maid atop Jackie's suitcase and swapping lies by candlelight, a surfboard fin biting at my ass as hundred-mile-per-hour winds sandblasted the door and the ceiling beams rattled like bad teeth.

The day the storm broke, we sidestepped fallen tree stumps and coconuts down the beach path and lost our breaths at a most unlikely sight: ten-foot, hot-glass, absolutely reeling point waves at a spot we didn't even know was a spot, not a soul in the water. Jackie and I surfed for six hours without a break. Everything I knew, every maneuver in my repertoire, every pent-up expectation that had gone wanting on fifteen previous years' worth of crummy, overcrowded, wind-chopped mornings—all of it was brought to bear out there among those spinning racetrack walls, all I had to offer, really, laid over in an instant, set on a rail in an extended bottom-turn, an arcing cutback, a hypnotic, needle-threading tube ride. The sun rose higher and the oily surface glass shattered into ten million sparkling shards and the jungle birds screamed their approval, and Jackie and I looped and banked and trimmed and ducked without a care or a worry or a boast or a regret, and not a word passed between us, for there was nothing to say. One late-morning set I paddled into delivered the finest wave I have ever ridden, and when I kicked out a few hundred yards later in the channel I was oddly numb, the way you feel when you find a place you've been seeking for days on a map and it doesn't resemble anything you'd imagined, and immediately you just want to go back the same way you came. The horizon was still throbbing with lines of energy, but suddenly, paddling out for another wave seemed pointless and vain. I belly-rode a line of whitewash in, walked up the beach without looking back, packed my things, and caught a flight to Miami that night, then home the next day.

Tossing the bags on my living-room couch, I could still feel that hollowness, a knockabout pressure in the chest, that damned helium balloon scraping to get out. I suppose it took me that year on the road to learn that surfing may offer a hell of a lifestyle, but it is not, in itself, a substitute for life. I didn't get around to unpacking my wave-riding gear for a month.

Not long after my great wave-hunting odyssey deposited me firmly back on square one, I took a job selling office copiers for a company that reputedly owned about half of Japan. The business plan was to cold-call thirty small businesses a day, and I stuck to the plan, which was about as fun as it sounds—enough said. I was still in training when the sales manager, a reedy former ladies shoe wholesaler named Swede who was actually Jewish and from Brooklyn, invited me out for a friendly beer one afternoon. I should have known it wouldn't be friendly, but Swede was smiling when he told me I was too laid back, and that if I didn't step up my game he'd be canning me at month's end. Then he bought me another beer, saying something about there being no hard feelings as I tipped my suds and wondered why I couldn't stop smiling like an idiot. So this was the world of business. He kept smiling right back at me, muttering something about positive thinking and what he had learned in Alcoholics Anonymous, and I felt like the butt of the Swede from Brooklyn's private joke and contemplated quitting on the spot, yet I held my tongue. I knew I wasn't much of a huckster, but I wanted to go out on my own terms.

Then luck intervened. That night, a summons for jury duty was waiting for me in my mailbox. When I showed it to Swede the next day, I thought he'd explode, but instead, he just shook his head and said son of a bitch, over and over, all the way back to his office. Apparently the company that owned half of Japan was big on civic responsibility here on American soil—they paid for unlimited jury service.

A week later I was sitting in a jury box, captivated by the eloquent, even-handed counselor for the People of the State of California, Deputy District Attorney Dale Bleeker. I pictured myself in his shoes, making my objections, the learned judge nodding, thanking me for my erudite clarification of the evidence code. I saw myself expertly framing a point of fact as a dozen jurors scribbled notes, saw myself boldly contradicting a lying witness with the truth. I couldn't tell if this lawyer thing was shaping up into an actual calling, but in my meandering life, at least it felt like a direction. Maybe even a path.

How I came to overstep is harder to pinpoint. My father died of a heart attack when I was six, and my mother disappeared when I was just turning seventeen, forcing me to become self-sufficient pretty much overnight. I have no other relatives, a lot of acquaintances in the small-town surf scene tradition, and few real friends besides Jackie, who is a world-class loner in his own right. I've basically been alone since before I became a legal adult.

When you learn to do for yourself to survive, your mind can play tricks on you, fooling you into believing that you're doing a damn fine job when in truth you're skirting the essentials. Starving. People say I look like my father. When my mother left I groped for a reason, and for a long time all I could come up with was that maybe she'd grown tired of me, that I reminded her too much of her dead surfer husband. Years later I learned that this was not the case, but by then I'd learned to avoid the intimacy, if not the touch, of a giving woman. I was determined, I suppose, not to be left behind again, by anybody.

Sometimes I think I reach out a tad too forcefully as a way of overcompensating for my own self-imposed isolation. Perhaps I'm trying to silence a little voice in my head that whispers to me when I'm alone in my car on Pacific Coast Highway at night, nothing on the radio, or paddling out at first light, ducking through a pitching wall of golden green. Not worthy.

This all feels vaguely like bad guesswork, built on amateurish research and influenced by half-baked reflection. But I do try to keep the noise level in my head turned down in the event that an important transmission might come through. I don't waste my time or my money pursuing consumerism, that greatest of modern-day mind-fucks, nor do I read self-help books or write bad poetry. I've never seen a shrink, although I did date a leggy therapist a few years ago whom I dropped flat when she told me that my collection of vintage big-wave surfboards shaped by my father was actually a troubling manifestation of phallic insecurity. Of course, I did feel obliged to point out to her that the ten-six balsa model with the offset redwood stringers could easily fetch six figures today at a surf memorabilia auction, but hey, why be a dick about phallic insecurity? But I also can't claim that I am inching closer to any breakthroughs. In the meantime, Carmen is dead right whenever she sighs silently, flicks a loose strand of fine black hair off her shoulder, and points out entirely without irony that my good deeds rarely go unpunished.

We headed southbound in the early twilight, toward Christianitos. Rudy was fairly loopy again, heading into Mitch Miller territory, apparently with nary a worry about the wife, her glowering boyfriend, and Silver the not-quite-lawyer, all of whom were fervently devoted to making him destitute. Dale motioned for me to light him another smoke, which I did. He nodded to me in thanks, puffing with the satisfaction of a man reclaiming his life again.

"I'm feeling good," he admitted, as if he'd forgotten how until now.

I heard the words "I'm happy for you" issuing forth from my lips, but I knew I didn't really mean it, and I wondered if I was just using this man to work out something so personal that he really didn't figure in at all. But Dale hardly noticed my comment.

"Gotta hand it to you. You really know how to do an intake interview. Thanks."

The words "My pleasure" issued forth.

I gazed at the view out my side window, hoping that I hadn't already overextended myself—or Dale, for that matter. Thinking about that faded green sign outside my office window, meditating on the message it spoke, and—oh, what the hell—making the meditation into a prayer for a little direction. Silently watching the day fade into night, ten million tiny lights popping on, one by one, showing the way to go home.

Five

Main Street in Christianitos is a bit of a throwback, a solitary strip of commercial buzz slicing through the center of town like a racing stripe down the hood of a '57 Chevy. For outsiders, I suppose, the wide sidewalks, antique lampposts, and quirky local shops on Main hold a certain charm that's absent from the antiseptic multilevel shopping malls in the area. Throw in the expansive ocean view—free of charge—just beyond the main drag at the foot of the pier, and you've got the closest thing in this area to a tourist attraction. But weekend window-shopping goes only so far, and foot traffic fades whenever the creeping marine layer smothers the coast like a damp wool blanket, which is often. To make it on Main year-round, you need local support.

Driving down Main is like perusing a spice rack: there's one of everything. A lone hardware store. A fish restaurant—the ever popular Captain's Galley. There's one used-book store, a bank, a Laundromat, a liquor store, the Bay Surf Shop, an art house movie theater, the Food Barn market. Then again, Clancy's and the Marmaduke are both windowless dive bars, so I guess they break the Main Street Rule of One. Shit-faced inebriation holds a special position in this town.

"Drop me at Beach Motors," I told Dale. It's the only auto repair shop in Christianitos.

"Your car ready?"

"I doubt it. It's a Jeep wagon, older model. Don't know what the damage is yet. Either way, tomorrow we should report our situation with Rudy to the Glendale police." I got out of the old Buick and leaned in the passenger window.

Dale did his best to appear nonchalant, his left arm slung over the steering wheel like a self-conscious teenager on a first date. "Sounds like a plan."

"Call me in the A.M.," I said.

"Make a new plan, Stan," Rudy muttered from the backseat.

I shook Rudy's hand through the open window. "Dale's gonna look after you, buddy. Take it easy."

Rudy winked at me. "Just drop off the key, Lee." A regular Paul Simon.

I scanned the half dozen or so cars parked behind the high chain-link fence in the Beach Motors yard, but I couldn't locate my ride. Damn, that meant it was still in the garage and wasn't ready.

Dale blew some carbon out of the idling Buick's pipes. "How you getting around tomorrow?"

"Maybe with you again." I wrote my home phone number on the back of a business card and handed it across to Dale. His hand shook slightly when he took it, and in the same instant, he caught the look on my face.

"Can do." He offered me the hand, as if he wanted to solidify a deal that until now had felt sketchy, and we shook. "Hey, thanks for the vote of confidence . . . you know, for today."

My face felt hot. I wanted to tell the man, Sure, not a problem, but the words wouldn't form. Inside, I was knotted up over what I'd done. Volunteering as his probation monitor was one thing, but bailing him out of an illegal employment situation was something much more. Throw an incompetent millionaire into the mix and the whole thing could foul in a hurry. What if Dale Bleeker was no longer the principled DA man I'd built him up to be way back when? Maybe he'd deserved to get canned. And what if he knew that those law center people were using his license illegally and he was only too happy to collect a monthly check for doing nothing? What guarantee did I have that he could resist fleecing his hapless new client?

No guarantee.

"Don't mention it," I said to Dale, sans enthusiasm.

"Sorry, already did. And I mean it." He shot me a thumbs-up sign, and with the gesture I caught another glimpse of the smooth operator I'd remembered gliding to and from the podium in that paneled courtroom years ago. I stepped back from the Buick, mumbling a prayer of sorts. Lord, watch over these two; God knows I mean, you know—they need you now. The car pulled away and into traffic, rattling down Main toward the ocean, a torn piece of vinyl top on the roof curling back in the breeze like a hooking wave.

I was halfway across the asphalt lot fronting the garage when Mickey Conlin, an old surfing cohort and my longtime mechanic, stepped out of the shadows to greet me, a greasy rag in one hand, a silver hunk of carburetor in the other. A crazy tumbleweed of brown hair half covered his eyes, and when he smiled his missing front tooth made him look like a hockey player, a beefy defenseman who lives to hear the sound of body parts crunching against the boards.

"Where's my machine?" I said. His frame was naturally well muscled, but he was thicker in the middle now, probably pushing into my weight range at well over two hundred.

He hefted the hunk of shining carburetor. "Where's your checkbook?"

I've known Mick as something of a tough guy since the first time he pushed me down on the playground in the first grade and demanded my lunch money. I'd surprised him and the circle of kids jeering the action by popping him a good one on the lip, a first for him. On that day my display of moxie did little more than guarantee me a beating at the hands of a bigger, stronger boy, and I accepted it tearfully but without major complaint. But the flogging intrigued Mick. The next day at school I found him trying to pry a shiny quarter from my fingers yet again, and instead of running, I got in three or four good shots before the other kids even had a chance to make the bloodthirsty cry of "Fight!" I took another beating, but afterward, Mick's nose was in worse shape than my face, and when we both returned from a week's vacation courtesy of the principal's strictly enforced demerit policy, he didn't come looking for any shiny quarters of mine again.

What Mickey Conlin could not have known was that I had already learned something about dealing with the threat of violence, specifically that it is all about fear. Not denying your fear or attempting to be fearless, which is sheer stupidity, but knowing it is there, inside you, screaming at you until you can't think and robbing your mind of its powers of assessment and strategy. I learned these lessons at home against a much larger opponent with whom I never fought, but the fear was there just the same, in the back of my throat, where your breath will snag at the halfway point between the mouth and lungs, right where the gasp originates.

Years later, when I took up wave riding in earnest, I found that by chance Mick had been bitten by the surf bug at precisely the same moment. We were the youngest pair of grommets on the beach, backs to the wall against the older boys, who tormented us with the standard hazing rituals. Our heads had been stuffed upside down into trash cans, Indian burns twisted deep into our skin, bodies masking-taped like human splints to the pair of flagpoles anchored in a small flower bed just behind lifeguard headquarters. We'd carted the pier crew's boards, wetsuits, and soggy towels to and from the parking lot like a couple of wobbly pack mules, loitered outside Pier Liquor in the hot summer sun, hopping about on burning bare feet, panhandling change from tourists, then finding someone with an ID who could score us a twelver of brew to smuggle back onto the sand.

"What's with the shit-eater, J.?"

I didn't know I'd been smiling. "Nothing. Just . . . you always remind me of our early days of servitude down at the pier."

"Quite the bottom-feeders, weren't we?" he said, the gap in his teeth flashing.

Mick and I bore those petty indignities together, biding our time and subsisting on humble pie. We stuck around because we loved the ocean, and, I think, because we both had no place better to go. I was an only child and had already lost my father before I started the second grade. In spite of the steady company of a loving mother, my home life was stiflingly lonely. For me, going surfing was like escaping to another place, an exciting new place full of challenge and fear and beauty and tanned girls in the sand and colorful characters in the lineup and endless rounds of surf checks brimming with ongoing passionate discussion and reflection upon the vagaries of wind and swell and tide. It was keg parties and pot and late-night junk food, waiting in line all night for concert tickets that always seemed to put us in the nosebleed section anyway. It was somebody's long-suffering girlfriend buying a ticket to the movies, then cracking the emergency exit so ten more of us could slip in and partake, the alarm buzzing and ushers running down the aisles with flashlights blazing as we laughed and stepped on feet and stumbled through the darkness and into some seats. It was lying in cool night sand that felt like a rumpled sheet, and staring at the stars while tossing off marginally accurate tidbits about Polaris, Cepheus, and Cassiopeia in hopes of impressing my date, the moment shattered by a nearby friend's not-so-subtle suggestion that we all run down to the sea, lose the clothes, and *really get raw*. It was head-splitting, hungover dawn patrols and long fruitless drives to distant windy shorelines, and the pure joy of the occasional perfect day.

And it felt like belonging.

To Mick, surfing was liberation from a home life far worse than mine. Johnnie Conlin, Mickey's dad, was a handsome, gifted grease monkey who'd never put his engineering degree to use like he probably should have. You could just see the guy simmering under the surface. Johnnie also had a thing for Wild Turkey in the morning, liked to flirt with married female customers, and was quick with a socket wrench for any outraged husbands who found their way down to the shop to call him out. Sometimes, when his frustrations were running high and he hadn't been in a good fight in a while, Johnnie would come after Mickey for an unmade bed or a toilet seat left up or some other bullshit, anything to pick a fight. Though Mick never shrank from violence and was good with his fists, he lived by a personal code that kept him from ever swinging on his dad—a code I could understand, although my father never worked me like Johnny did Mick—and this left him essentially unprotected. Mick's mother, a shaky housewife who wore a nightgown all day and was rarely seen out of doors, was no help. It was said that Doris Conlin was a fine schoolteacher before she married Johnnie, a taskmaster who knew how to apply the firm hand to bring about order in her classroom. But Johnnie was a far greater challenge than some kid who'd forgotten his textbook, and slowly, brutally, he stole her confidence. Now she was just as much a victim as Mick, an undiagnosed schizophrenic who lived with a constant, needling fear of when Johnnie would go off next.

Home was an ugly deal all the way around for Mick. One time I was over there, goofing on a guitar and teaching Mick a few chords in the garage, when Johnnie came home and instantly got after his wife over that evening's dinner menu. "Meat loaf a-gaaiinn!" he kept shouting. A door slammed and furniture started to clatter. Mick's mom was crying and screaming through it, and the next thing you knew, a whole set of dishes was flying out of the kitchen like bats from a cave.

For both Mick and me that first summer, surfing was our ticket to a new life, and if subjecting ourselves to an endless series of juvenile pranks was the price of admission, we were more than willing to pay up.

"We were groms," I said.

"Lowest life-forms on the beach," he said, reciting the standard refrain. "But they were some pretty fun times."

Which was true. Until one packed-out day at the pier, when the game got a lot more serious. A dry offshore wind had whooshed out of the inland flats during the night, carrying with it a whiff of sage and the exhaust fumes from ten thousand tailpipes roaring along Pacific Coast Highway. Full-moon weather, the cosmic stuff that supposedly spikes murder rates. The left off the Northside pilings was forming up thick and finely tapered, and each swell was hotly contested. As the morning session progressed, a muscled, cocky-looking surfer from out of town began to lose his cool and started hogging waves, shoulder-hopping local riders and generally acting badly. A challenge was imminent. Rod Weesun, an older pier guy who'd come back from Vietnam with blank pits for eyes and a generally unhinged manner, paddled in, snatched my beach towel from under me, and ordered Mick and me to deal with the interloper.

It was an invitation to a beating, and I said as much to Mick while Weesun hissed about what a pussy I was. I didn't care—although I was already a big kid at thirteen, it was not my way to throw my weight around, and I was not inclined to start trouble. But with the abuse Mick took from Johnnie on a regular basis, he was probably a lot more sick and tired of grommethood than I was at the time, and he didn't hesitate to throw the first punch when he caught the guy coming up to the showers. The other surfer looked twice his size when he squared off red-faced on Mick, and Weesun and the pier boys cackled as Mick absorbed a series of clean shots to the face and head. But he knew what I knew about fear, found his focus amid the tumult, and somehow hung in until the guy's arms tired, then paid it all back and more. A few minutes later, the lifeguards were loading the cocky guy feet first into the back of their Jeep down on the sand and Mickey Conlin was copping his first assault and battery arrest in the parking lot. After that the crew took to calling him Mick the Brick for the way he doled out punishment with those meaty guns of his. He was in the group, and despite my nonexistent backup that day, my status mysteriously rose along with his. We were grommets no more.

As we got older, Mick became an enforcer at the pier, using his reputation to maintain order in the lineup, though he rarely came to actual blows with the perceived offenders. But that was a lot of years ago. I couldn't remember the last time I'd seen him in the water.

"What's the story on the Jeep?" I said.

Mick's rap on my car was ominous. Too many of his words started with "re," which, coming from a mechanic, is not a good thing. "I'll have to repack those bearings," he said, "replace the drum, save you some money if I can find a reconditioned one. You want, I could redo the whole front end while I'm at it."

I rubbed my eyes, staring at the list he'd written on pink carbon paper. "Right, while I get *really reamed* with the bill."

He grinned. "Yeah, well, when your rectum recovers, you might recall my reputation for remarkably reasonable rates." Then he paused. "What, no rebuke?"

I shook my head. "I want a receipt I can read," I managed.

Mickey rubbed the blackened rag into his palm. "Seriously, though, have you thought about giving it a decent burial?" He peered into a remote corner of the yard, where an old pickup caked in dirt sat on blocks, a motorcycle sans engine leaning against it. "Got a little room over there for it."

"You're quite the businessman, Conlin. I get a new car, I won't need your services."

"It's all right, I've got too much work anyway. It's just me and Turd, the great Norse dipshit."

I peered into the garage and made out the outline of my Jeep mounted five feet in the air. Tord the Norseman was hunched below the undercarriage, studying something. "Tord's good," I said. He'd done nice work on my most recent major tune-up.

"Yeah, he is, but his poetry stinks."

"Tord?"

Mick stared into the garage with me. "Dude won an award last week for this poem he wrote about a yellow flower. Wants to hang it in the shop."

"The award?"

"No, the fucking poem."

"You going to?"

He gave a tiny chuckle. "I would if it was any good, but like I said . . ."

I didn't doubt his assessment. For an auto mechanic and former enforcer, Mick was quite the literate bastard, my only surfing friend who frequented the used-book store on Main more than I did and was always reading something. Well versed in the classics even in high school, he'd once helped me with a senior-year term paper for our English lit class, a tortured analysis of the nature of betrayal as explored in *King Lear* that had run aground way back in the first act. Methinks that dog of a paper would have netted a big fat F without his guidance, and I bought him a used *Riverside Shakespeare* in gratitude. My guess is that reading provided a handy escape hatch for Mick when he was growing up, but I have no guess as to why he decided to spend his life poking his head up under the greasy metal asses of automobiles.

Tord looked out from beneath a chassis and saw me. I nodded hello but he ducked behind a wheel well, his lips tasting something sour. "What's eating the poet?" I said.

Mick squinted into the garage. "He's been in a pissy mood all week. Think the award went to his head. He says ever since he got the news about it, he can't locate his muse."

"Tough break." I paused, watching Tord skulk around beneath a chassis. "Know what you should do?"

"Can his ungrateful ass?"

"There's a sensitive approach. But you'd be stuck without a mechanic, so that's no good."

"No shit, I'd be buried." He tucked my estimate under his arm. "What do you propose, Counselor?"

"Easiest thing to do is just let him hang the poem."

"Damn. I knew you'd say that."

"I'm your lawyer. I know what's best."

"Yeah, and the thing I love is how you're so modest about it." He turned toward the garage. "Turd!" he bellowed. Tord's pointy blond head emerged from the dark and nodded at us. "One of our best customers here is sick of reading those old *People* magazines we got in the waiting room. Wants something more highbrow."

Tord's face was flat, as if he was unsure if his boss was fucking with him. "Yaah, okay." He eyed us cautiously.

"Go ahead and stick the yellow-flower poem up on the wall across from the clock. And the award."

Tord looked like a kid in a toy store. "Really? You want . . . now?"

"Better do it before I change my mind."

Tord dropped the pneumatic wrench he was holding and scrambled toward the office, then stopped suddenly. "But, boss, what about the motor oil poster?" I knew the one he meant; a trio of swimsuit gals in white one-pieces and matching Stetsons, phony six-guns smoking—among other things. I've studied it a few times before.

"Just take it down. Fold it up gently."

"Yaah, okay, boss."

"The sacrifices we make for art," I said, flashing my friend the old shit-eater.

"Put a sock in it, Shepard." We watched Tord gallop across the yard to his red Volvo, car keys in hand. "So, you really want to keep the Jeep alive?" Mick said.

I hesitated. "I don't know. Hadn't thought about a burial just yet."

"You're supposed to be the big-time prosecutor," he cackled.

"Hardly."

"You telling me you can't swing a new vehicle?"

I thought of Carmen, what she might think if I tooled up Porpoise Way in a shiny new SUV. My salary at the state bar was decent and the mortgage on my dead parents' house had been paid off long ago. All I had to do was make the property taxes and pay for upkeep. I was also making money managing the business affairs of my middle-aged surf-legend friend, Jackie Pace. In the past few years the vintage surf memorabilia market had exploded, and Jackie and I had worked a deal with a well-known local surfboard shaper to reproduce a series of classic Pace Potato Chip models from the sixties, signed by Jackie and sold at collectors' auctions twice yearly. The first boards netted two thousand apiece, but the most recent batch went for three times that. I was cleaning up on these funky pill-shaped early short boards, these instant relics that were destined not to ride waves, but to hang above fireplace mantels. This last year the money had gotten so good that I was able to bank half my bar salary, sit back, and watch my 401(k) plan grow.

Carmen had no idea that I was doing this well financially. I figured if she did, it might make her more reticent about marrying me, what with her proud streak about making it on her own and her current financial woes. One of these days I would have to tell her, but not yet.

"Just get it back on the road," I told Mickey.

He flashed the gap in his teeth at me. "Gonna take some doing this time, J. We're not talking tune-up, as you know." The bottom-line total he gave me was in the neighborhood of a down payment on a new car, but my mind was made up against that because of Carmen.

"Just give the good poet the word," I said.

"He already ordered the parts this afternoon." Mick nodded as I shook my head at that little revelation.

"Nice call, Svengali. You could have been stuck if I'd said no."

He shrugged. "Something told me you weren't ready."

"I want to drive it to work tomorrow."

"Not likely," he said. "Won't be ready till noon, maybe eleven if Tord is quick about it."

Not a problem, I thought. I was long overdue for a surf, and that was all the excuse I needed for tomorrow morning. "Guess I'll have to go slide a few by the pier."

Mickey Conlin gazed down the street and into the whistling breath of the Pacific. "You still into it pretty heavy?"

"Not like we used to be, of course, but yeah, I still make an effort. When Jackie's around I tend to get out more often."

"Who you surfing with these days?"

"The usual gang of idiots." Actually, most of the crew from our day was gone—moved away, dead, or in jail. I stopped keeping track years ago.

These days I just didn't have the time to hang at the beach, and my surfing forays had been reduced to quick tactical strikes of an hour or two at most. More often than not I surfed alone.

I had a thought about tomorrow. Perhaps I could take Carmen's brother, Albert, out for a paddle. He was a total novice but he loved the thrill of catching a wave, and a nice little session would probably help get him adjusted to his new surroundings. Yet Albert was so far beneath my experience level that surfing with him felt a little like baby-sitting. It would be nice to hit it with Mick, who had been an accomplished rider in his time.

But there was more to it than just surfing with someone on my level. These days I was noticing more than ever the lack of familiar faces around town and in the water. When I was sixteen it seemed like my friends and I owned the beach, the peak on Northside, the half dozen best parking spots for drinking without the cops seeing you in the beachside lot on Friday night. The sidewalks on Main were our private skateboard park, and we slalomed and banked in and out of cars and bodies wearing scowls that let people know they were in *our* way. Of course, we had to grow up, and the more I traveled to surf breaks in other people's backyards, the more I realized that I couldn't rightly lay claim to a damn thing for my own in a world so diverse. That is, not if I wanted to be anything more than a rank hypocrite, and surfing is too full of those already. I'm talking about guys who will vibe you like heavy locals the minute you set foot on their beach, but can't wait to jump in the car and go crowd out someone else's spot when the swell is hitting better there.

But growing up around here was a good time while it lasted. Then came college and a lot of hours chained to a desk, then law school, and what felt like double leg irons anchoring me to that desk, a three-year sentence to late nights in a hard chair under a hundred-watt reading lamp. After that came increasingly complex legal work up the freeway in L.A. I first represented parents losing their kids, because of abuse or neglect, in juvenile dependency court. As parents, most of my clients were simply clueless. Convicts, drug addicts, unrepentant wife beaters, teenage moms. Most of them weren't too keen on personal accountability, which meant that they usually depended solely on me to set their worlds right again. The responsibility weighed on me day and night. That is why, when I came to the state bar, I was so tickled that my "client" was the agency and its principle of protection of the public, not some poor loser with a bullshit sob story and a heart full of unrealistic expectations—for me, distance represents safety. But Christ, a dishonest attorney can cause phenomenal havoc, as a three-hundred-exhibit paper case will quickly teach you. In this kind of litigation, the details can swallow you whole if you let them. I know because it's happened to me plenty, and in a system in which the flow of new cases is seemingly endless, winning does not always feel like quite enough. All too often I am left with nothing more than aching eyes, a pulsating headache, and a long sit on the freeway after dark, alone. Peeling off the Pacific Coast Highway and heading down Main, I pass storefronts closed up hours ago, hear a skateboard clicking by on the sidewalk just out of view, catch a hint of salt air and french fries, see the flash of an old pickup with a pile of surfboards poking over the tailgate hanging a left way down the block. Without thinking I speed up—was that someone I know? Doubtful. So I slow down again, knowing these are just flashes of a played-out dream tripping by, fragments of a lifestyle that once was so vital to the question of who I am, but is now just slowly, inevitably slipping away.

Which makes me sad.

Christ, Mick might not even surf anymore, but he knew what I knew about the life we once pursued, and he'd valued it just as I had.

"Meet me at the pier at six," I said. "The weather's supposed to clear. There should be some wind swell left over from the storm that just blew through."

He scratched the toe of his boot on the pavement. "I don't know, man. It's been quite a while."

"Come on. As your attorney I'm telling you, you need to do this. I'm *advising* you to hit it with me at the crack."

"That's fine, but I gotta open up around here at eight."

"Let the poet do it. He thinks you walk on water right now."

Through the smudged office window. I could see Tord pulling down the old motor oil poster.

"We'll see." Mick's tone was noncommittal. "Think it'll be crowded?"

I didn't know. Weekdays you used to be guaranteed uncrowded surf, but lately the pack near the pier seemed to be ever present. "I hope not . . . for their sake," I said.

Mick didn't respond to my little wisecrack, but instead gazed across a row of shining car hoods at the white brick wall backing the property. His eyes seemed to be reflected inward, like those of an older man studying yellowed photos of his former self.

"We'll see."

Six

I walked down Main toward the pier and stopped at the Food Barn, where I picked up four steaks, garlic bulbs, extra virgin olive oil, fresh angel-hair pasta, a bottle of balsamic vinegar, and a halfway decent Chianti. The storm clouds had passed and the stars shone a cold white in the night sky, the wind salted and brisk off the sea. Outside the market, I stood next to the community bulletin board to avoid the chill as I counted my change. Thirty-nine bucks at the register—damn, that happened fast.

An older woman in a clear plastic raincoat emerged from the market and thrust open a huge black umbrella, eyeing me harshly as if to discourage any smart-ass observations about the rain having stopped hours ago. She clicked down the sidewalk past dark storefronts, struggling to lead with the umbrella against the whipping onshore winds, her rigid posture reminding me of Mary Poppins, awaiting liftoff with the next powerful gust. Then she paused and glared over her shoulder as if to ensure that I wasn't following her. I nodded affably and called out good night. The dear lady flipped me off. Christ, this town seemed to be getting meaner by the day. Mary Poppins picked up the pace, still shooting me the stink-eye, then disappeared behind an overstuffed Dumpster.

A hundred three-by-five cards chattered like a tiny wind-powered engine. Tonight I wanted to make a nice dinner for Carmen and Albert, to help them feel more at home, but I knew Carmen would feel uncomfortable sitting around and watching me cook on the same day she unpacked her bags. She's too proud and independent for that and would at least insist on helping. My plan was to marinate the steaks and grill them outside on the barbecue while she made a Caesar salad and boiled the pasta. Give her something to do while letting the house fill up with the smell of cooking food.

My change count tallied two nickels, six pennies, and a rumpled dollar bill. I hate being without any cash. I'm not fond of the credit card hustle, so if my wallet's empty, I really feel it. I headed across the street to the ATM, thinking, Christ, it's cold and this suit jacket may be wool but it's worthless against this breeze, and what the Mary-fucking-Poppins was with that old bag anyway, and damn, I should've bought the tri-tip that was on sale as long as I was there . . . a typically high-minded procession of thought. I drew closer to the money machine, which was bathed in overhead light like an altar in a shrine to capitalism, and now I was rationalizing about the risk involved in withdrawing cash on a dark street at night, not a slick idea, partner, but wait, I was in a small town not known for crime, *my* small town, that is. So on and so forth.

My bank card was buried in the machine, my grocery bags set around my feet like cement shoes, when I heard a male voice. "Um, excuse me, but—"

I whirled. "What do you want?" I sounded paranoid, heart thumping in my ears. In L.A., you don't approach people using an ATM at night. Ever.

He stood beneath an awning in front of the bicycle shop next door, well out of the glow of the orange floodlight the bank had installed high above the machine I was using. In the shadows he looked tall and rangy, his long hair jagged about his shoulders. "I was wondering if you could help me out a little, bro."

Bro. A clichéd term of endearment some surfers use on other surfers.

"Sorry. No." I tore three twenties from the machine and stuffed them into my wallet.

"My girlfr—we . . . I just, need a little, um—"

"Listen, man," I said, cutting him off and still sweating the situation. "This isn't the time or place to hit people up, get it? You could get shot."

"Oh. Yeah." The silence of recognition hanging in the air between us. "Fuck," he muttered, though out of fear or disappointment I could not tell. I gathered up my bags and got out of there fast.

• • •

Every time I see my house on Porpoise Way I just walk right past the memories. I see a father who looked a lot like I do now and died too young for me to remember him much more than you might recall a friendly neighbor who packed up and moved on rather suddenly one day a long time ago. A mother who split early one morning without a good-bye when I was just seventeen, quietly so that she wouldn't disturb my sleep. The gorgeous spearlike surfboards my dad shaped by hand for riding big waves, valuable relics now, hung along the walls like big-game fish. My mother's offbeat tastes reflected in a seashell-encrusted lamp in the kitchen, a beaded rainbow rug in the upstairs bath. Chilean rococo, she'd say with a wink. Just objects, I tell myself. Forget nostalgia; home is not a place, it's a state of mind. One that I've located through the act of dialing the ocean's rhythms, of understanding and, with years of practice and absurd dedication, mastering the complex mechanics involved in riding a breaking wave while standing upright on a surfboard. Home is not this stoic house that greets me in the shadows each night as if it hadn't enough faith in my return to shine a light down the front walk. Not hardly, thank you. Home is the many friends I've made in the lineup and on the beach, the commonality of experience, the shared addictions, the early-morning surf checks and evening glass-offs, the half-baked, wave-greedy safaris to Mexico, the wrong turns, blown engines, and encounters with banditos. The rush and stoke and walk-on-water beauty of the act.

I feed myself this kind of bullshit all the time. It helps make the empty spaces inside this house less noticeable.

But tonight the little two-story with the narrow brick path, overgrown roses, and upstairs dormers staring down onto Porpoise like a pair of gentle eyes was aglow from every window, and I slowed my steps up the front walk just to soak in the odd sight. Inside, Albert was sprawled in front of the tube in the living room, catching a video from his extensive personal collection—Tom Hanks in *Big,* the same film he'd been watching when I showed him how to work the VCR that morning. Albert can sit through a film five times in a row, mesmerized.

I called out a greeting.

"Hi, J.," he mumbled, fixated on the movie, which was almost over. Hanks was back at the amusement park, face-to-face with the magic wish-granting genie that had made him an adult. Wishing now to be a kid again. I caught my half-lit reflection in the hall mirror, and it almost didn't seem real, my image there in the mirror. Nor did the passage of time. But here you are anyway, I said to myself, and you can't fight change. My brain was saying, Don't just stand there, you might as well come inside, but the feet weren't listening. Maybe this was why Albert watched his damned movies over and over again. Maybe he was aware of the same slippery passages of time and had found a way to hold on to something a little bit longer, or at least *feel* like he was holding on. Then he looked at me self-consciously, as if suddenly aware that he was in my living room, watching my TV, and my feet started to move again.

The kitchen lights were blazing and the door was open to the backyard. No sign of Carmen, or Max, my pet Rottweiler. I put the groceries on a counter near the refrigerator and thought I heard a female voice calling out.

"J.?" Coming from the backyard. I opened the kitchen door.

"Help me!"

Max was halfway across the yard, standing under the pepper tree and peering into the branches with great interest.

"Max!" I shouted. He's one terrifying dog when he wants to be, but he's a smart one, and he usually picks his places to be ferocious. This wasn't one of those times, and when he saw me he bounded over, his big tongue flopping. I gave him a quick pat and went to the tree to get Carmen down. She was about six feet up and looked at me queerly when I reached for her.

"Not so fast . . . what about him?" Max had fallen in behind me.

"Sit, Max. Stay." As always, Max obeyed.

"Thank God."

I lifted Carmen down. Her faded blue jeans were baggy and torn at the knees, but not from this latest little adventure. Even in a loose navy blue sweatshirt, her black hair in a plain ponytail, she looked just right. She was shivering and I wrapped an arm around her shoulder, her cocoa brown eyes never leaving Max.

"You okay?"

She nodded. No point asking her what had happened, she'd tell me soon enough.

"How long you been up there?"

"Couple of minutes. Man's best friend there attacked me." She said it like she was shaming Max in the process, and when I turned and shot him the old stink-eye, he lowered his massive head and slunk away. "I had no choice but to run for it."

Despite Max's awesome physical stature, I'd never known him to attack anyone absent provocation or a direct command.

"Bad dog," I scolded Max. He settled onto the bottom porch step and rested his chin on his paws. I can tell when he's upset or embarrassed, and right now he was both. Like me, my dog has a sensitive nature. "He won't bother you," I told Carmen.

"He'd better not." She seemed flustered by Max's sudden and convincing display of passivity, and she glared at him until he had to look away. Oh, Max, I wanted to whisper to him, what I could tell you about women.

"So—"

"I thought I'd help you out tonight by feeding him before you got home," she said.

"That was very considerate of you. Thanks." When I kissed her on the cheek, I spied Max's shiny metal chow bowl lying upside down a few feet from the base of the tree, empty, a few loose nuggets of dry kibble nearby. He must have been hungry tonight. Cold weather affects his appetite that way.

Carmen's smooth brown face was still screwed up tight. "He was lying here taking a nap a little while ago."

"Loves his spot under the tree."

"Right. So I brought his food to him, put it down, and right then I remembered, you feed him over there, on the path by the garage."

Which was true, and by now I knew how she'd goofed.

"You tried to move his food."

"I didn't want him to make a mess on the patio." She nodded at the used brick surrounding us.

"It's no big deal, Car. You didn't need—"

"It was to him! He practically lunged at me! I just dropped it and got up the tree. What's the matter with your dog, J.? I've never seen him like this."

"Nothing," I said, finding just the wrong word at the wrong time.

She pulled free from my hug and crossed her arms. "Nothing?"

"I mean . . . no, it doesn't matter. Let's go inside."

"What?" Waiting me out. "Tell me."

It was simple. "It's not a great idea to take a dog's food away while he's eating." Her look was blank. "It's a survival thing. You remove his food, a primitive part of his brain sees red. Dogs are territorial."

"Territorial."

"Max wouldn't attack you, Car, he loves you. You just threatened his space at the wrong time and he ran you out of it."

She eyed Max again. "Interesting." Across the yard he was faking nonchalance, but I know that big boy, and his ears were burning. "I've never had a dog. Don't think I want one."

I tried a warm smile on her. "Pretty soon what's mine will be yours."

"That thought crossed my mind while I was seeking traction on the side of the tree trunk." A good sign. Her sense of humor was coming back, along with the color in her cheeks.

"Max loves you, Car," I assured her, nodding at the big black beast. "Isn't that right, buddy?"

Max perked up instantly and loped over to make amends, Carmen wrapping her arms around my waist like a lifeline as he approached. He sat at attention, tongue sliding over those big pointy pearly whites that, regardless of his master's rap on animal instinct, were all business, all the time.

In a gesture of her trust in me, Carmen reached out and patted him on the head. "I love you too, boy. Just don't eat me, eh?"

Max was so happy he barked, making Carmen jump. But she held her ground.

God, how I love them both.

Dinner went smoothly enough. Albert didn't say much when I laid an invite to go dawn patrolling on him, but he's not exactly a wordy fellow. Down Syndrome casts an opaque haze over his personality and emotions much of the time. Then again, Albert will surprise you with a sharp observation when you least expect it, and a good sense of humor, like his sister's, is at work beneath the surface, if you listen closely.

Last July I took his sister and him to the on-the-sand wedding of a local friend and pier regular named Ted Strunk, a guy we'd affectionately called Dead Skunk since about the second grade. Fifty or so invitees huddled on the Southside beach down near the South Jetty near sunset on a windy late afternoon, the scalloped high clouds out past the surf going flamingo pink as a smiling young minister in a Hawaiian print shirt presided over the nuptials. Earlier, on the walk down Porpoise Way, I'd related to Carmen a few vital stats about the Skunkster. His silky smooth goofy-footer's style on the Southside lefts peeling into the pier in the winter. An ingenious practical joke he pulled in junior high involving a visit from the superintendent of schools, a pair of black pumps and fishnet stockings, and a blow-up sex doll levitating in our tight-assed gym coach's office window at precisely the right moment. Skunk's gift for mimicry, and his up-and-down—but mostly down—employment status as a jazz saxophone man and local stand-up comic. Albert trailed along behind us as I spoke, saying nothing. As usual, I forgot he was even there, and wisecracked to Carmen that Skunk didn't need two toasters and a crystal gravy boat to help ease him into matrimonial bliss, he needed some steady work.

Down on the sand a half hour later, the smiling minister got to the part where he asks if anyone knows why the two lovebirds should not be joined, and if so, to speak now. A few seconds of bloated, obligatory silence followed, broken only by the faint cries of seagulls floating high above the wet jetty rocks. That's when Albert, in that slow, stammering voice of his, said "J. says S-s-s . . . Skunk . . . n-needs a job."

That was easily the loudest laugh I'd ever heard anyone get at a wedding, and man, every last one of Skunk's friends and family offered to buy Albert a drink at the luau reception that followed. For his part, Albert seemed happy but mystified, sipping on a fruit punch until his lips were stained red and dancing with Carmen a few times to some live reggae in that funky slow-mo style of his.

Typical oblique Albert, content to wait quietly for the payoff we'd both promised him: that big slice of wedding cake, icing piled high, a scoop of vanilla ice cream on the side.

Albert likes weddings. Ask him why and he'll look at you like you're the one who's slow. "Everybody's happy, and the cake is good," he'll tell you. I guess that's why I bristle—as does Carmen—when people label him "retarded" or the more PC "special." Albert is just Albert.

As I cleared the dishes away, Carmen noticed him grinding his teeth a little as his eyes stared into his empty pasta bowl. He does that when he gets overexcited. She gently brushed away the coal black hair from his forehead and let her hand caress his wide cheek. His eyes were still intent when she said, "Baby, what's the matter?"

Albert said nothing, but he looked out of sorts. Damn, I thought. First night here and he's homesick already. Not good.

Ever since we'd met two years ago in juvenile dependency court, this had been a mighty sticking point between Carmen and me—what to do about Albert. Would he just live with us always, as if he were our own adult child? Or could he live in a structured home environment with other men like himself—and, most of all, would Carmen ever be able to let him go? None of this would be worked out tonight, or any time soon, for that matter. I took the dishes to the sink.

"*Papi,*" Carmen was saying to her brother, "*está bien. Sana sana, colíta de rana . . .*"

A home for Albert apart from us. I'd actually heard of such a place through the local pastor at St. Ann's, Father Ashton. Father had seen the three of us at mass last year when they spent Labor Day weekend at my place, escaping a late-summer heat wave. A few weeks later I bumped into the old priest in the paint section at the hardware store. There he was, a man of the cloth, toting a gallon of "virgin white" in each hand. I had to laugh, and bagged on him a bit, which he handled with good nature. But we got to talking, and he commented on the dark, disarming beauty he'd seen me with at mass. Almost without thinking, I brought up the other half of the Carmen equation. There was a home, Father Ashton said, where adult men like Albert lived in rooms of two, eight to a house, fully supervised by caretakers trained in caring for special-needs adults. A Catholic home called the St. Regis. Not that I gave a shit about the religious qualifier, but apparently it was the only ticket in, since some heavyweight Catholic donors had fronted the start-up bucks, currently sat on the home's board, and had the last say about who got in. Fine by me—I liked the sound of a home where Albert could be with his peers. Carmen didn't. Last month Father called to tell me there was an opening. I phoned Carmen, gently pitched the idea, tried to set up a visit. She hung up on me—twice. We haven't spoken about it since.

All was quiet in the dining room as I loaded the dishwasher, Max laid out a few feet away on his mat by the back door. When I came into the living room Carmen was reclined on the couch; she'd found my old hardbound copy of *Lord of the Flies* in the bookcase and was reading it on her back, one long leg on the cushions, the other dangling to the floor. She had to be bone tired from the early-morning move and dealing with her mother's illness and Albert's full-time supervision, but I liked seeing that she apparently felt free enough to slouch in my home, and I didn't care about the reason. Albert was on the floor in front of the set, searching his bright blue L.A. Dodgers gym bag for another video, the nightly local news on the TV screen. He looked up, hesitant.

"W-wanna . . . w-watch one together?"

"Sure, buddy." I peered into the bag and didn't like what I saw: A Travolta flick involving a talking baby, a few Chevy Chase duds, a bony freckled kid named Pippi Longstocking riding a smiling big-lipped camel, some second-tier Disney musicals. Christ. My instincts told me Carmen needed some maintenance, but my first evening at home under the same roof with her was about to go Chitty Chitty Bang Bang. Maybe *Big* is still in the VCR, I thought as I made for the TV.

"Look, J.," Carmen said, pointing at the screen, "that's the state bar's building, isn't it?"

It was. I found the remote and cranked up the volume. A local news reporter named Marty Handlesman was staked out in front of my place of employment, talking about the new blue-ribbon panel of bar evaluators and the "mission" they were embarking on beginning next month. "Their mandate comes directly from the governor," Marty intoned soberly. "To clean up a disciplinary agency that's supposed to be cleaning up the profession of law."

Supposed to be. Nice slam, Marty. His walrusine jowls flapped on about reform and accountability and budgetary this and that, the bottom line unchanged: we were in for another shakeout, this one by a hand-picked group the governor had dubbed "ADEPTT." A strained but nifty acronym for Attorney Discipline Evaluation Panel for Timely Transition. A heavyweight panel made up of a few retired superior court appellate judges, a TV-friendly ethics professor from UCLA Law School named Bernard Schmidt, and the former city attorney from Riverside, Norma Erstad. Marty was telling the viewers at home how great it was that the panel was headed by the "esteemed" former state senator, attorney, and businessman Miles Abernathy.

"Great," I said. "Miles Abernathy. Two years ago he sponsored a bill to cut our operating budget in half. He should be very fair-minded." Abernathy was talking on tape now, his hair thick and pewter-colored, the tips like polished silver. His face was wrinkled but tan and handsome—a deal maker's face—and his teeth were white and straight, but a size too small.

Carmen and I stared at the tube, Albert an afterthought once more. "The guy looks pretty confident," Carmen remarked.

My dinner felt like a brick in my stomach. "He does, doesn't he."

Marty was interviewing Abernathy now, asking for elaboration on the panel's mission.

"The state bar has often been criticized for being bloated and arrogant, Marty," Abernathy said. "And rightly so. In the past, they've operated on an ever increasing budget, and have failed to listen to calls for reform." He paused to stare straight into the camera. "If the bar doesn't heed the call and follow the panel's recommendations this time around, the only alternative might be to shut it down."

"Do you think it'll ever come to that?" Carmen asked me.

"I hope not. This guy and a handful of other gadfly attorneys in Sacramento have been saying that for years. They'd like nothing more than for lawyers in this state to be unregulated. They hate the bar but they don't have a single alternative to offer when they talk about blowing it up. It's bullshit." As I changed the channel I caught a flash of consternation on Carmen's face. Oops, no cursing in front of Albert. "Sorry about that," I said. "I meant, it's baloney."

"Be more careful, please," she said. Albert was cross-legged on the floor, inspecting a comic book I'd put on his bed before he arrived this morning: "Space Replicants Invade!" It was full of muscled action heroes repelling alien invaders with insect faces. As usual, I couldn't tell if he'd been listening. "Maybe the others on the panel will be more fair," Carmen added.

The news show shifted to another story, a piece on the mudslides the rain was causing in Malibu Canyon. I changed the channel just as a Mediterranean hillside mansion was shown slipping partway down a disintegrating hillside. Christ, the fundamentalists would love that. As I suspected, *Big* was still in the VCR, so I hit rewind.

"Yeah, maybe they'll be fair," I said. "I don't want to look for another job anytime soon."

Carmen sat up enough so I could slide in beside her. In the lamplight her brown skin emitted a subtle glow, like burnished wood. "You've got your hands full as it is, Mr. Shepard."

"Don't I know it." It was the first complete thaw since the Max episode, and I took advantage, leaning over to kiss her on the mouth. The doorbell rang.

"Look!" Albert shouted, pointing out the living-room window at the spinning red lights atop a police car out front. "The Replicants are here!"

Cops on my doorstep are nothing new. I've lived alone here since I was barely eighteen, a circumstance that provided for freedom of expression and debauchery on an epic scale. This was back in the day when partying with nothing to celebrate except getting wasted one more time was *the* thing to do every Friday and Saturday night. I knew all my neighbors and they knew me, and typically they tolerated the rumbling stereo thunder, the intoxicated war whoops from the upstairs balcony, and the rustle of ripped kids peeing on their front lawns in the dark. Then an anonymous call would be made and before long a Christianitos PD black-and-white like the one out front right now would cruise by to look in on the situation.

The inquiring officer was always reasonable enough, nodding and grinning through the screen door mesh as if reminded of a tanned girl in a print skirt and sandals he'd once known, a night when he himself had shotgunned one too many cold ones and got a bad case of the whirlies. Usually they would ask me to give the word, I'd give it, and within a half hour the whole show would be history, Porpoise Way black and speckled with litter like an empty fairground just after the circus blew town. Then I'd be alone, plunging a backed-up toilet and plucking butts and empties from the rose beds out front, wondering, again, why I ever believed that filling this house with virtual strangers would make it feel any less empty to me.

The officers on my porch tonight delivered their good evenings with a deference I rarely saw back in my party prankster days. The smaller one, a Latino named Terraza with slicked black hair, stood a few feet behind his partner, Officer Hale, and let Hale take the lead. I'd seen Hale around town for years, fishing off the pier on his days off, hoisting one in the Captain's Galley at happy hour, buying a smoke alarm at Christianitos Hardware. He was big, standing eye to eye with me as he talked, his furry white eyebrows contorted as he adjusted the ample roll hanging over his belt to his satisfaction. I asked them to come in, Carmen and Albert wedged behind me in the doorway. But Hale nodded over his shoulder at the street as if he didn't want to take his eye off something.

That's when I saw Dale Bleeker's tattered old Buick parked a dozen feet up from the squad car, bathed in rays of ethereal spotlight glow.

"We picked them up at the pier, in the parking lot," Hale said. "Guy driving is a regular down there."

"How's that, Officer?"

"Loiterer. He uses the toilet facilities for shaves and spit baths at night. I've never seen the old man, though. The owner of the vehicle says the gentleman is his 'client.'" At that, Hale exchanged a smirk with his young partner.

I opened the screen and, stepping onto the porch, peered into the street. I couldn't make out Rudy, but I could see Dale's dark silhouette, a cigarette pulsing red as he puffed hard, his big hand atop the steering wheel like he was still cruising down the fast lane the way he'd done earlier tonight.

"He also says he knows you, you can vouch for him," Hale told me.

"I can," I said. "He's okay." That wiped the smirk off of Terraza's face. "I thought he'd be putting the old guy up in his house tonight," I explained. "He lives not far from here."

Hale's handheld radio chirped out a muffled dispatch that he ignored. "Apparently he's going through a split. Wife's got him sleeping outdoors, on the pool furniture."

Jesus, I wanted to say. "They're not under arrest, right?" I asked.

"Nah. Technically they were loitering, but you know, this is a small town." My cue to step in.

"What can I do to help?"

Hale folded his arms and sighed, doing his best Andy Griffith. "Well, if you can see fit to get them off the street tonight, I think that'll be the end of it."

"Sure," I said, committing to two more houseguests almost without thinking. As soon as I spoke, I thought . . . Damn, should have talked it over with Carmen a little. Of course she would have said help them out, because, like me, she's the helping kind. But this was her first night in what was presently my home but would soon be ours, and I should have checked with her, got a female temperature reading, if only as a gesture of respect. "I mean, just a minute."

But by the time I turned toward the house Carmen had slid an arm around her brother and slipped back into the living room.

"There a problem?" Hale said.

"No," I said, hoping I was right. "We've got room." Sure, for me on the downstairs couch.

"Good. We'll send them in." The two cops gave me the old sign-off nod and headed for the street.

J. Shepard, probation monitor, career counselor, innkeeper, victim of his own good intentions.

"What a day," I muttered.

"You have a nice day, too," Terraza, the Latino cop, called out, matching my latest knee-jerk response with one of his own. He gave me a small-town wave, which I didn't return, then receded back into the night.

Seven

People surf for all sorts of reasons. To look cool, or at least attempt to look cool. Getting chicks, or—again—straining hard to get there. For sharing a smoke and talking story in the parking lot with friends. For the splendid cardiovascular exercise and a vigorous upper-body workout to boot, old sport—that is, if you tend to be wound as tight as a miser's ass, count your calories using a chart on the refrigerator door, and are prone to missing the point of things altogether. Or perhaps for a sublime communion with Mother Nature, a pure tap-the-power-source, soul-tripping epiphany and slip-slide boogie back to the watery womb—oh, sure thing, if you happen to be totally full of shit, which is a certainty if this is how you describe your surf sessions. (Then again, if you are one who employs the soul-tripping, live-to-surf, surf-to-live rap with more than an ounce of brio, you are probably also getting your share of chicks, because many an otherwise rational female will check said rationality at the door and go whole hog for this particular brand of Mother Nature's sun-child beach-boy babble. This I know from years of personal research.)

But really, if you ride waves with any seriousness about the act itself, you do it to catch that familiar—if fleeting—feeling, the adrenaline-buzz high you get from a rail-to-rail, wind-whistling magic-carpet-ride speed dance along a meadow green wall of point-wave bliss. From whipping a tight power-carve in the sweet spot just under the cascading lip—thwack!—like a fulcrum grinding a mill wheel or a revolutionary cracking a Liberty Bell. From groping and tunneling through a sucking, hissing, twilit low-tide chromium-glass cylinder from way, way back. From sacking up and paddling out on a double-thick, tremors-in-the-sand day—a day when everyone else is passing—and meeting the challenge. From locating an inner peace you didn't even know you had through the exercise and discipline of sustained intense concentration. And, probably most of all, from just having a kick-ass good time.

Friday morning I surfed for yet another purpose: to escape from dry land for a while. Surfing can be good for that as well.

Last night Carmen had been too quiet as we got Dale and Rudy settled. I'd offered her but the briefest summary of Dale's troubles, rewound the scenes at the law center and the bank, described Rudy's apparent senility and scheming new baby-doll wife. Tomorrow we would go to the police in Glendale, get in touch with Rudy's daughter again, begin to sort this thing out. Carmen listened to it all without comment, then told me she trusted me, her brimming lips pursed as if she was withholding on me in more ways than one. The thought of her upstairs in my bed, alone, made the lumps in the couch feel like stones in a riverbed.

I'd wanted to hear Dale's account of the matter, ask him why he hadn't told me he had nowhere to go, what he thought his decision to park at the pier could have come to short of a midnight thumping by thieves or a ride in the back of a squad car for trespassing on public property. But he wouldn't even look at me as we tucked the sheets into the pullout sofa bed in the den, and I didn't push it. The man was visibly in the throes of something biting and inward and wholly miserable, a rusting Buick out on the curb his outspoken legacy to personal and professional achievement. Across the room on the china cabinet sat a row of bottles—Wild Turkey, Mescal tequila, Dewar's, Ron Rico, Tanqueray, J.D.—my good stuff on display. I wondered what kind of bonehead principle of home decoration I'd been following with that little touch, hoping Dale wasn't already jonesing for that one drink he knew he could never take again. Plugging in a spare night-light and clock radio upstairs in the guest room, I had decided Dale could do without a speech from his monitor. But I wished his AA sponsor was around to warn him off of any sleepwalking.

I slept like hell on the couch, tossing all night, thinking of Carmen upstairs without me, what to do about Dale and Rudy, and Eloise Horton and her stupid F-due reports. Listening to the last storm's slender tailwind blow cold and hollow through the cracks in the house and wondering if it would shift around offshore and make for surfable waves by morning. I didn't need the alarm clock, for when I heard Albert taking a leak sometime around six-twenty, I was already awake, watching the shadows of leaves tickle the ceiling, and I zipped upstairs and quietly grabbed him before he could stumble back to bed. We pulled on our wetsuits in the kitchen, got our boards down from the garage rafters, and headed down the alley toward the sea. Max was pissed about being left behind. I told him too bad. Although Albert had surfed with me probably thirty times in the two years I'd been seeing his sister, he was still a novice, and I needed to keep a close eye on him. The last thing I needed was Max eating some early-morning carpe diem yoga boy's bamboo mat or chasing a surf fisherman up a lifeguard tower just as Albert took an unexpected tumble. The big Rottweiler didn't take it well, turning his back on our expedition by the time we reached the garage, and I made a mental note to make it up to him.

The wind had died sometime before dawn and the air had a bite. It hadn't poured in hours, but the ground was still damp, the leftover rain puddles swimming with dead leaves. We walked in silence, listening to the upwelling rhythms of the surf, and had to scale a huge protective sand berm on the Southside beach to get a precious first glimpse. No one on the beach or in the water—Max would've given me his I-told-you-so look if he'd been here. Southside was thick and junky, the swells shifting and weaving as if the ocean were seriously hungover from last night's howler. As we watched, the full dawn crept across the sand and striped our shadows down into the shorepound.

"N-n-no good, J.?" Albert asked.

"We'll check Northside," I said. "It's never as big, and it might be cleaner."

Northside was in fact smaller and better looking, but we had to wait another half hour before it cleaned up enough to ride. Shifting peaks were popping everywhere on the outside sandbars, mushing out, then re-forming into spinning little walls near shore. A few locals were out near the pier, riding the biggest outside peak. I stayed in the re-forming shorebreak with Albert for about an hour as the sun climbed over the pier railings and the seagulls came looking for sand crabs in the shallows. At some point my session started clicking, and it seemed that everywhere I paddled, a nice line would lift before me and I'd spin and go, spin and go. Inching nearer to the best peak under the pier, each ride was like another groove sliding to center in an LP record. Slowly, I forgot about Albert.

"J., whas hapnin'?" a reedy young local named Stone Me Stevie called out, stroking past me, a wet thatch of blond hair half hiding his face. A wan mustache and the faintest shadow of a goatee had sprouted on his angular face since I'd last seen him in the water a month ago on Southside. It looked funny on him, like a kid playing with a marking pen to make himself Charlie Chan on Halloween. "You see Conlin?" he said. I looked about but couldn't see my old friend Mick through the blinding morning surface sheen. I shook my head no. Stevie grinned. "Well, he's out here, man! About fuckin' time, you ask me."

But I hadn't asked him. "How's that?" I said, knowing what the little prick meant but pushing him to say it. Mouthy little trolls like Stevie have a bad habit of engaging guys like me and Mick in their private little surf-zone battles, expecting us to back their occasionally boorish acts of aggression against outsiders just because we share the same zip code. I don't surf to fight, nor does Mick, and I resent the suggestion that I am bound by my very nature to repeat myself.

Stevie shrugged. "Kook City out here every day, man. Gotta lay down the law sometimes."

I met him with a glare. "Wow, Steve. Really taking a stand there, aren't you."

His oily blue eyes were vacant before the barb hooked into him. "Whatever, man." He turned and paddled away toward the pilings, hooting at a rising set of swells.

I needed to reconnect with Albert, so I swung around and dug in for the first swell. Stevie had changed direction and was now coming hell-bent for the same wave, only from farther behind the peak. In surfing etiquette, this meant he had priority, but after our little exchange, I didn't give a damn about priority, and when he saw the shit-eater on my face he pulled up instantly. Stevie probably knew I was planning to make him pay for his lame remarks with a fading bottom turn right across his shins—which was accurate, by the way.

"Aargh! Fuck, J., hey!" Then, "Go for it, J.!" The quick change of heart shouted in an obvious attempt to save face, as if he'd decided to give an older guy a free pass. I took a steep, rushing drop, thinking, Yeah, right, Stevie, I'll go for it since you mentioned it. Pier rats like him never, ever share a wave with anyone. The peak spun off and I rode low and tight to the wave face, powered forward as if cupped in the palm of a giant's hand. Then the hand disappeared in a patch of deeper water farther inshore, but I pumped my board and stayed with it until the palm rose again over the inside bar, sweeping me through a series of speedy green sections until I was on the sand. Albert was eighty feet up the beach sitting on his board, almost doubled over it and looking winded. I checked my waterproof watch: 9:22. We'd been out a solid two hours by now and I figured he'd had it. My Jeep wagon would be ready at eleven. I unhooked my ankle leash. Time to head home and face the day.

The sand was moist and heavy from the rain, the texture of cold, gritty oatmeal, but it was warming by the minute. Albert was still immobile, head down as if he didn't see me yet. He did something funny with his hand, like he was trying to blow his nose with it. I say funny because Albert is particular about his habits, fastidious even. He wouldn't blow his nose on his sleeve, even in a wetsuit. Then I saw the streaks of red flowing out of his nostrils, the confusion on his face, and I began to run.

Dumping my board, I slid in, dropping to my knees. "Albert, what happened buddy? You okay?" Blood oozed through his fingers. He opened his mouth to talk, his teeth outlined in red. "Your stick hit you?" I was guessing he could've had an odd tumble in the soup, gotten whacked underwater. Freak accidents happen in surfing. My nose is a little flat in the bridge, like a boxer's, from a whack I took underwater from a fallen rider's loose long board years ago. The blow had nearly knocked me unconscious and broke my nose in two places.

"H-he, he h-h-hit me!" Albert sputtered, teary eyed. His shoulders quaked spasmodically.

My temper flashed. I wanted to shout something incoherent in the vein of What the fuck, what kind of cheap-shit, outrageous stunt was ... But there was no one around, just Albert and his bloody surfboard and nothing but a shining February morning, a handful of distant heads bobbing like seals in the surf. I glared at the black figures with something approaching pity, the kind you feel when you come across a dying moth fluttering on the patio bricks and crush it under your boot to end its misery. Somebody was going to pay, and pay dearly.

"Who, man, who hit you?" My heart was revving beneath the black neoprene stretched across my chest.

"I . . . d-dunno, J." I wrapped my arm around him to console him, but he kept quivering miserably. "Out there!" He pointed to the surf. "I didn't. . . . I c-c-couldn't s-see!"

I studied the wounds on his face and noticed the right nostril was far bloodier than the left. A contusion the size of a dime was swelling his upper lip just above the right corner of his mouth, where the fist had smashed into the thin layer of skin covering the upper gums and teeth. Albert said he hadn't seen the guy who hit him. The damage to his face had this odd, sideways angle to it, as well. I figured he'd been punched from behind.

My jaw was clenched as I flexed my hands into fists. Pumping up. "I'll find him," I said. "Let's go see the lifeguard, get you feeling better." I helped Albert to his feet, carrying his board and mine under both arms. "Just keep an eye out for the guy. You see him, you tell me. Okay?"

He wiped his eyes and sniffled hard. "Okay."

We trudged up the sand toward the pier parking lot. Across the lot at the foot of the pier stood lifeguard headquarters, a plain two-story cinder-block job with a narrow observation tower ringed with slanted black windows. That tower always made me think of prison yards and guards with machine guns, but now I was wondering whether someone up there had seen Albert get attacked, and I decided I would inquire while they fixed Albert up. Goops of blood dribbled down the front of his surfboard as we lurched through the sinking tufts of sand, grim as casket bearers. Christ, this was Albert's first full day in Christianitos. Some welcome.

The Northside parking lot was sprinkled with cars with empty surf racks on their roofs, their owners at play. A pea green pickup loaded with fishing gear idled two rows back from the beach, a pair of Japanese men smoking cigarettes inside the cab, windows down. Nearer the pier and parked straddling two spaces was a dirty white van that used to be a mail or delivery truck of some sort, the kind with a big, low windshield, high-backed seats up front and double tires in back. Some amateur artist had hand-painted on the side of the van a black serpent hemmed in by a stylized, diamond-shaped border. Vaguely reminiscent of a rock-and-roll band's insignia, the kind of stuff that was big on heavy-metal album covers in the seventies. A handful of guys milled about beside the van, some in wetsuits, the others in old jeans and faded tees. I didn't recognize any of them. Inside the van and through the side door, rumpled clothes were piled high and a yellow box of Cheerios sat on a plywood countertop. Two of the surfers' hair glistened and their feet were wet and sandy, the pavement puddled where they stood. One of them, a thick dark-haired guy with a three-day beard, puffed a cigarette with one foot resting on the front bumper and glared at me as we passed. He shook his head slightly and smiled coldly, as if to say, You can't touch me, fuck. That was invitation enough for me.

I set down the boards, walked right into their space, and stepped up to the smirking one, startling him.

"You got something to say to me?"

"No." He sounded defensive. "The fuck's your problem, man?"

The others stepped back, sizing me up for a fight. Shit, four against one. A little too late to be calculating odds, but I was still so jacked that the numbers hadn't made me turn and retreat, as they should have.

"Hey, man, we can surf here if we want," a tall, longhaired guy in a black Peterbilt ball cap said from behind me, his tone defensive. He looked familiar, like the panhandler from last night, but then, it had been dark by the ATM, so maybe not. "You don't own the beach."

"Did you swing on that guy?" I said to the one who'd smirked at me before, nodding at Albert. He didn't answer. I made mental notes about whom I might be able to hurt first, and how. If I could disable two of them quickly, they'd have me two on one. By now the bravado that had marched me over here and into this thing was fading. Four on one, genius. Better put on your diplomat's hat before you start eating your teeth.

Common sense was now screaming for me to get the hell out of there with a few strong words and a warning.

"I said, did you swing on—"

But then a third one, a big guy about my size frame with roly-poly arms and shoulders, had to go and pop off.

"Yeah, sure, man." Nervous, but conjuring a smirk for my benefit. "Look at him, dude's a retard," he went on. "Yeah man, we're real big on beefing retards." All of it said loud enough for Albert to hear. Someone else snickered.

I hate that word.

The big roly one attempted to stare me down. It didn't work. Well, fuck diplomacy, I told my rational self.

"You shouldn't have said that," I said. With that, the others spread out around me, but I stayed intent on the big one. I might well get worked, but he was going to pay first.

Maybe not—my peripheral vision caught the dark-haired one rushing me from the right. I snapped into a quick cross-step and a side-kick to his chest that cracked his breastbone with a clap and dropped him flat on his back. The big one was on me now with a right that had something on it, but I ducked and it glanced off my shoulder, spinning me. When he followed through on his right too far I stomped on his front foot, trapping him for a hard upper shot to his chin with the butt of my palm. "Kurt, what's happening!" a girl wailed nearby. Two down and two, maybe three to go, I was thinking as a blow clapped my neck and right ear. My head was dizzy and my ear stung like hell as I fought to keep my feet. Another pair of hands, cold and clammy, clawed at my eyes from behind, and I reached up and broke a pinky, then maybe an index finger, snapping the bones until my attacker cursed and fell away. Someone kidney-punched me and my breath was suddenly gone. I swung viciously, missing, but my free hand caught a handful of long hair on the backswing and I yanked the guy's head down and punished him with a knee to the face. Pure luck, but I'd take it. Three down.

I still couldn't get my breath back as I swung about-face, but too late—another blunt shot thumped the base of my neck, and I spun and lost my balance. Falling, I saw Albert's terrified face twenty feet away, his black eyes lit up. The guy who'd popped me twice from behind was moving in, dancing around me, the fool. Tilting hard, I hit the pavement, and rolled to avoid a kick coming at my head. "Kurt! Oh my God!" The girl's screams again. Pain throbbed like a brass gong clanging in my ears and I heard a police siren scream.

The black-and-white splashed through a huge rain puddle and skidded to a halt, tires smoking. Two uniforms jumped out, their billy clubs ready, but no one was ready to fight back. The surfer I'd kicked in the chest remained flat on his ass, gasping as he stared up into an even paler ocean of blue. Fat Boy's face was a mess. He'd bitten his tongue when I clocked him and was spitting up blood, his eyes glazed. The recipient of my knee to the face was on all fours, inspecting the asphalt like it was an archaeological find. I wish I could say I was just standing there, buffing my nails on my Superman tights and cape, but it wasn't exactly like that. My head was too clouded to find my feet just yet, so I stayed down on one knee and worked on my breathing.

The cops rousted everyone against the van.

"Cool out, you idiots!" an angry voice barked. "Hands along the van, palms out! Legs spread! Hey, stupid, I said against the van, did I tell you to turn around? Do not turn around!"

There was some grunting and groping among the ones I had injured to find their feet. I wobbled gingerly into place.

"We could arrest every last one of you pricks right now for disturbing the peace, and don't even think about trying us, 'cause we will if even one of you starts mouthing off."

Nobody did.

"Shepard?" a softer voice said. I turned around. The Latino cop from last night. Officer Terraza.

"Morning, Officer," I said agreeably, a note of apology in my tone. "Pulling a double shift, I see."

He started to speak, then frowned. I'd probably guessed right. "That's none of your business. What happened here, Shepard?"

My neck was throbbing and it hurt to move my jaw. I'd broken a knuckle and my forearm still vibrated up to the elbow from the greeting I'd laid on the roly-poly guy. My knee ached right where I'd high-stepped the longhair in the face. My right ear was like a ball of flame. But I had some explaining to do.

"This was my fault. My future brother-in-law, Albert here, was attacked in the water. I wanted to know who did it. You can see why."

The cops turned and spotted Albert, took in his flat Mongolian features, his blood-encrusted nostrils and fat lip.

"You did that to him?" Terraza asked the surfers along the van, agitated. They all denied it. Vehemently, spitting at the pavement. Listening to them protest, an ugly notion seized me. I'd come storming in based on a single sideways stare-down. Nothing any of them had said to me actually implicated them in Albert's beating.

Five feet away, three clear surfboards lay in a pile. The foam blank of a new clear surfboard tends to sparkle like Miss America's teeth, but these sticks were soft yellow in places, waterlogged beneath the fiberglass. Dimpled with pressure dings. The board on top had a logo from a shaper named Mr. Zag. Nobody I'd ever heard of, this Mr. Zag, certainly not a well-known area board builder. Surfboards are like guns: make, model, and caliber are very noticeable to those in the know. This crap was strictly second-rate.

The local crew would not be keen on embracing these characters, had probably given them a thousand subtle signals that their kind wasn't wanted around here. That's never been my thing, but then again, I tend to move around town like it's my own backyard. The beach, too.

Shit. These guys could have been merely defending themselves. Well, too bad the big one used the word *retard,* I rationalized. His mistake.

"Take off, Mr. Shepard," Officer Terraza told me, nodding but keeping it stern. I took my cue, went back to Albert and scooped up the boards. "Gentlemen," I heard the cop say to the others as we walked past the van, "this is a small town, a nice place. If you think you can come down here and . . ." Lecturing them. My status as a local resident had bought me a free pass this time. It wasn't exactly fair, but then, neither is life.

"Did you see the guy?" I asked Albert. "Look at them. Do any of them—"

"I du-dunno, J.!" Albert said, still sobbing. Watching a punch-out probably hadn't done much for his already rattled state. "I'm sorry, J., I'm s-s-sorry!"

"It's okay, man," I tried to reassure him, my mind unable to process what had gone down in the five short minutes since I'd ridden a wave to shore and walked up the sand to find Albert. I stood beside him, an absent touch to my stinging ear resulting in a mess of bloody fingers. Then I wiped my hand on my black wet-suit, Albert's eyes tugging at me, the latest betrayer of his trust, from behind.

The sun was high in the winter sky now, the air so crisp and temperate as to make a mockery of the morning's chaos. Twenty miles offshore, Santa Catalina-Island lurked behind a gauzy strip of brown air. That clunky old Deep Purple riff came to mind. Smoke on the water, a fire in the sky. I always hated that song.

We walked up the parking ramp toward the town, and home, Albert silently beseeching me to make things better. But words failed me.

"It's all right," I said at last.

Like hell.

Carmen came suitably unglued at the sight of us and took the news of Albert's beating like a body blow. She assumed my banged-up state resulted from a spirited defense of Albert, and I wasn't inclined to tell her I actually might have jumped the wrong guys. Not yet, at least.

Rudy and Dale were in the kitchen. Every last cereal box in the house was laid out on the maple dinette table near the window, Rudy reading ingredients and manufacturer come-ons like a radio announcer on speed.

"Alzheimer's, I'm guessing," Carmen quietly told me. "Probably in its onset."

"You sound like you know firsthand," I said.

Carmen leaned closer as we stood together in the doorway, watching them. "I had this relative once. Uncle Victor. Technical writer for Hughes Aircraft, former Airborne Division infantryman in World War II, survived D day and something like a yearlong march through German ground forces."

"Impressive."

"Rock solid. Used to visit the house almost daily. Then it happened."

"Wheat starch, sugar, salt, calcium carbonate . . ." Rudy read on.

Carmen smiled at Rudy. "Uncle Vic had the same sudden childlike regressions," she said, "the odd eccentricities surfacing as his lucidity slipped away. A rapid disintegration. One day he's helping me research a book report on the state of infant care in Third World African nations, the next, he's wandering his neighborhood block, knocking on doors to ask directions to his own home."

"That's harsh," I said.

"Yeah, harsh."

Sure, Rudy would have to see a specialist for a diagnosis before we knew for certain, but I had no reason to doubt Carmen's speculation.

Carmen took me to the bathroom and cleaned up my ear.

"The guy at the shop called," she said.

"Mick?"

"No. Some other guy. With an accent. The car is ready."

I pulled away. "Hey," Carmen said. "I wasn't finished."

"It's fine," I said.

"That's not what I meant." She put the damp washrag she'd been using on the bathroom counter. "I wanted to talk to you. About today. What happened."

"Listen, Car," I said hastily, "I think we've been over it enough, don't you?"

She folded her arms. "I'm worried."

"This thing was an aberration, a freak," I said. "Albert never should have gotten punched. I'm going to find out who—"

"You misunderstand. Of course I'm upset, who wouldn't be? It was horrible." She looked away, studying the bloodstained washrag in the sink. "But the way you handled it, the way you respond to these kinds of things. The violence."

I'd heard it before. Carmen is something of a pacifist. I am not. I've never seen the point in arguing.

"I did what I had to do," I said. "I'm not apologizing for it."

Her arms remained folded. "I didn't ask you to."

A little later I told Dale he and Rudy could drop me at Mickey Conlin's garage, then follow me to the Glendale PD. Dale looked like he hadn't slept much, kept rubbing his hair back on his scalp as if it was a smudge he couldn't clean off.

"Bye, sweetie," I said to Carmen, stealing a glance at the liquor bottles while I hugged her close. The cabinet looked undisturbed.

"Oh, I forgot to tell you," Carmen said, "someone from work named Ellen, or maybe Hortense, called just before you came back. Rather curt and fast-talking. Hard to even get her name."

Ellen or maybe Hortense. I frowned.

"Eloise Horton."

"I think so."

"My manager."

She probably was unhappy about something—a late filing, my failure to attend a staff meeting. I nodded. At the bar, management is constantly cooking up reasons to meet, taking us away from the real work. Protecting their hustle. I told Carmen I'd deal with Eloise later, but her feeling was that, judging from their conversation, this situation couldn't wait. I trusted Carmen's perception, put down my briefcase and called Eloise, told her about my car and that I was on my way in. Eloise wanted me in her office, soon as I got there. Wouldn't say why, but I figured it was the usual management shakedown. Filings, filings, filings.

Dale fidgeted with his hands at the dining table.

"Just relax here awhile longer," I told him. "I'll call you later."

"What about Glendale PD today?" he said.

"That'll have to wait."

I thought I saw Dale stare right at the bottle of Jack Daniels as I headed out.

Mick was not in the shop when I picked up my car.

"He came by a little while ago," Tord the grease-monkey poet told me. "Surfboard on the roof of that sixty-nine Mustang fastback he keeps in the garage at home. Said he'd be in before noon." He grinned as if he and I shared a secret, but only he knew what it was. "Looked very, very happy."

"Let's square this away," I said, checkbook in hand.

Tord noticed the bruises on my neck and bandage on my ear.

"Heard about a bad scene down at the pier. Two guys in the hospital. The Sirens, they come right by here going down Main." He pointed a hand, outlining the route.

"Interesting."

I didn't say I was involved but he seemed to figure it out on his own.

"Yaah. Interesting."

I paid for the repairs and got the hell out of there.

Eloise was in her office when I got to work, and I went straight there, dumping my briefcase just outside her door before knocking lightly.

"Shepard, where the hell were you this morning?" she said through the back of her head. Mesmerized by a bunch of numbers on her computer screen.

"Morning, boss. I'm fine, thanks. How are you?"

She swiveled toward me in her black leather captain's chair. She was in another one of her black pantsuits, tight fitting, with a crème-colored silk blouse, her dark eyes burning. Those legs looking long as stilts.

"It's afternoon, and don't get smart with me, Shepard. We had a unit meeting. You missed it."

"My car broke down. I told you that yesterday, remember?"

"You could have taken the Blue Line."

"I did. Yesterday. But today I didn't have an extra two hours to sit on that thing. I had to pick up my car."

"You missed an important meeting."

"I didn't know you were having one."

"That's because you weren't here yesterday afternoon when I announced it. Honey Chavez says you left early. Without my knowledge or permission, of course."

"I was doing a little investigation on a case," I said matter-of-factly, as if that would say enough. With Eloise, keeping your calm and keeping her in the dark are equally important.

"And what case is that?"

"A case involving UPL." I made a face like I was grasping at a name. "New case. What's it called . . . um, Conlin." Thanks, Mick.

I was betting she wouldn't take a minute to check the case name, and she didn't. What, and miss a prime opportunity to kick a board up my butt? No, Eloise Horton wouldn't wait for that. "I see. You know. That is what we have investigators for, or have you forgotten?" she snapped, her arms folded. Like a schoolmarm.

This was getting old. Mea culpa time had come. "Sorry I missed the meeting," I said with a little feeling. "And you're right, I should have used an investigator. But I'm a little like you that way." That perked her eyebrows. "You know, I just wanted the job done right." The classic brownnosing compliment.

Eloise gazed out the window of her corner office. Down below, the Santa Monica Freeway snaked west in the pale sunlight. "I may not have a lot of courtroom experience, you know."

Try none at all, I wanted to say.

"But I do care about a job well done."

"Sure, doing it right," I said, commiserating. "It's what you're about." Judas Priest, if flies could land on bullshit words, this office would be swarming like an outhouse right now. But Eloise was digging it.

"You're a good lawyer, Shepard." Running those long fingers back over her short Afro, massaging her temple. Sighing. "Just keep me in the loop. I don't need any extra headaches."

Right. As if that caseload of zero was making her reach for the Excedrin. I managed a tight little smile and went back to my office.

Honey Chavez was heading to lunch with five or six other legal secretaries, her *m'ijas*. A close bunch known around here as the Mexican Mafia. She looked particularly nice today in red cashmere and matching lipstick, a tiny wrapped gift coming out of her purse for friendly inspection by the girls. Somebody's birthday today.

I briefly told Honey about my car. "Surf's up again, huh?" she wisecracked, handing me my phone message slips.

Why fight it? Honey knew the deal. I just stood there smiling as the ladies enjoyed a nice chuckle at my expense, I glanced at my messages. One was from a detective with Glendale PD, a guy named Tamango Perry. In by 3 P.M., could see me then. Shit, I'd have to figure out an excuse for bailing early from work again.

"Make sure you see Eloise before you go to lunch, she's looking for you," Honey said over her shoulder, the girls making their exit. I was about to say Eloise had found me, but Honey added, "She won't be here this afternoon."

Oh, really. "What's she doing?"

"Dental appointment," Honey said with a tiny wink. She knew I did things my own way, and she was good enough to slip me whatever inside information she had on Eloise's goings on.

"Thanks. You ladies have fun."

Problem solved.

I flexed my fingers to wave, but my broken knuckle wouldn't work. Then I rubbed my hand until the burning sensation dissipated, thinking maybe the day was salvageable after all. Eloise was cool for now. I hadn't even eaten yet, and a bite at that Salvadoran place around the corner would be excellent. Big plate of the beef stew with rice. After lunch, I'd stop in on Therese Rozypal and see about Bobby Silver's reinstatement trial on Monday.

I pulled that day's *Times* from my briefcase and snapped the case shut, sliding it under my desk. Looking up, I saw the judge's decision sitting in my in-box: *In the Matter of the State Bar of California v. Eugene Podette.* Nervous, sweaty little Eugene Podette, the good Christian flimflammer, Von Trapp family jack-off. Christ, that was fast. I flipped through Judge Renaldo's analysis, saw all the right factual and legal findings, laid out exactly as I'd done it at trial. Good work, Your Honor. Disbarment, right? Had to be—had to be. Then, on the final page, the order of a thirty-day suspension with probation. I read it again: thirty-day suspension. The words hitting me harder than anything I'd absorbed that morning in the pier parking lot.

I sat down at my desk, flexing my fingers, too angry to give a damn about the pain.

Eight

Therese Rozypal was on the phone in her office, twisting the long white cord through her fingers as she waved me in. She looked smart and prosecutorial in a charcoal pinstriped dress suit, sitting there, telling some defense attorney that she didn't care where else he had to be that day, the matter had been calendared months ago, so no way would she stipulate to a third continuance. Damn, I thought, how many times have I heard that one?

"Then make a motion, sir," she hissed into the phone. "No, I never said that. I don't owe you anything of the sort." Rolling her blue eyes at me. "I take that as a threat. Do not threaten me."

I didn't really know Therese, because she was a recent hire, but I liked the way she sounded just now. Nobody's pushover.

Waiting, I studied the only two photos mounted on her desk. Both were pretty interesting. One was a picture of Therese in a red Santa's helper hat, gorgeous furry white sweater, perfect teeth flashing, cheek to cheek with a glassy-eyed tiger-striped cat wearing the same kind of hat. Cute. No boyfriend—then again, maybe he was the photographer. Therese struck me as too good-looking to be unattached.

Parked behind the Christmas shot was the photo I'd heard others at the bar talk about outside Therese's presence. Heavy silver frame, black felt around the edges of a vintage black-and-white of a pig-tailed little Girl Scout shaking hands with Richard Nixon. The subjects looked stiff and a bit posed, but on closer inspection, a lot was going on: Tricky Dick, jowly and bent at the waist, a big incisor poking out the side of his grin as he employed the classic politician's two-hander on his nubile future constituent. Even in the old photo he looked older, near the end of his run as President. She was no more than twelve or thirteen, I guessed, the hand embrace from a man of his experience and years somehow out of place. The young lady's forest green Girl Scout sash was peppered with badges. Impressive, and maybe a tad swanky, the way it hung free below the breast line, like a beauty contestant's banner. A holy river of silky blond hair running shiny and free. No glasses on the future Republican's face—or maybe she'd removed them for her photo-op with the Quaker from Yorba Linda.

Therese finished her call and parked her gold wire-rimmed glasses a bit higher. The rushes of blond locks were braided into a tight bun today, but the face was as fresh and ready as in the old Nixon photo. Judging from the photo, I guessed Therese to be in her early thirties, like me. But she looked about twenty-five. She cracked a smile.

"The old one's not a fake, if you're wondering," she said.

"You mean the photo, or the politician?"

"Ha-ha, very funny. They're both originals, smart guy."

"You can say that again." No time to be teeing off on Nixon, I thought. I was here to talk about Bobby Silver. "So, where was the picture taken?" Shifting gears.

"Newport Beach. The Balboa Bay Club."

"I know the place." Therese seemed to be awaiting my explanation. I was recalling an incident that could not be counted among my finer moments as a man-about-town. "I sort of got thrown out of there once."

She perked right up. "Well. Please, do tell."

"It was a retirement party for my sales manager, Kenny Vakoutas. One thing about salesmen is they love to drink even more than they love to talk. Anyway . . ." She looked at me a bit askance. "What's wrong?" I said.

Between us was an empty desk blotter, and I began to notice that this office was about twice as clean and organized as mine. Of course, I have a much heavier caseload, boxes full of paper stacked waist-high against every wall, the Legal Warehouse Deco look. Therese and I were in the same trial unit, Eloise's group. On the corner of the desk, a plastic in-box tray sat empty. No doubt she submitted her F-due reports on time.

"I just . . . can't really picture you in sales," she said.

"Neither could very many buyers."

She laughed. "So what happened at the party?"

"It seriously bogged when they ran out of spirits, so some of us adjourned outside to take in the view. Wow." I shook my head at the memory. "A lot of stars in the sky that night. You know that long dock they have in back, right on the harbor?"

She nodded. "Of course."

"Well, there was this yacht, pretty big, took up half the dock, just sitting there, the keys right in it."

"You didn't."

"You have to admit, Therese, it was a strange setup. As if somebody left it that way, just begging us to take it for a spin. Almost like it was some kind of a test."

"How far did you get?"

"Not very. I didn't know the police had boats in Newport."

"Harbor patrol," she said quickly.

"Not the friendliest bunch."

"They're not so bad. I grew up on Lido Island," she explained.

Lido was one of the artificial islands enclosed within the harbor, a place ringed with dockside mansions.

"Yeah, not so bad." This time I smiled back.

She sat back, assessing me, her big eyelashes rolling like soft fans. "So, J. Shepard. Yacht thief."

"We just borrowed it, no intent to permanently deprive. Where would we park it anyway?"

"I've heard you live at the beach."

"Right, in Christianitos. I assure you, there's nowhere to park a yacht there." Suddenly I felt like I was talking too much about myself. It was time to discuss Bobby Silver's reinstatement trial. "Anyway—"

"I was wondering, how do you square a life of crime with being a prosecutor of bad guys here?" Needling me a little, but good-natured.

"I'm a master of self-deception."

She leaned forward, mock serious. "Good thing I found out. You probably don't know this, but last week I asked Eloise if I could co-counsel with you on a trial or two. Imagine that."

I went along. "Close call, Therese." But this was news to me. I couldn't imagine Eloise endorsing such an arrangement, not with the way she felt she couldn't control me.

"She said no," I added. "Right?"

"Wrong. She actually suggested it when I was hired."

"I have a hard time believing that."

"Well, she didn't exactly use your name, but she said I should try to pair up with the strongest trial lawyers in the unit." Therese gazed at the picture of the Girl Scout with the president. "You know, as a way of getting my career here off on the right foot."

"What gave you the impression that I was one of those lawyers?"

"Don't be so modest," she cut me off. "You know your stuff. I've asked around. Everybody says so."

Obviously, Therese's poll excluded Eugene Podette and his lovely wife Trixie, who, had they heard this little tribute to my legal stature, would doubtless be on the floor, writhing in breathless laughter right now.

"I need to talk with you about something." I said. "The reinstatement trial for Bobby Silver."

She sat back in her big chair. "Okay, but can I get your opinion on something first?"

"Sure." She'd probably been working on the Silver case for three months, her entire career at the bar thus far, and I was about to put it on a completely different tack. Even if I was about to significantly boost her case, it was still her case. Lawyers tend to be proprietary about the matters they handle. Every case is like a problem, a riddle, and when you're locked into solving that riddle, it's none too gratifying when someone else comes along and whispers an answer into your ear. "Fire away," I said.

"That was Lars Gerbel on the phone a minute ago, asking for another-continuance of a trial that's set next month. He accused me of giving him a hard time just to 'assert my womanhood,' said I was trying too hard to prove myself just because I'm a 'woman in a man's world.' "

"Sounds like Lars."

The man was a bit quick with the personal cracks for my taste. Last year at a pretrial conference, he'd told me I was "too tanned to work full-time," which explained why I seemed "a little slow" to appreciate the finer points of his fuzzy little motion *in limine,* a maneuver defense lawyers make before trial to exclude damaging evidence against their clients. But my opposition was solid. When the judge said motion denied, Lars rolled his eyes, acting as if I'd been handed a gift, like I was just another lucky bastard. I took special pleasure from winning that trial on every count I'd charged. To me, Lars Gerbel was a major blowhard.

"What was your question?" I asked her.

She blushed a little and waited. "You don't think there's anything to that. I mean, me asserting myself too much in that way."

"Lars Gerbel talks a lot, Therese, that's all. He's just trying to get into your head to work an advantage. Look around you. Half our prosecutors are women. Blow it off."

I knew what Gerbel was working up to, the suggestion that Therese Rozypal had made it this far based on looks, not ability. A common insult laid on attractive women everywhere. But I didn't say more.

She sighed and folded her arms. "You're right. Thank you. So, what do you want?"

"To help you with the Robert Silver reinstatement."

"Oh my god, that's great! We'll . . . you can co-counsel!" She turned to her credenza and started pulling out a thick file folder. "Let me get his witness list." Flipping through papers. "I'd love to see you take some of his witnesses on cross. Maybe you can do—"

"Actually, I can't," I interrupted. She put down the pleadings, instantly deflated. "I mean, I can't co-counsel with you, Therese. Not on this one."

"Oh. Why not?" The insecurity that Lars had nicked was right there in those pale blue eyes again.

"I could be a witness. I know some things about this guy. Bad things."

"Oh my God," she said again, this time more softly. "I didn't realize."

I would explain, of course, but already I felt lousy, seeing those eyes fade like the last calm reflections off the pier at dusk. "The point is, this guy's not getting his license back," I told her. "I'll help see to that, Therese. But it's still your case all the way."

"Okay, J."

I looked at that old photo of Nixon and actually felt something for the guy, pressing the flesh of the moneyed Newport crowd until his hands were numb, then suddenly, reaching out to this . . . vision of a Girl Scout. The blood pumping in his ears, tongue-tied—well, then! A simple affable nod suddenly veering into a thirsty perve on her loveliness.

J. Shepard, yacht thief. Good one, Therese, I was thinking. I must have been smiling a little because she asked me what was so funny. Nothing, I told her.

Nixon and I silently watched as she took out a legal pad and pen. Then I told her everything I knew about Bobby Silver.

If I was going to meet that Glendale police detective after three I had about an hour to kill on more mundane projects, the first of which was a pretrial statement coming due on a case going to trial in March, the matter of Rodney Dortmunder. A personal-injury solo practitioner from Burbank, Dortmunder had a thing for settling his cases for lowball, sellout sums, then stiffing his clients' medical providers so he could still retain a fat contingency fee. Months later, unwitting clients would get a phone call from a friendly collection agency or, worse, discover new black marks on their credit reports. They'd dial up Rodney demanding an explanation, but invariably get brushed off with the I'll-get-right-back-to-you runaround routine. Then they'd call the state bar and make a complaint, at which time their former attorney would sue them for defamation of character in a cheap attempt at intimidation.

Pretrial statements take time for prosecutors because you're required to set forth your entire case by listing your witnesses and what they're going to say and listing your exhibits and which witnesses are sponsoring their admission into evidence. The rule is that if you don't name a witness or exhibit in the pretrial statement, it won't come into evidence later at trial. But when you're taking away someone's livelihood, judges tend to go overboard to be fair to defending lawyers. Typically, the accused attorney on trial won't even file a pretrial statement, claiming ignorance of the rules. If he's representing himself, judges will often let it slide. It's a nice advantage, putting on your defense by surprise.

Rodney Dortmunder was representing himself. Just as Eugene Podette had done. Imagine that.

Three o'clock came and went, with Eloise back early from her damn dental appointment and prowling the halls outside my office like the doc had forgotten the novocaine. Another early exit would not be possible, so I rang up Glendale PD and was put through to a detective with a lilting Caribbean accent named Tamango Perry. Official but friendly manner, and an intelligent way of speaking.

"Tell me the full story, Mista Shep-had, and I will puh-sunnily do what I can." Sounding Jamaican, which I commented on, but he said I guessed wrong. "I am half African, my fatha's side, half Haitian, from my motha."

"You have an interesting first name," I said.

"I was named Tamango in honor of the Yoruban spirits Exu and Shango."

Which left me with not a damn thing to say, except a most witless "Cool."

He laughed. "What about this office you went to, Counselor?"

I filled him in on our visit to the law center, Dale's situation, Rudy's marriage to Angie. The glowering boyfriend Carlito, Bobby Silver, and the straight-arm attempt they'd made at the savings and loan. He told me there wasn't much he could do about Rudy as yet.

"It sounds like potential elder abuse," he explained, "but if his marriage to the girl is valid—that is, if he wanted to marry her and knew what he was doing, and she hasn't yet stolen his assets—I don't know. Sounds like no crime has been committed yet."

"What about the law center?"

"I will look into that place for you. If they are engaged in unauthorized practice of law, we can do things. Get a search warrant, make arrests on the employees." His last remark just hung there between us. "What about your friend, Mr. Bleeker?" he added.

"Not much he can do," I admitted. "We don't know how many cases they've used his name on. Probably quite a few. But obviously, he'll be cooperating."

"I would certainly hope so."

Then I found myself doing something that surprised me: I went out on a limb for Dale. "I know it might look shaky, his involvement, but Mr. Bleeker was just recently hired on. He'd been out of work a long time before that. He really needed the job. I think it clouded his judgment."

The detective paused. "I see."

"When I first met him, he seemed unaware of the situation."

"When was that?"

Shit. "Yesterday."

I told Perry about Dale's probation—had to. Then I asked him why Dale would tell me about a UPL scam if he was really in on it. I realized as I spoke that the Dale Bleeker I had glimpsed years ago, the high-minded courtroom stalwart and prosecutor of criminals, was still a presence, if only in my memory.

"He didn't know they were using his license, Detective," I concluded.

Another pause. "Are you are sure about that?"

"Yes, I am."

"All right, good enough, Mr. Shepard. So, where is Mr. Kirkmeyer staying?"

"With Mr. Bleeker."

"Here in Glendale?"

Man, this guy and his questions—which, of course, probably made him a good detective. "In Christianitos," I said, not inclined to reveal the depth to which I'd sunk myself in this mess. But if I wanted to maintain my credibility, I had to tell him straight. "In my own home. We expect that his daughter will be coming in from Washington State in a few days. Of course, we can bring him in for an interview anytime you like."

Tamango Perry took his time with that little piece of information. "Thank you. I'll let you know." The sound of fingers drumming on a desktop. "What will you do in the meantime?"

"Keep him safe, I guess." I couldn't think of anything else to tell him.

"Thank you again, Mr. Shepard. That is very good of you."

Apparently I'd said the right thing. "Call me J., Detective."

"All right. Thank you, J., and you may call me Tamango. You are doing a good thing for this gentleman."

"Don't mention it, Tamango." I could feel an objection coming.

"But please, J., do be careful. These kinds of people . . ." He sighed. "These people, who would steal from the elderly, the infirm, take everything, leave them with nothing, they are very dangerous. They won't think twice about pushing aside anyone who stands in their way."

I thought about Carmen, alone in my house with a handicapped young man and a broken-down former prosecutor as her only protectors, a solid one-hour drive from my office. She was also still too leery of Max to let him close enough to run interference on an intruder. Carmen was potentially helpless if Angie and Carlito happened to ring my doorbell on Porpoise Way.

I thanked Detective Perry and got off the line, then dialed my home number with the receiver still stuck to my ear. Eloise Horton floated by my open doorway like a faithful apparition, peeked in, and probably noticed the case file documents splayed across my desktop, the pleadings on the computer screen behind me, because she gave me a contented nod, as if pleased to see me buried up to my eyeballs. Gee, thanks, Eloise. But the Rodney Dortmunder filing was the least of my concerns at the moment.

My home phone rang. Five, ten, fifteen, twenty times.

No answer.

Nine

At times I build these false barriers in my mind regarding what is truly important and what isn't. I wake up in hell, feeling totally shot, thinking, God, I'd like to call in sick, just this once . . . but no, I shouldn't, I'm needed at work and there's this case, a brief due, another filing I really should file by . . . Right, as if a single day removed from the grind would alter the world's rotation by so much as a hair. I see my face frozen before the closet, certain I can't wear the blue oxford shirt again, I just wore it last week, people might notice. Never mind that those same people are too busy sweating their own little lists of private details no else cares about. Checking my watch in a stacked freeway lane, I guard the sliver of space between my bumper and the van in front me from line jumpers, sweating about . . . let's see, five minutes and forty-five seconds of scheduled commute time, now misplaced. A line jumper emerges in a lowered white Honda Civic, his tinted windows quivering amid an angry rap lyric and serious woofer distortion, and as he dive-bombs the spot between the van and my wagon I brake hard and mutter a rhetorical "What the fuck was *that*?" Five minutes and forty-five seconds late already . . . but late to do what? To walk into a building and anchor myself in a chair behind a desk all day, of course, those first five minutes and forty-five seconds indistinguishable from the four hundred and seventy-four minutes and fifteen seconds more to come before quitting time. I flip on my computer, the fluorescent light flooding my pores. Fucking line jumpers.

Yes, these are false impediments, blown up with the hot air of self-absorption and seriously out of whack with reality. But just now, another apparent phantom impediment was looming large. I had to tell Eloise I was bailing from work early, this time because of an unconfirmed crisis at home. I wondered what she would say, while simultaneously thinking: Why should I care?

I stressed over that one for half an hour, my throat a little tighter each time I replaced the receiver after dialing home and getting nothing but ring after hollow ring. So I banged out witness and exhibit lists for the Dortmunder case, my mind fixating on that punk thug Carlito and the threat he'd made at the savings and loan. Ringing home again, I had no success. I began to picture Carlito backing Carmen into the entry-hall wall with a forearm across her neck as Angie stormed inside and grabbed Rudy, the phone ringing impotently in the background. That image was enough to get me out of my chair and down to Eloise's office. I was bailing, regardless.

Eloise was on the phone with her back turned when I got there, but she saw me and didn't even react. Another subtle message that the waters between us ran chilly. This had been our history from the beginning, since that first day we'd taken her to lunch following her surprise hiring. I say surprise because nobody I know even saw it coming. Eloise Horton materialized like that relative you never knew you had who turns up right before the will is read. Out of nowhere.

I leaned against the doorjamb outside her office, my neck stiff from the shot I'd taken in the pier parking lot that morning with Albert. Five more minutes crawled by. Screw it, I decided, the situation at home is real and this business about whether the boss will be annoyed if I cut out a little early just doesn't rate.

Eloise's secretary, Monette—which she pronounces Mo-nay, like the Impressionist painter—was sorting a pile of letters at her desk ten feet from Eloise's open door. Monette is a very dark black girl. She may look as wide of one of Claude Monet's pastel haystacks, but she's definitely not French. I slid in next to her cubicle and watched her thick fingers riffle through the letters as she silently bopped to some stereo sounds on a small headset. Despite my loitering presence, Monette gave no indication that she knew I was alive.

I rapped my knuckles on her armrest. She grimaced and tugged back her headset. "Tell Eloise I've got a problem at home and I'll see her tomorrow," I said.

Her eyes returned to her work. "You should tell her yourself."

"She's on the phone."

Monette turned and checked it out for herself, in super slow mo. "Then put it in a memo."

"I don't have time. It's an emergency."

"She prefers memos." Shaking her head.

"I don't have time. Just tell her, please."

Monette didn't say she would, she just stared at me, vacant as a naked billboard. Remember the important things, I silently counseled myself. As I made for the exit, I thought I heard her say, "Oh, I'll tell her," in a low voice, but when I looked back, she was sorting letters again, her head bopping to a tune I could not hear.

The house was dark when I cruised down Porpoise Way, no signs of life at all through the living-room glass down below or the twin dormers up above. I drove around back and double-parked across the garage door in the alley, then rattled through the gate and into the small, square backyard.

"Max," I called out.

A few seconds later, my Rottweiler rolled from the shadows, teeth flashing, like a prehistoric shark rising from the deep.

Max came to me a few years back via a former client that I represented in juvenile dependency court named Darla Madden. She was a mountainous woman, a widow raising two kids in a two-bedroom apartment that, with the addition of Max, had devolved into something of a shit hole. The day I met Darla, I told her that the only way she could keep custody of her kids was to choose between them and Max. You would think it was an easy choice, but Darla was reluctant to make a move. The thought of two kids marooned in a foster home unnecessarily really ate at my insides, so in a rather softheaded moment, I offered to take Max—temporarily, that is, until Darla found a bigger place to live and got the county off her back. The kids went home to their mom, but Darla never returned to reclaim her dog. That suited me fine because I've come to love Max like the brother I never had.

The big guy licked my hand and sat up, begging for a little affection. I was instantly relieved by his nonchalance. Had something nasty gone down earlier, Max would still be bristling from it.

Inside, the house was intact. No note on the fridge or by the phone in the entry hall. I went back outside and opened the back gate into the alley. "Come on, buddy," I said to Max. "Let's see what's shakin' in town." Wondering where to start. The police department? Fire station? Maybe just by cruising down Main first. I had no idea, but the thick scent of salt and wet sand swelled my lungs, and something, perhaps an instinct, like your brain ordering you to scratch before you even feel an itch, well, something like that was directing me to head for the pier, and I was off.

Max hopped in the front passenger door. I slid a heavy-duty choke chain around his neck as his stub of a tail thrummed the seat. To him, this stuff was fun, but I welcomed his backup. People think twice about advancing on you when you've got close to two hundred pounds of chewing machine by your side. I leaned across the seat to roll down his window for him and caught a tongue-licking that felt like a raw steak slapping me across the cheek.

"Cool it, boy."

Night was coming, black and moonless. A few anglers were fishing off the end of the pier. The parking lot was empty and lifeguard headquarters was well lit but closed down by now. A local wino slouched against the observation tower, wrapped in a blanket and creased like a half-eaten burrito. Above him on the tower, the chalkboard that displays daily wind, tide, and surf conditions was wiped clean, as if the ocean, too, had closed for the day.

I crawled the Jeep wagon toward Main, windows down, barely accelerating. The shops and sidewalks on both sides of the street were dead quiet. In front of the Marmaduke, a guy in a leather vest sat on a chopped Harley and fooled with the strap on a helmet that was shaped like an old Nazi SS job. The biker made strong eye contact with me when he heard the car. For some reason I didn't look away, even when his face twisted into a scowl.

"Hey, who's your girlfriend?" he called out. An old, unfunny joke.

I tapped on the brakes. The biker swung a leg out over the gas tank. Tough-guy tats adorned his bare shoulders, but he was a runty one and I could see him straining to increase his stature by puffing his chest. Not worth it, I thought, I'm busy with other things. I took my foot off the brake and the Jeep inched forward.

"She's as ugly as you are," the biker added.

Sometimes the assholes of the world just wear me out. I braked again.

"She is a he, clown. Care for an up-close meeting?"

Max didn't much like the guy's looks either and let off a lion's roar of a growl that wiped the attitude right off his stubbled face. I sighed, arm slung over the steering wheel, doing my best to register zero concern. This approach tends to work well with bullies.

The dude was quick to reassess his options, and Max and I watched him swing that leg right back over the tank and settle onto his bike again without another word. Nothing personal, I guessed. He was probably pissed about the new mandatory helmet law in California.

But there it was again. Just amother stupid comment from a stranger, and yet, I would have been all too ready to go.

We continued to creep north toward PCH, seeing nothing unusual. The Food Barn market glowed like a nighttime oasis through broad glass windows, a row of empty check-stands inside. Kitty-corner across the four-way stop the Captain's Galley restaurant was having a slow night. Nothing but empty parking spaces lined the front of Pier Liquor. I began to feel foolish, like this was an absolute waste of time, when Max fixed his gaze on the Beach Motors lot and let out a hefty bark.

Dale's Regal was parked across the open garage, the front doors wide open. Mick Conlin was standing a few feet in front of the hood, Carmen next to him. She waved when she saw me.

I swung the Jeep wagon in and cut the engine, leaving the headlights trained on the Buick. The garage's recesses were dark, no sign of Tord, but the office and waiting area were flooded with hard overhead light. Inside, Rudy and Albert were hunched in one corner, backs turned, Dale slumped in a plastic chair a few feet behind them. The electronic pops and gurgles of a video game followed a fat column of light out into the yard.

"Stay," I commanded Max. He obeyed but fudged a little, craning that granite head of his out the window to catch what action he could.

Mick was in his navy work pants and shirt, no jacket against the descending evening chill. Carmen was in old jeans and an oversize gray sweatshirt of mine, looking ravishing in an offhand manner you just can't plan. I gave her a peck on the cheek, which she didn't return.

"I guess you two have met," I said.

"My pleasure, too," Mick said. Carmen smiled.

"I called the house and no one answered," I told her. "A bunch of times."

"Oh."

"Got here as soon as I could."

"Rudy decided to take a stroll," Carmen said. "About two hours ago. Right out the front door, alone."

"Where was Dale?"

Carmen shrugged. "Asleep, I think. On the living-room couch. Albert and I were upstairs reading stories. If Mickey hadn't come by and rung the doorbell when he did we might never have caught up to him."

Mick nodded. "I heard about what happened at the pier this morning. Thought I'd stop by to see if you needed any help with anything."

"Thanks, man. How'd you find Rudy?"

"We drove up and down every street in town," Carmen said. "He was nowhere." She seemed to lose her breath. "It was pretty terrifying, J."

"Jesus. I'm sorry."

"I was pretty scared for him, but I thought if I called the police, it might cause a problem for you." Her downcast eyes made me feel ashamed of the confusion I'd caused her these past two days.

"Rudy and Dale had a problem last night too," I explained to Mick.

"With the city's finest?" he said.

"You guessed it. So where was he?"

"Dale figured it out," Carmen said. "I guess they stopped in at the liquor store last night."

"Great."

"Dale said it was just to buy some snacks," Carmen said. "Anyway, Rudy noticed the video games by the door and wanted to play. Dale said he didn't have change so they had to pass, but they could come back."

"He must have been wandering around town awhile when he recognized Pier Liquor," Mickey said. "We found him spinning the wheel on that Grand Prix game, just watching the track peel by on the screen. No quarter in the machine. Guy behind the counter was ready to toss him, said he and his buddy did the same thing last night."

Carmen shook her head. "I think Dale's broke, J."

"Sounds like it."

"So we brought him over here, let him play on my machines," Mick said. "He seems happy enough." He nodded at Carmen. "Your lady was pretty certain you'd find your way to us before too long."

I took out my wallet and handed him a ten. "Let me pay for the games at least."

Mickey declined the gesture. "No worries." But his eyes told me he'd picked up on the tense vibe between Carmen and me. He checked his watch. "Tord's gone home. Think I'll head inside and wrap things up."

"Thanks, Mick," I said. "For everything."

"Forget it," he said over his shoulder. "Hey, sorry I missed you this morning. I was having so much fun in the water I didn't even see what went down in the parking lot."

"Never mind, at least you had fun," I said. "That was the idea." I tried a meek smile on Carmen. She deftly turned it away by looking past me to Albert and Rudy. Together we watched Mick enter his office and disappear through an open door back into the garage.

"Don't try to sell me on the joy of surfing, J.," Carmen said quietly. "Now is definitely not the time."

"I'm not. What I meant was . . . ah, never mind." I could feel an argument bubbling beneath the surface and figured that now was not the time to start philosophizing on the free-and-easy essence of surfing. Patching up Albert and me this morning, Carmen simply couldn't fathom how anyone could actually come to blows over something as fleeting and trivial as a breaking wave.

"Never mind what, J? Tell me about it, I'd like to know. There's a whole lot I don't understand right now." Her pinpoint gaze never left my eyes.

"Just, I don't know, it was probably better that Mick didn't see me when I faced off with those guys this morning. More bodies would have ended up in the hospital." I briefly explained Mick's old role as pier enforcer, how he'd grown tired of it over the years, fighting other people's battles for them, how he'd chucked off the whole endeavor over time. I mentioned my invitation to him last night to join Albert and me for a little dawn patrol. I did what I could to make her see that today should have been a special occasion, just for Mick to be back in the water, having a gas after a lot of years away.

Her forehead grew lines. "How do you know it wasn't him, J?"

I was lost and my face showed it.

She exhaled. "You know what I mean. This morning. He was there. How do you know he's not the one who slugged Albert?"

I hadn't thought of that, but my mind wouldn't allow for any progress on the subject. It was like looking at a math problem that's not right, but you don't know what part. For a time I just listened to the roaring echo of cars rolling down PCH a block away, toeing my wing tip on the blacktop.

"No, I know him," I said finally. "I've known him a long time. That's not Mick. No way." I wanted to explain, but I knew she wouldn't understand how a person like Mickey Conlin could credibly maintain a certain social order by virtue of his presence and reputation alone. How he could enforce an unwritten set of rules in the water without victimizing a hapless soul. I'd never known him to light upon anyone weak or defenseless. Even when he'd taken on me as a schoolkid, I realized later that it was that thing I had that drew him to me, that ability to temporarily override my fears. And for all his fearsome rep, Mick was not one to look for trouble, ever. It was just that, over time, trouble seemed to find him more and more, until he just walked away.

Then again, what if he had just snapped this morning? I pictured Mick streaking through a section, Albert unwittingly cutting him off, a collision, Mick reading it as intentional and dealing a quick retaliation. It was not entirely impossible. Mick never looked for trouble, but he was prone to violence. Or he had been, long ago.

Could he have temporarily lost his temper, misplacing his judgment with it? Would he be too ashamed now to admit it to me, the friend who'd invited him to go slide a few? Like it or not, was he still the pier's enforcer?

Mickey Conlin was capable of plenty, I knew, but I was still staring at a math problem that was wrong. He would not have done Albert this way.

"I suppose you're going to tell me all the people he's beaten up had it coming," Carmen said, her eyes fixed on her brother and the old man playing their games.

I knew enough not to answer. Albert should never have been attacked by anybody for any reason. Regardless of who popped him, Carmen would stay upset about it for a long, long time over this.

"Car, he's not a thug. Look at the way he helped you find Rudy tonight."

She folded her arms. "Maybe he feels guilty about Albert."

I folded my arms, mirroring her stance. "He's not the guy."

We endured an uncomfortable silence, staring across the blacktop at an inventory of broken-down cars. I thought about starting over with Carmen—completely. Later tonight, maybe making the last twenty-four hours up to her with a warm bubble bath, a little champagne, a foot massage. Whatever it took.

"Sorry about this business with Rudy. I got here as soon as I could."

"I called you at work," she said. "Your secretary said you'd left early. Said to tell you to call your manager, too, she wants to talk to you." Carmen dug her hands into the back of her jeans pockets. The temperature was dropping by the minute. "Are you in some kind of trouble?"

Christ, we were sounding like a married couple, the burned-out kind.

"No. That's just her thing, riding roughshod on her people."

Carmen waited as if she'd come to a conclusion. "This is getting to be a problem."

"I'm telling you, Car, Eloise Horton is not a problem. All she wants . . ." But I stopped. Carmen had raised a hand and pointed a long finger toward the glass.

"I mean those two, J. That old man needs care and real supervision, not the kind he's getting."

"I know. But it's not that simple. Apparently he's quite well off, stands to lose it all if Angie and Carlito got hold of him." I explained what the detective, Tamango Perry, had said about no crime having been committed as of yet.

"Where the hell is his family?"

"His daughter should be here soon, by Monday. Don't worry, I'll help Dale keep an eye on him this weekend."

"He really blew it this afternoon."

"I know. You said he was asleep. He was probably pretty gassed from last night."

"He's homeless, J. It's no wonder he's exhausted."

I pondered the difficulty a man like Dale would encounter sleeping in a Buick during winter. I've crashed in my car a few times on surf trips up north when heavy rainfall washed me out of my tent. It sucked. I woke up feeling like a broken accordion. A man over six feet like Dale can't fold his body in enough places to fit across the seat of a standard automobile, even a boat like that Regal.

"Just a few more days, baby," I said, gentle as a lullaby, stroking the fine black hair behind her ear. "We'll get Rudy home safe, and I'll make it up to you and Albert." Carmen's poised loveliness always stirs something fiery and possessive in me. I grabbed her waist and pulled her close.

"You'd better, mister." Her tone had softened ever so slightly.

I hugged her tight, my chin resting on her shoulder, weary of doing damage control, yet knowing that I was damn lucky to have her and not wanting to let her go—ever. Beyond the impossibly bright office windows, the garage door stood wide open and the shop sucked in the night like a cave. In the shadows I could barely discern various shapes: the cylindrical shaft of a hydraulic lift, a car chassis suspended in midair, coils from a hose hung on the rear wall. A long workbench. Against the bench stood another dark vertical column, thicker and not perfectly shaped like the hydraulic lift. An upright figure, one the general size and shape of Mickey Conlin. Looking right at me.

Ten

A new swell hit Saturday morning, a west-northwest that barreled through a narrow window of open ocean between the Palos Verdes Peninsula to the north and Catalina Island to the south at just the precise angle to strike the sandbars off Christianitos like a tomahawk drumbeat. The sea was playing my song, and not one that I often hear at home this time of year. Winter swells are generated by far-off storms bearing either north or west off the California coast; those from too far north lose something when they bend around Palos Verdes, while swells straight out of the west are blocked by Catalina Island, which lies twenty miles straight offshore from the tip of Christianitos pier. But when a swell like this, from just the right angle, manages to shoot the gap—as locals call it—the drumbeat rises. Bands of energy refract off the long south jetty and collide with undiluted incoming lines to form thick peaks that pack twice the juice of a typical wave. In double-up conditions, takeoffs are touchy because the wall is sucking up hard, turning inside out as it breaks. But if you can make it to the bottom still standing you're going to get wickedly slotted, and, as anyone who surfs can tell you, a good tube ride is unbeatable.

I heard the first muffled detonations while lying in bed late Friday night, the house otherwise silent but for the groaning of my mattress as I shifted endlessly in search of sleep. By dawn the air was vibrating with energy. I slid downstairs without a sound, found Max in his spot near the kitchen door, and jogged down the block and across the sand.

Southside was alive with wedging green peaks pitching and bowling into an early-morning sunshine that made the shorebreak sparkle like white wine. Two riders were already out about a hundred yards south of the pier and Max was shadowing their movements in the sand. A big set lifted out the back, and the two rose over a stacking wall of water that devoured their trails as it unloaded on the bar. Through the mist another peak was hooking, and I saw a slash of white descending through its heart, a rider up and caroming off the bottom now, arching his back as he slipped beneath a canopy of falling water. I hooted, Max barked, and the surfer, locked inside, felt his way through the glorious glass-blown belly of the wave until it spat him out onto the shoulder. I turned and ran for my board.

My giddiness was short-lived. Surfwise, this was easily the best day of the winter, a no-brainer for any serious surfer. Days like this, you drop everything else in order to log as much water time as possible. But as I stood in the garage and stared up at the two dozen surfboards that float beneath the rafters like a school of colorful big-game fish, an odd paralysis set in, and I found that I could not decide which board to bring down. Typically it would be the 7'2" semigun for thumping overhead beach break, or maybe the seven-six for extra paddling speed, but I left the boards undisturbed in their stirrups and leaned against the wooden workbench as the sun cracked wider and wider through the open door. Not moving.

I never made it back to the shore that weekend. I just couldn't. Too much was going sideways at home. Albert's cheek was tattooed purple and his lower lip was as fat as a hand-rolled cigar. Since the mishap at the pier, he'd beaten a full retreat into the Wonderful World of Disney, camping in front of the TV set with a stack of G-rated videos in heavy rotation. By Sunday night I was gripping from two days of nonstop musical glee, pondering whether Mary Poppins, with her magic powers and ability to speak to animals, was perhaps the Antichrist.

Rudy had another regression and spent Saturday afternoon chanting like a Hindu priest as he inventoried the contents of the kitchen pantry—pap-reee-ka, pap-reee-ka! But he wasn't hurting anybody so I let him empty the shelves, then put everything back after we tucked him into bed. Dale mostly sat around all weekend, silently brooding in the bench seat beneath the living-room window as he gazed out onto Porpoise Way at his sagging house on wheels. Something was really killing him inside, something that lay beyond that window, but he wouldn't talk about it. Twice on Saturday and once again Sunday he pried himself away, dutifully phoning Rudy's daughter, Kimberley, to inquire as to when we could expect her arrival. But Kimberley was beginning to read as a flake, and no definitive date was forthcoming.

" 'Soon,' she says, 'really soon,' " Dale reported before heading back to his spot near the window.

Carmen didn't ask me, but she knew the surf was pumping, could sense it in my keyed-up manner. Both days she tried to give me permission to go slide a few, but both times I said no, unable to bring myself to leave her there alone to watch over three men who were carrying on like three boys in their own distinctive ways. I'd set this thing in motion, which made them my responsibility, and that meant sticking around at all times to prevent any further chaos. Explaining myself, I felt shallow, having to give voice to a sense of duty to look after these men that was second nature to her, thinking: Funny, not long ago I actually believed riding great waves to be the end of the rainbow. Carmen nodded without comment, content, I believe, to let me stumble onto my own discoveries without adding to my discomfort.

By normal accounts it should have been a shitty weekend, sitting around the house those two days, just a spoonful of sugar not helping a single damn thing go down. Four times the phone rang with surfing friends on the line wanting to know if I was on it, itching to talk story about the day's stellar rides and nasty wipeouts. I let the answering machine catch every message. Something had happened. For the first time in my life I had consciously overridden the reflex to surf, determined as I was to avoid taking undue advantage of my fiancée's generosity. Before this weekend, my impending marriage to this girl had seemed an abstraction not yet within my grasp, like a fistful of pretty postcards from a foreign land I'd never been to. Now at least I felt like it was a place I could locate on a map.

So I missed a good swell—well, a cooker. Still, it wasn't so bad. I would recover. Three thousand miles at sea an ill wind would kick up once again, a building front pinwheeling east below the Aleutians. A new swell would rise up and shoot the gap, the drumbeat pounding in the false dawn. Another time.

The thing is, there is only one Carmen, and this weekend felt like our time.

I took Dale with me to work Monday morning, had him wait downstairs in the cafeteria while I met with Therese Rozypal before Bobby Silver's reinstatement hearing got rolling. Therese wasn't looking too chipper and had her office door closed, her notes spread across that otherwise spanking clean desk.

"What's the problem?" I asked after I'd settled in, raising an eyebrow at the Nixon photo all over again.

"I don't know," Therese said. "I don't know." She stared at the notes in apparent frustration. Therese seemed like the type who liked to control things, which is good if you're a prosecutor, because you have to. But this one seemed beyond her grasp.

"Maybe it would help to just talk it through," I suggested.

She sighed. "Okay. I've reviewed Silver's petition for reinstatement again and again. I can feel it, something's missing. It just seems . . . too clean."

"What's the work history read like?"

Therese flipped a page on her copy of Silver's petition. "That's a perfect for instance. Look at this, he shows a five-year history of these 'business consulting' gigs that are just too loose, you know, too convenient, too hard to track down."

"Too elliptical," I said.

"Exactly. I mean, how many disbarred attorneys do you know whose 'consulting' services would be in significant demand?"

"Not too many."

"What advice would a man who's misappropriated a half dozen clients' settlement funds have to say that any sane person would want to hear?"

"So, is he lying about the jobs?" I said.

"That's another funny thing. The companies he listed as clients checked out, and although none would comment on specifics, all of them verified having done business with Silver."

"What kind of companies were they?" I asked.

"Interestingly, all four are investment-services outfits, limited partnerships with slick names like Capitol Consolidators and Homeowners Fidelity Trust. I say interestingly because Silver has no MBA or business background per se, not as far as I can tell."

"So naturally you're skeptical."

Therese rubbed her forehead with an open palm. "Of course I'm skeptical. But you know, my dim view of the case isn't evidence of anything. There's more. I've just got a feeling I'm missing a connection."

Apparently Silver had fared quite well as a consultant, well enough to repay the bar's Client Security Fund every last cent the fund had shelled out to the former clients from whom he'd stolen. Financed by a small portion of yearly bar dues, the Client Security Fund is like a safety net that keeps bilked clients from crashing to the ground headfirst, awarding up to fifty thousand dollars per claim in cases in which a client can show that her lawyer separated her from her money through dishonest means. Restitution is a key component of rehabilitation, and any fallen lawyer seeking reinstatement must demonstrate as much by repaying the fund if it has made payouts in that lawyer's name.

In Silver's misappropriating wake, the fund had forked out a whopping $147,264 to six clients that had gotten the royal bendover, all of the awards paid out during the first year following his disbarment. Most lawyers seeking reinstatement have trouble making ends meet during the down years; losing your principal livelihood will do that to you. Not Bobby Silver. Fourteen months ago, the fund received a check for $24,544 from him, the first of six checks in the exact same amount to roll in once a month, each dated the first of the month. One day after the last payment was received, Silver filed his petition for reinstatement. Like clockwork, Therese said.

"Impressive," I agreed.

She leaned forward over her papers. "I guess so, but what do you really think?"

"It's too good to be true."

Most thieving attorneys make only halfhearted stabs at restitution, casting themselves as victims, their good intentions thwarted by their inability to make a decent living as nonlawyers. They look for ways to get back in the club without paying those steep back dues. If they make it back in, great; if they don't, hell, what's a few days in court spinning a tall tale or two? It was worth a try. But this guy wanted back in the worst way. Which didn't make a lot of sense.

If Bobby Silver was swimming in green as a so-called consultant, why bother reclaiming his law license? He was near sixty, creeping up on the traditional age of retirement. As long as he wasn't a lawyer the state bar had no jurisdiction over him, which meant they had no practical basis to collect the hundred forty-seven grand they'd paid out of the fund. Something was not right about this synchronized method of repayment, the fat checks rolling in. Silver was the picture of cool efficiency. It just didn't jibe with the concrete cowboy I'd seen waddling in to the law center four days ago, face red and spit flying as he realized that Dale and I stood in the way of his plans to fleece a befuddled old man. By all outward appearances he was no better equipped to make a living outside the practice of law than any of the other wannabes whose reinstatements I'd handled.

"My guess, the restitution money he's been forking over is ill-gotten," I said.

Therese took her time thinking that one over. "But restitution is restitution, the judge will say."

"That's true," I said. "Were it not for our chance encounter with Silver last Thursday, he likely would have breezed today."

"Too bad for him."

We shared a smile as we stood to go.

The thought of my chance meeting with Silver as a lucky break put an extra click in my step as Therese and I made our way down to the fifth floor and through the state bar court's security check. The place was quiet, as usual, and the long, carpeted hallway outside the courtroom lay before us like an open fairway as we walked to the last door on the left and entered Department 6. Because the department case calendars are manageable and the judges handle only a few matters each day, state bar court is devoid of the usual courthouse hubbub. Today not a single soul lingered about the fringes.

Inside Department 6, the Honorable Anita Wachter had not yet taken the bench. Wachter's clerk, Wayne Fong, sat at an adjacent desk to the left of the judge's big leather chair, fooling with the recording equipment the state bar court uses in lieu of live court reporters to memorialize the proceedings. Wayne and I play pickup basketball in the basement gym a few times a week. I broke off from Therese to sit in the gallery.

"You playing at lunch today, J.?" Wayne asked as he slung a sleek headphone around his neck. His white shirt and oversize navy blazer made him look like airport security.

Bobby Silver was at the defense table with a man in an expensive black suit who was presently hunched over the table reviewing notes. Neither so much as glanced at Therese as she settled in opposite their table, but when Silver heard Wayne speak my name, he turned and eyed me, looking none too pleased to see me.

"Probably not, I've gotta be here today," I said, not coming out and saying that I'd be testifying, but letting Silver, who was straining to listen in, know that he'd stepped in something last Thursday in Glendale by running into me.

I smiled at Wayne, then glanced at Silver. His face was in full blush, his eyes flaring. I shot him the classic shit-eater in return. He whispered something to his lawyer that started with a few loose "goddamns" and trailed off into an extended hush-hush rant. His lawyer is a cool one, I thought, still writing his notes with his back turned to me as Silver's neck puffed and corded. Across from the defense table I saw Therese stop unpacking her things long enough to pick up a thin pleading someone had left on the corner of the prosecutor's table. She scanned the front page of the pleading, stopped short, and surveyed Silver's table with a frown.

Bobby Silver's lawyer finally turned and showed me a row of perfect white teeth I would know anywhere. "Counselor."

Roger Turnbull, one of the most high-powered criminal defense specialists in the state, and his simple greeting wiped the smile off my face like a hard slap.

"Morning," I managed.

I watched him introduce himself to Therese with the greatest of ease, apologizing for the last-minute substitution of attorney he'd dropped on her and promising to cooperate so as to make the hearing proceed as smoothly as possible.

"How have you been, J.?"

My lips were moving. "Fine, just fine," I think I said. But the whole time my brain was screaming: Roger Turnbull? What in hell is Roger Turnbull doing representing Bobby Silver in a routine little reinstatement hearing?

Therese finished unpacking her file box and caught my eye. I nodded to her to step outside. The hallway was deserted as usual. Therese brushed at the perfectly coiffed bangs on her forehead, a nervous gesture.

"Oh my God, that's Roger Turnbull," she half whispered. "*The* Roger Turnbull. You know him?"

"We had a conviction matter together last year. He was representing the mayor's son. You know, the cocaine addict."

"Oh. Right, right. I read about it in the papers."

I guessed Therese was a bit freaked by the fact that she was about to butt heads with a legal luminary. Now was the time to let her know how he operated.

"Interesting case," I said. "Had some lesser charges, a couple of solicitation misdemeanors to go with the coke possession for sale. The guy was on a weird power trip. We located the call girls who got busted with him on the sex counts. They told us he'd flashed a gold badge on them when it came time to pay, acted like he was a cop. Said he wouldn't bust them, they were 'way too hot' to get arrested. Apparently when vice popped him they found a gold honorary city inspector's badge in his wallet, had his dad's name inscribed on it."

"Nice guy," Therese said. "Impersonating law enforcement. Not too bright."

"The way I saw it he was also committing an illegal act under color of authority."

Therese nodded. "Yeah, I like that. Hey, that's good." The color coming back to her face now.

"Thank you."

"How'd it go?"

"We were all set to go to hearing, I'm figuring he might get disbarred. Then Roger comes riding to the rescue. I'd talked to Eloise about settlement on this before, and she'd said no way, take his license, this is a statement case. Felony possession for sale, under the influence, the two solicitation counts. For once I had to agree. Then Roger tells me wait until next Monday, he'll make a few phone calls, see what he can do. Monday morning, I get a call from Eloise to make a deal."

"You're kidding," Therese said.

"Serious. She told me she'd consulted the chief, and after further consideration, this was—how did she put it? Said the case presented a fine opportunity for the bar to show it could be 'firm, yet fair,' whatever that means."

"What did he get?"

"Nothing much. Stayed suspension, three years' probation, the usual terms and conditions."

"For three convictions? That's a joke." Shaking her head.

"But he still managed to break his old man's heart. I guess his dad thought he was something he wasn't." I remembered my surprise at seeing the mayor slide into the back of the courtroom at the last settlement conference we'd had on that case, his face ashen but the chin thrust forward as if to provide moral support for a son who refused even to make eye contact with him.

"So, how do you think I should handle this?"

I didn't want to crowd her with my opinions, but I knew a few things about Roger Turnbull, so I was relieved she'd asked. "He's a deal maker, Therese, so don't worry about it. As you know, there's no settlement in a reinstatement case like this. Silver has to prove his case, not you. His lawyer shouldn't have much of an impact."

Therese sighed. "I hope not."

I glanced back down the empty hallway that led to the lobby, scanned it anyway, as if someone who could hear me might be hiding there.

"What's wrong, J.?"

The last-minute substitution of attorney still bothered me. I hate courtroom surprises. They always seem to turn out badly.

"I don't know. Bobby Silver and Roger Turnbull. Guess I just can't picture those two together," I said. No need to undermine her confidence.

Therese leaned in so close that I could smell the apricot body wash she must have used that morning. Then she smiled like a self-assured young woman who didn't concern herself with phantom eavesdroppers in empty hallways. I should have felt relieved, but was instead swayed back on my heels as a chemical reaction altered my senses. My knees locked and my face felt hot—animal attraction. I held her gaze, assuming an utterly false calm.

"Don't worry," she said. "They probably can't picture us together either."

Not waiting for an answer, she turned and went back inside.

Dale came in and sat with me in the gallery, and we watched Roger Turnbull guide Silver through his bid to start anew as a reformed lawyer. Therese did just fine, making the right objections and keeping out of evidence three "new" exhibits Silver hadn't listed in his pretrial statement. Judge Wachter was polite enough to both sides but her manner was merely perfunctory, as usual. Today she was wearing a new wig, a deep reddish brown thicket of curls that made her heavyset face appear tired by comparison. The synthetic hair seemed to tilt a little too far forward, like an ill-fitting hat. She bore down on her laptop computer, tapping out a steady stream of notes. Not that she would have cared about the sliding hair. Judge Wachter rarely looks up from her keypad, and almost never smiles. The judge has always struck me as someone who doesn't much enjoy her line of work, or the company of lawyers for that matter. This probably made her the best jurist Therese could have drawn in a contest with a smooth operator like Roger Turnbull.

The early portions of the hearing were predictable and dull. Silver testified about his consulting experience, which by his description sounded less like business counseling and more like ground-floor pitch making for various "investment opportunities." As he spoke, I noticed the caressing effect his Texas drawl had on words. He tended to stretch each suffix like saltwater taffy, his voice low and even, the consistency of pitch somehow soothing to the ear.

"We-yall, yessirrr, the project wuzzz a bit on the sma-wall saahde, but it wuzzz verrry, verrry succ-ssessful for all pahh-teees in-volllvved. In fay-acttt . . ."

Although I was consciously thinking this guy probably has the moral makeup of a sock filled with horse manure, his steady vibrato had a lulling effect, like a persuasive undertow constantly threatening to pull me under. Bobby Silver had some serious sales skills.

The action heated up briefly when Therese got her turn to cross-examine him. She began by surprising him with a quick counterpunch to the sanctimonious claims of reform and rehabilitation he'd made at the close of his direct examination.

"Mr. Silver, you just described yourself as a man who has learned from his mistakes."

"That's correct." Silver's gray eyes were blank.

"You just described yourself as"—pausing to check her notes—"here it is, a 'solid citizen, with a lot to contribute to society.' Isn't that right?"

"Aah said that, you heard me right, dear," Silver said with a touch of sarcasm, glancing at the judge for approval. He didn't get it.

"Ask your next question, Counselor," Judge Wachter said without looking at Silver.

Therese stood up, pulling what looked like a magazine from her file box on the floor, contemplating it as if for the first time.

"Now, when you talk about making a contribution, Mr. Silver, does that include writing articles for a magazine called *Modern Outlaw*?"

"No," Silver spouted over his lawyer's objection.

"Specifically, an article, well, more of an editorial I guess, called 'Leave a Vapor Trail'—"

"What is this?" Silver barked. "Why is she showing me some dumb magazine? She can't—"

"Mr. Silver, contain yourself!" the judge responded. "Now—"

"Objection!" Turnbull yelled.

Therese lifted the magazine in offering. "Your Honor, I was only—"

"Hold on, hold on, everybody," Judge Wachter said more evenly. "Counselor, what is this?"

Therese handed a copy of the piece to both the judge and Turnbull, and both silently pored over it for a minute. Roger Turnbull betrayed no emotion as he read, but I saw a tiny grin crease the judge's lips as she turned the page.

"Objection," Turnbull said. "No foundation."

Judge Wachter looked amused by the challenge. "Ms. Rozypal, why don't you lay some foundation for Mr. Turnbull."

"Yes, Your Honor. May I approach the witness?"

The judge put down her copy of the article and folded her arms. "By all means."

"Mr. Silver, I'm showing you page thirty-one of a magazine by the name of *Modern Outlaw,* April 1992 issue. The article is entitled"—pausing for effect—" 'Leave a Vapor Trail, Not a Paper Trail.' To summarize, it describes a method of cheating the IRS out of otherwise taxable earned income using various means of nondisclosure."

Silver did his best to look bored.

"That's nice. So what?"

"The author is a 'Bob Silverstein,' " Therese continued, "and the italicized byline describes Mr. Silverstein as a 'legal rustler par excellence' who plies his trade in California." Therese let the magazine drop to her side. "You wrote this article, didn't you, Mr. Silver?"

"I did no such thing, ma'am."

I was thinking Therese would be stuck by now, unless she planned on calling someone at the magazine who could testify that Silver was the author, which I didn't expect, since Therese had not even mentioned the article in her office this morning. But Silver did something stupid: he kept talking.

"I look like a Silverstein to you?" he said, gazing up to the bench.

"Let me get this straight," Wachter said slowly. "What you mean, Mr. Silver, is not 'Do I look like a Silverstein' but 'Do I look like a Jew,' isn't that correct?" Glaring at him now.

"Your Honor," Roger Turnbull said quickly, "I don't think Mr. Silver meant—"

"He can speak for himself about what he meant, Mr. Turnbull, so please be quiet and allow him to do so."

"All aah mee-yeen, Yurrr Honorrr—Was that thi-yiss Mr. Silverstein, whoever he may be, is not me. Aah did not write that article. Never e'en seen it before. Aah swe-yerrr."

The judge sat very still, her face tight. Wayne Fong tried to make himself busy at his desk beside the bench.

"You don't have any more questions on this issue, do you, Ms. Rozypal?" she said, signaling to Therese that her intent was to move on.

"No, Your Honor."

I was relieved to hear that response. For an inexperienced prosecutor, Therese seemed to possess a pretty good set of courtroom instincts.

Silver straightened up from his chair as if he were finished as a witness.

"What are you doing?" the judge asked him.

Silver glanced at Therese, then the judge. "I thought she said she was done."

Wachter allowed herself a flicker of a smile. "Are you through questioning the witness?" she asked Therese.

"No, Your Honor. I'm finished with the magazine, but there's more."

"Very well. Sit down, Mr. Silverste—" The Judge caught herself. "Stay there, Mr. Silver. You're not done yet."

Silver eased his carcass back down and frowned into the chrome microphone. Therese, who'd been camped before the witness stand all this time, slowly floated back to her seat at counsel table.

"Let's talk about an office in Glendale you're affiliated with, Mr. Silver, a place called the Glendale Lo-Cost Law Center."

Roger Turnbull's murky gray eyes took a run from the blond prosecutor on back to me. Twice in a row now he'd apparently lost his way, which for him, I figured, was probably closing in on some kind of a record—and of course I knew there was more confusion in store for old Roger. But my face showed nothing. Up front, the judge was typing away, getting it all down on her laptop.

Eleven

Therese cross-examined Silver about the events of four days earlier beginning when Dale and I had popped into the law center in Glendale. Silver paused, then admitted that he had been there last Thursday, but he stared right back at his questioner as he denied having had any involvement with Angie, Carlito, or Rudy Kirkmeyer. If he was trying to intimidate her, it didn't take; Therese went down her list, asking all the right questions and setting the stage for my rebuttal testimony.

When Roger Turnbull's turn came to question his client on redirect, he asked Silver only two questions.

"Mr. Silver, what were you doing there, at this office in Glendale?"

"Well, ah'd heard there was a possibility aah could pick up some paralegal work there. Thought a legal job might be a good idea, even if ah wasn't actually practicing, you know, to help ease me back into the law."

"Were they hiring that day?"

Silver made a nonplussed face. "Nah, turned out the rumor was false."

Judge Wachter tapped more notes into her computer. Turnbull told her "Nothing further" as if he was tired but satisfied, as if mining the truth was a taxing endeavor. The explanation had a reasonably convincing ring to it. I might even say it was believable, if I didn't otherwise know Bobby Silver was totally full of shit.

Therese didn't bother with recross, not with me about to give my side of the story.

Turnbull rested Silver's case.

"Rebuttal?" Judge Wachter asked.

Therese sucked in a deep breath and called me to testify. I took the oath, settled in, and waited for Therese's questions, slowly recounting for the judge my experiences of last Thursday afternoon. "Let me get this straight," Turnbull asked me first on cross. "You were out there, at this legal center, with this Mr. Bleeker." He paused to stare at Dale, who sat up straighter in his gallery seat, eyes on the judge, who was taking full notice of him for the first time that morning. "Because you were his probation monitor?"

"Yes."

"And he was in trouble?"

"Yes. Without knowing it. As I said earlier, he'd accepted a position as an attorney. I thought it sounded like an operation in which they were using his license to—"

"Objection, hearsay, and the witness is speculating, Your Honor."

Judge Watcher overruled the objection. "You asked a question that invited just such speculation, Mr. Turnbull."

Turnbull thanked the judge as if she'd ruled in his favor. This was how I'd remembered him from before: unflappable.

"Is this how it's done around here, Mr. Shepard?" Turnbull went on. "Prosecutors like yourself, handling the probation oversight of . . . *disciplined* lawyers like Mr. Bleeker here?"

"Right," I said. "Disciplined, just like your client was, sir. But actually Mr. Bleeker never got disbarred."

"Objection, nonresponsive."

"Answer the question, Mr. Shepard," the judge ordered me.

"No, it's not how it's typically done," I said.

Turnbull rubbed his forehead, which was about as shiny as his wing tips, as he paced the floor behind his chair. "So this little . . . outing you had, it wasn't part of a state bar investigation, was it?"

"No."

"Did you make an official report of some kind?"

"Yes. I telephoned the Glendale Police Department and spoke with a detective about it."

"I mean, here at the bar?"

"I looked up Mr. Silver on the bar's computer system and saw he had a hearing scheduled for today, saw that Ms. Rozypal was the attorney assigned to handle it. So I went to her office and told her what I told the court today."

"I see." He tilted his head toward Therese as if he'd just made a connection. "Mr. Shepard, do you and Ms. Rozypal work together?"

"Yes."

"I see." Raising his eyebrows. "You work together closely, don't you?"

I remembered the powerful charge that had briefly passed between Therese and me earlier that day. Christ, could that hidden attraction be apparent to an astute observer like Roger Turnbull? Not possible, I thought. At her table, Therese sat placidly writing a note on a white pad, nothing happening on her end. I bit my bottom lip. Not possible.

Then I began to consider whether I might have imagined the heated moment that morning. Maybe it had to do with Carmen's moving in with me the week before but sleeping in another part of the house instead of my bed, our constant close proximity at home leading to nothing but frustration, false starts, and interruptions by my three other new houseguests. Perhaps my physical yearning for Carmen had manifested itself in a displaced projection onto an attractive coworker. Suddenly I felt better about myself. Ah, but of course, Therese was a mere symbol.

Just then the mere symbol crossed her legs, and I felt my heart skip like a windup toy with a broken spring.

"Mr. Shepard?" I heard the judge say.

Some fucking theory.

"We belong to the same trial unit," I said.

Turnbull's gray eyes were shining on me. "Well, how convenient."

"Objection, argumentative," Therese said.

"Let's limit the sarcasm, shall we?" the judge said to Turnbull.

"So, you bring this information to Ms. Rozypal on the eve of trial, and . . ."

"That was just how it worked out. It wasn't planned."

Turnbull acted offended. "I wasn't finished, Your Honor."

I shrugged at the judge. "Sorry."

He paced behind the cherry-wood lectern that stood between the two counsel tables and directly faced the bench, waiting for the judge to give him her full attention.

"After eight months of trial preparation in this case, four months in which the state bar investigated my client and found nothing, and four more months of discovery, you ask us to believe that you came to your coworker"—stopping to glare at Therese—"on the eve of trial, with this outlandish tale?"

I folded my hands in my lap, no expression. As talented as he was, Roger Turnbull was shadowboxing phantoms right now.

"As I said, that's just the way it worked out," I answered. "I had no control over the timing, didn't know your client was going to be there until he pulled up in front of the law center in his Cadillac."

"He showed up on his own accord?" Wachter asked me.

"Yes, Your Honor. About five or ten minutes after Mr. Bleeker and I had arrived."

I eased back a little from the chrome microphone I'd been talking into, feeling pretty untouchable. Then Roger flung something of a wild punch.

"You said there is no state bar investigation into this matter as yet, correct?"

"That's correct."

"I'm wondering." Pacing, making the judge follow his movements. "Did you take this issue up the ladder, so to speak, to a supervising attorney?"

"No. I mean, not yet."

"Oh, really. Now, you're a deputy trial counsel, aren't you, Mr. Shepard?

"Yes."

"You are subject to a chain of command in your office, aren't you?"

I told him I was. He asked me who my boss was. The judge was typing in her laptop when I said the name Eloise Horton.

"Does Ms. Horton know that you chose to monitor Mr. Bleeker's probation yourself?"

"No."

"No?"

"I saw no need to tell her."

Enjoying himself fully now, he beamed a wide toothpaste-ad smile my way. "What about this business at the place in Glendale, the law center, did you tell her about that?"

"No."

"How about today? Does Ms. Horton know you're here, trying so desperately to hit a home run for your coworker?"

Therese was on her feet. "Objection, relevance, and it's argumentative."

"Withdrawn, withdrawn," Turnbull said before the judge could sustain the objection. I could feel my teeth grinding in the back of my mouth.

"I think I can get an answer to that last question by asking it in a different way, Mr. Shepard. Now, you haven't told your supervisor that you would be testifying today, have you?"

"No. I was called to testify on rebuttal, only *after* your client lied about what happened last Thursday."

"That's enough, Mr. Shepard," the judge said.

"Very interesting," Turnbull said, slipping back into his chair. "You're quite the free wheel, Mr. Shepard, aren't you?" I didn't answer as he turned to the judge. "Your Honor, I request that the court take judicial notice of a certain known fact."

"That fact being?"

"The fact that this is precisely the kind of activity that the newly composed bar discipline system review panel will be most interested in."

Judge Wachter's face was stony, the way it looks when she's somewhere between perturbed and angry.

"Request denied, and you can spare me the editorial commentary, Mr. Turnbull." Without looking, I felt her turn her gaze on me. My inquisitor crossed his legs very casually, as if he were chatting about classic novels on a cable TV show. I thought he had more for me, but he waited too long.

"Any further questions for this witness?" she asked him. This is code for a judge saying she has heard enough.

Turnbull said he had concluded his line of questioning and, ever cordial, thanked both the judge and me.

Therese passed on asking me further questions on redirect, which I guessed she did to avoid giving Turnbull another run at me. Then she rested her opposition.

It was well after twelve, but the judge made no mention of the time and asked the parties to make their closing arguments. Turnbull paced the floor behind counsel table as if he wished a jury were present to appreciate his performance. Raising his voice for underlining effect, he dismissed my testimony as an untrustworthy, unethical insider's attempt to harpoon Silver's petition for reinstatement based on nothing more than hearsay. Since my story conflicted with Silver's, and since there was no corroboration offered to support my version of the facts, Turnbull argued, the testimony should be thrown out. Furthermore, he intoned, his arms spread and palms gliding out as if he were Moses addressing a convention of Philistines, the bar prosecutor's surreptitious acts should raise serious ethical concerns for the court, perhaps even warranting a finding of prosecutorial misconduct.

"Thank you, Your Honor. Thank you in advance for your impartiality, for giving my client the opportunity . . ."

I chewed on my lower lip as the high-priced gasbag signed off ever so slowly, ever so cordially with the judge.

Therese gave her closing standing ramrod straight at the podium, her tone formal. She wasted no time in reminding the judge that I had testified under oath, my story was consistent, and Silver had admitted to being at the law center the previous Thursday. What mattered most was that a bar prosecutor had witnessed firsthand Robert Silver committing a violation of the rules of professional conduct, and most likely a crime. Plain and simple, Robert Silver had attempted to practice law without a law license, which is strictly prohibited. How could he say he was rehabilitated from the lawbreaker he had been back when he'd been disbarred? In what way had he changed for the better? None that the state bar could see, none at all.

Judge Wachter fixed on her laptop for a good ten minutes, scrolling back and forth and jotting extra notes by hand before she finally spoke.

"I am going to provide a written decision in this matter, of course," she began, "but I know you have been waiting patiently for nine months now since you filed your petition, Mr. Silver. So I am prepared to make a tentative ruling pending my final written decision."

"And aah do thank you, Your Honuhh," Silver said, laying it on thick one last time. He was literally on the edge of his seat, crimped in a position that pushed up the shoulders of his gray pinstripe suit. From the side he looked like a kid dressed up in Dad's clothes.

The petitioner's heartfelt thanks seemed to roll right off the judge, who didn't bother to say "You're welcome." Wachter nodded gently at her clerk as if to say, Hang in there a little longer, we're almost done. Then she zeroed in on the petitioner, Robert Silver.

"When your attorney rested his case, I was prepared to rule that you had met your burden of proof, Mr. Silver, that you had shown by clear and convincing evidence that you were rehabilitated from your former misdeeds, and that you were currently fit to practice law again in this state. Then, when I heard that business about the magazine article, I was given pause. However, my job is to deal with evidence"—she briefly looked Therese's way—"provable, admissible evidence. Now, I find that there is no evidence that you wrote the article, because your name is not Silverstein."

"That's absolutely right, Your Honuhh, and aah didn't mean to—"

"Mr. Silver, do not interrupt me while I'm making this ruling. If you persist in doing so I will have you removed. Understand?"

"Uh, yes, Your Honuhh."

Wow. The judge was in a shitty mood all right. I hoped it was not because of what I'd brought to this case, or the way I'd brought it.

"So I was willing to give you the benefit of the doubt on that issue, Mr. Silver. But I didn't like the way you answered the question when you were asked if you'd written the piece. Your answer, sir, was most indirect."

"B-but aahh didn't—"

"Quiet, please!" Glaring at him. "Now, as I was saying, your answer was less than direct. In fact, you answered the question with a question of your own." Checking her notes. "You said: 'Do I look like a Silverstein?' Now I thought that was peculiar, and it got me thinking. You see"—she nodded at the empty witness stand—"I watch people stand up there and take the oath pretty close to every day, and I have to admit, even someone who has seen as much as I have—and I have seen plenty, let me tell you—that those words, 'Do you swear to tell the truth,' they *do* have an effect on people. Even people who intend to be less than truthful in the testimony they give."

"Your Honor," Turnbull said, "I can assure you my client—"

"Save the assurances, Counselor." The judge held up her palm like a cop halting traffic. "You've had your say, now I'm having mine. Please don't interrupt."

"Yes, Your Honor. And I thank you, Your Honor."

Christ, I thought. Roger Turnbull might be a high-profile deal maker, but this was just low-grade brownnosing.

"At any rate, that oath does something to witnesses. Oh, I know it doesn't prevent witnesses from lying, but I like to think it makes them think about lying before they do it. And quite certainly, that simple oath seemed to have had just such an effect on the petitioner today. Twice it was very noticeable. The first time, as I mentioned, when he gave that cute answer about whether he'd written that article in the outlaw magazine. And then again when Ms. Rozypal asked him a very simple question: Were you there, at that place in Glendale called the law center, last Thursday?"

Turnbull was out of his chair, a hand extended. "Your Honor, I'm sure Mr. Silver would be glad to testify further, if the court would like to ask him additional—"

"No, and do not interrupt me again, Mr. Turnbull."

Wayne Fong loves it when Wachter chews butts, and he raised an amused eyebrow from beside the bench. I did my best to ignore him.

"When asked that second simple question," the judge went on, "the petitioner paused, long enough that it became apparent to me that he was measuring an answer. I gave some thought to what it was that he might have been trying to determine, in that brief few seconds. What might have brought on that pause? Then the answer became clear when the bar put on its rebuttal witness."

The judge stared straight at the defense table. Silver and Turnbull were so quiet you would have thought they'd stopped breathing.

"The petitioner paused because he had no idea what kind of evidence the bar had in rebuttal of his petition. Of course, how could he know at that point? No rebuttal evidence had been presented as yet. Now, apparently he knew something significant was forthcoming due to Mr. Shepard's presence last Thursday at the law center, and because he observed Mr. Shepard seated here in the gallery this morning."

She looked up at Dale. I didn't turn to see him, but I knew just where he sat, in the back row of the gallery, the seat nearest the courtroom door.

"And although the bar chose not to question Mr. Bleeker, he was here in court as well, in full view. What I realized was that you paused to make a decision. And I can now infer from the rebuttal testimony I heard that in that moment, you decided, Mr. Silver, that you had better at least admit you were at that law office, since at least two other people present in the courtroom could place you there. But the rest of Ms. Rozypal's questions about what you did while you were there were damaging, so damaging that hearing them one by one, you knew you couldn't possibly answer them truthfully, for your petition for reinstatement would have no chance. So you denied the rest."

The judge studied her notes again. Therese found a second to cast a sideways glance my way. Her demeanor was reserved, the chin held high, as dignified as a princess in waiting, her back straight against her chair. Still every bit the serious lawyer, but I could tell she was beaming inside, ready to burst. I knew that her beauty was growing on me, and I felt a pang of guilt. An inner voice gave counsel, delivering a simple message to my frontal lobe and parts further south: You're getting married, dipshit, keep it zipped.

"Around here we take the unauthorized practice of law very seriously, Mr. Silver," the judge said. "Now why, after nearly six years, you couldn't have waited a few more weeks to get your license to practice law back—well, I just don't understand that."

To me, the answer to that riddle was easy: He couldn't resist taking Rudy Kirkmeyer for all he was worth.

"It's truly a shame that you jumped the gun the way you did, but by asserting that you were counsel for that elderly gentleman, you committed a serious violation of the rules of professional conduct and very likely even committed a crime. Therefore, you give me no choice but to deny your petition for reinstatement."

Silver and Turnbull leaned close together and shared a whisper. I checked my watch. Almost one. Wayne could forget about shooting hoops in the gym today. The usual noontime game would be breaking up in a few more minutes. When I looked up from my timepiece, Judge Wachter was dead set on me.

"As for Mr. Shepard, I have to say that although I found his testimony to be credible, I was not pleased to learn that he was apparently acting in such an independent, unorthodox manner. I have not yet determined what I might do to follow up on these concerns."

Christ, that sounded ominous. My throat was suddenly parched. I swallowed painfully.

"That's all I have for today," the judge concluded. "The parties will receive my written decision by mail within thirty days. Counsel for the bar and the petitioner, I thank you both for your courtesy and professionalism. Court is in recess."

"We're off the record," Wayne announced, tearing his tiny headset off. "All rise."

We stood in unison as the judge left the bench, and it was over.

Dale Bleeker and I slipped outside to wait for Therese. Dale was wearing the same slightly dusty suit he'd had on the first day I met him, and I wondered if it was the only suit he had. Different tie, though, a bloody red one with a quiet diamond pattern. His eyes seemed different, too, more disturbed, like a pair of high windows reflecting incoming stormy skies.

"Hey, thanks for not calling me as a witness," he said quietly.

"Don't thank me," I said. "That was Therese's call. It's her case."

"Maybe, but you stole the show, man." He extended a large hand and we shook. "Nice job."

For the first time since the police had escorted him to my front door, Dale appeared outwardly encouraged.

"What now?" he asked.

Inviting me to simply obliterate his good vibe.

"Silver can't do much to get to Rudy now," I said, "but Angie and Carlito won't quit."

"They'll just find another shyster, won't they?"

"If they haven't already. And we still have to deal with getting you extracted from any law center messes—I mean cases—in which they used your name. That hasn't gone away."

"Damn," Dale said, leaning back against the wall.

"We should also think about getting Rudy to a doc if the daughter keeps dragging her feet getting down here. I don't feel comfortable looking after him much longer, not without a professional opinion on what we're dealing with."

"It's some form of dementia," Dale said. "Carmen said it looks like Alzheimer's."

"She was guessing." Four days now, harboring an elderly man I knew precious little about—not good. "What if it gets worse? What if he were to have a seizure?"

Dale nodded. "Walk out in the street and get hit by a car."

I didn't even want to think about the complications if the old man were to go and die on us.

"We've gotta do something," Dale said after a pause.

"Any suggestions?" I said. Then I waited. Rudy was his client, after all. But Dale seemed frozen in place. What had become of the catlike courtroom predator whose sanguine air I'd once dreamed of emulating? Or was the image a fiction, a product of a certain acute lack of vision on the part of one young juror who happened to sit in front, where the spit flew, the fiction then further distorted by the soft-shuffle steps of ten years' time?

"I'm thinking," Dale said, "and don't look at me like that, all right?"

"Like what?"

"Like that. You know, washout, disappointment. Even if that's what you think, and you have every right to at this juncture. Just go easy." He looked away. "I don't need the grief."

He was right. Fiction or not, this was not the time to sort out my feelings about what had become of Dale.

"Don't sweat it, I'll figure something out," I said. "But you're backing me all the way."

He nodded. "Goes without saying."

"I may have to open an SBI—a state bar investigation—on the law center to see those records. You can be the complaining witness, admit to what you know, cooperate."

"Right," he said, "and get disciplined for my trouble if a mess of abandoned cases have my name on the papers."

"We don't know that to be the case. Not yet, at least, so don't worry about that part. It may be the best we can do."

He jammed his hands down into his pants pockets. "Don't worry. Easy for you to say."

He was wearing me out, watering down my patience.

"Easy? Wrong word, partner. I'm sweating a shitload of details here and at home, in case you hadn't noticed. Right now nothing's very easy."

His head drooped on his shoulders. "You're right. Sorry."

"Forget it."

"What else?"

"As far as Rudy is concerned," I said, "we might try getting his home address and stopping by his place. If Angie and Carlito aren't hanging out there, we can check his records, see if there's any medical information in his files. Even a family doctor's name could help."

"Sounds like a plan."

Ten feet behind us the courtroom door was yanked open from the inside and Bobby Silver and his lawyer burst into the hallway whispering loudly. Silver's face and neck were a watermelon pink.

"I don't care who's payin' the goddamned bill for your services," Silver hissed in Roger Turnbull's face. "You're fired! Got that?"

Turnbull stood frozen. "Bobby, please, let's just go down the hall, we can get a conference room and discuss—"

"Good-bye!"

Silver stalked past us but caught me checking him. "You think you're so smart," he said to me. "Let me tell you something, son."

"Bobby!" Turnbull shouted after his client.

"You don't know nothin'!' "

"Anything," I said, reflexively correcting his piss-poor grammar. His forehead was beaded wet and his eyes were flaring.

"Huh?"

"Never mind."

Without another word he strode toward the lobby, bulging pant legs swishing down the long hallway.

Turnbull had already recovered, with a natural smile. "Obviously my client is rather upset."

"Obviously," I said.

"Gentlemen," Turnbull said, excusing himself with a dip and fleeing after Silver.

"Didn't sound like the concrete cowboy is Roger's client anymore to me," I said.

"Me either," Dale said. "What do you think Silver meant, saying you don't know nothing?"

Good question. It could have been a standard insult, but then, he might have been referring to the situation with Rudy. Or possibly the law center.

"I don't know. Maybe we're missing something."

"As far as I'm concerned," Therese said from behind me, her file box loaded onto a chrome cart, "you're not missing a single thing, Mr. Shepard." With that she leaned forward, smiling hugely, and hugged me with her free hand.

I just stood there, smelling that marvelous apricot body wash, feeling confused and happy and guilty and dumb at the same time. Struggling to recall that handy bit I'd worked out before about Therese Rozypal being just a symbol of something else, the rationale escaping me now.

Twelve

Therese was so pleased with the judge's tentative ruling that she insisted on buying Dale and me lunch. We settled on the Persian place down on Eleventh and Hill you can see from my window, walked outside and down the sidewalk like a team of fictional legal superheroes in the opening credits of a prime-time melodrama. Dale and I flanked Therese as we shared our takes on the hearing. It felt liberating just to be outdoors, the stressful anticipation of the day's legal contest behind us. As we walked, Therese did most of the talking, which was only right, since the victory was hers. Dale seemed to be warming to her company nicely. Regardless of whatever punishment he'd subjected his body to of late—I say this recalling the hulking bag of Coors empties in the Regal's trunk—his mind could still produce the odd incisive observation. For one thing, he had studied Silver's face throughout the proceedings, noting a host of subtle expressions that told him Silver was putting up hefty resistance to his lawyer's advice and counsel. It was as if Roger Turnbull, for all his fame and notoriety, was a burden to Silver, his presence more an imposition than a godsend. Hearing Dale, I pondered what we'd seen outside the courtroom. Silver had told Turnbull he didn't care who'd paid for him, he was fired.

The sky was a soft winter blue creased with vapor trails from streaking jets headed east over the mountains. Cool air filled my lungs as we continued nearly in step with one another. A lifeless breeze merely hinted that a great ocean lay to the west. The light was almost artificially brilliant, the rooflines and lamppost shadows and speckled tree shade on the cement leaping forth in painterly contrast to the sun's steady beam. The light in Los Angeles is extraordinary. Days like this are the reason the early filmmakers came out here, and stayed.

Therese commented on the afternoon's beauty. Perfect earthquake weather, I said without thinking. No one disagreed; the big shakers always seem to rattle our world on pristine days.

We had stopped to wait at the signal just across the street from the restaurant. I asked Therese the name of the lawyer who'd represented Silver before Turnbull had subbed in at trial. Tad Rizzo, she said. I shuddered when she said the name. Tad Rizzo, known by his many dear friends at the bar as "Ratzo," was a bottom feeder of the first order, a lazy, whiny obstructionist who loved to drag out settlement discussions and go to trial on loser cases just to inflate his fees. A guy whose monthly ad in *California Lawyer* magazine posed the crass, rhetorical question "Why Pay More?" (The obvious answer is that you get what you pay for.)

Here was Silver, upgrading from Ratzo Rizzo to Roger Turnbull in a single day. Like doing zero to sixty in three seconds flat. Then making a stink about it after the hearing. It just didn't make sense.

The light changed and we made our way across Eleventh and into the restaurant, which was beginning to empty out at this hour. A very dark waiter who nodded too much came and took our orders, then went away. Therese and I sat directly opposite each other, eating flat bread and finger-painting the beads of sweat on our ice waters. Dale sat back and rested his eyes. We rehashed the hearing a bit more, then tired of the subject and began to talk movies, sports teams, and that ultimate evergreen L.A. topic: traffic. Just before the waiter brought a sizzling tray of kabobs to our table, Therese took a breath.

"Tell me about yourself, J."

"Not much to tell," I said, conscious of her intense gaze and enjoying it, I must admit. But by the time the nodding waiter slipped us the check, it was as if that oath I'd taken in Wachter's court had kicked in again, for I was deep into a description of Carmen.

Carmen is, well, striking, which became apparent the first time I saw her. She was at work, a computer screen lighting her face, fingers twisting phone cord as she gave directions, a stack of paperwork staring up at her from her crowded little desk inside the children's court building in East L.A., calmly providing information on the classes that Las Palomas, her employer, offered to address any and all manner of deficient parenting. I had waited as she smiled her way through the endless flow of aftercourt drop-ins she received from many of society's more accomplished fuckups. Knock, knock, who's there? Child molesters, addicts, wife beaters, kid beaters, mental cases, each one gripping a signed court order and a defensive attitude, saying, I do *not* want to be here, lady, I do *not* need or deserve this shit, okay? Each one departed the Las Palomas office ten minutes later just as cynical, but maybe a tad more hopeful than before. Some of them even thanked this young woman that had looked into their hangdog eyes and somehow located in them a certain dignity that even they had forgotten was there. Carmen is trained as a social worker, but her gift is her ability to make you believe that you alone are unique, even special.

I, too, was at work the day we first met. I'd been short a Spanish-speaking interpreter on a case, my last of the afternoon. The court had assigned me to represent a father who spoke little English and punished his kids with a flick of his cigarette lighter on a trembling open palm. At the time I considered it rotten luck, bogging down like this on my final case. That was during my third year representing wayward parents in dependency court, and by then I was pretty sick of the whole damned thing. I remember that day as a rough one, how badly I wanted to snag an interpreter, do the hearing, flee the building, and tear back down the freeway to Christianitos and the sea. But the interpreters' office was empty.

I was stuck. There was nothing to do but slide back down to the courtroom and sit around and rot while my afternoon died a slow death. But just as I started back toward the elevators, I heard a young woman's honeyed voice emanating from an open door a few yards down the deserted hallway. Stopping, staggered by indecision, I remember feeling sorry for myself, lamenting my situation. But what the hell, I thought, maybe I can ask the honey-voiced woman if she's seen or heard anything about the vacant interpreters' office not thirty feet away. It was worth a try. I walked to the open door and went inside.

Lucky me.

• • •

The eye contact between Therese and me waned a bit after I told her about Carmen. Therese offered nothing in return about her personal life when I was through talking about mine. I didn't push it, knowing that if it were not for Carmen, I'd be on Therese like a suction cup. Some women have that certain something, a feminine magic that can wreck a man, steal the words from his tongue, turn his brain to runny oatmeal. Carmen possessed a warehouse full of that magic. No doubt Therese Rozypal had some in store as well, but I could scarcely recall the impression she had made on me as a new hire. Not much of one, at any rate, just that of a quiet, conservatively dressed young attorney with a rather uptight hairstyle and a goofy picture of a Girl Scout and Richard Nixon on her desk.

We left the restaurant and crossed the street again, both of us content to walk back to the bar offices with Dale in the middle, like a human firewall. I wished I could tell Therese I'd underestimated her, that she had that something very special, how it was too bad our timing was off, how . . . Right—not in this lifetime could I say anything of the sort. All I could do was compliment her, colleague to colleague, on the fine job she'd done on the Silver matter, and leave it at that. So I did. We walked on, and when Therese thanked me for the kind words, her eyes were fixed on something down the block, well away from me. Nobody's fool.

It's funny, I was thinking, how attraction can turn on and off like a faucet. Funny, and terrifying.

Dale hung out quietly in my office the rest of the afternoon while I read the investigative file on another new case due for filing. Just before five the phone rang. Tamango Perry, the Glendale police detective, was calling me from his car on a mobile phone, his voice rattled. He started and stopped a few times, as if he was distracted.

"Everything okay, Detective?" I asked.

"Yes, sorry . . . well, no, not really."

"Where are you?"

"I am at the site of a homicide. Gang related."

"Oh."

"I'm upset about it."

I waited.

"A newspaper boy on his bicycle route was wearing a San Francisco 49ers jacket," he said, "red being the favored color of a rival gang. Shot dead, left in a gutter, and for what? Wearing the wrong color on the wrong street of some dump of a neighborhood not even worth fighting for, let alone dying for."

I didn't know what to say. "I'm very sorry."

"No, I am," Tamango said. "I am sorry and I shouldn't go on about it. Sometimes it gets to me."

"Must be hard."

"Yes."

A siren rolled by in the background. I wanted to break the silence but didn't know what to say. I didn't even know why he had called.

"I'll be here awhile," he said, "taking statements and writing it up. But I wanted to let you know, on my way over here I came down Brand, went by the Lo-Cost Law Center. I stopped by earlier today, late morning, but they were closed up. Odd to be closed like that, you know, midday. No one was answering the phone either. I thought maybe they figured the situation with you and Mr. Bleeker was trouble for the operation. Maybe they closed up shop and moved on."

"I see." I didn't like the sound of that. If they were gone already it would be much harder to trace the cases they'd handled using Dale's name. He could be on the hook for months as new complaints from jilted clients trickled in one by one.

"But when I drove by a little while ago on my way here, I saw a light on. Hard to tell, I was speeding through traffic, but I thought I saw someone inside."

"Want us to meet you there?"

"Who is 'us'?"

I told him Dale was with me.

"Yes, perfect. I'd like you there when I question them. If Mr. Bleeker is there, we can ask to see their files without a warrant, since he is their staff lawyer."

"Figuratively, Detective," I said.

"Yes, of course."

I'd not yet met Tamango Perry in person, but I liked the fair-minded approach he seemed to take to his work.

"We'll be there. Might take half an hour at least from downtown, with evening traffic."

"Try taking Broadway up to San Fernando Road."

"I know the way." It's a nice no-freeway route that cuts north through Chinatown, then jogs left along the L.A. River bed.

"And please, Mr. Shepard, wait for me. Don't go in until I come over. This is a police investigation at this point."

"I understand."

Dale was out of his chair by the time the receiver hit the cradle. I told him what the detective had seen as I shut off my computer. "Outstanding," he said. "Let's get this thing resolved."

"Don't get your hopes up too high. They may be gone before we get there. We gotta boogie." I grabbed my jacket and turned out the lights.

My phone rang. Dale and I exchanged a frozen glance standing in the doorway. "Might be the detective again," I said. I picked up the call.

"J., glad I caught you."

I winced. "Tell me, what can I do you out of, Eloise?"

"Very funny. I heard you testified on rebuttal in a reinstatement this morning. Heard you were quite effective."

Her tone was level but had that usual pinprick twinge of challenge in it. I turned my back from the door and gazed out the big windows at a patch of sky the color of malt liquor fading in the twilight.

"That's nice of Therese to say, but—"

"Who said anything about Therese? I heard it from Judge Wachter."

Great. The judge had already called to complain.

"Oh."

"We need to talk," Eloise said.

I imagined the self-satisfied smile on her face. Nothing seemed to bring more pleasure to Eloise than having something on you.

"We're talking," I said.

"In person."

"We will, first thing tomorrow, okay?"

"Now!" she shot back. "My office, now! Got it?"

I felt like chains were snapping inside me, something I'd held back a long time finally busting loose.

"Don't shout at me again," I said, straining for calm. "I won't stand for it." Silence. "It's the end of the day," I went on, "and I'm on my way out to an appointment."

"You listen—"

"I said I will see you first thing tomorrow."

"I told you . . . to get down here now. N-O-double-U." Her voice quaking a little through the spelling. "Your job depends upon it, Mr. Shepard. Understand?"

Fuck this, I thought, this is wrong and it has to stop.

"Don't threaten me, Ms. Horton, it's a mistake. I have rights as an employee. Keep it up and my next meeting isn't going to be with you, it'll be with a union steward, then the chief. Do you understand that?"

Christ, what a hollow counterthreat. Our employee union was best known for a long history of befuddled contract negotiations and unjustifiably steep mandatory member dues, not for fighting tough labor disputes with management. And the last time I'd spoken with the chief was at last year's Christmas party, about three seconds' worth in the buffet line. Something like, "Hey, try that jalapeño dip, it's got quite a kick." God knows I had no special in with Reginald Hewitt, none whatsoever. But Eloise didn't counter me.

"Are you openly defying me?" she said at last.

I looked at the digital clock radio on my desk. "My clock reads five-oh-one," I said, fudging by a few minutes. "Standard business hours are over. You can look it up in the bar manual."

She snorted like a bull. "Don't you get smart with me, Shepard."

"I will see you in the morning. Nine o'clock. Your office." I hung up the phone before she could respond. "Let's bail," I said to Dale.

His smile was small and reserved. "Back door?" Already hip to my evasion tactics from his previous visit to my office.

"Definitely."

I grabbed my briefcase, said a hasty good night to Honey Chavez, and we headed out fast.

No one was waiting at the rear elevators when we got there. "Yeah, I'm a back door man," I crooned in a low voice, heart still thudding in my throat from the exchange with my boss. "I'm a back doe-arr maaayannn." The old blues classic helped me decompress a little. She can't fire me, I told myself, I haven't done anything wrong. Maybe a transfer to another unit would be good for both of us. Maybe . . .

"I'm a back door man," Dale piped in. He seemed dialed in to my apprehension. "I'm a back doe-arr maaayannnn."

I appreciated the gesture.

"Well, da men don't know," we sang in unison. Just then the elevator doors swung open, a crowd of stoic faces, all eyes suddenly upon us as we shared a quick grin that said hey, what the f———. "But da little girls under-staaannnnd."

Bodies parted, people making all kinds of room for us. Dale frowned as we stepped in and took our places. I was reminded that he was homeless and unemployed, by now quite used to being greeted with silence and cold stares. But they were looking at me the same way. Hell, I was thinking, it wasn't *that* bad.

No, I knew it wasn't the mediocre singing.

The doors pinched shut four inches from my face. Unseen mechanisms creaked and whirred inside the elevator shaft. I stared straight into my hazy reflection in the stainless steel, pulse quick, green eyes unblinking. We descended to the lobby in silence.

Dale sings with me because he knows, I thought. This is just how it is when you're desperate. Saner folks can smell it on you.

The Glendale Lo-Cost Law Center sign on the brick facade was dark, as was the reception area, but a lone light shone from the back room. I idled on Brand Boulevard in the northbound lane outside the office, waiting to cut across and park. No one seemed to be inside the law center, at least no one we could see from the front. The print shop next door was closed for the day, as was the nail salon. The flow of oncoming traffic finally slowed and I swung my Jeep wagon into a space a few doors up the street, by the Cuban bakery. No sign of Tamango Perry yet.

"What now?" Dale said.

"We wait."

"I'm hungry. That kabob at lunch was fine and all, but it went down like an appetizer."

"Amen. You can't spear a full meal with an oversize toothpick."

We'd both been polite about our puny servings, since Therese was buying and had insisted on ordering for us. But Dale and I were both probably twice her weight. Our plates were clean before she finished her cucumber salad and reached for the main course.

"This place sure smells like heaven," Dale said, his window half down. The bakery looked devoid of customers. A bald guy in a white apron was mopping the black-and-white squares of tile near the glass counters stacked high with pastries. The chrome stools were balanced on top of one another to one side, like a row of miniature radio towers.

"This place knows how to make a Cuban sandwich," I said. "They toast the bread in this special press."

"Lead the way."

We got out. Night had fallen, so I didn't bother to feed the parking meter.

Dale stopped me on the sidewalk. "J., check it out." Pointing to the law center. "I think someone turned off the lights."

Through the glass, the front room did appear darker than it had been just a moment before. Strange shadows flickered in the background. We forgot our sandwiches and walked closer.

"Jesus!" Dale cried.

The back room was on fire, a black cloud of smoke smothering the light from a lone ceiling bulb as it spilled into the reception area. I ran to the front door and shook it, but it was locked. Then I ran to the bakery and shouted at the guy mopping the floor to call 911. That shocked the hell out of a swarthy woman seated behind the register, and she dropped a stack of bills she'd been counting and picked up the phone as if it was the thing that was burning. When I got back outside, Dale was in the street, craning for a view of the structure's rooftop. No flames were visible, but the night sky just above the store was starting to pulse with an orange light.

"That doesn't look promising," I said.

Black smoke began to snake out of a silver turbine on the roof. "Or that," Dale said. "What now?"

"We wait, I guess," I said.

Dale looked at the asphalt, then at me. "I mean, what now about me? You know, my situation. What if the fire department doesn't get here before all those client files with my name on them go up in smoke?"

I hadn't thought of that. "Well, you don't want to see innocent people be put out by losing their files forever."

"Course not."

"But I'm not exactly inclined to dash in there to get them out. Most likely the people running this place already burned a lot of people, no pun intended. At least their clients will go elsewhere from now on."

"I'm happy with this vantage point, then. You?"

A wisp of burning ashes arced up against the dark sky.

"Ecstatic."

Somewhere in the distance the sounds of sirens whispered at us. Above the Cuban store, a young man in a tight white tee appeared, yanking hard on his end of what looked like a garden hose and yelling, "Vámos, vámos!" until a burst of water shot forth. We stood in the street as the law center burned, watching the man hose down the bakery's roof like he was watering a front lawn.

"So we wait," Dale said.

I nodded. "That's the plan."

The sound of sirens was growing now, punctuated by the occasional honk of a fire-engine horn. I craned for a look up Brand, checking for flashing lights coming our way. That's when I saw the yachtlike Cadillac parked across the street not fifty feet away—Bobby Silver's tacky rig, minus its tacky owner. The hair on the back of my neck bristled.

Bobby Silver was the man Angie and Carlito had dragged Rudy in to meet that first day Dale and I had come here. When Dale and I made our entrance, the pert little receptionist had known instantly that something was wrong, that even if Dale was the new chump Mr. Julian had hired, he was *not* the man Angie and Carlito were here to see. That meant that the receptionist knew what Bobby Silver looked like, which meant that Silver had been here before. Which might give him a reason to double back here now if the place was shutting down, as Detective Perry believed it might be.

Why else would that big boat be sitting there across the street?

Silver was in there right now. Had to be.

"Christ," I gasped. My next few breaths came short and painful.

My legs felt like they were operating independently, and I found myself running in to the bakery to grab a stool. It was a lot heavier than it looked, with thick chrome legs and a welded steel plate under the cushion. The guy who'd been mopping started yelling something at me, but I was too fast for him and bolted back down the sidewalk, already gassed from hefting the awkward load on my hip.

"*Ay, Dios mío!*" a voice cried from behind as I flung the stool with everything I had and the glass front door exploded.

"J!" Dale shouted from the curb. "The smoke!" Headlights flashed behind him as traffic poured indifferently down Brand.

"I know!" I shouted lamely. Then I turned and stepped into the law center through the jagged new hole I'd just made, and instantly, everything went black.

Thirteen

In urgent circumstances the rational part of my brain typically generates a lot of noise, calculating the odds of my own imminent success or failure based on variables like speed, distance, and velocity. The size, strength, bulk, and fury of an opponent. The intent and duration of a smile on the wetted lips of the woman seated alone at the bar. The extent of my alcoholic and romantic impairment, and the likelihood of my sparklingly witty opening remark harpooning the moment. Rapid-fire counsel from a hundred tiny voices. I typically settle on the loudest voice, then make my move, buoyed by the slimmest belief—like a climber who has lost his rope but still clings to the rock—that, well, hell, at least I've got a plan.

Most of the time, that is. Far less frequently I will find myself diving headlong into risky situations hearing nothing but my heart's rhythmic thud in my ears, as if the chorus of reason has gone temporarily mute. Paradoxically, these moments of seeming fearlessness scare the hell out of me because I know too well the trouble they can bring. I suppose that I am not suitably wired to be a man of action.

A mushrooming cloud of hot gray smoke clawed at my eyeballs and forced me to the floor. I crabbed past the receptionist's desk on all fours, whacking my shin on a table leg as I passed. No fearless oblivion this time. The Big Question screamed inside my skull: Why, man, why risk your ass to save a walking douche bag like Bobby Silver? Shin throbbing, I crawled past a water cooler—old-style metal, the kind with a big upside-down water bottle up top—and peered into the back room.

The layout was rectangular and went deeper than I had expected. The back wall was brick with a tan metal door. It was the only wall that wasn't burning. The long wall to my right was lined with storage cabinets blanketed in flames. Stacks of metal chairs stood before the wall to my left. Patches of fire flickered along the baseboards, but it wasn't torching yet. Above the burning files, white ceiling tiles were going black and dropping out in sizzling chunks, but the roof above must still have been sound, because the smoke seemed to have nowhere to go.

I coughed hard and lost my breath, sucking in a lungful of overheated air. Bad idea. Crabbing in reverse now to the water dispenser, I dipped my tie in the tray, shot it with cool water, and stuffed it into my mouth. Another chunk of ceiling gave out overhead, and as I watched it fall, I spotted a pant leg dangling off a mustard sofa in the near right corner. Or at least the flames were making the furniture look mustard-colored. The pant leg belonged to Bobby Silver. As I crawled forward, I could see his distinctive shape—pointy boot tips in the air, the belt lost beneath a slab of gut, a nothing chin dropping off the face as if in its creation God had worked his way down from the top and just quit when he finished the nose—slung horizontally across the cushions. Not moving.

The water bottle was nearly full and heavy, but plastic, so I bounced and half rolled it into Silver's corner and used it to douse the flaming cushions. Silver looked unharmed. I couldn't tell if he was breathing, but in these conditions it didn't much matter, as mouth-to-mouth was out of the question. As I leaned over to lift him, sparks shot out of a wall socket and a glass coffeemaker on a table next to us exploded, splattering us with cold water and coffee grinds.

The man was heavy like a fat man would be. No way I could carry him out on my shoulders, not with this visibility. Another section of ceiling gave way, a chunk of bubbling tile landing between Silver's legs and igniting the couch again. I grabbed his shoulders, turned my back on the room, and dragged him backward with everything I had.

Outside, a fire truck had pulled up, and the hoses were reeling up the sidewalk. A pair of paramedics took Silver from me, rolled him onto a board, and were gone. I sat on the curb, spitting into the gutter. Staring up, I took in the view of black sky with a newfound appreciation for the vastness of deep space.

My head was spinning, so I stayed put until Dale brought help in the form of a stout female paramedic. She gave me oxygen, bottled water, and a few wet towels for my face and hands. As I started to feel better, the scene around the law center grew busier. Dale told me that the black man out front answering questions for a few local TV news crews was Tamango Perry. I figured the news-people must have heard the calls on their police-band receivers and rushed over to cover the action. When I felt better I walked over and talked to Tamango. For a cop, he looked quite dapper in a navy suit and burgundy rep tie. He had a broad, handsome face and a buzz-cut Afro, was six-four, with a tilted posture that told you he'd been stooping to be at eye level with people all his life. My first impression was that he was friendly by nature, but with the shit detector switched on at all times. I gave him a full state-ment, which he took down on a small pad. Under the streetlamp's yellow glow, the lines on his wide forehead seemed as elegant and permanent as wood carvings. When he spoke, every third or fourth syllable tripped off his tongue like a lilting dance step. I recounted all I knew about Bobby Silver, his reinstatement hearing, and what I'd seen inside the law center tonight. Tamango stopped me at times to ask questions, but mostly he listened and wrote.

"You know, you could have waited, like I asked you to," he said finally as he closed his book.

Behind us, the fire had been put out, and the back room of the law office whispered with foul chemical smells I could not identify and creeping fingers of white smoke. Firefighters scuttled about on the sidewalk, packing up equipment. A guy who looked like the fire captain picked through debris inside. A dozen Hispanic folks, some who looked like regulars and some in white aprons, milled in front of the Cuban bakery, muttering and folding their arms tightly against the night air. A pair of uniformed policemen stood near the law center's door, their faces stoic. Across the street, a TV newswoman's silhouette was front-lit as she taped a segment, the smoldering office providing a dramatic over-the-shoulder backdrop.

"We did wait," I said. "But then I saw his Caddy on the street and pretty much knew he was in there."

Detective Perry peered up Brand in the direction the ambulance had driven twenty minutes earlier. Silver's yacht of a Cadillac was still there, just across the double yellow.

"The man was lucky you two came along when you did," he said.

Dale was leaning against my car door in the street, smoking a cigarette. I thought of all those client files, perhaps all those that had his name sprinkled through them, destroyed.

"So, what now?" I asked the detective.

He shrugged. "Go home. I'll call you when I know something about Mr. Silver." Then he shook my hand formally. "And be careful. Please. I don't like the looks of this fire." Staring at the blackened facade, he stashed his notepad in his coat pocket and said good night.

Tamango Perry walked away before I could ask him what his warning was about, but a moment later the fire captain emerged from the law center's front door, and the two stiffs in uniform snapped to life. As the fire captain and Tamango spoke, Dale walked over and stood next to me.

"How you feeling?" he asked.

"Like I cleaned out a fireplace with my tongue."

He smiled, then cracked his knuckles, letting off nervous energy. When he asked his next question, I experienced a wave of déjà vu. "So, what do you think this, um, means, you know, for my situation, J.?"

"I don't know. It could simplify your life, if that's what you're asking." Then I frowned. "Of course, that doesn't change the fact that a lot of people whose files got torched probably got screwed by this place and have absolutely no recourse." I shook my head. "It's still a bad scene."

He lowered his head. "Hadn't thought of it that way."

When I looked at Dale, he was straining for some stoicism, but his face practically shone with relief. "You're probably off the hook," I said.

"But it's not like this is over. I've still got a client who's in real trouble."

I pictured Carmen inside my house, noticing the front door ajar, then having to give chase down Porpoise Way, Albert loping along behind her as Rudy Kirkmeyer roamed the neighborhood at will.

"We have to settle this thing with Rudy fast," I said.

The smell of smoke and damp soot permeated my clothes. I wanted to get out of there, go home to Carmen, and forget about Bobby Silver and the law center for a while.

"Think it was an accident?" Dale said.

"I have no idea. But the detective said he didn't like the way it looked."

Dale motioned toward the front door. "Check it out."

The fire captain and Tamango Perry were nodding as if some sort of consensus had been reached, their faces serious but unfazed, like men who in their daily work had seen far too much that was wrong with the world. Then Tamango turned and gave instructions to the two uniforms.

We watched the officers reel out the yellow crime-scene tape and secure the area.

At dinner, Carmen asked me about my history with Mick.

I drained my second glass of burgundy, still shaken by the fire at the law center.

"Well, certain days at the pier, there are just too many guys in the water and too few waves. So you have to share. Sometimes a guy will take more than his share. Occasionally, way more. When that happens, you've got to do something to maintain order. Otherwise it's a free-for-all. Mick was known to be able to maintain order."

Carmen picked at her green beans. "Oh, and just how was it that he was able to maintain order?" she said, emphasizing the last two words.

I glanced at Albert, but he was talking to himself in a low voice, which he often does. He wouldn't be upset by the topic, I decided.

"Mostly through his presence alone. You know, like a police presence."

Carmen dropped her napkin on the table. "I know all about police presence, J. They talked about it a lot in East L.A. when I was growing up." She sipped her wine and swallowed slowly, but without any apparent enjoyment. Her face was hard looking, even in the candlelight. "There was a lot of police presence on my block. All it meant was the cops had carte blanche to take a nightstick to any brown face they didn't like."

"Mick wasn't that way. He never ran roughshod over anyone just for the hell of it. He's more of a peacekeeper. He merely ensured that a certain level of respect was maintained."

"With what, his fists? That sounds like my father." She sipped at her wine again. "Some peacekeeper."

"Mick usually didn't even need to fight," I said, sounding ever more unconvincing. I poured myself a third glass of red, avoiding Carmen's fixed gaze.

"So, he used physical intimidation," she said. "That somehow makes it better?"

"I didn't say that. I—"

"It's the same thing with the wife beater," she said, cutting me off. "Even when he doesn't smack her a good one, he's abusing her, using her fear to tie her up. Might as well use a rope, 'cause it's no different." She held out her wineglass, which I cautiously refilled.

I was intent on damage control at this point. "This is not like domestic violence," I said.

"Wife beating," she said through narrowed lips.

I felt my frustration level rising fast and had to take a moment just to breathe. "Whatever. But the fact is, at every surf spot in the world there's a pecking order. It's human nature to stake your claim."

"Wrong, she said. "It's an animal instinct to stake your claim, one that leads to violence against your neighbor, war, and death. We're not animals. God gave us the intellect to rise above animal instincts."

I fiddled with my wine, not drinking.

"Your friend Mickey Conlin stopped by a while ago, a little before sundown," Carmen told me after dinner. We were in the kitchen doing dishes alone. Rudy and Dale were reclining in the living room with Albert, watching *Wheel of Fortune*. Every minute or so, Albert could be heard calling out a word or phrase, trying to solve the puzzles aloud.

"That why you were asking about him?"

She kept her eyes on the leftover salad, which she was covering with plastic wrap. "Maybe."

"What did Mick say?"

"Not much. That he was just checking on Albert, to see how he's doing." She handed me the big pot I'd used to cook the pasta. Her lips were taut the way they had been at dinner.

"You don't believe that."

She moved closer and rinsed a dish; her brown eyes fixed on the tub of soapy water.

"He's almost too concerned. I think he's got the guilts."

I stopped drying the big pot. "The guilts." My tone was slightly incredulous.

She threw down the sponge.

"Oh, what difference does it make? What do I know about surfing, right? I'm just a girl from barrio East L.A. I don't know a thing about this strange 'code of the waves' everybody goes by around here, you know, the one that gives a guy who lives here the right to pounce on any poor kid from out of town who takes one too many good waves. You call that 'enforcing'? Sounds like punk thug stuff to me."

I'd been thinking about our argument at dinner ever since it had happened. Coming from a neighborhood that was subdivided and controlled by no fewer than three street gangs, Carmen was no stranger to the territorial nature of young males. The concept of localism at the beach that I'd so lamely laid out couldn't possibly have been new. No, I knew what was really bothering her: the sight of Albert's bloody face coming up the walk. That's the thing about violence; it's usually just another abstract topic to discuss over dinner, wineglass in hand, like talking about the economy. But when you or someone you care about gets pummeled, your theories and social perspectives will be tested without mercy. And those theories and perspectives will fail and fail miserably because you cannot analyze and categorize and intellectualize the dark side of human nature with any real effect on the ultimate truth that remains. It is too immense and prevalent and elemental a thing—salvation's gateway, God's great gift to mankind crowned with thorns and drooping dead, nailed naked to a cross.

But there are endless choices along the road. Sometimes you kill the insects to save the crop. Sometimes you wage war to stop a Hitler. And sometimes you fight back because the choice to not fight back is no choice at all.

"Listen," I said, putting both hands on her shoulders, "I told you, I know Mick from way back, and he would never, ever punch out someone like . . . I mean, someone—"

"I know what you mean, J., someone like my brother. A gentle, sweet, trusting, helpless . . ." She started to cry. I put my arms around her shoulders from behind. "Kindhearted little *pobrecito* who wouldn't hurt a flea," she said, sniffling hard, her body shaking.

The past few days had ground us both down—what with my worsening job situation, Albert's beating and subsequent foul mood, Carmen's having to watch Rudy while Dale and I were gone for long stretches, and her unfinished business involving an invalid mother and title to the family house belonging to a long-gone, no-good father. All of it hanging over us like the oppressive coastal gloom in June.

"You need some serious maintenance," I said. "Tonight." I kissed her up and down her neck and on her ear.

She softened in my arms. "How about an ice-cream sundae, some of those macadamia nuts?"

I nodded. Carmen is a careful, conservative eater. I've learned that serving her an elaborate dessert works as an excellent prelude to romance. Consuming all those extra calories makes her feel reckless, which stokes her burners.

"The whole shot."

I flipped off the fluorescent lights overhead and pulled her even closer, kissing her face softly at first, then her lips, hands groping and squeezing as her lithe body pressed against mine. With a whisper, I suggested we try the counter tiles, but the phone rang before I could make my move. Tamango Perry.

"Robert Silver passed away," he said without emotion. "About an hour ago."

So much for my moment with Carmen.

By reflex, I told Tamango I was sorry, but the truth was I didn't feel much of anything about Bobby Silver's life being over. The only way I knew him was from the untold grief he'd caused those who had entrusted him with their legal representation. I also felt a certain burden lifting, though I knew that that was an illusion. Angie would find another Bobby Silver to assist her in fleecing Rudy Kirkmeyer—that is, if she hadn't already.

"Did the smoke get him?" I asked.

There was a pause. "It certainly didn't help."

"Heart attack?"

"That's what I thought, at the scene. But the primary cause of death was blunt trauma to the head."

"I guess part of the ceiling could have fallen and hit him. Except . . ."

"Except what?"

It didn't fit. "Well, the couch I found him on was mostly clean. Just a few chunks of burning tile."

I felt Carmen recoil when I mentioned the tile. Shit. I'd successfully downplayed my role in the incident at dinner, writing it off as a right-place, wrong-time deal and nothing more, complaining about my sooty duds and the obscene dry-cleaning bill that was sure to result. Choosing my words with care, not wanting her to worry needlessly or lecture me again about overstepping.

But by now she'd figured out that someone had died in the fire, someone I'd tried to pull out in time. Which meant that I, too, could have been injured, or worse.

"Ceiling on fire, huh, J.?" Carmen whispered acidly. "Must've missed that detail at dinner." Carmen hates being bullshitted, even when it's justifiable.

"It wasn't a falling object," Tamango said. "Someone smashed in the back of his skull with a heavy object, probably left him there to die. The coroner said he never regained consciousness. That's why he looked asleep when you found him."

"Jesus."

Bobby Silver had been murdered. Had his bungling of the Rudy Kirkmeyer situation cost him his life? Then again, God knows how many clients and former clients the man had bilked in his time. Perhaps one of the betrayed that had never gotten over the sting of being flimflammed had finally caught up with him.

Contemplating the news, I almost didn't notice Carmen slipping free from my grasp. The fluorescent lights came on overhead, assaulting my eyeballs. Squinting, I turned toward the light switch near the door, but Carmen had already left the room.

Damn. Another opportunity to improve my standing with my fiancée shot to hell. I'd probably have to throw in a bubble bath on top of the sundae just to get her to listen to my apology.

"J.?" the Caribbean voice said over the phone.

I shut my eyes. "Yes. You were saying."

"The fire marshal saws signs of arson," Perry went on. "They found traces of residue from a low-grade, highly flammable liquid, probably lighter fluid."

"Any idea who did it?"

I heard him sigh.

"What's wrong?"

"I'm not happy about this, not at all. But you'll know soon enough. Your role in this is also being examined."

A wave of shock rolled up my spine. "What the . . . Tamang . . . Detective, with all due respect, that's ridiculous. You called me. I went over there because you called me. How could you think—"

"J., wait, I don't think anything of the sort."

"Then who's saying this?"

"Chief Conforti."

"Your boss."

Nicholas Conforti had been chief of police in Glendale for about three years, and had landed in the pages of the *Times* on several occasions. Unlike the LAPD, which was always being criticized for using too much force, Conforti's department had a well-known reputation for not doing enough. A few years ago he'd failed to quell a spate of armed robberies in parking lots and structures adjacent to the local shopping mall, loudly insisting that the problem would be solved if merchants paid more for increased security. Then he took the worst of those crimes, a knifing murder of an old woman for thirty bucks and an old Timex, and used it to publicly demand more budget money to hire additional men. He got his money from the city, $3.5 million, but then hired not a single new man, citing a serious need to "retool" within the existing force. His opponents would say that "retooling" was merely a code word for bolstering the perks attendant to the job, but the chief was always quick with his rationalizations. When a spending audit last year revealed that two cops in vice had blown nine thousand bucks on Internet porn from their desktops in one month alone, Conforti explained that in order to catch deviants, his cops had to learn to think like them. This was why he'd listed the expenses as "educational" in the books.

"When I got back to the station Conforti asked me for my report," Tamango said. "As soon as I wrote it up, he took it into his office and shut the door. I can only surmise that he came up with a list of suspects without my knowledge or consent."

"A list of suspects." I didn't like the sound of that.

"So far, you and Mr. Bleeker are the only names on that list."

I was too stunned to speak for a time. "Will I be arrested?"

"Doubtful. There's no real evidence linking you in my report."

"No shit," I said.

"Try not to get too upset, J. I will tell you, between us, I also know that someone with access to the place did this. Both the front and back doors were locked. Keys had been broken off in the locks, to make sure Mr. Silver couldn't escape. I had a locksmith remove the remnants. Both of them fit the locks."

"So why Dale and me?"

Another pregnant pause on the other end.

"I don't know, although I might venture a guess. I think that your and Mr. Bleeker's involvement with that law center could cause undue attention to be paid to it, and that has made somebody very uncomfortable. I see this as an attempt to shift the focus away from the law center and onto you."

"You mentioned this to your boss, I hope."

"Unfortunately, Chief Conforti is more a politician than a cop. And he knows a lot of people."

"So he wasn't exactly receptive."

"That's a good way of putting it."

"I still don't get how Dale and I fit in."

"Plan on watching the local news tonight, Channel Three, Channel Six. They both interviewed the chief."

Great. I can think of no worse source of accurate information than local TV news.

Tamango muffled his phone to talk to someone. Then he came

back on. "I am sorry, I have to go. You have my cell phone number, use it. Don't call me at the station anymore." The man sounded concerned for his own job.

"I won't, don't worry."

"And please be careful. Understand?"

"Fully," I lied.

I hung up the phone. In the living room I could hear Pat Sajak and Vanna White saying their good nights over the delirious cheers of their studio audience. I called Dale into the kitchen and told him everything, the two of us leaning against the long counter, staring into the darkened dining room. He didn't flinch when I told him the part about his being a suspect. I suppose that by that point in his life, he'd grown accustomed to bad news.

Dale wanted to know what he could do, but, since I had yet to determine the extent of our problems, I just asked him to keep an eye on everybody for a little while. The late news wouldn't come on for a few more hours, and my brain was on overload. I wanted to fixate on Carmen, run a mental tape of our kitchen embrace on rewind, forget about this mindbender of a day I'd had, salvage the night. All I could see was Bobby Silver's dead legs on that burning couch, a judge angry about my involvement with Dale's probation, Roger Turnbull sheepishly getting his ass fired in the hallway outside court, Therese Rozypal's doelike eyes when I passed her the basket of flat bread, Angie clawing at Rudy's hand at the savings and loan.

Dale was staring at me.

"What?" I said.

"Your face. When I was prosecuting crimes, I used to see that look all the time."

"With the criminals or the victims?" Dale looked stymied. I flashed him the old shit-eater with not a whiff of confidence behind it. "Don't answer that, I don't want to know," I added.

Dale managed a hollow guffaw or two. I was thinking: Christ, I've got to get out of here, and now. Fleeing my own fucking house, for God's sake. I found a jacket, put Max on his choke chain, and lit out toward Main to pick up a can of whipped cream, maraschinos, and some macadamia nuts.

Fourteen

Carmen and I lay sideways across the king-size bed in my room, still panting from a pass between the sheets that I will describe only as athletic. My head was swimming in the afterglow of that sweet release, but I was wondering, staring at her hourglass shape, if the unhinged, wham-bam-thank-you-ma'am quality to our coupling was a sign that we were drifting apart. Tenderly, I stroked her hair. I wanted to tell her things, remind her that I loved her, thank her for helping with Rudy, apologize again for Albert's mishap, and I waited patiently for her to face me so that I could say my piece with my eyes as well. But she didn't turn around, and when the clock radio clicked over to eleven o'clock on the bookcase near the door, she sat up, plucked the TV's remote off the big oak dresser beside the bed, and pointed it at the set.

"J. Shepard, fallen hero, that story and more news at eleven," she said, mimicking a promo teaser. "This I've gotta see."

Earlier, I'd told her Tamango Perry's news as she devoured her ice-cream sundae. She'd said little, refraining, thankfully, from any editorializing about me needing to mind my own business. All she wanted to know at the time was what I expected to get in return for feeding her such a splendid confection. I told her, figuring she didn't want to hear any more about my deepening entanglements with the law center. Apparently I was mistaken.

Carmen went to my closet and found a blue cotton dress shirt, pulled it on, and sat back down on the bed. The Channel 6 newscast rolled along for about ten minutes without mention of the fire. The anchor, a white-haired, smiling dandy named Phil Newton, promised a look at the weather, "but first, a look at a developing story in Glendale that was literally sparked"—ha, ha, ha—"earlier this evening by a fire in a legal office on Brand Boulevard in downtown Glendale. Our Channel Six field reporter Deidre Sharpe has the story."

Deidre Sharpe was a bright-eyed, statuesque blond thirty-something who used to model and once dated Hugh Hefner before becoming a hard-hitting news reporter. I'd seen her interviewing Tamango tonight in the street. She was easily six-two and stood eye to eye with the detective. The inside skinny was that Deidre always reported from the field because Phil didn't fancy looking like a runt sitting next to her at the Channel 6 anchor table. The way-inside skinny was that Phil had once tried to make it with Deidre, but was too small for her in more ways than one.

Deidre's good looks were downright distracting.

"Hugh Hefner is a god," I muttered.

"What?"

"Nothing."

Deidre related the basics about the fire, declaring that a man identified as Robert Silver, a lawyer who'd recently run afoul of the State Bar of California, was dead. Fire officials were investigating the blaze as possibly the work of an arsonist. At this juncture, Phil Newton—no relation to Isaac in the brainpower department, to be sure—furrowed his famous caterpillar eyebrows and began lobbing in-studio queries at his reporter. Instinctively, I reached for a pillow and used it to cover my privates, as if in anticipation of the swift kick to the balls I felt coming.

"Why do the police suspect arson, Deidre?"

"That hasn't been ascertained yet, Phil. What's more, police are indicating that they've opened a murder investigation. They believe that Silver was killed by a sharp blow to the head, and that his body may have been left to perish in the fire."

"Can you tell us, are there any leads, suspects, or arrests yet, Deidre?"

"No, Phil, but sources tell us that police may be looking into a possible link, an unusual connection between Silver and two Los Angeles lawyers, one a state bar prosecutor."

Carmen sat up straighter. "Here we go." I felt the bites of ice cream I'd pilfered from Carmen's sundae an hour ago inching their way back up my throat.

Deidre laid out the basic facts behind my meeting Dale, handling his probation-monitoring duties, Dale's employment at the law center—which was merely "alleged" at this point. My testimony at Silver's reinstatement hearing this morning. Notably absent was any mention of Rudy Kirkmeyer, Angie, and Carlito.

"How the hell did she get this?" I said. No one from the press had seen fit to observe Silver's hearing this morning, and there was no way Channel 6 could've gotten hold of a transcript.

"All she said was 'sources say,' " Carmen observed. "She's keeping it confidential."

Then Deidre tied her story together in a way I hadn't seen coming.

"Glendale police are looking into the possibility that the fire may have been part of an attempt to destroy client files, files that would have implicated Bleeker as an attorney who took his clients' money without performing services. Apparently the city has had complaints."

"Tamango didn't say anything about any complaints," I said.

"Maybe Deidre got that part herself," Carmen said.

The report wound down.

"Although no one has been arrested or charged, Phil, police are confident that the perpetrators will be brought to justice. Glendale police chief Nicholas Conforti had this to say."

The chief's forehead shone like a collector's nickel as he stood on the steps of the police station, a microphone under his chin.

"Deidre, I can assure both you and the viewers at home that Glendale is a safe community and will remain a safe community."

"What a relief," I said. Carmen shushed me.

By now I had an idea about what was going on. Tamango Perry was probably right: I'd stumbled onto something with this law center, and obviously, somebody wanted me out of the picture. What better way than to get me shit-canned at my place of employment? That little opera would likely play out tomorrow.

"This going to cause a problem at work?" Carmen said.

"No."

She'd find out soon enough if I got suspended or fired. No need to cause her additional worry tonight.

"I should sue Channel 6 for slander," I said only half seriously.
"It's owned by that billionaire Aussie, Shelby what's-his-name.
I'm sure they won't put up a fight if you sue, J."
Carmen's mild sarcasm brought a smile to my face. I'd been
hammered by the press before and had lived through it. A hidden
camera once caught a distraught female client of mine hugging me
in gratitude. That night, a Channel 6 reporter used the footage to
speculate as to whether I was having impermissible sexual relations
with the client. I was nearly thrown off the client's case, but I told
the judge the truth and the controversy died.

Just now, I hoped the truth would be enough to get me through
this little tight spot as well.

On the tube, Deidre said, "Back to you, Phil," and was replaced
by a walrusine weatherman with a handlebar mustache and a grin
shaped like a quarter wedge of watermelon.

"A new low-pressure system is headed across the Pacific, Phil,
and . . ."

I'd have to check the surf in the morning. What difference did
it make if I got fired at nine or ten, anyway?

We watched more news. They cut to sports; a slow night with
no scheduled contests for the local college or pro basketball teams.
Cut to the Laker Girls promoting a new calendar to raise money
for MS research. Major cheesecake shots to help plug the product.

"Well, what do you think?" Carmen said.

"What can I say, they're goddesses, but they probably couldn't
spell 'multiple sclerosis' to save their lives." Ducking the obvious.

Carmen persisted, yanking the pillow from under my leg and
thwacking me on the head with it. "Not that, smarty."

"Someone inside the bar fed Deidre Sharpe that information.
How else could she connect the dots so quickly?" Watching the
Laker Girls do their hardwood boogie was not exactly speeding my
mental processes, so I rolled onto my side and looked at Carmen.
"I think this crap is just a diversion."

"Maybe so, but it's a pretty powerful diversion. Like the sundae
you made me tonight."

I shook my head. "That sundae was a catalyst, my dear, not a
diversion." Reaching for the remote, I turned off the TV. Carmen's
bare legs ran off the bed, and my eyes ran after them, all the way

down to her toenails, which were painted in the French manicure style. In spite of the mounting chaos, all I could fix on now was how much I wanted to make love to her again. The bedsprings creaked as I leaned forward and wrapped her up from behind.

"No," she whispered. "I don't want to be just a diversion from your problems, J. That's what it felt like earlier."

I had no response, save for a feeble apology for the rough sex.

"You could lose your job," she said.

"I haven't done anything wrong."

Her eyes were downcast. "Neither did Albert. Look what happened to him."

I got up early for work the next morning, reaching for the alarm long before it was time. Thought about getting fired again and decided to surf. Twenty minutes later I was alone on Southside, groping through a fog so thick it looked like another dimension. But the surf was a touch overhead, clean and well focused on the sandbar, and the dull green shadows kept coming through the mist at me, forming up like the curved back of a breaching whale. I rode to forget my troubles, but the fog and the empty lineup had me straining for something that seemed missing, and my rides, though technically proficient, lacked that creative spark that good surfing requires, that feeling of freedom from which a coherent style emerges. And if you don't surf with style, you've missed the point.

The sound of rising swell followed me home and upstairs, where I laid out on the bed my best prosecutor's suit, the black one, draped a red foulard power tie over the lapels, and stood back. It was the suit I wear the first day of any important trial, the time when projecting a no-bullshit, all-business aura to those with whom I will tangle is paramount. But today it looked lifeless and rather ordinary, as if the last dry cleaning had shaken the magic from the threads. I knew that wasn't it. Today I would not be prosecuting. The first act was not mine to orchestrate. Today the allegations would be aimed at my head, my job, and my reputation. The fuckers were going to shit-can me.

Hell, what's the use? I stuck the suit back into the closet, then hesitated, and pulled it out again. I stood there a good long while, immobile, watching the first hint of sun find the sweat-beaded windowpanes, the growing light casting minute variations on a dozen shades of gray. My legs were tired from the jog up the wet sand following my surf. I sat down, wondering how I had brought myself to this point.

It had all begun with the urge to assist Dale Bleeker, a man I felt I knew, but honestly didn't. Did I really give a shit about helping the man? Or was I merely trying to preserve a memory that was best left alone, like a crushed flower folded into the pages of a book whose petals turn to dust if you ever touch them again?

I was meddling with the past on several fronts these days. Straining to ensure the rehabilitation of a once great criminal prosecutor whose entire career had been scuttled by an inexplicable impulse to free Willy. Luring a violent old surfing buddy who'd long ago soured on the Life back into the water, then maybe—just maybe—seeing the results in the bloodied face of my future brother-in-law. Holding fast to the notion that I was still the J. Shepard that Carmen had come to know and love, a guy defined in large part by what he did for others. Perhaps I hadn't recognized in time that this approach had left me critically lacking in the self-definition department. I could see the frustration building in her eyes: How do you deal with an inaccessible so-called partner?

Time to make some decisions without looking back, I concluded. The black suit was first on the list.

Twenty minutes later Carmen knocked on my door. She was barefoot, in a white terry robe, her dark hair swept over and down her left shoulder.

"Hey, nice suit. The IRS auditing you today?" My inquisitor leaned against the door frame, arms folded.

"Very funny." I finished fastening my wristwatch and straightened the knot of my tie in the mirror above the dresser. "Actually I'm just going to work. That is, if they still let me in the place. Might as well look sharp."

Carmen slid behind me and hugged my shoulders. "Sort of like looking good at your own funeral, huh?" She let out a small giggle.

"Something like that."

She squeezed me a bit tighter, sighing. "Sorry I ducked out on you last night. It was . . . rather crummy of me."

"Forget it."

"Let me make you a nice breakfast. Waffles, sausage, eggs, whatever you like."

"Thanks, but I gotta roll in five minutes. I left a message with my union rep to meet me downstairs before I go up to the tenth floor and deal with my manager."

"Wow. You think that's necessary?"

I shrugged. "All I know is I've worked hard at this job. They're not going to bend me over without a fight."

"Promise me you'll eat something when you get there."

I told her I'd get something in the cafeteria. Carmen followed me downstairs to the door, watched me retrieve the fog-dampened *Times* from the front walk. When I handed her the newspaper, she rolled her eyes and said, "Least today I'll get to do the crossword."

"I don't do the daily crossword," I said. She looked at me funny. I figured Dale must have been knocking them out the last few days.

We kissed, and I held her and kissed her again. "I love you," I said, surprising myself as much as her. Those words have never rolled from my tongue very naturally.

Carmen's gaze was steady on me. I thought she waited way too long to say "I love you" back, but there it was. When I kissed her a final time, I saw a trace of regret in her eyes that I hoped was there because she knew that I might lose my job—not because she might be sensing I was losing her. I felt an urge to set down my briefcase and tell her more, to make some needed reassurances. But the words didn't exactly leap forth.

"Car."

"Yes?"

"Nothing. I'll call later."

Still no more than a hint of sun lurking in the battleship gray sky, but I was blinking hard as I started down the walk.

The word was out before I stepped out of the elevator on the tenth floor. I'd barely made it down the long row of offices to my door when Honey Chavez got up from her desk and cut in front of me, said a shaky good morning, and apologized for having to tell me that my office door had been locked.

"I heard about the fire, J. You okay?"

I mustered a wafer-thin smile. "Never better." Glancing about, I saw others going about their business but watching me at the same time. "She in her office?" I asked my secretary. Honey nodded yes.

Then, feeling a lot of eyes on me, I casually retraced my steps, retreating through the security doors that lead to the elevators. George Burrows, my union rep, was there, right where I'd left him. George is about six-one and gangly as a giraffe, with thick prescription frames and a freckled face that makes you wonder if a ten-year-old is locked in that beanpole body. He's also an outspoken gay rights advocate who spends more weekends than anyone I know walking and jogging and rallying to promote everything from breast cancer research to increased suicide-hotline funding. The man may not look like a tiger, but he's got passion, which I suppose makes him an excellent members' representative.

"You're on, George," I said with a nod, holding the door open for him. "She wants me in her office. Ready to boot some butt?"

George's eyes were alive. "Let's do it." He seemed amped for a showdown.

Eloise barely knew what hit her. She started by trying to remove George, which only made him pop open his briefcase and cite Article 3, section 1(a) in the state bar Memorandum of Understanding, reading straight from the employees bill of rights. I settled into a chair opposite my manager's desk and let George get it on, enjoying her heightened state of distress. Good show, Eloise, I was thinking. You don't want to kick off a meeting with George Burrows citing the MOU to you.

Half an hour later I was shaking the guy's hand for ensuring that I would only be suspended with pay. Eloise had failed even to write me up, which is a prerequisite to any official action, and had yet to gain the signed approval of Reginald Hewitt, the chief, to begin an inquiry. Apparently she was so overjoyed to have something on me that she hadn't bothered with formalities, and George, sensing she would do anything to avoid having me return to work that day, brokered a most advantageous deal. Full pay and continued benefits, nothing placed in my employee file without a fair hearing, and confidential proceedings in keeping with the MOU. George also made sure I could collect my personal items from my office before I left. Eloise had her wide-body secretary, Monette, follow me with the express orders that I had five minutes to clear out and under no circumstances was I allowed to remove any state bar property, including files. When George and I stood up, he thanked her for her time, briskly offering his hand. I thought Eloise would bite the tips of his fingers off, but she held it in check, her lower lip quivering in anger. Noting an opportunity to further seal the deal, I flashed her the old reliable shit-eater on my way out the door.

Back in the elevator, that last order Eloise had leveled at Monette had me wondering. Despite the ample TV news scoop on my situation with Dale, it sounded like Eloise still didn't really know what I'd been up to, since I knew there was nothing significant to be found in my workspace. Last night I'd assumed she'd been the one to tip off the press. Maybe I had been wrong. Maybe I'd underestimated the intensity of the woman's long-standing dislike for me. Then again, perhaps she'd already searched my office and therefore knew there was no harm in allowing me back in there.

But she'd blown it this morning, probably guessing wrong that I'd show up alone, lose my cool when she tried to dictate what was what, and in so doing, hand her perfectly good cause to let me go. I might be suspended for now, and I was probably facing a termination proceeding in the near future, not to mention the blow to my career aspirations here at the bar. But thanks to my inept manager, at least now I had time to look into the law center and settle this thing with Dale and Rudy.

Honey Chavez had an empty file box ready for me. George stood sentry at the door as if to ward off any repeat incursions from Eloise. Monette had followed us back and was now standing two cubicles away, watching George. I was scooping up my picture frames, admiring the view of a clear blue winter morning over downtown L.A., when I heard George issue a brusque hello.

"I'd like to talk to J. Do you mind?"

Therese Rozypal.

George hiked his wristwatch and told me I had three minutes remaining by his count, rolling his eyes like a jealous girlfriend when Therese slid by him. She wore a navy cardigan sweater over a pleated knee-length plaid skirt and leather boots. Her hair was in a braided ponytail—the first time I'd seen it down. Those eyes matched the sky I'd just glimpsed out the window. Very fine.

She'd missed the news last night but heard plenty of gossip when she came in this morning. Had I been fired? I told her about my meeting with Eloise, and what had happened last night at the law center.

"What now?" she said.

"I go home. Look at this thing from a few different angles, hopefully sort it out."

"What about me?"

She must have noticed me swallowing hard. "I mean," she added quickly, "isn't there anything I can do to help you? Silver was my case, after all."

"If I need you, I'll ring you up."

Therese handed me a business card. "My home number's on the back. Call me anytime."

My knees felt weak all over again. "I will. And thanks for stopping by."

We lingered behind the door as if caught in a magnetic field. "Bye, J.," she said. "Don't be a stranger."

George Burrows looked at me after he watched Therese pass by. "What?" I said, feeling a rush of guilt.

"Nothing."

"Say it, George."

"Well, I've always heard practicing law is a pretty stodgy affair." He glared at Monette, who had crept closer and was now taking momentary refuge in Honey's cubicle, her big bottom resting on a patch of desktop. Monette scowled right back at George. "Not with you," George said to me. "With you, boy, it's never a dull moment."

"Thanks, George."

"You're an original, J."

"You should talk."

Then I thanked him properly for negotiating so well earlier. "Next time you march for money, I'll fill the cookie jar," I said. He smiled as if he was about to thank me back, but said, "I know."

I reached back into my office and shut off the lights. George motioned me to follow him, hissing at Monette, "Move it, sister. Coming through."

Fifteen

The line inside the bakery wasn't bad for midmorning. A security guard ordering a birthday cake for pickup tomorrow. A pair of old ladies, their hair wrapped with black scarves, selected their bread by committee, in Spanish. Just ahead of me, a smiling, bearded priest who looked like a pastry-counter regular danced back and forth before the glass display case, pointing—two of these, three of those—as a helper filled a white cardboard box, hustling to keep up.

It's too early for lunch, I thought, but when I got to the counter, I ordered two Cuban sandwiches and a coffee anyway. At least when I got home I could tell Carmen I'd eaten.

When I asked for the owner, the woman seated on a stool behind the register gave me the stink-eye she probably reserved for bill collectors and shirtless patrons. "Esteban!" she bellowed.

His name was Esteban Carpio. He was thin for a bakery proprietor, with a medium gray long-sleeved silk shirt, untucked, and a gaudy gold bracelet. He smelled faintly of flour, which I suppose comes with the territory. Stopping to pass on tiny greetings as more customers trickled in. He answered yes, in heavily accented English, he recognized me from last night. Then he wanted to know, suddenly dead serious, what brought me here.

I took out a Franklin and handed it to him, told him I wanted to pay for the chair I'd used to break the law center's window. He pushed the money back at me, shaking his head.

"No, my friend, the chair is insured, and besides, it was used to save a life."

I decided not to tell him that by the time I tossed that stool through the glass in front, Bobby Silver had been brained so hard that he was probably dead already. A gold tooth flashed inside his mouth as he recounted a blaze I'd witnessed firsthand.

Esteban Carpio leaned in. "Maybe the fire, it was an act of God. Maybe, my friend, He hear our prayers."

My sandwiches were ready. Carpio had them brought to a small table near the counter and sat me down. Then he got himself a coffee and joined me. I ate the first sandwich in four bites. The pickle and mustard made me sweat, it was that good. I asked what he meant about the act of God.

"Miriam," he called. "Bring me the flyers from the legal office that burn down."

The cashier frowned and cursed quietly in Spanish. Sliding off her perch, she hobbled through the swinging metal door into the back. We sipped our coffees. "What kind of people, eh?" he asked. "It should not happen in America." His face was full of pain.

I nodded dumbly.

Miriam the cashier appeared again, dropping a manila folder on her boss's side of the table. He held her up, asking if I wanted a coffee refill. Miriam stood over me, flicking daggers at me with her eyes. I passed.

Carpio spread several letter-size advertisements on the white Formica between us. The ads were announcements for investment seminars, hosted by the law center, the most recent event dating a few months back, another flyer from last July. Educate yourself! Learn to beat Uncle Sam at his own game! Tax shelters for retirees! Estate-planning advantages you can't afford to miss out on! Why pay expensive attorney fees when you can plan your own future? Each flyer plugged a free seminar. Absolutely no obligation! Drawings for door prizes! A week on Maui! Romantic Puerto Vallarta! A Jamaican adventure!

I asked where he'd gotten them. Carpio pointed to a small bulletin board behind the double doors facing Brand.

"They put them up there. Right under my nose."

Two of the flyers had "Homeowners Fidelity Trust Presents . . ." in bold print across the top. The flyer with the July date was nearly identical, but listed "Capitol Consolidators Presents . . ." as the event's sponsor.

I'd seen the names above, on Bobby Silver's petition-for-reinstatement application. He'd claimed to be a hazily defined "consultant" with both companies.

"What did you mean about this not happening in America?"

His face was red now, his eyes wet. "My friend, you should have let the place burn all the way to the ground."

"You going to tell him, you fool?" the cashier growled at Mr. Carpio. I realized then that she was his wife.

"Yes, I going to tell him," Carpio said. "So be quiet, huh?"

"Oh, fine, why not?" she muttered, ringing up another purchase—the priest with his box of pastries. "Why not?"

Carpio had attended the seminar in July, heard the speaker, an "estate-planning specialist." Sounded good. They had a way you could beat the estate tax when you die and your children inherit. Carpio liked the idea.

I asked him how it worked.

He twirled a plastic spoon in his cup of coffee. "You have to understand, it sound so good. I work hard all my life. In Cuba, the government there take everything, give the people nothing. I don't want that to happen here, too."

Carpio exchanged pleasantries with the departing cleric. Then his wife the cashier approached our table, told him in Spanish that he was needed in back, *urgentemente.* I got after my second Cuban sandwich, this time savoring it in five bites, my chest aching. Nothing like a midmorning carbo hit big enough to pop a pant seam.

I could hear the man and his wife arguing in back, a little about what he'd just told me, and a lot about the fact that he'd gone and told me at all. They sounded like they were going to be at it awhile, so I went out to the street, bought the *Times* from a rack, and brought it back to my table. The place had emptied out. I sipped my coffee, enjoying a warm slant of sunshine across my back, and started reading a feature about a hot-guy screenwriter who'd written a novel about power and greed and sex and couture—apparently in that order—on the Left Coast. The author, who'd grown up somewhere in the vicinity of Bumfuck, Iowa, came here five years ago and was now a self-appointed cultural expert on this city and its denizens. The hard-hitting tone of the reprinted passages from the book made for some unintentional hoots. Evil valets lurking among the Beemers and Benzes like gators in a swamp. A mysterious Euro-boy hairstylist with leather pants and lethal scissors. Snarling French poodles. Gorgeous Amazons toting derringers in their Louis Vuitton bags. Heavy product placement. People drinking rum and Pepsi, for Christ's sake. Beverly Hills noir, they were calling it. Make-believe snapshots of the dark side of the soul. Oh please, I thought, you shouldn't have to strain so hard to make this shit up. The good and bad is all around us, all the time.

Carpio returned to my table, apologizing for the delay. "Before we talk more, my friend, I like to . . . wonder if, can you help me get my money back?" His wife was watching me closely from behind the register.

I told him I didn't know if I could, but I'd spoken with the Glendale police about problems associated with the law center and they were looking into it. I'd see what I could do.

Never mind that I was a murder suspect and had been suspended from my job.

His eyes were teary again, but he nodded to his wife, who'd perched herself back on her stool behind the register. In short, he told me he'd done well with the bakery the last twenty-four years since he bought it, built it up into a local gathering place of sorts, each year yielding a few percent more profits than the last. He had paid off his home a few years ago, a small but nice Craftsman a few blocks off Pacific Avenue north of the freeway. Had a few slow-growth investments, some safe stuff like Public Storage and GE stock. About ten years ago he'd bought a distressed apartment building nearby, eight units. Sunk thirty grand into repairs, but saved a lot by doing most of the work himself. Now it was worth half a million, yielding about thirty thousand a year in income after expenses. Not bad for a baker from Havana.

I sheepishly agreed, knowing the punch line was yet to come.

Then this place opened up two doors down. Word was they did a lot of things you thought you needed a lawyer to do, only way cheaper, and without the lawyer. Customers talked about putting deposits down for family law and bankruptcy filings, name-change applications. They were told the paperwork could take months, but were happy to wait it out at such a bargain rate for services.

Classic UPL, I was thinking.

Carpio thought it sounded fishy, but he was never one to argue with customers. Then one day the young girl who sat up front answering phones came in and asked for permission to post a flyer announcing an estate-planning seminar. It sounded interesting, so he went, and liked what he heard: When he died, he could leave his estate to his heirs tax-free.

The scheme had an alluring ring to it. The Carpios would give their apartment building to a charitable trust, which would sell the property tax-free and use the purchase money to buy an annuity, which would pay the Carpios a cool forty grand a year. Carpio would then buy five hundred thousand dollars in life insurance to be held in a separate trust. That way, when he and his wife died, their heirs would get the full half-million value of the apartment property from the life insurance payoff.

Carpio's wife approached with a coffeepot and refilled my cup, which gave her the opportunity to glare at her husband from point-blank range. He reached out and grabbed her hand. "Stay," he ordered her. Sulking, she parked herself behind his chair.

The confidence men running the scheme left out a few key facts during their presentation. The cost of the life insurance policy was about thirty-six thousand dollars a year. Subtract that expense from the forty thousand dollars yearly the annuity would pay them, and they were netting only four grand, way short of the thirty thousand a year they saw in profits when they owned the apartment. That property was now owned by the trust, as well, meaning the Carpio's could no longer sell it if their future expenses unexpectedly spiked.

"Then, when we know this is bad, we go to a real lawyer my son knows to straighten this out."

The wife rolled her eyes. *"Ay, Dios mío."*

The attorney looked over the deal, inquired into the value of their investments, and reviewed their last three income tax filings. Then he told them something they could not believe: Their estate was small enough that it would never have triggered estate taxes when they died. But these people who had sold them the annuities and life insurance had made out very, very well, making fat commissions on both transactions. The lawyer was looking into a lawsuit, but he doubted whether they could ever recover a cent from confidence men like these, even with a legal judgment.

I knew the attorney was right. Accomplished scammers are experts at hiding their assets.

"Our lawyer say this happen all the time," Carpio told me. "Miriam's cousin, he live in Miami, same thing happen to him two years ago."

Mrs. Carpio huffed. "Different plan, but that one, they use annuity and life insurance, too. We wish they tell us before he . . . before we do this thing." Her husband reaching up to take her hand.

"But they were ashamed," Carpio said. "I can understand."

A new wave of customers stepped in off Brand, perusing the pastry case, and both the Carpios seemed relieved at the sight. "Don't ever sell this place," I said. "It's a gold mine."

Mr. Carpio asked me to come see them again anytime. I asked if I could keep the flyers and he said take them, please. I got up, promising to be in touch if I found out anything about the scammers two doors down. Mrs. Carpio walked over with a white bag filled with pastries, holding it out in offering. I thanked her, but said it really wasn't necessary.

Her black eyes were hard as glass. "I know, if you have a chance, you will do something about this."

"Ma'am, I didn't say that I—"

"Is not about the money!" she snapped. "Not anymore! You find these people. I hope you get them back. Jus' . . . you get them back for what they do." She saw, over her shoulder, a customer ready to be rung up. "Tha's all is left to do. You understand?"

I thought of Albert's bloody face on the beach, Rudy Kirkmeyer waving at me from the backseat of Bobby Silver's Cadillac, Monette standing watch as I cleared the pictures off my desk at work.

"I understand."

She handed me the bag of pastries.

Out of habit, I called my voice mail at work and found that it wasn't yet disconnected. I wondered if they'd go that far. There was one message, from Skip Greuber, the bar manager I'd worked for before Eloise Horton was hired. He said he was shocked at what they had done today, knew I'd gotten the short end, and wanted to see what he could do to help. He wanted me to call him, which I did. When his secretary asked who was calling, I gave the name Peter Nunn.

Skip Greuber and I had prosecuted Peter Nunn as co-counsel a few years back. Nunn was behind a statewide insurance-fraud ring that specialized in staged accidents and false medical claims. By the time the trial date rolled around, Nunn had fled to South Africa, where he couldn't be extradited. South Africa is a fabulous surfing destination. Skip used to ride a longboard way back when, and he and I joked that the bar should have paid our way to go get Nunn and bring him back.

I had liked working for Skip Greuber.

"J.?" he said cautiously.

"No, man, it really is Peter. Guess what? J-Bay is six foot and perfect right now."

"You're quite the comic. But seriously, we need to talk. How about lunch?"

"I just ate two Cuban sandwiches. But I'll let you buy me a Coke."

I suggested meeting in half an hour at Yang Chow, my favorite restaurant in Chinatown. I might be hungry again by then, so what the hell? A stop there might make it worth my while. The state bar owed me that much.

Greuber took his time arriving, leaving me waiting at a small table for twenty minutes or so, sipping warm tea in a small ceramic cup. The place was busy as usual, and I felt uncomfortable holding down a table without even ordering. It was a relief to see a Chinese woman half his size leading him back to me. He gave me a major handshake.

"You're looking sharp," he said. I was still wearing my best suit from this morning.

"What, for having my balls removed with tin snips?"

Greuber laughed, settling in with a menu. Skip was average in size, with a long face that looked too large for the rest of his body. His dull blond hair was so thin and combed over that it was catching the reflection of outdoor sunshine on Broadway. He pinched at his small mustache in a compulsive way that made me wonder if he was nervous about our meeting.

"So, what's good here?" he asked me.

"The company."

"That was pretty slick, J., saying you were Peter Nunn when you called."

"I figured you wouldn't want it known that you were fraternizing with the kind of attorney who gives the agency such a black eye."

"Oh, please. You think I don't know that disciplinary review panel is just the latest dog and pony show?" He put down his menu. "So, is that what we're doing, fraternizing?"

Skip was a skilled lawyer who chafed at the bureaucratic bullshit the bar threw at him. He dabbled heavily in investments and stock market trading, his stated goal to retire at fifty, which for him was three years off. I knew he wasn't fond of his work, but still, he was management, and I wasn't comfortable spilling my guts.

"You tell me," I said.

Skip told me he was concerned that people would wreck my career, make me a scapegoat just to have the bar look better. I couldn't exactly disagree. He asked me about the law center. I told him the business about my monitoring Dale Bleeker's probation, Bobby Silver's reinstatement hearing, the fire. Nothing he wouldn't already know.

"What were you doing out there when the place caught on fire?" Skip asked.

"Just trying to follow up on the Bleeker thing," I lied. "Talk to the office manager, see how many cases had his name on them, what could be done to take care of those clients. Obviously, that didn't work out."

"Yeah. Obviously."

A thin young Asian man in a pressed white shirt appeared with a pad and pen. Skip let me do the ordering. I put us down for two plates of slippery shrimp—their specialty—the equally fabulous pork with green beans, and a side of steamed rice. The waiter poured more tea into our cups before retreating to the kitchen.

"Look, man," he said. "You may need some help navigating."

"Maybe."

He glanced both ways. "Anything I can do in the meantime, just call."

I wanted to ask for permission to use a bar investigator to look into a growing list of questions I had, such as who owned the law center and whose name was on the office's lease. Who was behind these seminars? Who ran Capitol Consolidators and Homeowners Fidelity Trust? But I knew that this kind of intervention—the kind I needed—was beyond Skip Greuber's notion of help. A friendly, supportive word over lunch was one thing. Hanging your managerial ass out on a line to aid a line attorney whose credibility was in question, and doing it three years shy of retirement, well, that was something else.

"So, what do you say?" Skip asked, gripping his tiny teacup like a shot glass.

"I say thanks, but I'm not gonna screw up your future, buddy." He looked disappointed and began to protest, but I held up my teacup to his. "That's not to say you can't buy me lunch anytime."

He half smiled as our teacups met. "Right. Cheers."

Sixteen

A raw west wind blew off the ocean that afternoon, chopping a head-high swell to pieces. I cruised by the pier parking lot, intent on taking my mind off things with a surf check, and didn't bother to stop. That is, until I saw Dale and Rudy coming off the pier toward the crosswalk on Main, followed by Carmen, Albert, and Mickey Conlin.

Carmen saw me first, came over as I rolled down the passenger window. She wore flannel under my navy ski jacket, her black hair tamed by a wool beanie. They had decided to take a walk, having gone a bit stir-crazy earlier from looking after the guys at home. Dale had suggested a stroll on the pier. I asked how Max had missed out on this excursion. Carmen said please, that was just what she needed, more responsibility.

Mick was hanging back, pondering the watery horizon, posed like a wood carving of some sea captain. He'd stopped by again to look in on Albert, Carmen told me. Yeah, right, I said to myself. I'd heard that one once too many times by now.

"Hey, buddy," I called to him. "Did I tell you I'm getting married?"

Mick stopped cold for a second but recovered and dipped his head so he could spy me through the window, then said: "No! God, I'm so happy for you, J. What's his name?" He turned to Carmen, raising an eyebrow.

Carmen dug her hands deeper into the pockets of my ski jacket. "You're right, I should've brought Max. The conversation would've been better."

Mick came around to the driver's side and offered an assessment of the surf. "You look closely, there's a decent west-northwest rolling in under all this chop. Add the leftover wind swell from this gale . . ."

"Good size and peaky tomorrow morning?"

"Good chance."

Mick had a light load at his yard, so I leaned on him to join me, and we agreed to go for a paddle early the next day. I offered to give everyone a ride home, but Carmen preferred to walk. Mick peeled off hastily for his repair shop. I'd probably embarrassed him a little with the marriage comment, but so what, he had it coming. He wasn't the first friend of mine to be sucked into Carmen's vortex, and he wouldn't be the last.

Dale and Rudy crowded in behind Carmen outside my car window. "How'd it go this morning at work?" Dale said.

"You still gainfully employed?" Carmen asked.

"Yes and no." I clammed up after that.

She looked at me as if slightly wounded. "What, that's it?"

I said I'd fill in the details at home, then shut up again.

The silence felt like a curse. I'd been all set to tell Carmen about the suspension with pay, but I didn't want to sound too ecstatic because, honestly, I didn't really need the money. Then again, carrying on as if the bar had just cut me a huge financial break struck me as a shameless, bullshit pose.

The signal at Ocean and Main changed to red as I pulled away from the curb and rolled up two cars back. My four houseguests passed through the crosswalk on their way home, Carmen leading Albert by the hand, Dale by Rudy's side, turning their backs to the whipping onshore. I was struck by the urge to call out to Carmen, to tell her we'd talk at home—defuse the tension a bit—and I rolled down my window. Leaned out, but no words came to mind. The light turned green. The guy behind me honked. I dutifully moved through the intersection, feeling the sting of lost opportunity.

Kimberley Kirkmeyer-Munson called late that night to tell me she'd finally freed her schedule enough to take a morning flight from Seattle the next day. It's a good thing she did, because if she had stalled any more, I would have let her know where else she could go. She asked me how Rudy was doing and I gave her a report that sounded familiar by now: friendly, benign, and incoherent at times. She paused long enough for me to say, Ms. Munson, you there? then told me she just couldn't get over how quickly her father had declined, as if she didn't believe it, even asked to speak to him as if to verify his decline. What did she think, we were kidding? Hell, we love putting up old men with Alzheimer's. I didn't fight her, though, because I knew her father needed her. I told her I would gladly have put Rudy on the line to have a semi-coherent conversation with her, let her make her own conclusions, but it was ten-thirty and he was in bed asleep already. She could see for herself tomorrow. The last thing Kimberley did was thank me, telling me how she trusted my judgment. It sounded like a line.

Albert had another punch-out nightmare that night, waking up shrieking and stammering and calling for his sister in the dark. S-s-stop hitting! I d-d-didn't do anything! Carmen! This was the third one since the day at the beach. The sight of Albert sitting there on the bed shaking got me angry all over again. Frustrated, I vowed to tap the guy who slugged him. Bad move. That is *not* the answer, Carmen scolded me. Then what is? I shot back. After that exchange we both went silent. It took a half hour for her to soothe and cajole Albert back to sleep. I stayed up, sat right by her side, held her hand, and told her I was here for her. Got no response.

The next morning's dawn patrol with Mick paid off nicely, and on first view from the berm, I felt better about luring him away from the yard for a few. Beefy overhead peaks churned and spit for shore. The wind was nil, the wave faces satin smooth. Nobody out at first light. We rode for an hour on Southside, the bigger sets pushing ten feet, but the rising tide eventually swamped the surf with lines of rippling backwash, so we came in, walked up the beach, and paddled back out under the pier on Northside. The surf there was smaller than Southside, as usual, but the tide wasn't hurting the shape, and the crowd was lighter than expected. We soon found out why.

The best peak just north of the pilings had only five or six regulars on it. The only faces I didn't recognize were farther up the beach, away from the pier. At least one local congratulated me on helping clear the water of kooks. How's that again? I asked. By dealing with those imitators in the parking lot. I tried to explain that it wasn't that way but was winked off, as if I had to be joking. Mick fared even worse. His return to the lineup, coupled with the incident last week, was apparently being lauded as a virtual act of aggression toward anyone not from Christianitos, as if he was skulking around not to line up the shifting swells but to run off interlopers. Mick was pissed, and he paddled away from the pier and surfed alone until he cooled off.

Later in the morning I rode a long right straight toward the pier and kicked out well inside, just off the small cement seawall that runs about twenty yards out into the surf along the edge of the pilings. Someone had painted a crude skull and crossbones, along with the message: "If you don't live here, don't surf here." The classic locals-only cliché.

The creeping high tide improved the surf steadily all morning, and slowly we shook off the grimness and lost ourselves in the bliss attendant to riding good waves. By eleven my arms quivered like jelly from fatigue and I took a wave in. Mick was already on the beach, sitting in the wet sand near shore and sunning himself with his wet suit peeled down to his waist.

"Nice wave in, law boy," he said. "Too bad you look like a cripple with that stance."

"Bite me, motor head."

Mick picked up his board and we started across the sand for the showers. "Wait," I said, grabbing his arm. Staring up at the parking lot, where fifty yards away, Angie's boyfriend, Carlito, had just stepped out of a lowered Chevy Impala, three *vato loco*–type dudes in white tees and pressed chinos piling out behind him, gang tats all around.

"What, you're afraid of lowriders?"

"They're looking for me. I had a disagreement with the one in the beret last week. His girlfriend is the old guy Rudy's wife."

"They're the ones after his money?"

I cocked an eyebrow at him. "I didn't know you knew about the money."

"Carmen told me."

"Well, isn't that nice."

"Look, man," Mick said, "I'm not out to steal your woman. It's just been a while since I met someone I could talk to."

"I've got a couple of nine hundred numbers you can dial, can take care of that."

"Ha-ha," Mick said, peering at the lot. "Think he's looking for Rudy?"

"Not right now, not here. We have a bit of a history. I met him in a bank lobby. He wanted Rudy's money, had to be turned away by force."

"I see."

"I think I hurt his feelings in the process."

"Look at that badass stare. He seems to be overdoing it."

"He tends to run toward overdoing things."

Carlito was presently vibing a family of pale-faced tourists who looked liked they'd just come off a weeklong jag at Disneyland, the kids still in their mouse ears, stretching beside their rent-a-car and gaping at the spectacle of the great Pacific.

"Hurt his feelings, huh?" Mick said. "Guy like that, how could you even tell?"

"He kind of swore revenge on me."

"Oh." Grinning. "So, is this why you lured me out of retirement? Beach protection?"

Mick had turned his back, shielding me from view. I wasn't looking for a melee, not after what had happened with Albert last week.

"They haven't spotted me yet," I said. "We could head back into the water, paddle through the pilings to Southside."

Mick snorted. "Listen, J., my hassling days are long gone, but I ain't runnin' from these baggy-pants bozos in my own backyard."

"That's fine, Rambo, but there's four of them and two of us. That's two to one."

Mick cracked his knuckles. "I've always admired your math skills."

"Look at that garb," I said.

"Definitely going for the full hoodlum look."

"Achieving it, if you ask me. Bet they're carrying."

That stopped Mick. "Think so?" he asked. His voice had gone cold.

"Guy in the beanie was pretty helpless the first time we met.

I'm pretty sure he's not concerned about a fair fight this time around."

"Well I still ain't sneakin' through Southside to get away. What's your Plan B?"

"I'm working on it."

Hunkering down in the wet sand, I gazed into the lineup, which was emptying out, now that the wind was on it. The surfers who had ridden lesser-quality waves up the beach were paddling south, moving in on the best peak off the pilings as the local crew dispersed.

"Any thoughts yet, Einstein?" Mick said.

"You'll be the first to know."

Perhaps I could build a little strength in numbers. A few guys in the water knew me well enough to want to back me, but how do you ask someone for that kind of favor? Not to mention, recent events aside, this was a generally peaceful beach, the crowds coexisting with little disagreement about who stood where in the pecking order. I'd already upset the social balance last week with the fight over Albert's punching. The graffiti on the seawall proved that much. But Mick was right; I couldn't run away in my own backyard. Besides, if they were here now at the pier and I slipped away, they'd be pulling up in front of my house in an hour. Then I'd really be alone.

Carlito was calling me out in public, looking to humiliate me in dramatic fashion.

"Thank God that asshole's proud," I said, "or I'd be lying in some alley a block away from home."

"Probably," Mick said. "We're better off facing 'em here."

I was through hiding and straightened up beside Mick. Carlito was fixing on us now, his chin pointing us out, the grin cocky.

"The guy's a bit of a showman," I said.

Mick said, "Well hell yes, look at that beanie, way it's cocked on his dome. Foot on the bumper like he's fucking Patton or something. Think they'll try to take us down here?"

"No, they'll stay by the car so they can bail fast when they're done. Sorry about this."

"About what?"

"We're gonna get our asses kicked," I heard myself saying.

Mick squinted back into the sun at me. "Thanks for the vote of confidence, brother."

"J., Mickey, hey, what's the haps?" a voice called out from up on the pier. I squinted and saw a shadow leaning on a one-speed bike, the kind with big knobby tires, against the metal railings. He looked like the kid who delivered the local paper weekday afternoons on my street, a thickset local grommet named Charlie, better known as Chubs. He didn't really know Mick or me, but was merely trying to ingratiate himself with two older, well-established surfers, the way grommets often will to gain more of a toehold in the local surf scene.

The timing couldn't have been better.

"Hey, Chubs, what's goin' on, man?" I said, laying it on.

I asked him if he'd surfed today, why he wasn't in school. He rode a few on Northside earlier, he said, saw me get a good left into the pier. Teacher conferences today, so no school. Mick rolled his eyes at me, no doubt wondering why in hell I was wasting my time with a lowly grom.

"Anyway, I need a little favor, Chubs. See those guys next to the Impala up there?"

Chubs looked. "Who? The beaners?"

I pictured Carmen's reaction to being called a beaner.

"Yeah. They're trying to move in on a friend of mine's business. His name's Rod Weesun. He should be at the Marmaduke on Main, that's his spot. You need to go get him, now, fast as you can, tell him those dudes are setting up shop, and I need his help to run them off, like right now. This minute, Chubs."

Mick stifled a chuckle. "You are really asking for it, man," he said under his breath.

"I dunno," Chubs said, his face a lighter shade. "That guy Weesun's a biker, and I heard he's crazy."

"He's a surfer, too," I said, "and like I told you, he's a friend of mine."

What I said was quite a stretch. Rodney Weesun hadn't been seen in the lineup since before he went to prison in '81 on felony possession-for-sale charges. It was common knowledge that if you needed black market pharmaceuticals or high-grade crystal meth, Rod was your man in Christianitos. I'd heard that in order to survive in prison, Rod had taken up with a white Aryan clan, most of whom were also bikers. He'd said it was either that or be left to fend off the black and Mexican gangs by himself, which wasn't much of an option. I hadn't spoken with him in two years, since the night he'd phoned me, drunk off his ass and in jail with no other lawyer to call. That night I bailed him out myself, Rod looking like he'd been through a meat grinder, headfirst, muttering something about a deal being a deal. The Marmaduke was out a plate glass window, a few pool cues, and several bar stools, but Rod was quite sure he'd held his ground. Whatever. I took him home, set him up on my couch, and poured coffee down his throat until he could sit up by himself. As he snapped out of his stupor, Rod began to get nostalgic on me, reminiscing with heartfelt but mostly distorted stories about the old days surfing with the local crew. I let most of it go without comment, since, truthfully, I'd never liked the guy. He'd been a major asshole to me when I was a grommet, hazing me relentlessly. Later on, he became outwardly jealous of my skill at riding Holy Rollers, a hairball big wave reef a half mile off the beach that, for all of Rod's landlocked bravado, he'd never had the balls to ride. But that night he acted as if we were blood brothers.

The next day I got a call from Rollo Bernardino, one of the better criminal-defense practitioners in Long Beach, thanking me for my dispatch and discretion in aiding his client, Mr. Weesun. My dispatch and discretion—that just killed me. Two days later I got a check from Bernardino's client trust account for the bail money, and an extra grand, calculated on the check stub as two hours' legal services at five hundred dollars an hour. Rod had his lawyer on one hell of a retainer, which was no accident. In his business, you don't skimp on the quality of your legal representation.

Chubs pedaled his beach cruiser off the pier like a little madman, the voice on the PA system off the lifeguard tower coming to life with a booming directive that riding bicycles on the pier was strictly prohibited. Mickey just shook his head at me.

"Hey, Weesun owes me," I said. "Shit, he owes both of us. Remember how he used to try to involve you in his little surf battles?"

"I'm way beyond that stuff," Mick said, checking on Carlito over his shoulder. Then he turned to me. "Let's get this over with." We picked up our boards. As we did, I noticed a few of the guys I'd fought with over Albert last week. They were wet-suited and dripping and standing around near the same white delivery van, sharing a smoke and enjoying the warming sun not more than a dozen spots over from Carlito and his boys. I thought about warning them, but how? Me telling them to leave, they'd take it at face value, get defensive.

"Forget it," I said absently.

They'd just have to use their heads and stay clear.

We decided to go straight for Carlito, not let him follow us under the pier to the showers, where the guy in the lifeguard tower might not see a gun or knife come out, might miss a falling body. The parking lot was about a third full, the pasty tourists still closest to the Impala, oblivious. I walked up to the father, a short fellow in a Universal Studios tee, pleated shorts, and rubber sandals, and quietly told him there was going to be a confrontation and he needed to clear out. "Honey? Kids?" he said. They got the message and split within seconds, the wife looking like she'd just sucked on a lemon.

Carlito smiled. "Told you this wasn't over." He took the measure of Mick, standing by my side, and told Mick to mind his own fucking business. Mick didn't bite, said this was his beach, he'd do as he pleased. Carlito's homies stepped around the side of the car and seemed ready to engage us.

The deep rumble of Harley-Davidson machinery never sounded so sweet as it did the next moment. Rod Weesun and two other bikers rolled past the tollbooth up on Ocean without stopping to pay and opened up their throttles when Rod spotted the lowered Impala.

"You're hosed," I told Carlito. "Better bail now, while you can."

But Carlito was stuck, having probably popped off to his bros about how easy it would be to roll me, and now not wanting to back down in front of them.

Weesun tipped his aviator shades at Mick and me as he got off his bike. His hair was balding but still long and dirty brown down the sides and back. He'd grown a beard since the night I'd bailed him out, and his gut looked bigger under his black tee. The two guys he'd brought with him wore ancient biker boots and greasy jeans and were as big as bouncers. One had a hawklike nose and bad acne scars, a slack, nothing-to-lose look about him. The other one calmly unwound a heavy chain from beneath his bike's seat, smiling like a born sadist.

Weesun told Carlito he was way out of his neighborhood and gave him the order to split.

"*Vámanos muchachos!*" Weesun cackled in their faces.

Carlito said he had business to settle with me. I thought that remark would blow my scheme and make Weesun realize I was using him, but he didn't catch on. Next thing you knew, the biker with the chain had swung and connected with the side of Carlito's face, putting him down. Weesun whiffed a punch past the guy in the red headband, who made him pay for his miss by tagging him hard in the ribs, knocking Weesun on his ass. But the hawk-nosed biker was coming in fast, fists flying in every direction. Mick and I stood back, eyeing the two Mexicans across the car's hood. One looked suitably freaked, but the other, a guy with big tattooed forearms under a creased white tee, was reaching for something in his waistband.

Mick must have seen part of the gun before it was out, or he wouldn't have dived across the hood and onto the tattooed Mexican the way he did. Then the scared one found some sack and pounced on Mick as he struggled to get the gun away. I moved in and pried the guy off with a chokehold and a pair of thumbs raking his eyes. The gun flashed silver in the sunlight, jammed, and exploded, flattening the Impala's left front tire.

The Mexican Mick was wrestling with screamed, his hand gnarled and bloody. Mick kicked what was left of the gun, which looked like a tinny Saturday night special, under the Impala. Then a squad car pulled up sideways not ten feet from us, the doors flung open, and two cops drew their guns, shouting orders to freeze.

Just like that, it was over.

I didn't fare as well with the local police this time. They arrested all of us for public disturbance, took statements, talked about charging the biker with the chain and the Mexican with the gun with assault with a deadly weapon. Weesun apparently was toting a rainbow of Schedule III and IV controlled substances in his saddlebag, so he had problems of his own. After a few hours of stewing in a windowless cell, Mick and I were led to an interrogation room where Buzz Hammond, the chief, was waiting to lecture us on citizenship. Brushing off our claims of self-defense, the chief said he was charging us with one thing and one thing only "for life, boys," and that was to set a fine example for others, to keep the beaches of Christianitos safe and peaceable. Then he let us go, complaining about the stench a wet wetsuit can cause indoors.

We picked up our boards in the dispatch center, then headed toward the lobby, feeling pretty fortunate all the way around. Passing the same interrogation room, I looked inside. There, where I'd been seated not five minutes ago, was the ragtag crew of surfers I'd fought with over Albert. Silent, awaiting cups of water that a detective was handing around the table, but you could see the outrage in their eyes.

I didn't get it. They'd had nothing to do with the Carlito episode today, aside from hanging nearby in the parking lot. A young Hispanic uniform, Officer Terraza, the same guy who'd given me a free pass the week before, stepped up to the door from inside and nodded at me officially before he pulled it shut.

"Well, thanks for a fun little surf session, Counselor," Mick said outside. "Next time you want to go for a paddle, J., please, do me a favor, let me go to work instead."

"Mick, if you don't mind, I don't want to hear it right now." My wetsuit, peeled down to my waist, reeked of sweat and salt water and itched like hell in the crotch. Carmen was probably going out of her mind again at home, wondering where I'd disappeared to, and I wasn't relishing having to lie to her about today.

Mick paused when we reached the sidewalk in front of the station. It was a beautiful day for February, no clouds, the sunshine lighting a smogtinged sky that was the color of faded turquoise, and an easygoing sea breeze tilting the palm trees above us.

"Ah, forget it," he said. "All things considered, we were lucky to get off so easy."

I was picturing those other surfers in the interrogation room right now.

"Luck's got nothing to do with it," I said.

Seventeen

Carmen leaned with her back against the sink in the kitchen, listening to my summary of Carlito's ill-timed play. We were sipping coffee, which was my idea, since six hours encased in wet neoprene had left me shaking and clammy, even after I'd showered and thrown on jeans and a tee. Dale sat at the dining table, nursing an ice water. His eyes were sunken as if he'd slept poorly again. Last night was the second time I'd awakened during the night and heard him rocking in a chair downstairs.

Albert and Rudy were in the living room, watching *The People's Court*. When I stopped talking, I could hear Judge Wapner chewing a motel manager's ass for inflating the plaintiff's room bill.

Carmen's face seemed to have tightened.

"What?" I said.

"That last part is pure bull, J.," she said. "Don't tell me you didn't enjoy having to deal with them that way. Of course you enjoyed it."

"Car," I said, "it's not like they gave us a choice."

"Oh, please. Of course you had a choice." She dumped the rest of her coffee in the sink. "You could've . . . paddled away. Or sat out there in the surf until they left."

"Really? Left for where? They'd have come right over here next. Then what would I have done?"

"You're right, you'd just have to punch 'em out right here, too, cowboy." Sarcasm was not her style, and she looked away, regaining something in private. Outside the kitchen window, the branches of the peppertree screened out the sun. Carmen sighed as if she were waiting for me to catch up. "You could try calling the police, J. That's what normal people do."

I was stung, having thought I'd handled a dangerous situation with a certain degree of skill. "Hey, it's not like I haven't tried.

But the only cop I've talked to on this case got kicked off of it, through no fault of my own, or his, for that matter." I finished my cup off, squeezing by a frozen Carmen to drop it in the sink. Getting angry, feeling she was judging a situation she didn't fully understand. "Lemme tell you something else you may not appreciate."

She leaned back, pushing my pointed finger away. "Take it down a peg. I don't like being talked to this way."

She was right. "Sorry. The thing is, I'm beginning to realize the cops in this town don't seem to mind a scrape or two here and there as long as the natural order of things is preserved. They have this knack for always showing up just a tick too late to make a difference."

"What do you mean by 'natural order'?" she said.

I paused to find the right words. "Maybe this only applies at the beach, but it seems like, if you live here and they know you, they don't mind if you try to set matters straight."

"Yeah," Carmen said, "and if you're from East L.A. and have dark skin, you're out of luck."

"Those guys came down here for one reason: to hurt me. I don't care if they were purple with pink polka dots."

"I'm guessing the police would've cared. You just said so."

"No I did not, and this is not about race," I said slowly. We were at it again.

Dale seemed to sense our bad vibe, because he stood up quickly and said, "J., you mentioned Detective Perry, how he gave you his cell number. Didn't he say you could still call him?"

"That's right."

"Well, why don't you call him and tell him about those flyers?"

Why not try Tamango Perry again? I had nothing to lose.

"Good idea. I'll call him later." I looked at my watch, which was at almost three. "Does Rudy know his daughter's coming for him today?"

Carmen said yes, she'd already packed his things this morning.

"Thank God they didn't get to him this morning," Dale said.

The doorbell rang, and the three of us exchanged frozen stares. Max began to bark, rushing down the side yard for a peek through the fence at the front yard.

Dale said, "What do we do if it's them?"

I wasn't sure what Angie and Carlito were capable of, but this morning in the beach parking lot hadn't been too encouraging.

"Stay by the phone," I told Carmen. "We'll call the police if we need to, I promise."

Carmen lowered her eyes. "Okay."

I went outside, called Max over, hooked him onto the choke chain, and led him in through the kitchen. The doorbell rang again and he barked low and throaty, his stub tail wagging like a twitching thumb. "Be cool," I told him, petting him between the shoulders, where the muscle was as dense as bedrock. Then I directed Dale to go be with Rudy and Albert in the living room, to keep them away from the front entry hall. "Sit, Max," I commanded. Sucking in my breath, I jerked open the front door.

She was a tall teenaged girl in torn blue jeans and an oversize gray sweatshirt with a surfwear logo in red across the front. She jumped a little at the sight of my pet Rottweiler, cheeks red from sun and her face still a little chubby. I recognized something in the set of her straight nose and green eyes, the even cheekbones.

"It's not Angie," I said over my shoulder. Carmen came away from the kitchen, stepping up behind me. "Max, stay." My dog dropped to the floor and relaxed.

"You're him," the girl said, standing back even more.

"Do I know you?" I said.

"You're the guy who put Kurt into the hospital."

"Kurt who?"

Still eyeing my dog, but gaining confidence, the girl said, "My boyfriend. And now his friends are getting picked up by the cops for fighting, when it was you again. They didn't even do anything, and they're getting hassled. They're still down there, and it's three o'clock. Jim and Riley, they gotta go to work. I had to move the van, got kicked out of the parking lot."

She nodded behind her at the dirty white delivery van, the one with the heavy-metal logo, parked out on Porpoise Way.

"I'm sorry," I said. "Last week, someone punched my future brother-in-law, for no good reason. When I tried to ask your friends—"

"Don't even try to justify it," she said. "I was in the van. I heard everything."

"Then you heard what the fat guy called—"

"They were scared of you. It's your beach, you're the big local guy, and we're not part of that." She swallowed. "That's pretty obvious."

"Look," I said.

"No, you look! I just came here to say one thing, and since I'm a girl I figured you wouldn't beat me up or something." She took another step back, one foot on the lower brick step now. "Just leave us alone. Just leave us the f-" She stopped in midsentence, and her face went pale. "Daddy?"

Dale stood behind me at the door. "Leanne? Honey?" Expectant, his eyes watering.

"Please, come in," I said to her, opening the door wider.

Leanne glared at her father. "You're with him?"

Dale stepped by me. "Honey, can you come in a minute and talk. We need to—"

But Dale's daughter let out a shriek and retreated, running, down my front walk, losing a yellow rubber sandal as she banged through the gate, not bothering to come back and get it. Max trailed behind her curiously and sniffed at the sandal. Dale followed her out to the street but let her go. He stood there, frozen, as the blue smoke from the van's exhaust floated back to him. Then he looked at Carmen and me with that same hangdog face he would wear when he stared out my living-room window at night.

"Better get him inside before a car comes," Carmen said. "I'll take Max."

She was giving me a subtle I-told-you-so look, which, to me, was not at all well timed.

"Know what I could really use right now?" I said. "A little support."

Carmen paused before she spoke. "I said I would take Max."

Dale asked for a drink as soon as we got him inside. I knew what he meant but told him we had some iced tea in the fridge and started getting it without missing a beat. Whatever we'd just seen with his daughter, I felt sure alcohol wasn't going to help sort it out. Carmen sat him down gently at the dining table, guiding him by the elbow. Rudy and Albert had fallen asleep in the living room. *The People's Court* had given way to a *Kung Fu* rerun. When I walked in to shut off the tube, Caine was trying to leave a mining town peacefully, but a trio of company thugs wasn't going to let it happen. Caine bowed his head, got his hat knocked off, and went into the beautiful centered stance you see before he starts beating someone senseless. By the time I found the remote and switched it off, the quiet priest had splattered two bodies in a dirt road in poetic slow motion.

Dale took a sip of his tea and said, "What can I say?"

"Whatever you haven't said so far," I suggested.

It wasn't exactly a life story for Dale, but it could have been one for Leanne.

"Only child," he said. "After my wife, Georgette, and I had tried to conceive for so long we'd lost track. Leanne came along quite by surprise; a solid decade after Georgette had gone off the pill. We'd forgotten about birth control altogether. She was a big baby, nine pounds and change, grew up into a happy, pink-cheeked little kid that could do no wrong at home or in school."

"What happened that changed her?" I asked.

Dale sipped his iced tea, then waited. "Fast-forward to age fifteen. Leanne was still a straight-A student, but quieter, developing more of an interior life, I supposed, taking on a Gothic look, a lot of black clothes, a long overcoat she wore day and night, even when the weather was hot. And Jesus, the eyeliner, like some kind of ghoul. Just an adolescent phase, we figured. Then Georgette gets the call."

"The call?"

Dale stared at me, nodding. "One morning, phone rings. It's the school vice principal. He says Leanne was truant fifteen times last month alone, picked up with an off-campus boy this morning, smelling of marijuana, a crack pipe in the young man's pants pocket. I was arguing against a motion to suppress that morning, had to rush to school as soon as the judge took it under submission. Georgette was already there, semihysterical, saying I don't understand this, I don't understand this, the man says my baby won't

222 ≣ John DeCure

even talk to me, won't talk to us." His eyes moved to a stoic Carmen, then back to me. "That man being the psychologist the district brought in to talk to Leanne, a social worker in there with her now, interviewing her about something."

"Carmen's a social worker," I said, trying to be conversational at exactly the wrong time.

"Is that right," Dale said, politely handling the intrusion on his narrative.

I exchanged a glance with Carmen, an Are you thinking what I'm thinking? look. She and I met in juvenile dependency court, where county social workers bring in cases by the truckload involving minors who have been harmed or are at risk of harm, that harm typically being physical and sexual abuse in the home. Dale sipped his tea again. So far, nothing I knew about the man's easygoing nature suggested he was a wife or kid beater, and besides, teens are too old for corporal punishment. By that age they can fight back or run away, or at least tell a cop or a schoolteacher that they're being hit. That meant sexual abuse was the most likely punch line here. Immediately I thought of his conviction for wienie wagging. Christ. Dale sucked a long breath as if he were gathering wind to push on. Carmen's face I couldn't read. She's always better than I am at hearing someone out, withholding judgment. Not me; my mind was leaping.

So this was my role model, my image of a great attorney, what I had wanted to aspire to all those years.

"So it was the social worker who talked to us," Dale said, "not the psychologist. Georgette first, alone for five minutes, the girl's VP offering me coffee in the meantime, nervous as hell, which meant that she was in on the secret already, whatever it was. Next thing, the door swings open, and Georgette is being restrained, cursing her head off—a woman who wouldn't say crap if her mouth was full of it, you have to understand—railing against 'that lying, disgusting little slut' . . . confusing the hell out of me until I realized she was talking about our daughter. Then Georgette's free, and yanking me out of my chair, saying, 'Get up, get up now!' I'm saying, 'Why?' 'Because we're leaving,' she says, 'that's why!' Threatening to sue the school, the county, and the whole district.

Shrieking at the poor VP, 'You think that little liar is at risk, then take her, take her!' "

"How awful," Carmen said.

Dale acknowledged her with a tiny nod. "Georgette was the homemaker, so I was used to deferring to her judgment on domestic matters, but I was scared by her flip-out, lemme tell you. It was the first time I'd ever seen that kind of an outburst. Hell, she was calmer during childbirth."

"What did you do?" I said.

"Tried to smooth her out, pretty unsuccessfully. But I also knew I had to go back in there to find out for myself what was going on. Georgette, she was already rushing to her car, saying, 'If you're going back for that little slut, then you better not come home either, Daddy!' Spitting the words at me."

"You went back," Carmen said.

Dale rubbed the stubble on his face. He probably hadn't shaved that morning.

"Talked to the social worker. Nice lady, Spanish accent. Chose her words carefully. I appreciated it, believe you me." He grinned a little, obliging us to grin back a little. "What the nice lady told me was that she understood Leanne had been going back to visit relatives during the summer, two weeks at the end of August, right before school started back, for the last seven years. Visiting Leanne's mother's family in Schaumburg, Illinois, outside Chicago. All true, I told her. That was Aunt Jenny and Uncle Pat; their two boys, Mark and Danny; and a girl of their own, Mary Kate. Nice people, big swimming pool in the backyard, lived not far from that mall, Woodfield or Whitfield, one they said was the biggest in the world. 'What else do you know about them?' the social worker wanted to know. 'Any serious problems?' Not really, I said, but two years ago they did suffer a terrible tragedy. Mary Kate, who was roughly Leanne's age, had died accidentally, suffocating when her head got caught in some of that gauzy plastic they wrap your dry cleaning in. Well, the social worker got pretty interested in Mary Kate's death, based on what Leanne had said happened to her each trip." His voice got snagged on something. "What her uncle Pat would do to her when Aunt Jenny and the kids weren't around."

"Oh my god," Carmen said quietly.

"Yeah," Dale said. "You guessed it, sweetie. I was practically numb when the nice social worker laid the progression of specific terms on me, terms I knew vaguely from the penal code. Digital penetration, penetration with a foreign object, oral cop' on the perpetrator, by force or fear. Vaginal intercourse. Sodomy. The cops showed a little later and said of course they would have to contact the authorities in Illinois, since it cast a new light on Mary Kate's accidental death. Not to mention, Uncle Pat could be criminally prosecuted if Leanne was willing to testify. But honestly, I didn't hear much more of what anyone was saying that day. I was too angry. My first thought was to board a plane for Chicago, go back there and take a machete to the motherfucker's genitals, hack them off and stuff them up his . . ." His hands were both fists now, and his breathing came heavier. "I was mad. But I knew I couldn't murder the guy, even if I wanted to. I stayed mad. Still am. Then my analytical mind clicked on, and this deep, deep confusion set in, like a fog. And I thought, why had Georgette reacted so strongly to the news, so viciously against . . . of all people, Leanne? Her little girl, the victim in all of this. Unless . . ." He stopped, and Carmen and I waited without moving.

"Dale," I said. "You don't have to be telling us all this. It's none of our business."

He looked at Carmen, then at me, his face calm, the way it had been the first time, when he'd put Thelma Ruffo away.

"You kidding? The way you look at me all the time, like I just spoiled a party I didn't even know I was invited to?"

"Dale," I said.

"Dale nothing!" he snapped. "Just let me say my piece, will you? And don't act like you don't want to know, because you do."

"Sorry," I said.

He played with his glass of tea, rolling the bottom edges like it was a spinning top wobbling down.

"I thought of my sex life with my wife. Her, uh, detached manner. The way she'd always refused to wear the lingerie I gave her for Valentine's Day, or maybe our anniversary." He shrugged at Carmen as if embarrassed about the topic, but went on. "The joyless way she'd go about it between the sheets, slowly cutting back once we had Leanne, until about three years ago, when we stopped having sex altogether. Georgette was acting as if she'd done her share for the marriage by then, not wanting to discuss it. Even inviting me, when I complained, to go and 'get serviced' by someone else, if that's what I wanted. I'd always wondered before why there seemed to be this huge physical barrier between Georgette and me."

"Most molesters were violated themselves, when they were kids," Carmen said.

Dale agreed. "I didn't know that at the time. I do now. Georgette and Pat had grown up in the same house with a father she'd never said so much as two words about."

So that was it. Georgette's father was the original perpetrator. "That must have been a hard secret for your wife to hold in all that time," I said.

Dale's face was almost too calm. "I think it was just too much for Georgette to face at once, the secret she'd repressed for all those years finally out. Her shame over what had happened to her, what it had done to her marriage, her brother's ruined life."

"You called the authorities," I said.

"Did they prosecute him?" Carmen asked.

Dale shook his head. "Never had a chance. He was driving home from work a week after they arrested him. There was this railroad crossing he'd pass on the way every day. Train was coming. They said he tried to beat it across the tracks and didn't make it. I don't believe that for a second. He was a goddamned coward, all the way to the end."

Dale went silent for a time. Max barked twice in the yard at something, then apparently lost interest.

"What happened with Georgette?" I asked Dale.

"The whole awful history of it just crept up on her and sort of swallowed her, I think. Pat's death, Mary Kate's likely suicide, Georgette's guilt over Leanne's victimization, the way she'd sent the kid back there every year as if she couldn't have known this might happen. But old ways die hard, I guess. Georgette held her ground, wouldn't budge."

"She disowned Leanne," Carmen said. In dependency court, where Carmen and I had met, we'd both seen plenty of mothers wed to child molesters do precisely the same thing.

"That's right," Dale said. "Leanne promptly ran away. Georgette threatened me with divorce, started flying into a rage over God knows what whenever I was around, really changed her ways. Started keeping the shades down, draperies shut. Letting the house she'd spent the past eighteen years beautifying go straight to hell. Spiking everything she put to her lips with a double shot of vodka."

"Major depression," Carmen said.

"Right again," Dale said. "Eventually, I got around to drinking, too. It was the only thing that could numb the pain. I'd lost the two most important people in my life in about a week's time." His eyes looked swollen, and he closed them for a time, but he kept talking. "When I was ripped, we'd fight, and the anger I'd feel toward her, for being such a . . . a weakling . . . God, it was so strong, it was like lightning passing right through me. Scared me, what I might do. Nights like that, I'd stagger outside and sleep on the patio furniture to stay away." His chest heaved quietly with slow, deep breathing, and we waited again.

"What happened to Leanne?" I said after a time.

"Leanne was gone for six months without a word. Every time I'd announce that we had to do something more than just report it and wait for word, because Christ, we were her parents, weren't we? We'd both just drink and wind up having another battle royal. I started drinking during the daytime—to calm my nerves, I'd tell myself. My concentration at work went to pot. For a time, I was getting by on my reputation alone, but pretty soon other people in the office started getting the tougher cases. Next thing, I find myself without any real caseload, doing the goddamned arraignment calendar, mornings, three days a week. That's what the newbies to the office usually got, a stack of arraignments each day, their first assignment. The other two days a week I'd do traffic court, misdemeanor trials the city attorney should have been handling anyway. Afternoons, I took some pretty long lunches. Sit in the Regal and get blasted."

"I'm sorry, Dale," I said.

"I did not flash those girls," he said quickly, pointing a finger at me. "Know that."

He drummed his fingers on the table, staring at the empty space across the kitchen. "I was drinking beer that afternoon, needed to relieve myself like you wouldn't believe. There was this hillside dropping off the edge of the cul-de-sac where I was parked. No trees or cover. So I thought I'd be discreet, climb down the hillside a few feet, at least below belt level, 'fore I did my business." He blushed. With the light coming in the side window, his rough whiskers cast an uneven blue shadow across his face. "The hill had this thick green stuff growing all over it, with these little purple flowers."

"Ice plant," I said, knowing where this was going. "You slipped on it."

"With my johnson hanging out. I think the hill had just been watered. Anyway, when I slipped, I landed flat on my ass, slid about twenty feet straight down the embankment, over this retaining wall at the bottom. Came down like boom, right smack in front of those two girls walking home from school." He shrugged, frowning. "Pretty slick, huh?"

Dale almost chuckled. "Right. They started screaming, ran off. So here I am, scrambling back up the hill, which I can't do because it's wet and slippery, so I gotta walk all the way around the block, way down the street then back up this steep incline to get to the Buick. A cruiser pulls up just as I get there, and here I am, drunk at three in the afternoon on a weekday."

"What'd you tell 'em?" I asked.

"The truth. I knew I was fucked."

He was fired the same week.

The rest of the story I knew, since I'd been involved in it. What I didn't know was that some months ago, Dale had seen a kid Leanne used to be friends with, a girl she was on the drill team with freshman year. She came up the walk one afternoon when Dale just happened to be out front, checking the mailbox for past-due notices. Said she'd seen Leanne down here, in Christianitos, at the beach. Dale drove down a few times, hung around, tried to talk to some of the kids in the parking lot, on the pier, asking after Leanne. Most of them were beach kids, surfers, telling him to get lost, acting like he was a pervert, a dirty old man looking for a teenage girl. Aren't we all looking for a girl, you fucking geezer, they'd say. Then he got a call from a state bar prosecutor who knew him from his DA days, wanted to help him comply with his probation. He was leery, because not too many people wanted to help him these days, but the prosecutor just happened to live in Christianitos.

"I thought, maybe this was meant to be. Maybe the time has come to redeem myself a little. Max barked out in the yard again. Dale kept gazing into empty kitchen space. "Hasn't happened that way just yet, has it," he said, not phrasing it as a question.

There was nothing to say for now. Dale looked wiped from recounting his story, and when he excused himself to use the facilities, his back looked stiff and his shoulders hunched forward like an old man's. Max was still agitated, and I took Dale's glass of tea to the sink and peeked out the window over the sink to see what was up. Max was there, at the base of the peppertree, balancing on one paw as if he was about to climb the trunk. A cluster of brown sparrows sat on the lowest branch, taunting him, letting him know it was their yard, too.

I rinsed the glass, then felt Carmen's hand on my back, and turned around as her arms slid up around my neck. What is this? I wanted to ask, but those brown eyes were boring into me at close range.

"I love you," she said. Then she kissed me, and I kissed her back, like we hadn't done since she and Albert had come to stay with me.

The doorbell rang. "You think?" I said, hoping Leanne had returned. Carmen didn't venture a guess as we came back through the dining room. Dale was there at the doorway, his hand on the knob.

"Mind if I get it?" His face was expectant, and I imagine he was saying a quick prayer that it was she. I told him to go ahead.

She was standing a few steps back on the porch, dark sunglasses hiding half her face. Hands on hips, head forward, aloof and insouciant, like a model at the end of the runway.

"I'm here for my husband," Angie said to Dale. "And I don't want no trouble about it either, old man."

Eighteen

My father was dead before I finished the first grade, so my memories of him are brief and somewhat time-worn. A handful of his exploits are documented in the annals of surfing—albeit the back pages. The early trips with the Christianitos crew to the Islands in the fifties, the suicidal cliff-hanging drops on waves too immense to ride, but then again, when you made one . . . The big wave guns he shaped by hand in our garage. Details in length, thickness, fin placement, rail configuration, rocker. The quiet legacy of an underground shaper who never lifted a finger to market himself, and these days, a story known only to resident old farts, surf historians, and true disciples of the Glide. But as his son, I tend to remember the less public aspects of the man. More than anything, I recall the way he carried himself. Which could sometimes surprise you.

One such time, an untalented but popular shaper from Huntington Beach had tried to put him out of business by duplicating his boards down to the last degree while gleefully knocking a bundle off the price. For a month or so it worked, and the orders for Shepard originals were way off. Something had to be done, so when my dad sent the guy an open invite through the board-building grapevine, people expected a major showdown. That's why, I was later told, the H.B. shaper pulled up in front of our house one windblown afternoon with a vanload of buddies with him as backup. And why a sizable contingent of my father's local friends seemed to be on hand within seconds of the van's arrival.

We were on the front porch together that day, my father reviewing my first-grade reading homework before letting me split for a bike ride. I remember watching the H.B. and Christianitos boys sort themselves out on our lawn like alley cats, lots of silent stare-downs going on. Is that guy gonna get it? I asked my dad, pointing at the offending shaper, a pudgy dude in granny shades and a tie-dyed ball cap. My father sighed, said, Nah, its not that way, then squatted and looked in my eyes as if to make sure I would remember what he was about to tell me. When your enemy shows at your doorstep, he said, you invite him in. That way he's not your enemy, he's your guest, get it? I didn't, but I went along, watched him cross the porch and lay a big howzit with a powerful handshake on the H.B. guy, who looked now to be in a mild state of shock, his cap coming off out of deference to his host. My father invited him back to the garage to talk design, the guy looking relieved and just plain stoked now, the situation defused. The word later was that after his visit to my old man's garage, the H.B. shaper got inspired and took on a new direction of his own, and a reasonably fruitful one at that. The Robert Shepard knockoffs were history.

"Invite her in," I muttered to Dale, still hanging on my father's words from twenty-five years ago.

Angie shrugged. "Whatever." She adjusted her black tank top, grimacing like it was cutting off her circulation, her faded jeans just as tight down below. Her movements were unself-consciously crass, but then, she was a good-looking girl who'd probably learned what she could do with her God-given gifts a long time ago. She caught me checking her out, smiled a little as she glided past me and into the short entry hall. "Where's Rudy?"

Thirty feet outside in my yard the front gate clicked, and I saw Carlito, his head bandaged under his beret where the biker's chain had struck him. Coming up the walk as if he were invited. No, I thought. Even my old man had his limits.

"You," I called out the open door. "Stop. Get the hell offa my property. Now."

He halted as if to think about it, then smiled defiantly. "Eat me."

My fists balled, my first thought being Screw it, he's dead, but decking this trash on my front walk in front of Carmen wasn't much of an option, considering the level of mayhem I'd caused of late. Carlito's remark gave me a much better idea.

"Funny you should put it that way," I told him. "Because I can arrange it, if that's what you want."

"Fuck you, beach boy." Carlito stood there, arms folded, the dumb turd not wanting to back off, but not getting my drift either. Hell, how could he?

He'd never met Max before.

I zipped around the side yard and opened the gate, waited for that big black head to poke through like a bull coming out of a rodeo chute. The dog eyed me gleefully, then fixed on the stranger on our brick walk.

"Max, get him!"

There may be no finer sight than a badass thug running for his life, except perhaps when that badass thug trips over his own two feet just before he can hurdle a fence to safety.

"Yah!" Carlito shrieked, I think as a result of his balls pancaking into the fence top. But it was hard to tell, since Max was ripping into his pant leg down below, yanking him backward and onto the ground.

"Max! Down! Down!" I shouted.

Backing off, the dog growled at me, gave me the Rottweiler version of the old stink-eye, like he wanted to know why I was cutting short the fun.

"Good boy. Let's go." I stuck him around back again, the big head drooping between his shoulders as the wooden gate closed.

Angie was attending to Carlito at the gate. His pant leg was shredded, but I didn't see any blood. He was covering his nuts with both hands, moaning into the brick.

"You prick, we could sue you for that," she said.

"Go ahead, sue me. I'm a lawyer."

"Your mutt attacked him. I saw it."

"He was on my property against my wishes. That's called trespassing."

"Look at his chinos. They're ruined."

"They didn't fit him anyway. Too big."

Carlito was having difficulty getting his wind back. "He's hurt," Angie said. "Fucking King Kong mutt almost killed him."

"Not exactly. Your boy is just out of breath from polishing his jewels on the fence post."

"It's the dog's fault, man."

"Really. I'll bet your boyfriend wasn't a hurdler on the high school track team, was he?"

Her face tightened into a scowl. "He's not my boyfriend."

"Right. And you're not after Rudy's money."

"And you are an asshole. Just lemme see him."

I stood over her, casting a shadow on Carlito, who was starting to breathe more normally. I said, "No. Tough guy goes in the car first, and he stays there during the entire visit, understand?"

"Yessuh, meesta lawya," she said like a snide servant.

I opened the gate first, then reached down and hiked Carlito to his feet, plucked his beret out of the shrubs lining the fence and propped it on his dome. His head bandage was coming loose at the bottom, white tape jutting out like broken spokes on a wheel. I slung his arm over Angie's shoulder, stood back and watched her help him back to her car, a brand-new black two-door Lexus she'd probably purchased with whatever they'd found in Rudy's safe-deposit box.

"They're awake," Carmen said when I came back inside. "Max's barking did it."

"He was a little upset," I said.

"Is that guy all right?" Looking toward the street.

"Yeah, unfortunately."

Dale was in the living room, sitting close to Rudy. Albert was curled up in the leather easy chair, still groggy from his nap. "Someone's here to see you, buddy," Dale told Rudy. Turning to me. "J., you think we should let her see him? I mean, with his daughter on her way here today?"

Rudy's head jerked oddly when Dale mentioned his daughter, and for a moment he seemed more fully alert. Then that hint of a silly grin crept back onto his face. "Where's my daughter?"

I told him she wasn't here yet, just as Carmen led Angie into the living room, where she stopped by the big window. "Hey, papa. How's my big daddy?" A plastic smile clicking on.

"Angie?" He was on his feet, Dale rising beside him, awkwardly standing by. She stayed where she was, though.

"Wanna come home with me now, papa?"

Rudy shook his head.

"Why not?"

"J.," Dale said, "we can't let this happen."

"Rudy," I said, "Kimberley is coming here to see you, later today. Why don't you stick around a little longer, until she gets here."

Angie turned on the charm. "I'm leaving now, papa. Right now. You coming?"

"Okay. Sure."

"Just wait until you see Kimberley, Rudy," I said. "Then if you still want to go with Angie, we'll give her a call."

Rudy paused, his eyes meeting mine. "Okay."

"Huh," Angie muttered. "Call me, my ass. That's bullshit, daddy, they won't call me. You wanna come home wit me, we do it now, that's it."

Angie and I were shoulder to shoulder with Rudy now, like bodyguards. "I . . . think I wanna go home," Rudy said slowly, as if he knew what he was saying.

"J.," Dale said.

I put a hand on his shoulder. "Listen, Rudy—"

"Let him go," Carmen said from the doorway.

Dale's face went a shade lighter. "What?"

"I think you should let him go." Carmen folded her arms. "She's his wife, and you can't keep him against his will. He says he wants to go, you need to let him go."

"Car," I said, not sure what I was hearing.

"J., trust me on this. I think I'm right."

Angie nodded. "Fuckin A, the lady's making a lotta sense to me." Walking over to take Rudy by the hand, leaving Dale marooned between the couch and coffee table.

"Bye-bye," Albert called softly from his chair. Rudy turned and waved meekly.

Something felt wrong, but I couldn't place it. All I could do was stand by as Carmen handed Rudy his gym bag, giving him a quick kiss on the cheek before Angie whisked him outside.

"God," Dale said. "This is awful."

But I know Carmen's instincts for people to be very good, and

I wanted to know what she'd seen that Dale and I had obviously missed.

She raised an eyebrow when I asked. "Know what first got my attention? The crosswords. I know you never bother with them, J." Then she nodded at Dale. "Apparently, neither do you."

Dale said he didn't get it. "Well," she said, "I like doing the one in the newspaper every night, before I go to bed. It helps relax my mind. So, the last week, with you and Rudy here, too, it was starting to bug me. I'd flip to the crossword and it would be done already. Wait a sec." She slid into the dining room, where I could hear a cabinet door open and close. Then she came back in carrying an armful of half-folded newspapers from the recycling pile I keep, selected a few pages at random, and held out the solved puzzles.

"Rudy was doing the crosswords," I said.

"So what?" Dale said.

"He's supposed to be suffering from dementia."

"Yeah, but how do you know he can't still do crosswords?" Dale said.

"It's not just that," Carmen said. She told us the crosswords had got her thinking, so the last few days, she'd concentrated on watching Rudy's behavior when he thought no one else was looking. "The only times he exhibited true signs of dementia were when we were with him," she said. "But when he thought he was alone he seemed to act more normal. I even caught him watching *60 Minutes* a few nights ago."

"But why would he fake it?" Dale said. "That girl is still out for his money regardless."

Carmen admitted she didn't know.

Something I'd just seen bothered me. "I'll tell you what got him out the door right there," I said. "Did you notice, as soon as I mentioned Kimberley showing up here, he seemed to get hot on leaving."

"That's right," Carmen said.

"I did notice that," Dale said. "But why would he want to avoid seeing her?"

"Don't know," I said. "If she ever shows her face around here we'll ask her."

"Well, I've got to follow them," Dale said. "We know they want to legally rob him, but they could hurt him, too."

"Let him go, Dale," I said. "Whatever he's up to, it's his decision."

"I don't buy that," Dale said. "I think he's just confused. Horribly confused. And he needs me." Dale lowered his gaze. "As you both know by now, the last person who really needed me was in for a major letdown. I'm not going to let that happen again."

"Dale, she's your daughter," Carmen said. "Not a mixed-up client."

"Big difference," I said.

"Oh, really? I don't see how." His voice quivering.

"Okay," I said. "It's your call."

Carmen went upstairs to gather Dale's things, brought them down in a small suitcase I no longer used. Dale and I tried to make a plan, agreeing that they wouldn't be headed for the savings and loan this afternoon—they'd never make it by the five o'clock closing time. He knew Rudy's home address, had copied it from Rudy's expired driver's license one evening while the old man was taking a bath. We figured that Angie would take him home tonight, then maybe get him to an unscrupulous M.D. in the morning, someone who, for a sweet cash payment, would sign off on a document declaring Rudy incompetent. That would pretty much pave the way for Angie to get power of attorney over his finances. It was the simple step Bobby Silver should have taken in the first place, but that day at the law center they'd been too greedy and impatient to make a more intelligent play for the money.

"I don't know what you think you can do for him," I told Dale. I also seriously feared for his safety if push came to shove with Carlito and him. But I didn't tell him so; he knew he'd be in danger.

He smiled like a fatalist. "Don't know what I can do either, but I do know I've got to do something. 'Know what? I feel better already."

Carmen and I mustered a pair of thin smiles between us. Then Carmen wished Dale good luck. I told him to stay in constant touch, to call me collect whenever and wherever he had a need.

"I was wondering," he said to me. "Could you do me a favor?"

"You got it."

"If you could go down to the pier for me every now and then, keep an eye out for Leanne."

I hadn't seen that one coming. "Sure, Dale."

"Who knows, maybe she'll come back by here again," he said.

Fat chance. "Maybe."

Then Max barked from the side yard and the doorbell rang. Dale's face was suddenly so full of hope that I shuddered as he jerked the front door open. Could it be?

It couldn't.

"Mr. Shepard?" That velvety croak in her voice sounding even better in person than it had on the phone.

"No, he's right here," Dale said with a long, tired face for my newest visitor.

Kimberley Kirkmeyer-Munson was tall, almost Dale's height, with soft pink cheeks and enough red curls to fill a pre-Raphaelite portrait. Expensive-looking tailored black pantsuit, gold necklaces and watch, clear fingernails, subtle lipstick. Maybe ten years my senior, but very finely tuned. Her black organizer was cracked open like a menu, three long fingers fanning the page that was tabbed S.

I shook her hand and did a brief introduction with Carmen and Dale, then led her into the living room, where she met Albert with a strained hi across the room. Albert muttered something of a hello, hugging a throw pillow to his chest as if he wished we'd all just leave him alone. Believe me, pal, I wanted to say, I know the feeling.

"So," she said, taking a liberal look around, "where's my father?"

Dale was loitering near the door. "I'm . . . gonna get rolling now," he said. "I'll see you later." Then he slipped out without another word, completing what had to rank as one of the slickest exits ever.

"Rudy just left," I said. "The new bride came by a little while ago and got him."

Her face was hot. "What? Why didn't you stop them?"

"We tried, but he wanted to go."

I thought Kimberley was going to chuck her organizer at my

forehead. "What do you mean, 'he wanted'? You said he's demented!"

"I might have been wrong. Apparently, he seems just fine when nobody's looking." I paused. "And when I told him you were coming this afternoon, his mind seemed to clear. That's why we had to let him go."

"Bastard!"

I held up a hand. "That really isn't necessary."

Kimberley smirked at me, calming down a shade. "No, not you—I mean him. The manipulative old . . . Don't you see? I'm here. He's got me right where he wants me, and now he's milking it." She walked to the front window and looked out at the swaying eucalyptus across the street from my house. "I'm sorry, but Alzheimer's? Huh." Turning to face us. "I think you've been had by a lonely old fool." Her curls shook as she sighed. "I think we've both been had."

Then she laughed without making a sound.

Nineteen

Kimberley stared at the coffee table, her eyes searching for something she wasn't finding. Finally she said, "May I, um, borrow an ashtray?"

I told her it would be better if we went out to the back patio. Carmen went to the kitchen and fished the big glass pitcher of sun tea out of the refrigerator. I went into the china cabinet and located a gold-rimmed ceramic coffee mug that had Elvis Presley's handsome young face painted on the side. The message "Long Live the King" was printed beneath the face. Kimberley did a double take when I handed it to her.

"Thank you."

The stone on her outstretched hand could've blinded me. Christ, the engagement ring I'd bought Carmen was a carat, but it looked like something out of a Cracker Jacks box compared to this rock.

Kimberley seemed to be calming down, which was good timing, because my patience was wearing thin, her crack about my being had still ringing in my ears. I had work to do, had to find out who was behind the law center and look into the so-called consulting firms backing the seminars. This business with Rudy and his daughter was beginning to sound like bad blood, a private matter best settled between them alone.

On the patio I made the obligatory introduction between my guest and Max. "I used to have a dog," she tittered when the color came back to her face. "He wasn't anything like this, though. Does he bite?"

"Only when he's hungry."

Kimberley seemed to get my vibe. Eschewing further chitchat, I watched her put her shades on and light a cigarette. Carmen sat down next to me, handing me a glass of tea.

"My mother died two years ago," Kimberley said. "Pancreatic

cancer, really sudden thing." Sucking on her smoke. "Three weeks after they saw it, she was gone. I barely had time to plan the funeral." She frowned, probably not liking the sound of that, being put out to have to bury your mother. Sitting in the speckled shade of the peppertree, her red hair seemed electrified. "My dad wasn't prepared for a lot of things. I mean, at all."

"You wouldn't know it from his portfolio," I said.

"That was all Mom's doing. She never worked, but she was a smart lady, grew up in New York City, father was a banker. Graduated from Vassar ages ago. After Dad retired, she knew his retirement wouldn't be much if they just sat on what they had, so she educated herself in investments."

"Rudy didn't mind her taking over?"

She shook her head no. "My father never wrote a single check, paid a single bill the whole time they were married, far as I know. Mom was the homemaker, but she handled all the finances, too. Dad's job was to bring home the bacon, mow the lawn on Saturdays, roll out the cans on trash night."

She told us that Rudy was a power-company guy, forty-two years, made a good but modest living, happy with his position and never pushing for promotion.

"An engineer?"

"Safety inspector. All the ladders and catwalks, plant lighting, railings, anything that could cause an injury—and a lawsuit—if it wasn't properly maintained." She looked away. "He was a glorified hall monitor, if you want to know the truth, but he was also a heck of a witness for the company if a worker sued. He has that . . . face. You know, the Look. Very innocent."

"We know," Carmen said.

"What's this got to do with you?" I asked Kimberley.

She tilted back her head and stretched her long, freckled neck, purging a smooth jet of smoke. "I think he's getting back at me for not rescuing him after Mom died. At least, that's my best guess."

"He thought you would take over once she was gone?" I said.

"I offered to move him up to Seattle with me, but he doesn't go for the weather up there." Flicking her ashes into the Elvis cup. "Tried to teach him how to write the bills, balance his checkbook. He took that really personally, and frankly, I got sick of his attitude, you know? I said fine, forget it, wrote to his creditors, got all his basic bills put on automatic debit. The rest I had Mr. Dobbs and the savings and loan handle for a small monthly fee. Dobbs has done such a good job with it, I'd almost forgotten about him until he called."

I chugged from my tea and leaned forward. "So what's the bottom line?"

Kimberley took her time answering. "You seem to think either he's fine, or maybe he's in and out. Well, I say he's fine. I think he's just punishing me for having left him alone." A tear shook loose, then another, and another. "That would be so like him."

"But you offered to take him," Carmen said. "You tried to help."

Kimberley wiped her eyes. "That's true, I did, but not on his terms. My father is a very stubborn man."

"You really think he'd go and blow his entire nest egg just to get to you?" I asked.

Her self-assured manner seemed to be failing her, and she stared up into the peppertree awhile, composing herself, then snuffed out her cigarette, little Elvis smiling on.

"Honestly?" she said. "I have no idea."

When I called Tamango Perry on his cell phone, he was at home doing laundry in his garage, having a beer while he folded clothes.

"First real break I've had all day," he said, sounding tired.

"Sorry. If this is a bad time—"

"No, no, don't mention it, I was going to call you tonight anyway. I thought you might like to know that my department's law center investigation is going nowhere so far."

"How is that?" I asked.

He paused, and I could hear the rumble of appliances behind him. "They took my statement. I don't know what they're going to do with me, because I resisted the many suggestions that were made during the interview."

"Suggestions?"

"That you were involved in that fire."

"You told the truth."

244 ≡ John DeCure

"About both you and Mr. Bleeker. The chief wasn't happy, but then, he shouldn't have taken my statement."

"Why'd they do it if they knew you'd hurt their case?"

"They didn't know what I'd say. It was a test." I heard him swig his beer. "I suppose you could say I failed."

"They're going to fire you," I said.

"We shall see." A long silence, then he said, "I am not afraid of that." As if he needed to convince himself.

"Listen, whatever I can do."

The line was silent, and I imagine that Tamango had stopped just to think, such was his deliberate nature. "The best thing you can do, J., is to find out what they're hiding."

I told him that was why I was calling, recounted my conversation with Mr. Carpio, the bakery owner. Then I described the flyers. He reminded me not to forget that the law center had been torched. Somehow, his cop's instinct was telling him, the arson angle might be important. There was a database the insurance industry used to track suspicious fires and the claims that arose from them.

"How do I access the database?" I asked.

"I can't help you with that," he said. "I can't really help you with anything right now, not with my chief watching me so closely."

"Oh." I didn't know much about the insurance business. This was going to be difficult.

"Can't you get someone at the bar to help you investigate?" he said after a stretch of silence.

"There's something I forgot to mention. I got suspended from work."

"Oh."

Then I had an idea. "But there is one guy, an investigator. He's good, too. And he owes me."

Duke Choi set down his chiliburger and stared at me, his mouth ajar. "You're fucking kidding me, right?"

"Jeez, Duke."

"And you still owe me lunch, it's still your turn to buy." Taking another bite out of his burger, the chili dripping out the bottom like mud sliding down a canyon wall. "This doesn't count."

We were at the original Tommy's on Rampart and Beverly, a place I felt was far enough away from the bar that no one we worked with would see us meeting. Eating our burgers and chugging cans of soda outdoors, standing up beside the chest-high counters that run along the walls of the place. Duke had his maroon knit tie draped over his shoulder so he wouldn't spatter it with grease. I'd gone casual in jeans and a Hawaiian print today. The air was warm and still and the noonday sun was so exacting that even the bum begging for change on the sidewalk was wearing shades.

With his weak mustache and a thin-lipped mouth that seems quick to smile, Duke looks more like the register guy at 7-Eleven than an investigator, but he's smart as hell and a very hard worker. Typically the smallest man in any crowd, Duke once told me he was so runty when he emigrated here as a teen that his Stateside relatives renamed him after John Wayne, thinking that might somehow boost his stature. Apparently it did nothing but identify him as a major pussy who thought he was a cowboy, and guaranteed him a steady share of thrashings on the way to and from school.

"What do you mean, it doesn't count?" I said. "These are the world's greatest hamburgers." I opened the bun on mine. "Look at the size of this tomato, it's like a manhole cover."

He belched. "Tastes like one too."

"Next time we'll hit that Thai place on Vermont."

Duke held up his hand. "Look, whatever you feed me, I can't get involved in this with you. I looked you up on the AS four hundred this morning." The AS 400 is the bar discipline unit's internal computer system. "You're classified. That means you're hot. Anyone checking you out will get checked out too."

I put down my food. "Know why? I stumbled into that UPL mill in Glendale. Now somebody connected to it wants me out of the way."

Duke chewed on his burger and waited. "You know that for a fact?"

I didn't know shit at the moment, but Duke didn't need to know that. "Call it an instinct."

He noisily vacuumed the bottom of his orange-soda can with

his straw. I thought he was weighing my proposition favorably, until he said, "I don't want to offend you, buddy, but you kinda gave the bar a bit of a black eye at just the wrong time, right when this disciplinary review committee's got us under a microscope."

"Oh, please."

"No, I'm serious. A lot of people we work with think what you did was pretty selfish, taking over that guy's probation monitoring without your manager's approval, and . . ." He shrugged. "You know."

"No, I don't know."

"Trying to destroy those files."

"You don't believe I would do that, Duke."

He smiled. "Course I don't. But that's only 'cause I know you."

Maybe I blew it by not buying him lunch at a fancier place, but I was getting tired of having my chain jerked. Duke can be persistent, which is good if you're an investigator, but he can also be obtuse. My plan had been to let him make the decision to assist me freely, but he didn't seem headed there anytime soon. Duke needed a nudge in the right direction.

"How's Lynn?" I asked. "She still living with your folks?"

Lynn Choi is Duke's youngest sister, a sweet round-faced girl who met exactly the wrong guy the first year she was in America. He started out as the classic nice-guy boyfriend, very bright, a senior, headed off to college in the fall. The kind who loves puppies and walks on the beach, a patient listener to whom the lonely Lynn gravitated like a magnet. But he had a darker side that wanted to dominate her, and it wasn't long before her parents began noticing nicks and bruises on their daughter's face and arms. By the time Duke tried to intervene, the guy had started her on ecstasy and crack, which he was apparently dealing to the privileged punks on campus with a taste for danger and way too much time on their hands.

I was working on a forgery case with Duke back then, and one morning when he came to my office to help me sort documents, I noticed a ripe shiner under his left eye, a deep scratch on his neck, and a cartoonish bump on his forehead. I said to Duke, I told you, don't mess with your cat's food when she's eating. He erupted in hysterical guffaws that quickly morphed into heavy sobs. I was pretty much taken aback, and my secretary, Honey Chavez, shot me a what-the-hey glance from her cubicle when I got up to shut my door. Then I sat back down and heard Duke's story.

He'd gone to see Lynn's boyfriend, found him at the local bowling alley lounge, where he conducted his business, told him he had a message from his sister, that the two of them were through, end of story, so leave her alone. In short, the message was not well received and Duke was followed out to his car. He tried to defend Lynn's honor, but he gave up a lot of size to the boyfriend and wasn't much of a fighter anyway. The goon had stood over Duke, telling him the prom was next week and Lynn better be ready, " 'cause we're gonna party, you know what I mean." Then he took a piss on Duke while Duke was facedown on the pavement, his eye swelling shut, a couple of the goon's friends laughing.

The last detail of Duke's story really frosted me, and I said so. Next thing you know, he's asking me—no begging me—to do this one thing for his sister. No way, I said, she's eighteen, I'm thirty-one, I'll look like a dirty old man. Well, how else will she ever break away? Duke asked me. A statement needed to be made, a simple one: Don't fuck with Lynn Choi anymore. He'd tried to make it himself, and failed. Their parents were immigrants, his father nearing sixty and even tinier than he. None of the big-talking relatives were worth a damn in a situation like this. She was still vulnerable, and Mr. Wrong knew it.

A week later I squeezed into a rented dinner jacket and took a somewhat bewildered Lynn Choi to her prom. The statement got made, and the live band wasn't halfway bad, either. That girl could dance.

Duke frowned. "Lynn's great, thanks for asking." Eyeballing me as if I was about to shake him down. "All A's her first year."

"Loyola Marymount, right?"

"She moved on campus this quarter. Going out for lacrosse." Dropping his burger wrappers and empty soda into a trash can next to us.

"I'm happy for her."

"Yeah," he muttered. "Me too."

I flashed him the shit-eater. "No, really, that is wonderful news, Duke. The folks must be proud. She dating anyone special?" Finishing my burger with one final chomp.

He sighed long and slowly, like an inner tube losing air. "Okay, J., I get the point. Like a goddamned stick in the eye."

"Come on, Duke. We're friends."

"Okay okay, just cut it, will you? What do you need me to do?"

"I'm glad you asked."

"Ho boy."

I think his burger was giving him indigestion.

I filled him in on everything I knew, gave him copies of the flyers, told him what Tamango Perry had said about the arson probably being important.

Duke said, "I know the database he's talking about, it's set up by the NICB." He noticed my blank expression. "Stands for National Insurance Crime Bureau. Any time a building gets torched, they enter data on the insurance claimant, the concerned parties, who the carrier is, losses claimed. The idea is to keep track of who's claiming what. The true scammers tend to buy their policies all over the map."

"What'll you do about the law center?"

"That'll be my starting point. I can go to Glendale, pull the business license, trace ownership on the address, take it from there. I'll do the same on these consulting outfits, check their slates, the statements of domestic stock on file, articles of incorporation, whatever I can get my hands on. See where it leads me."

I walked Duke back to his car, a dented black Toyota Celica that needed a wash sometime last month. We shook hands. Tommy's was still packing them in, a line ten deep calling out orders to the waiting fry cooks.

"Thank you, man," I said. "Anything I can do . . ."

Duke's reflexive quick smile was there, but the eyes were full of dread. "Just don't call me at work. The atmosphere there's really wacked right now."

I wanted to let him in on my suspicion that someone in management was working both sides of this law center thing, but Duke looked freaked enough for the time being. He started his engine and rolled down his window, then said, "How do you intend to keep me out of this? 'Cause I need my job."

I hadn't thought of that. Usually you use your investigator as your source when you mount evidence in a court proceeding, no questions asked.

"This isn't even a case yet," I said, "and the only lawyer involved is already dead. I wouldn't worry about it." Not now, at least. Not yet.

"What about that other guy, your probationer? He's involved."

"Not really. He's just the dupe whose license got used for the UPL side of it."

Duke smirked. "Oh yeah, I'm sure he had no idea. *How* much did you say they were paying him?"

I stepped back from the dusty Toyota, eyeing the chrome mud flaps. On a two-door Celica? Now there was a classic Duke Choi touch.

"Call me," I said.

He backed up, put it in drive, and pulled up alongside me as I walked to the Jeep wagon. "I forgot to tell you, Lynn says hi."

I nodded and walked on, muttered, "Not with a ten-foot pole, buddy," too low for anyone to hear me.

Twenty

Weeknights are league nights at the Sea-
shore Lanes, so if you want to bowl and aren't part of the program,
you've got to get in there and out of there early. Carmen, Albert,
and I arrived a little before four. I gave the counter guy an extra
ten to put us in lane 1, way over by the wall. That way Albert
could roll with his unique two-handed shot-put style with a min-
imum of embarrassment. The late-afternoon crowd was sparse,
maybe five other lanes taken. The nearest bowlers were in lane 6,
two thick-necked football jocks and a skinny blond girl with a
mouth full of metal, somebody's kid sister. The guys were perving
on Carmen as we headed past them such that I had to stare back
until they looked away.

Carmen knew how good she looked in just jeans and a tee under
a black V-necked sweater.

"Jealous," she said.

"Not jealous," I said. "Proprietary."

She held out the fingers on her left hand like a fan, displaying
her ring for me. "This doesn't mean you own me."

"You must not have read the inscription inside the band. Para-
graph two, line three. With this ring, I thee own."

She sighed. "Lawyers."

I caught her from behind and squeezed her, tried to kiss her
neck and ear. For a second or two, it felt like we were alone together on a date. Until Albert said, "Carmen, c-can I go first?"

I stopped coming on to her, having learned some time ago that
it's futile to even try to compete. She told her brother absolutely,
he could go first. Then she kissed him on the cheek, straightening
the collar of his Dodgers warm-up jacket.

We settled in, and I noticed that distinct bowling alley aroma, a
thousand sweaty, rubber-soled insteps behind the cashier's counter

area. Down here in the lanes, the secondary smoke from last night's action still clung to the furniture. A white banner hung from the ceiling above the rows of pins and said, "Seashore Lanes, Where Friends Come to Bowl." No friends of mine, I was thinking. We were not two miles from my house, yet I hadn't set foot inside these walls in probably twenty years.

The rest of the hanging banner, the part in smaller print, said: "Please Drink Responsibly." Hey, now there was an idea. Convincing myself that I needed a drink to take the edge off, I said I'd be right back and told Albert he could bowl for me in the first frame. A bar called the Tiki Room was built into the corner of the lobby nearest the parking lot, with smoked-glass windows and a mock awning covered with dead palm leaves ringing the place. The interior was so dark I had to stop in the doorway to adjust. Stepping in from the fluorescent glow of the alley was like falling down a mine shaft, and I could see only the general shapes of patrons recessed against the furniture as I found the bar and ordered. The place was devoid of conversation—just a smattering of Responsible Drinkers getting hammered after work.

I bought two longneck Buds, a Coke, and a bowl of popcorn to take back with me. As I turned to go, two men at a table in the back caught my eye, their figures pulsing red from a fake tiki torch that was slowly shorting out above their table. The guy in back, facing me, his forehead high, like Dale's. The other one with his back turned to me, a smaller man, gray hair. I squinted, which helped not at all, thinking: Rudy?

The bartender, a watchful fat guy with a mirthless face, handed me my change. My hands were too full to do a serpentine weave through a clutter of tables and limbs, and besides, it made no sense that those two would be together, here. Rudy was with Angie again, probably in Glendale. Dale was probably parked down the street in his ratty old Buick, watching them. I eased back out of there and down to lane 1. Albert was up, tiptoeing toward the line for another slow-motion two-hander, the ball rolling with a wobbly hum, eight pins going over like felled trees.

Carmen clapped. "Yes!"

"Nice shot, champ," I said, pulling on my smelly rubber shoes. Albert's black eyes widened as he mumbled something to himself.

He scooted back to the ball return, a smile forming, the first smile I'd seen on his sweet face since the day we went surfing.

When Carmen and I first met she was taking her brother bowling pretty regularly. Albert liked to bowl but she always chafed against the ritual, sitting indoors on beautiful days, surrounded by dirty ashtrays. I'd sprung her by taking both of them surfing, gave Albert a lesson, with help from my friend Jackie Pace. The session had been an unqualified success, the start of something exotic and new for Albert, who was stoked beyond words. It was a start, as well, for Carmen and me. But now, it seemed, he might not surf again for some time, if at all. These last two years I'd done my share of entertaining Albert with ball games and go-kart rides, miniature golf—the usual. But that stuff was designed to kill an afternoon, nothing more. Riding waves together was something far more challenging and meaningful. It hurt me to think it might be gone.

"Thought I saw Dale and Rudy up there, in the bar," I said. Carmen's brown eyes flashed. "I know, I know. It couldn't have been them."

She took her beer and set it down without drinking from it. "You're obsessing. I've seen you this way enough to know."

I took a drink as Albert lined up his next roll. "All I said was I thought I saw them. That's not obsessing. I haven't mentioned them all aft—"

"Shhh. Albert's up again."

Just like that, the mood between us had gone chilly.

Albert let fly with a shot so slow the ball could've left snail tracks. Willing the roll left, left, left, his body contorted into a question mark. His ball nicked the four pin, and pins seven and eight wobbled before they went down. A nice spare. Carmen clapped, as always. I took another drink.

Obsessing? My ass. I'll show you obsessing.

Carmen was next, left the six and ten, then rolled a gutter ball trying to pick up the split.

I got up and selected a heavy black ball from the rack behind me, lined up, and flung it down the lane with all the frustration of the past week behind it. The pins exploded in every direction, so loudly that the jocks nearby took instant notice. A strike.

Albert said Good one, J., then got up to take his turn. Carmen didn't speak until I slid in next to her at the scorer's table, her black hair covering the sides of her face. I noticed my frame was empty.

"You're supposed to put an X right here," I said.

But she stayed perfectly still. "Albert and I are moving back home. This isn't working out."

I tried to hold her hand, but she withdrew it. "Car," I said, "wait. Don't decide that now. Dale and Rudy just cleared out. Before them, you know how long I went without having a house-guest?"

"It isn't just that." She shrugged. "Although the packed house certainly didn't help."

I put my hand on her shoulder. "Look, you know how sorry I am about what happened to your brother. It's my fault, had I been closer by, no one would have touched him. But it happened. I screwed up." She was looking way down the lane. "When are you gonna forgive me? When are we gonna get past this?"

Albert's next roll had a lot more pop than usual, and he nearly fell over the end line letting it go. Gutter ball. Walking back he hung his head. Suddenly I felt like a jerk for rolling that strike.

"I don't know," Carmen said. "I don't know."

Driving home, we watched the lights along the Pacific Coast Highway pop on all around us, front-lighting a sky at dusk the color of red plums with the skins peeled away. I offered to make bow-tie pasta with sweet Italian sausage, one of Carmen's favorites. "That sounds nice," she said. Noncommittal, but it was something. We hadn't discussed the timing of their departure, but at least they were staying for dinner.

I stopped at the Food Barn market on Main and ran in alone to pick up a pack of sausage. When I came out again, the air was moist and salty and weighted with the hushed rumble of breaking waves. It was a shadowy night. Smoky clouds puffed their way across a white moon bright with scars. The ATM across the street stood empty beneath the yellow safety light. I thought of the awkward panhandler who'd hit me up for change there on that wet, windblown night not long ago. Maybe the same guy I'd knocked out in the parking lot the day Albert got punched. Something still gnawed at me about the way he and his friends had glared at me when I accused them of doing the deed on Albert. Something inconsistent with everything I knew about exploiters and the way they will delight in their own wickedness, as if it is part of their reward. There was too much indignation in those eyes that morning in the parking lot, not a trace of sadistic swagger in the faces around me as I formulated my patterns of attack and defense. I remembered the girl's shrill cry from inside the big delivery van. Crying out a name. Kurt.

I wondered now if the guy was all right, pictured him in a big hospital bed with a girl at his side. Someone to hold his hand, at least.

Inside the car, Carmen told me I looked terrible. I didn't want to tell her what was on my mind, so I didn't say anything.

The house felt bigger and colder now that Dale and Rudy were gone. I turned up the heater and flipped on some downstairs lights, hoping to improve the atmosphere. Albert got Carmen's permission to watch *Jeopardy* and settled in on the living-room carpet with a book about fire trucks of all shapes and sizes. I was in the kitchen, boiling water and mashing up the sausages with a fork, when Carmen answered a knock at the front door.

"You have a visitor," she announced with a seen-it-all face.

Therese Rozypal stood a foot inside the door, as if she feared entering any farther.

"Hi, J., don't look so glad to see me."

"No, I am. Just, I'm surprised." I smiled and took her overcoat, a full-length slate gray beauty from Bloomingdale's. Therese was in a navy dress suit with a white blouse buttoned all the way up, very smart, a black leather portfolio under one arm. Her hair was braided thickly down both sides and tied at the ends with thin blue ribbons. Carmen stood by impassively until I made a forced introduction.

"We work together," I heard myself saying, as if that would cover it.

Therese apologized for arriving without warning but said there were things going on at the bar she felt she had to talk to me about in person. Since she lived in Newport Beach and headed right by here on her way home, well . . . I thought her justification was a tad too eagerly delivered. Carmen took it in with the poker face she puts on when she studies a situation. I told Therese I was cooking and invited her into the kitchen.

"She's beautiful," Therese said, leaning against the counter. I pulled out a frying pan and put it on the stove.

"I think so too."

"When's the wedding?"

I told her we hadn't yet set a date. "So what's the bad news from work? My free vacation over?" I wanted to change the subject.

"Intake has six complaints on Dale Bleeker." She pulled a handful of documents out of her portfolio. I turned on one of the burners, poured a little oil in the frying pan and set it back down. The papers were complaint summary screens Therese had pulled up on her computer and printed. Each alleged nonperformance on estate planning and bankruptcy filings, and listed Dale's address as the Glendale Lo-Cost Law Center. Your standard fallout from a UPL operation. All of them mailed in to the bar over the last few days.

"They probably heard about the fire," I said.

She nodded. "That makes sense."

I dropped the sausage into the pan. "Thanks for the info."

"You're welcome." Her blue eyes seemed trapped inside a thought. "I should go. I feel like I'm intruding."

I told her she wasn't, asked her to stay for dinner. Therese said no but let me pour her a glass of burgundy, which she sipped standing up. The sausage gave off a sweet-and-spicy scent as I turned it slowly. "There's another case," she said, putting down her glass.

"Show it to me."

"I can't. I mean, I couldn't print it without them knowing. There was this classified code, um, next to your name."

I stopped stirring and took the sausage off the burner, not sure how it felt to be investigated. Me, investigated, the guy whose job it is to carry a bat on my shoulder against bad lawyers, to take aim and swing on the liars and forgers and cheats and psychos, those who fabricate and obfuscate and misappropriate for a living. I didn't feel anything but a slow, rising anger in my gut.

I'm not one of them.

"You okay, J.?"

I stirred the sausage some more. "What's the summary say?"

"It follows the basic outline of the story the news reported after the fire. You know, that you might have caused it to destroy evidence. To assist a probationer who might have paid you to become involved on his behalf."

"Moral turpitude?" That's the catchall charge for lawyer dishonesty.

"Multiple acts."

"That stuff about Dale paying me, I gotta give it to them, that's creative." I slugged down a mouthful of wine. "Has anybody bothered to look at his car? What money?" Christ, that sounded catty. "That's not what I meant."

"I know. Somebody's got it out for you right now."

"Who's the complainant, that Glendale police chief, Conforti? His detective, the one who called me and practically told me to go there the night of the fire? Guy knows I came along after and pulled that dirtbag Silver out of there, told me he thinks it was arson and maybe even murder. Conforti took him right off the case."

She shook her head. "It was an SBI." That stands for state bar investigation, which means a case opened from within the office as opposed to a complaint initiated by a member of the public.

Instantly I knew.

"Why am I not surprised?" I said. This was Eloise Horton's long-awaited shot at causing me permanent grief. "So, Eloise thinks she's finally got me on something worse than a late F-due report."

"J.," she said. "It wasn't Eloise. I checked the reporting codes."

"I didn't know that was possible."

She smiled a little. "It is if you know the right people in Intake."

I pictured a weak-kneed male complaint analyst gazing up from his keyboard at Therese, teamwork suddenly a hot concept to him.

"Stanislav Greuber."

"He goes by Skip," I said.

"I can see why. Stanislav's pretty terrible."

Skip Greuber, my former manager. Supposedly a friendly face, as recently as a few days ago at Yang Chow. Unless he was just stroking me to find out what I knew.

"I don't get it," I said. "Eloise is the one who wants my ass on a platter. You've seen her in action."

"I don't know," Therese said slowly. "Eloise is just . . . Eloise."

"Yeah, the original Ice Queen."

Therese stared into her wineglass and watched the grapes swish around the edges. Her eyes were pensive and a darker blue just now. "She's not out to get you."

"You don't consider this out to get me?"

She paused as if she was trying to gauge something between us. "Here's the thing," she said, straightening herself. "You're a good trial attorney, and she isn't, but she's the one who's supposed to be in charge." I must not have looked like I was sold, because she added, "Don't be offended." Working up to something bigger.

I dropped the pasta into the boiling water. Max barked outside, reminding me that he was hungry for his dinner.

"I'll try not to."

"I think you intimidate her. Probably without even knowing it, but you do."

I'd never looked at Eloise from that perspective. "She could still be after me. She did suspend me."

Therese's forehead wrinkled just above her eyebrows. "But look how she did it. With full pay."

"I can thank my union rep for that."

"Maybe, but that was because of how Eloise handled you. That was her response to a situation that had been building up a long, long time. She acted on emotion, not logic or reason. Women do that."

Our eyes were on each other briefly, as if we were both considering the subtext of Therese's words. An imagined scenario rushed forth, and I saw Therese setting down her wine, stepping up to me, her breath sweet and warm, shaking that blond hair loose as her lips sought mine. Hell, I'm engaged, I thought, I wouldn't grope her for a kiss, but then, what might I do if she was the aggressor? Wouldn't I be less culpable somehow, a victim of the moment? No, that was crap and I knew it. I couldn't picture myself in a chair opposite Carmen on the set of some cheesy talk show, explaining to Phil or Sally Jessie how my affair with another woman "just happened" as some outraged housewife the size of a line-backer jeered me from the front row.

But she was standing so close to me now, cheeks aglow, the pink tip of her tongue tickling her front teeth for an instant, stealing my breath away. It still could have happened—spontaneously—and I was not exactly doing any backpedaling. My brain tapped out an urgent message to the southern region: Down, boy.

"Okay, Skip Greuber started it up," I said. "Who'd they assign as the investigator?"

"Another weird name that was easy to memorize." Pausing for effect, as if she were about to make an important announcement. "Duke Choi."

"You're kidding," I said absently, thinking, *Duke Choi! I'm hosed! How could they know?* The L.A. office employed maybe thirty investigators, so the odds were thirty-to-one it was a coincidence. Maybe Duke had told someone he was meeting me at Tommy's, and it got back to Greuber. No, I'd expressly told Duke to keep it quiet, and Duke is not one to go looking for controversy.

How could they know?

She rolled her eyes. "I know, I've never heard of an Asian Duke. Do you know him?"

I told her I did.

"He any good?"

I drank the last of my wine. Across from me, Therese just kept looking extremely fine, the way her legs were gently crossed as she leaned on the counter, the graceful tilt of her head. Look away, the voice in my head boomed. Look away. I did, and my mind's eye hit rewind on a tape of my lunch with Duke. The voice asking, How much did you tell him, man? Ah, well, just about *everything,* man.

"He's good," I said.

"Why didn't you invite Therese to stay for dinner?" Carmen said, lighting a candle on the dinner table.

I was standing beside her, dropping salad onto Albert's plate as he tugged at the sides of his sweatshirt and grimaced. Albert is not big on greens.

"I did. She couldn't stay."

Carmen stayed silent a few beats. "Uh-huh."

"What's that supposed to mean?"

She lit the second candle and blew out the match. "I saw the way she looked at you. She's very attractive."

"I suppose."

Carmen sniffed at that. "She likes you."

"We work together. That's it."

"You and I met at work."

'That's different. I was available then, so were you."

As soon as I said it, I realized my approach was getting off track. This wasn't so much about how I felt about Therese as it was about telling Carmen how I felt about her.

"God," she said, "you're such a romantic. What are you trying to say, if you were available now and she was, it would be open season? And obviously, she is available."

I came around the table. "I'm sorry. That's not what I meant." I put my arms around her shoulders, but she pushed me away.

"Don't tell me you're not attracted to her," she said with a tone of bitterness that surprised me. "I know you are."

Christ, I was ready to tell Carmen what I knew she wanted to hear, but she seemed intent on making me suffer. I felt my temperature rising.

"Sort of the way you're attracted to my buddy Mick."

She stepped back. "After what he did? Dream on."

"Oh come on," I said, "cut it about 'what he did,' will you please? I'm not gonna even defend him again on that, it's so stupid." I backed off, turning to the stove, where a yellow ceramic serving bowl sat waiting to be filled. Damn. We never used to argue like this. I sucked in a deep breath. "The reality is, just because we're together doesn't mean we'll never be attracted to someone else. We're not living in a cave."

"Sometimes it certainly feels like it."

I paused again, stemming my anger. "You'll meet people you're attracted to, so will I. But that's not the point. The point is whether you act on it."

Carmen's arms were folded tightly across her tee. Shit, I thought.

All she was looking for was some reassurance, and I had to make my point, give her the old clinical assessment.

"As far as I'm concerned," I went on, "you're the only woman I ever see, Car. To me, you're it."

I waited for a response but got none. The electric clock built into the range buzzed quietly. Outside, Max was topping off his dinner with a little game of street hockey, batting his empty food bowl around the yard. I turned toward the stove.

"What? That's it?" Carmen said. "Keep going. I want to hear more." She was still upset, but a tiny glimmer of a smile was form-ing on her lips. Albert caught it—and laughed.

"Yeah, J., we w-w-wanna . . . hear more," he stammered. His demand made Carmen laugh, too.

I came back to the table without the pasta, looking into Car-men's eyes, point-blank. "Okay, then."

That's Albert for you. Retarded? Sure. Sometimes you forget the guy is even there, he's so reserved. Other times, like now, you realize he's the smartest person in the room.

Twenty-one

Dale called during dinner to tell me he was camped out down the street from Rudy's house in an old but nice neighborhood just north of the Glendale Freeway.

"Think Angie and Carlito are sitting on Rudy for now," he said. "The new Lexus is in the garage. Carlito went out briefly to a liquor store for cigarettes and a few groceries this morning in his own ride."

"What's he drive?" I asked.

"A rust orange Camaro with skinny low-profile tires. Looks older than the Buick."

That was it for the report.

"Oh, one other thing of interest happened this afternoon. Angie went around the house and shuttered all the windows, as if she wanted to hide what they were doing in there."

To me it was an ominous detail.

"I don't like it," I said.

"I know," Dale said. "The thing is, if they're just hanging around, biding their time before they try the bank with Rudy again, what would they have to conceal? There's nothing illegal about waiting, so maybe . . . I don't know."

"Unless they've figured out he's not really bats," I said. "Maybe he's doing their crosswords too."

Dale didn't respond to my little crack. "But why wait? Angie could still drain his account."

"Not without his consent. And that manager Dobbs, he's not gonna let her liquidate that much business with his bank if he can help it."

"But if Rudy won't give his consent . . ." I could hear Dale's breathing on the line. "Jesus, J., they could be torturing him in there, right now, under my nose."

"I doubt it," I said. That was a lie. I was fully confident that Angie and Carlito were capable of squeezing the life out of that old man to get what they wanted. I just didn't want to encourage Dale to do anything foolishly heroic.

"I'm thinking, tonight, when I go back there, I'll get closer and sneak a peek," he said. "Maybe even slip inside. Bet there's an unlocked door or window somewhere in back."

"Don't, Dale. Stay out of their way."

He chortled. "As if you would."

"What's that supposed to mean?"

A siren passed by Dale's pay phone, and he waited for the noise to die. "Nothing. Just, I feel great, that's all. *Doing* something for a change, instead of watching that big old train come down the tracks, waiting for it to run me over."

"What big train? This sounds like a Johnny Cash song." I paused. "A really bad Johnny Cash song."

I thought I heard him chuckle. "Ah, J.," he said, "I've seen you in action and I know you know what I'm talking about. If you were here right now, you'd do the same, maybe even figure out a way to do the situation one better. Hey, what can I say? I've come to believe that I actually got lucky having you monitor my probation."

"How is that?"

"I've learned something from you. Not to hold back. I want to say thank you for that."

"Well, don't take this the wrong way, but you're not welcome." I knew what this was really about. "Dale, this isn't a makeup test for other things in your life you wish you'd done. Listen to me, do not force the situation with those two, they're bad news."

There was a silence on the other end, and I thought I was getting through. "Say," he said, "I don't suppose you've seen Leanne again, have you?"

Christ, the man could be thickheaded. "Earth to Dale: Did you hear what I said?"

Another pause. "I heard. But lemme tell you, I do miss my little girl. And I need to see her again, to set the record straight. You know, start fresh. And you sort of *promised* you'd look for her, J."

I had my bargaining chip. "I will. Tonight, even, but only if you *promise* you won't play James Bond. That's the deal, boss."

"Fine, okay," Dale said slowly, sounding dejected. "I'll stay put and watch."

I hung up the phone, thinking about Leanne Bleeker's potential whereabouts, but not expecting to find her anywhere near Christianitos. Still, I should look. Not of a mind to reveal my latest entanglement to Carmen, I merely ducked my head into the living room and told her I was taking Max for a walk. Then I threw on a black ski jacket and hooked the big boy up. His tail was wagging so hard he nearly fell over, his naked enthusiasm reminding me of Dale. "Jesus, Max," I said, "don't tell me you're that lonely, too."

The evening was calm and very cold. No moon, and no offshore wind blowing out of the inland valleys, but the humidity was low and the lights of the Port of Los Angeles and Palos Verdes Peninsula rimming the sea to the west looked magnified reflecting off the oil-smooth water. I strolled out onto the pier with Max, straight past the sign that says no bicycles, skates, or pets on the pier— anyone who lives here knows those ordinances are winked at after dark. Two young Hispanic men with fishing gear were walking the other way. When they saw Max, they quickly crossed to the far side, their eyes on him as the big dog lumbered by. Max and I took up a spot just above the surf line. Row after row of white water hissed beneath the pilings. I leaned against the railing and scanned the Northside parking lot, which was not yet closed for the night. A bright orange VW Baja Bug was parked in the first row behind the sand, a guy and a girl leaning against the driver's door in an intimate embrace. A battered Volvo wagon and a nondescript American sedan bearing a county seal on its door took up two spots just outside the lifeguard headquarters. That was the entire scene. No white delivery van, no loitering surfers in the lot. No Leanne Bleeker.

"Hey, J., what's the haps?"

Stone Me Stevie had rolled up behind me on a bright red two-wheeler, a vintage Huffy with white sidewalls and chromed front forks. Despite the nippy weather, he wore only a pair of tattered blue jeans with giant holes in both knees, an unbuttoned Pendleton over a white T-shirt, and cheap thongs on his feet. His dirty blond hair was pulled back into a ponytail, which served to sharpen his angular features and highlight the acne scars on his face and neck. A confirmed surf rat, Stevie was less than a year out of high school but still suffered from a case of arrested puberty, what with his fluttery voice and cheesy mustache and goatee. He was said to be perfectly content living in the guest room above his parents' garage two blocks from the sand, unemployed and with no plans for the future. That is, aside from hitting the most happening parties each weekend, dealing some good-quality weed on the side, and surfing the pier every chance he got.

As usual, he smelled faintly like a roach. The kind you smoke.

I said a terse hello, not wanting to encourage a conversation.

"Great fuckin' run of waves we've had since the New Year, eh man?" he said.

"Mm-hm."

"Been keeping tabs on a tidal calendar at home, making daily entries about wind, swell, and tide. It's been head-high or better sixteen out of the last twenty-two days."

"Awesome."

"Riding a new stick this winter, a little longer for better paddling but really responsive. It's like, I can feel it in my turns, the way, like, on this one left I got this morning, I, like, hit this fat section with all this speed and just laid it on edge . . . And fuck, man! You shoulda seen this air I boosted in the shorebreak, we're talkin' wicked air!"

In my book, an aerial is a typically showy trick with a wretched success rate, and it's very hard on the average surfboard.

I felt I had to ask. "So, Stevie, you land it successfully?"

He stopped to catch his breath. "Well, okay, I fell, but dude, it was *so* radical! Some guy on the beach said he saw it and said he couldn't fuckin' believe I even went for it!"

Blah, blah, blah.

Surfers like Stone Me Stevie bore me to tears with their performance anxiety, as if anyone else gives a shit about how hard they're ripping it up. I stared into the black expanse beyond the surf line, teeth gritted. Good for you, Steve, you *shred,* bro.

Even Max, who loves his outings, looked bored, his coal black eyes glazing. I was ready to shrug Stevie off and stroll up Main, clinging to the slim hope that I might see Leanne or her panhandling boyfriend vying for change outside some establishment. Then I thought of Stevie's tidal calendar.

"You check it here every morning?" I asked.

He beamed. "Damn straight. I mean, you gotta be on it if you wanna score, brah."

I grimaced. "Right." There's nothing like getting unwanted advice, and from this punk, who wasn't even born when I started chasing waves. Shake it off, J., I told myself. "So, you check it in the afternoon and evening, too?"

He shrugged, lighting a cigarette and tossing the match into the foaming drink below the pier. "Yeah, sometimes, if there's swell. You know, pray for a glass-off."

A glass-off occurs when the prevailing afternoon westerly wind dies down, making for smooth wave faces and good surfing conditions. It's a rare treat in these parts.

Max tugged at the leash, looking up at me with a forlorn mug, as if even *he* knew this guy was dumber than the last big turd Max had deposited under the peppertree at home. But I tugged back and told my dog to stay. I had nothing to lose by asking Stevie a few more questions.

"I was wondering if you've seen these guys. Surfers. Not from around here, but they tend to congregate around this white delivery van. You know, like an old UPS truck somebody converted."

He rubbed his handlebars, hit on his smoke, and stared at the sea as if he was concentrating. "The one with the trippy design painted on the sides. Yeah, I've seen that van before."

"How about lately?"

Stevie's brow was still arched in contemplation. "Those dudes are fucking kooks. Shitbag equipment."

"You seen them lately?"

"Not the last couple . . . hey!" A big smile bloomed on his face.

"They're the ones you kicked ass all over! Fuck, man, that was *so* cool! I mean, sometimes you gotta make a statement, right? Like, what's ours is ours, locals *rule*."

"I've told you before, that's not what it was about," I said, raising my voice. "Anyway, you said you hadn't seen them since whenever. When was the last time—"

But Stevie wasn't listening. "Fuck, I wish I'd seen it firsthand. Bam!" He smashed a fist into his hand. "What a day for the local crew, man! You know what? I write shit in my calendar about crowd conditions too, and I swear, man, since that day—and the day those Mexicans got beefed, too—swear to God, the kook factor's dropped off a lot."

"No kidding." He hadn't heard a word I'd said.

He grinned. "I got your back, man."

"Nothing like making a statement," I said. This guy was hopeless. I turned to my dog, who was sitting obediently on his haunches. I tickled his leash. "Let's go, Max. Later, Steve," I said over my shoulder. "Keep the faith, *bro*."

"Hey man," he said, but I kept walking. "I know what you think of me. But you're wrong."

"Good night, Stevie," I said over my shoulder.

"You think I'm a pussy," he called out, "but you're wrong, man. I can back my act."

I stopped and turned to face him. Stevie was standing up now with the bike's chassis between his legs, doing his best to appear sincere. "You know," I said, "you talk so much shit, you end up believing it yourself." I shook my head. "That's pretty sad." I started to go, but pulled up short. "Your attitude stinks. Grow up. You don't own the beach. None of us do."

"You're wrong, man," he said. "I'm not shitting you, I made a statement of my own, kicked a dude's ass that day you got into it with those kooks with the garage-sale sticks."

"Oh, sure."

"No, I did." His tone indignant. "I was S-turning this re-form through to the shorepound, fading into the left, but then I see the right jacking better, so I thought, Fuck it. Changed direction, cut across the peak, then this total barney drops in right in my way. Blows the wave, even dings my rail." Stevie laughed to himself. "Shoulda seen the look on his face, the dork, like he could barely swim. Clueless, man." He caught his breath, looking as if he was enjoying my attention. "So I just, I dunno, like, I just blew it, man, fuckin' shoulder hoppers, not gonna take their shit anymore. I go: Bam!" Smacking a fist into his open palm. "Corked the fucker, sent him straight to the beach."

Stevie's eyes got larger with every stride I took toward that fancy bicycle of his. "Hey, whoa, dude, it's cool," he whined as I grabbed two fistfuls of Pendleton and hoisted him backward off his seat and into the air. He didn't start begging for his life until he was hanging upside down over the railings, staring, eyes bugged, at the walls of white water pancaking into the seawall below.

"What I do, man, what I do?" he cried above the rumble.

"That was a good friend of mine you 'corked,' you little shit. My fiancée's brother, who happens to be a very gentle, mentally handicapped young man."

"Fuck! Sorry, man! I didn't know!"

"Question is, how could a dipshit like you know anything?"

A splash of whitewater kicked up in his face. "Fuck, man, lemme up!" he panted.

"I gotta say, I don't like your tone, Steve. Are you telling me what to do? 'Cause if you are, you're gonna be having a barnacle sandwich for dinner, *bro*. I am not in the mood." I purposely loosened my grip on his ankles.

"Okay, okay, sorry! Please, man, lemme up."

"We have to talk."

"Sure, sure, you got it, let's talk." Still pretty scared as a big line of whitewater burst against the pilings below. "Jesus fucking Christ, man!"

"Don't be taking the Lord's name in vain," I said, letting him slip a few more inches. "He's the only reason you're still alive right now."

"Okay, okay, sorry, man! I'll shut up."

"Somehow I don't think that's entirely possible."

Max barked a few times, letting me know he was growing tired of this scene. I yanked Stevie up and propped him against the railings. His face was drained of color and his skin was shiny with salt water. Max and I stood by, watching him puff little white clouds up into the night. When he recovered, he made a move to pick up the bike, but I planted my shoe on the chain guard.

"Relax, you're not going anywhere yet."

Stevie seemed to be reflecting on his situation. "Look, J., hey," he said, hands out. I ignored him. "What can I say," he said. "I'm sorry, but fuck, man . . ." Twisting, his hands in his jeans.

"But what?"

"It . . . wasn't like I planned it or anything. The dude—" Stopping to think. "Your friend, he kinda cut me off."

I took a few slow, deliberate breaths in an attempt to stay reasonably calm. "You're such a pinhead." Shaking my head. "You said you were fading into the left on that re-form, until you saw the right jacking and cut across the peak. Did it ever occur to you that Albert saw you going left before he started paddling for the right, and maybe he just didn't look back in time to see you'd changed direction?"

Stevie studied my face as if he was trying to gauge the correct answer. "I guess it's possible."

"You guess? I taught him how to surf. He doesn't shoulder-hop. He knows the rules. Are you suggesting otherwise?"

He looked away. "No, man, not at all."

I nodded, frowning. "You have no idea how much trouble you've caused. You know, I told my fiancée, Albert's sister, that when I found the little shit that popped him I'd tap him hard. And don't deny that you tried to cold-cock him. He didn't even see you."

His shoulders quivered. "Hey, really man, I didn't know. I mean, don't—"

"But then my fiancée goes and tells me, 'J., violence begets violence.'" I shook my head. "How do you like that?"

In his only smart move of the night, Stevie didn't venture a comment.

"Right now, I can't say whether I agree or disagree with her viewpoint." I sighed, letting him stew in his juices a bit longer. "You could say I'm on the fence. But I do love her, so I guess I'm willing to try to see things her way." Stevie looked on dumbly. "Which means that for now, you'll remain among the living."

He exhaled like a pearl diver coming up for air. "Whoa. Cool."

"But you and I aren't done. In fact, you're just getting started."

He waited a respectful moment before asking, "Um, whaddaya mean?"

"Have you heard of atonement?"

Stevie looked stumped, then hit on a thought. "Yeah, had it in history class. The Japanese, how they got stuck in those camps out in the desert during World War Two."

My dog and I exchanged sullen eye contact. "You can see why I don't usually surf by the pier," I muttered to Max. Then I stepped off Stevie's fallen two-wheeler. "No, that's internment, Steve. Atonement means making amends for your fuckups."

"Oh." He shrugged. "Well, cool." Then he patted his shirt pocket. The Pendleton's breast pocket had a flap on it, and by some minor miracle, Stevie's Marlboros were still intact. He stuck a cig-arette in his mouth, cupped his hands around a match, and lit up.

The gesture was way too casual for my liking, and I pictured sending the little shit straight back over that railing ass-first. But then I pondered what Carmen would say if and when she found out about it. And she would know, because one of the stops along the path to enlightenment I had in mind for Stevie involved a well-timed apology to Albert. If Stevie showed up on my porch looking like a train had hit him, she'd put it together instantly.

Hit by a train—Christ, I was starting to think like Dale.

Stone Me Stevie puffed away, eyes darting as he fidgeted in place, as if he was sensing that he was not yet out of harm's way. I tried not to think about Albert's bloody face that day on the beach, or his subsequent nightmares. Straining for poise, I bit my lip. Then I righted Stevie's bicycle and handed it to him.

Max and I saw no sign of Leanne Bleeker on our stroll up Main from the pier. The strip was mostly quiet. No one was loitering outside either Clancy's or the Marmaduke, though you could smell the beer, sweat, and cigarettes and hear the pool balls cracking from the sidewalk. The Food Barn was deserted. Across the street, the local fish restaurant, the Captain's Galley, had a few patrons sprin-kled among a lot of empty candlelit tables, but the bar downstairs was bustling, as usual. The Galley bar is a cut above the rest, with lots of polished brass, a wall full of nautical antiques, a respectable happy hour, and a no-shirts-no-shoes-no-service policy that actually gets enforced. It's also the one bar in town with a reputation for attracting women.

My walking pace was leaden. The pasta was giving me heartburn. My conversation with Stone Me Stevie had left me feeling overstimulated but let down, the way I get when I see a horror flick with a lousy ending. The next long block up Main past the restaurant was lined with darkened storefronts and empty sidewalk. Leanne was not in the vicinity, not tonight at least. I wanted to go home. Then I saw, through the Galley's tinted glass, a simple gesture I recognized, and it stopped me. A woman in a black leather jacket on a middle barstool, flipping a pile of strawberry curls off her shoulder as she sipped a margarita. I ordered Max to sit next to the newspaper rack at the entrance and went inside.

I'd put Kimberley Kirkmeyer-Munson up in the Christianitos Inn about two blocks from here. She'd been so put off by traveling all the way from Seattle, then just missing her dad at my place that afternoon, that she didn't want to discuss her next move. At the time, I didn't feel it was my place to direct the action between her and Rudy. I told her I'd call as soon as I heard word from Dale, which had been only a few hours ago.

Kimberley was having a three-way conversation with Homer, the bald-headed bartender, and a fifty-something man in gray slacks, a blue university stripe shirt, and a navy blazer. Something about the guy in the blazer looked artificially handsome; for one thing, his skin was a tanning-booth gold.

"Evening, J.," Homer said. He picked up a glass pitcher and started drying it with a white towel. "What are you having?"

"I'll order in a minute," I said. Homer is a perceptive guy, which is why, I suppose, he's good at his job. He could tell I wanted a little privacy with Kimberley, so he floated away without another word.

Kimberley wheeled around on her barstool. She looked good in black denim jeans and a tight-fitting maroon turtleneck sweater. A tangle of gold necklaces hung around her neck.

"Well, surprise, surprise, it's Mr. Lawyer J. I was going to come see you tonight." Sounding a tad buzzed.

"Woo-hoo," the man in the blazer said. Flashing a thumbs-up at me. "Lucky dog."

"Then this nice gentleman started talking my ear off about his adventures in the local real estate trade, and what could I do but start drinking."

"Hey," the guy said, "thanks a million, honey." Lifting his drink, which looked like a whiskey rocks, in mock salute.

"Telling me his sob stories . . ." The booze flattening her smile around the edges.

"It's a jungle out there," he told me, winking. Then he held out his hand. "Ralph Pritchard."

"J. Shepard."

He handed me a business card. "So, J., you rent or own?"

"I own."

"Smart man. Whereabouts?"

"Old Town. Porpoise Way."

"Old Town. Me, too. Well, technically, I don't currently live in Old Town. Bought a place on Fifth Street last June, just before prices started creeping back up. Dumpy little turn-of-the-century Craftsman, but a helluva piece of land, so close to the sand and all. Knocked that puppy down, built four townhomes on the same lot." He leaned in conspiratorially, flashing a row of capped teeth. "Made a goddamned *mint*."

I knew the project, a pseudo Cape Cod monstrosity that eclipsed the afternoon sunlight of half the beach cottages on the west side of Fifth. Towering eyesores like that were common now in Christianitos. In recent years the city council had sold out on residents in a big way by rewriting the zoning regulations to accommodate such high-dollar, overbuilt developments. They defended their actions by claiming that change was inevitable. But, as Ralph Pritchard had so succinctly attested, it was really all about only one thing: money.

He sipped his drink. "So, when did you get in?" he asked me.

"At birth," I said. "I've lived in the same house all my life."

"Ah, a true local."

"As opposed to a false local?" Giving him full eye contact.

He was unflappable the way that people in sales can be, and he tossed off a phony laugh. "Touché, my friend. So tell me, you interested in selling? This is a great time to think about it, J., with values on the rise and interest rates cooling." Using my name to keep the now's-the-time shtick personal.

I looked at Kimberley. She seemed amused to see me having to fend the guy off.

"Not in this lifetime, Ralph." I flashed him the old shit-eater, forcing a viselike handshake back on him. "Great meeting you. Would you excuse us for a moment? We need to discuss some private business."

"Party's over, eh, deary?" he said right past me to Kimberley.

She shrugged and waved her long fingers close to her breast. "Toodle-oo."

Ralph Pritchard flexed his fingers and drifted down a row of empty stools toward Homer.

"I thought you were married," I said, watching the real estate man retreat.

Kimberley smiled. "Oh, please. Like you said, not in this life-time." She set down her drink. "A man like that thinks every no gets him one step closer to a yes." She raised her glass at Ralph. "Speaking of marriage, my father is getting a divorce." Taking a drink.

"You talked to him?"

"We made a deal this afternoon." I must have looked semi-shocked, because she said, "What? You didn't think I was going to sit around in that charming little bed-and-breakfast all day, just waiting for word on what he was doing, did you? Your girlfriend was right."

"Fiancée."

She swilled what was left of her margarita. "Whatever." Looking more intoxicated than before.

"So he was faking the Alzheimer's," I said.

"Well, he's lost some of his edge, but that happens to everybody. Old age sucks. But can you believe it? To think he married that hustler Angie what's-her-name just to get my attention."

"He told you that?"

"Not in so many words, but I didn't want to interrogate him, he's my father."

"I see." She wasn't quite selling me that she knew the complete score with Rudy.

"We had a nice chat after I got back from my meeting with Mr. Dobbs this afternoon." She cast a glance at Homer, tilting her empty glass.

"You went to the savings and loan."

"You didn't think I'd let him get wiped out, did you? My mother spent years building that portfolio."

"But it's your father's account."

"And it still is, only with me as executor now. I have power of attorney. I'll sign off on any and all transactions from here on. That little slut can't touch a nickel of it without my consent. Which of course she'll never get."

"How'd you get power of attorney so fast, and without Rudy there?"

She dropped her chin as if mildly taken aback. "You won't tell anyone, will you?"

I didn't answer.

"After forty years," she said, "I think I know what his signature looks like. And Mr. Dobbs knew a notary with poor eyesight with an office a block away."

"Dobbs helped you."

She gave me the sideways glance again. "You think he'd let that much business go out the door just standing by?"

Christ, I thought, so much for ethical dilemmas. Dale and I had sweated so hard to deal with the problem legally, and she'd dispensed with it in no time, without any apparent guilt or second thoughts. Suddenly I felt old-fashioned, out of step with the ways of the world, the things people will do for money.

"So, the end justifies the means," I said.

Her green eyes sharpened. "Don't give me that. It's the American way and you know it."

Homer slid her a fresh-blended margarita, no salt, then looked at me. I spied the Crown Royal bottle in its usual place along the wall between the Dewar's and Cutty Sark, could almost feel that righteous burn expanding in my chest, clearing away the post-Stevie funk, not to mention the splitter of a headache this Rudy business had caused me. Forget it, I thought, now is not the time for clouded thinking.

I ordered a diet cola.

"You called him after you did this?" I asked.

"At home. The little hustler answered, said he was asleep. I told her she'd better wake him up, 'cause this thing was over." Grinning, she sniffed her foamy white drink before sampling it.

"You told her what you did."

"Offered her fifty thousand to initiate the divorce, another fifty when it's final, otherwise I'd go to the police."

"She took it."

"Dobbs said her boyfriend came and got it this afternoon."

I remembered that Dale had thought Carlito was just going out for groceries in his Camaro.

"So what's your end of the bargain with your dad?" I asked.

"I'm moving back." She stopped. "Well, not right away. Lot of details have to be worked out when I get home."

This didn't sound quite right, based on what I knew about her thus far. Her whole life was in Seattle.

"Why the about-face?" I said. "I thought you two covered the same territory when your mother passed away."

Her painted eyebrow spiked. "I didn't realize how desperate he'd gotten." Shaking her head. "I mean, to do all this, for Christ's sake."

A tangle of feelings twisted my insides. Relief, that Rudy wouldn't see financial ruination. Anger, at being manipulated in this little father-daughter saga. Concern, for Dale, who was still hanging his ass out on a line to protect Rudy.

And disbelief. Somehow, it seemed too tidy a conclusion. I couldn't picture Angie bidding Rudy a tearful good-bye at LAX while Carlito idled the car outside the terminal, not even for a hundred grand. I'd seen the numbers that day in the savings and loan.

Rudy faking it completely? That idea bothered me too. I'd seen those glazed eyes, and that look in them, like the eyes of the boy you see being swept down the flood-control channel on the news during winter, a boy who knows his predicament, knows that all is lost and there isn't a damn thing he can do about it but wait for the end.

But I didn't have the energy to spoil Kimberley's little moment of victory.

Homer brought me my diet cola. Kimberley toasted her father, her glass clinking with mine.

"And here's to his attorney, Dale Bleeker," I said. "Who deserves a helluva lot of credit for keeping him in one piece through all of this."

"Here, here." Her tone was so upbeat that out on the fringes, Ralph Pritchard hoisted the fresh schooner of beer he was nursing high in the air, gazing at Kimberley with puppy dog eyes.

But I had on a straight face. "I'm serious, Kimberley. You owe Dale Bleeker a *lot*."

She nodded. "Maybe I'll hire him to prepare Dad's will."

I was stunned. "You're kidding."

"No, I am not kidding."

"A guy like your dad, all that jack sitting in the bank in his name, and he's got no will? That makes no sense."

She toyed with her margarita, stirring the crushed ice with a pair of thin red straws. "I know. Dobbs can't believe it either, but it's true. Mom had hers done five years ago. Dad too, same time, but apparently he took his home unsigned, said he wanted to sleep on it."

"He never signed it."

"Said he lost it. It probably went out with the Sunday paper." Shaking her head. "How positively just like him. Everything the hard way. I mean, look at me."

She tilted her head back, inviting me to have a look. Even drunk she looked well put together, such that Ralph Pritchard was still compelled to stare from his new spot down the bar. Her eyes were heading toward bloodshot but I could see the indignation clearly enough. Her jaw was set, lips pursed. I know this look in a woman. She was working up to something big.

"He jerked my chain all the way from Washington," she said. "What do you think of that?" Slopping some of her drink onto her chin.

Not much, I wanted to say. Jerking her chain? Jesus, look around you, woman. I wasn't up for hearing her self-pitying gripes, not after what Rudy had put Dale and me through. That Crown Royal was practically levitating off the bar shelf in front of me, mocking my shaky resolve. Homer the barkeep was ringing a sale on the antique register, grinning at the flirtation going on between the bottle and me. I shut my eyes.

"That's just *tragic,* Kimberley," I said with a bite.

"Tragic?" Kimberley stiffened. I hoped she was wise to the fact that I didn't want to hear her sob story. We sat there and diddled our drinks like two prisoners on a blind date gone bad.

"Yeah. Shakespearean, even."

Then she said in a more reasonable tone, "All I'm saying is, if he was that lonely, why couldn't he just pick up the phone and tell me? Would that be so hard to do?"

"You're not the most accessible person I've ever met."

"Well I'm here now, aren't I?"

I gave her credit for coming all this way.

"And I'm serious about hiring Mr. Bleeker to prepare my father's will."

"I suggest you do it fast, and pray that your dad doesn't keel in the meantime."

"Oh, he's fine. Sounded great on the phone today. Maybe Pop's a little sad, but he's in generally good health."

I set down my drink and swiveled to face her. "What I meant was, I hope Angie and Carlito don't kill him. If he dies intestate— you know, without a will—she gets half of everything. And a million beats a hundred grand anytime."

"Then we should do it tonight," she said, touching my wrist.

"Not with a phony signature," I said. "Dale wouldn't go for that. Neither will I."

"You'd stand by and watch my father lose everything instead? After all I . . . after all we've done for him?"

"It's a serious crime."

Kimberley's freckled white cheeks blushed pink. "Well, of course we'll do it legit," she said.

"Of course," I said, unconvinced. I was jonesing for a real drink, but I wanted to go home and crawl into bed with Carmen even worse. I was sick of other people's bullshit schemes.

"Now don't go making me feel guilty about what I did this afternoon," Kimberley said. She swigged deeply into her glass, as if she needed more ballast. "It's not like I had a choice."

That one made my forehead ache. Shit, the woman couldn't possibly know how often I'd heard that feeble rationale in my line of work.

"Don't kid yourself. You always have a choice."

She wagged a finger. "You shoulda ordered a real drink."

"Just do the will as soon as your dad splits with Angie. When's that supposed to happen?"

"She said she needs a week to move out."

My gaze narrowed on her. "That's too long. Gives them too much time to plan something."

Kimberley's face rumpled. "Don't sound so paranoid, you're scaring me."

"At least I've got your attention."

"Well excuse me, but I don't think it's necessary. I know a thing or two about the law, too." She said it like someone who always has to be right. "If the girl kills him, she won't inherit a penny."

I got off my barstool. Outside, through the windows, Max's huge head hovered near the door, poised like a sphinx. I peeled a five out of my wallet for the drink, flashing on Bobby Silver's lifeless form stretched across a burning couch. No longer feeling so out of step with human nature.

"You're right," I said. "That's why when they kill him, they'll make it look like an accident."

Twenty-two

The *Times* ran a piece in the Metro section the next morning that read like a follow-up to Channel 6's TV report on the law center fire. Headlined "Panel Reviewing Bar Activities Makes Early Headway," it was little more than a vehicle for Miles Abernathy, the disciplinary review panel's leader, to air the familiar beef that the bar had too much power to investigate and prosecute complaints. In Abernathy's view, the panel had already uncovered evidence of "a troubling tendency, if only on the part of a small minority of bar lawyers, to overreach, sometimes even flouting the law in the process." Of course, he was talking about me, and the *Times* reporter duly rehashed the facts involving my possible "role" in the fire, inferring that I might have started the blaze to destroy files. According to Chief Nicholas Conforti, the Glendale police were looking into the possibility that I had committed arson at the behest of a previously disciplined attorney whose involvement in the law center's business was as yet unknown.

Apparently I was unavailable for comment. I frowned.

"Well, that's bullshit."

"They called last night when you were walking Max," Carmen said across the breakfast table. She was reading "Dear Abby," sipping tea in a white terry robe. "Too bad you were out so late."

Last night. My back ached when I thought about it. Kimberley's inebriated state had not mixed well with the sudden realization that her dad was likely in great danger. She'd cried a little, begging me to help her father. The tears led to a quick, shaky cigarette and a hyperventilating anxiety attack. I offered to walk her back to the hotel, taking her hand, but Kimberley had barely cleared her barstool before a bad case of the whirlies descended, bringing on an indelicate reflex action. I saw it coming and ducked, but Ralph

Pritchard, who'd come over to lend a chivalrous hand, was slower. That snappy blazer of his was probably being plucked out of the Dumpster and fitted right now by a pier wino.

I'd carried Kimberley the four blocks over from Main to Fifth on my shoulder, laid her across the bed in her room, turned up the heater, placed a small trash can near the bed in case she had another urgent need, and left. By the time I walked back home, took out the garbage, and put Max away for the night, Carmen and Albert were asleep on the living-room couch, the eleven o'clock weather guy talking about a forty percent chance of rain.

I flipped to the back pages of the paper to read the rest of the state bar piece and got a surprise: Burton Webb, the governor of the state of California, was using Abernathy's claims to renew his threat to cut off the bar's funding if it failed to heed the call to reform. To Burton Webb, a slash-and-burn advocate of small government, bar reform meant only one thing: cutting the bar's dues budget in half. Never mind that the agency is charged by law with responding to each and every complaint it receives, that its 800 hot line gets maybe ten thousand calls a month, or that the volume of cases prosecuted has tripled in recent years. Forget the rising cost of labor and doing business in general. In Webb's view, the state bar is "like a bloated *Hindenburg,*" a redundancy illustrative of the man's linguistic shortcomings.

The whole thing read like overkill for a commercial fire at a small office in Glendale, a forced piece of reporting. I wondered who had fed this crap to the *Times* and what his or her connection was to a UPL outfit that backed investment scams targeting the elderly.

Today I would check in with Duke Choi. I put down the fish wrap and had a hopeful thought: Maybe Duke was already getting somewhere.

Carmen had read the disgust on my face. Unable to resist, I picked up the paper and reread the governor's quote aloud. "Quite the rhetorical genius, isn't he?" I said.

"Don't look at me." She'd pulled her bare feet up and wrapped her arms around her legs. "I didn't vote for him."

"Neither did I."

"You're being used," she said after a moment.

"I know."

"But I don't think you're important enough for them to ruin you."

"Gee, thanks."

She picked up the paper. "No, no, no, don't be offended. I really don't think this is about you, though, J."

I pointed to the article. "See that? 'J. Shepard.' That's me."

She took time to sip her tea, letting me wait. "You're being too literal. What I mean is, this ethics-panel thing is part of a bigger cycle. You know, like Mexican politics."

I stared across the table. "Mexican politics."

Carmen allowed herself a small smile. "That's right. Remember last winter when we took that trip down to Baja? The one-weeker that turned into a two-weeker."

"Sure. Good waves." We'd had a lot of weather on the way back up. Every road from the Seven Sisters turnoff to San Quintin was washed out when the rain came.

"And you were wondering out loud why they kept rebuilding the roads to go straight through the streambeds and washes, the Mexican men out there by the roadside with their picks and shovels, already starting the rebuilding process."

"You've got to admit, it makes no sense."

"But that's the point," she said. "They were already rebuilding when we came back through. Those men had jobs."

"So that's why they build roads right through streambeds in Baja, to create jobs."

She nodded. "It's a cycle. It might be stupid and inefficient and probably corrupt, but it is what it is. And Mexico is that way. A lot." She laid down the article. "This panel thing is no different."

The phone rang. It was Skip Greuber. "J., buddy. Glad I caught you. Thought you'd be out surfin', man. Howzit today?" Laying it on a bit thick.

I didn't trust anyone who would investigate me behind my back. "Awe inspiring," I said, "two foot and crumbly." I felt my heart thumping inside my T-shirt. "What do you want?"

"Nothing, just thought I'd call. You see that article in the *Times* yet?"

"If I had a bird, the bottom of the cage would have new lining already."

"Pretty wild how they got a quote from Webb and all, huh?" I didn't answer. Then he said, "We're getting some complaints on that Bleeker fellow now."

"UPL, yeah, I know, but it's no surprise. That place in Glendale was using his name and bar number without his knowledge."

"I dunno, J., doesn't look too good for him if you ask me." He waited for my response, but got none. "Say, you wouldn't happen to know where we can reach him, would you? We'd sure like to talk to him."

"Try his membership-records address."

"We did. His wife says he doesn't really live there anymore. You seen him lately?"

I was tired of his game playing. "This part of your SBI on me, Skip?"

He paused. "Now wait, buddy—"

"Quit with the buddy crap already, will you?" I said. Carmen sat very still, studying her section of newspaper self-consciously. "What do you want, Skip?"

"Okay, okay," he said, "act like a jerk-off if you like, J. I just thought I'd extend a little courtesy to you, that's all."

"Well gee, thanks. Have a nice day. Later, Skip."

"J., hang on a minute, wait!" he yelped. "You there?"

"Make it fast."

"Reggie wants a meeting with you." He was talking about our ultimate boss, Reginald Hewitt, the chief trial counsel at the bar.

"Then why didn't he call?" I knew Hewitt to be a straight-ahead type, even if he was somewhat removed from the day-to-day personnel like me. He was the kind of guy who would come around from behind his desk to shake your hand on your first day on the job, then surprise you by remembering you by name when you crossed paths again in a parking lot six months later. I couldn't quite picture the chief using Skip Greuber to set up his meetings.

"Jesus, J., quit busting my chops, will ya?" Skip said it as if he was down on himself for lacking the wit to cook up a decent lie.

"Sorry, but that's not good enough, *buddy*."

There was an unexpected pause before Skip said, "You listen to me," letting some agitation bleed through. "We know what you're doing. The chief wants to put a stop to it before the bar gets another big fat fucking black eye for the public to see."

"Skip?" I said.

"Yeah?" Suddenly hopeful.

"You tell the chief he'll have to follow the MOU and go through my union rep."

He half chuckled, letting out a long sigh. "Shepard, you do not know what you're getting yourself into."

I didn't care for the sound of that. "That a threat or a warning?"

He seemed to think about his answer. "You decide, smart guy."

I hung the phone up hard, stood there, staring through the window above the sink at the big palm across the alleyway behind my house. No wind yet. I felt the pull of the ocean again, the need to distance myself from this building mound of grief by the most reliable method I knew. I wondered what the swell was doing, whether the midmorning low-to-high tide was bumping up the surf. I'd checked it from the second-story balcony at dawn, balancing with one hand flat on the brick chimney as I stood spread-legged on the railing. Unless the surf is sizable, it's an unreliable, cheater's surf check, as plenty of good small days go undetected from this distant vantage point. But I just didn't have the requisite energy or desire to get dressed and slog down the block and over the berm for a true check this morning.

I thought of Stone Me Stevie's claim that the crowds had thinned near the pier of late, due in large part to the intimidation factor that the two beefs I'd been involved in had generated. The possibility that this was true simply robbed me of my present initiative to give it a midmorning look. At least for now, finding a few uncrowded peaks wouldn't seem like much of a coup.

I didn't hear the doorbell ring, but I heard Albert call out, "I'll get it!" from the other side of the house. Albert digs answering the door. Carmen says it makes him feel useful and more like an adult.

"Think the chief might want to offer you your job back?" Carmen asked me.

I shook my head no. "I still have my job. This is just a free vacation."

"Um, J.?" Albert called to me from the entry hall. "It's K-K-Kimberley."

"Free vacation, right," Carmen said. "And the fun never stops." Her voice weary.

I came away from the window and bent over to kiss Carmen on the head. Her black hair smelled faintly sweet, like vanilla. She hadn't said another word about moving out since the bowling alley, and I was glad for it. I wanted her to know I appreciated her hanging in so well through all of this craziness of late, but as I made my move, she closed her eyes.

I kissed her anyway.

The taxicab was still idling on Porpoise Way when I invited Kimberley Kirkmeyer-Munson into my living room. She wore tight blue jeans and a white top under a black V-necked sweater, red tennis shoes. Her hair was thicker and curlier than I'd ever seen it, as if she'd slept on the roof of a Greyhound bus all night. Dark sunglasses hid her eyes completely. A way casual look for her, and somehow the effect was to make her seem more vulnerable. Carmen seemed to notice the difference too; she'd crowded in behind me and had her arms folded, sending Kimberley the Woman-don't-even-think-about-it greeting.

Kimberley waved her hand at the yellow Ford Taurus. "Okay," she mouthed at the driver. The cab had a minibillboard on its roof advertising a new brand of cigarettes named Ocean Breeze. Christ, I thought, this world is getting more cynical by the minute.

"Wasn't sure you'd be home," Kimberley explained. "And I am not in any shape to walk back to my hotel, even if it is only on the other side of Main."

"Feel free to call first," I said.

Kimberley guided herself into the big leather chair near the front window, the one Dale liked to sit in at night. Everything nice and easy. She winced. "Ooh, my head feels like cement." She left her sunglasses on as she rubbed her temples.

Carmen and I took up on the couch and waited, but Kimberley said nothing. She seemed to be winded just from her trip up the front walk to ring my doorbell.

"I came here to thank you," she finally told us, removing her shades. Her eyes were almost as red as her hair. "For last night." Her eyes cut to Carmen quickly when she realized what she'd said. "I mean, for helping get me back to my room after I got sick. I was so zonked, I still don't know how you did it."

I wasn't about to volunteer any information in front of Carmen. "You're welcome."

"You made a helluva point about my father." Then she regarded Carmen. "Dad doesn't have a will."

Carmen raised an eyebrow. "So?"

"So, if those two find out, God only knows." She shuddered lightly—"Anything could happen."

It was probably a good time to reassure her, but quite honestly, I didn't feel obligated, not with the extended stroke job Rudy Kirkmeyer had apparently given Dale and me just to get his daughter to notice him again. I was still not completely sold on Kimberley's take on the situation.

I said, "Maybe a quick reunion is in order."

Kimberley straightened as if to shake off her hangover. "Can you help me?" Carmen and I exchanged blank stares. "I mean, I'd like to hire you. To do the will."

"He's already got a job," Carmen said.

Kimberley sat back a little. "Just barely. The hotel leaves a free copy of the *Times* at my door in the morning. I read today's edition while I was waiting for my cab."

"I'm not an estate-planning lawyer anyway," I said.

Kimberley clicked her tongue impatiently. "Then let's cut to the chase. I'll pay you a fee to help me get him back. Safely."

"Have you tried talking to him since you made the deal with Angie?" I said.

"The line's busy." She opened her purse and began to dig through it, probably looking for a smoke. "Truth is, I'm beginning to get concerned."

"You should have made handing him over contingent on them getting the first fifty grand," I said.

She found her cigarettes. "You're right. That's my point, I'm not good at this kind of stuff."

"You want to go outside?" I asked.

Kimberley waved off my gesture. "I want you to help me get my father back. I'll pay you whatever you want." She sighed, her lips puckered, and said quietly, "Please."

"I don't need your money," I said, walking to the front window. I thought of Dale, the way he'd stared through these same squares of glass at night, aching to somehow make his lost daughter found again. And with Rudy, how far Dale had gone to protect a client who'd lied to him and never paid him a cent for his trouble.

I could feel Kimberley's perceptive gaze on my back. "Then what?" she said.

"There's something else."

"Name it."

"Dale's in trouble, professionally speaking."

"According to the paper, so are you."

Wanting to stay in control, I ignored her comment. "I help you get your father back," I said, "you owe Dale and me. And I mean both you and your dad."

"Okay." She got up, wobbling a little. Standing beside me now, red curls aflame in the window light. "So, what now?"

"No violence," Carmen said from the couch.

Kimberley blinked. "Fine with me, sweetie."

Then Carmen rose and glided wordlessly out of the room, disappearing up the stairs.

Kimberley watched Carmen go. "What was that about?"

"Nothing. You feel well enough to take a ride over to Glendale?"

The last of the morning overcast was evaporating, and everything outside my window seemed tinted a pale, cold yellow. Kimberley turned away.

"I'm ready." She slipped her shades back on, coughing into her sweater sleeve. "For a cigarette." Hacking again.

"Yeah, I can see that," I said.

She smiled tightly, her face pained. "No, I'm serious. The nicotine'll help clear my head."

"You sure you're up to this?"

"I want my dad back."

"All right. Let's go."

I wanted to end this thing, to get back to tending to my career and Carmen and Albert, to shooting hoops again at lunch in the basement gym, to fixing an upstairs toilet that wasn't flushing quite right, to taming a front yard that was starting to look a bit tropical, even in February. To get back to doing my F-due reports (late, of course).

But we weren't going anywhere just yet. Kimberley stayed frozen, gripping my forearm for balance.

"Do me a little favor," she said, her voice no more than a wisp of the throaty croak I knew.

"Sure."

"Take this ice pick out of my ear."

Twenty-three

That forty percent chance of rain the weather guy was talking about last night seemed to jack to about eighty on the drive twenty-five miles inland to Glendale. A ceiling of ribbed clouds the color of wet cement stretched across the San Fernando Valley, shadowing the sun from the drizzled Hollywood Hills to the north and casting the cars and buildings and trees and rows of houses in a gentle half-light. It was as if the city were locked in an old-fashioned black-and-white photo, and it made me fix on a single thought: Everything dies.

Kimberley was mostly silent, wrapped in her own thoughts. I'd let her choose a tape from the glove, and she'd gone straight for Pearl Jam. As we pulled off the Glendale Freeway and headed due north on Pacific Avenue toward Rudy Kirkmeyer's home, Kimberley cranked up the volume just as Eddie Vedder capped the tale of a murderous flashback with a refrain that counterbalanced my fatalist perspective: I'm still alive.

I suppose. We rolled along, pinned to our seats by a wall of guitars.

Rudy lived about a half mile north of the Glendale Freeway, in a neighborhood of sensible homes that I guessed were built sometime around the 1920s. Smallish houses with a semblance of style, some with red tile roofs and Spanish arches, others with leaded glass and steeply pitched rooflines for an English twist. The uglier homes on the block just sat there like shoe boxes, as if the architect had taken a vacation.

"It's the white one with the green shutters," Kimberley said, nodding.

Rudy lived in one of the better-tended shoe boxes on the street, with a decent lawn, a cement driveway, and a brick porch. Oversize junipers lined the far side of the front yard like a row of missiles on a launching pad. Closer to us, a tangle of mature hibiscus obscured the side windows and spilled onto the wood shake roof. Nice fire hazard, I almost remarked, but Kimberley was keyed up enough about her dad's safety, so I let it pass.

Dale's Buick was parked just ahead, where the road began to curve away. I cruised past the residence and slid in behind the sagging Regal.

"Where the hell is he?"

Kimberley was talking about Dale. She tore out of the door before I even cut the motor, cupped her hands against the Buick's passenger-window glass to see better, then stood back, aghast.

"Oh my God, he's not moving!"

I came around the driver's side and opened the door. A McDonald's bag puffy with discarded paper rolled off the seat and onto the pavement. Dale was still in the pair of jeans I'd bought him last week and the blue cotton dress shirt Carmen had loaned to him from my closet. The top button on the jeans was undone and his shirtsleeves were rolled back. His mouth was open, a pile of gold fillings glittering in the dark.

"Jesus, what is that sound?" Kimberley said from across the hood.

The man was snoring like a hippo.

"Dale," I said, shaking his shoulder. His head rolled back, one eye sliding open. I couldn't smell booze on him, but Christ, I was certainly thinking about it. His other eye opened, and I thought he was swallowing his tongue when the snoring abruptly stopped.

He tried to sit up straighter, grimacing. "J., hey, J., where . . . Wow, what time is it?"

A chill wind buffeted the Buick's open door and seemed to help Dale wake up quicker. I let him get his bearings, and scanned the backseat for signs of alcohol. No empties in sight.

"Don't worry," he said, "I'm not sauced."

"I didn't say you were, man."

He shook his head. "You didn't have to."

Still an excellent observer.

"You didn't call," I said.

"I was up most of the night. That's why I'm so wiped out."

Kimberley came around the front of the big Buick and stood beside me, staring in at Dale. "They were up really late, lights didn't go out until two A.M.," he added, grinning at me.

"Don't tell me, you played commando," I said.

"No sweat, I played it safe. Waited an extra two hours, then I went around the side there by the hibiscus trees. Got a good look, too."

I frowned. "Exactly what I told you not to do."

Kimberley shifted her weight, leaning forward. "So, whatcha see?"

Dale paused as if to savor the moment. "You may not like this. The place is torn apart."

"Oh God!"

"They trashed it?" I said.

"Tossed it is more like it. Stuff everywhere. My guess, they were looking for something they couldn't find."

Kimberley pressed a hand to her forehead and paced in the street. "They know! They know!"

Dale eyed the strutting redhead quizzically. I filled him in on the fact that Rudy didn't have a will, describing the deal Kimberley had cut with Angie to get a divorce rolling.

"Well," Dale muttered.

"Well what?" she barked.

Dale took measure of her jumpiness before he spoke, then said, "As a DA I made plenty of bargains with bad guys over the years. They almost never worked out quite the way I wanted." Dale rubbed his chin, which looked like it had a good three-day salt-and-pepper growth going. "Don't know if I'd trust those two to keep up their end in any situation."

"What do you mean by that?" Kimberley shot back. "They'll get fifty grand more when the divorce is done. That's easy money for a criminal."

But Dale was already making the critical connection, and he jerked his thumb toward the house. "Inside, they were looking for a will that doesn't exist, weren't they?" Kimberley was too keyed up for me to agree with Dale out loud. "He dies intestate, she gets half, isn't that right, J?"

I nodded subtly.

Kimberley caught my nod, stopped pacing and slapped her hand on the Buick's hood. "Brilliant! Boy, you two are just too smart for words."

I realized that she had only half believed me when I laid out Rudy's situation for her both last night at the Captain's Galley and this morning at my place. I still couldn't grasp why Rudy Kirkmeyer would marry Angie, let her clean out his safe-deposit box, and fake a degenerative disease just to get his daughter's undivided attention. But I was beginning to see how remarkably obtuse Kimberley could be. Now it was as if she'd finally got the message and was kicking herself—and Dale and me—for not seeing it before.

"That's it, I'm going in there and getting him," she said. "Right now, goddamn it." Stalking across the street, eyes straight ahead.

I hustled up the curving drive behind her, Dale lagging back a good fifty feet as he tucked in his shirttails and combed his hair with his fingers. A fresh puddle of oil freckled the cement opposite the garage door. Probably from Carlito's rig, I thought, which meant he wasn't there. Not that I feared the idiot, but not dealing with him would be a plus. Kimberley mounted the brick porch, blew off the doorbell, and pounded the front door with her fist.

"They're probably not here," I said after a solid minute of intermittent knocking.

Kimberley swung around and glared at Dale. "You were supposed to be watching him."

Dale gazed into a planter of overgrown azaleas. "Must've slipped out while I was resting."

Kimberley shook her head. "Nice. Leave it to Dad to hire Rip van Winkle as his lawyer."

She was pushing it too hard. "Cool the sarcasm," I said, "it isn't necessary. If you'd have included us in your little dealings with Angie, we wouldn't be here right now."

Kimberley huffed, standing back from the big green door. "Guess I'm not used to dealing with 'bad guys.'" She paused and regarded Dale, who was still half out of breath from his scramble up to the porch. I suppose that what she finally saw was a tired old lawyer who'd spent a cold February night in his car, trying to keep tabs on her addled father.

"Sorry, Mr. Bleeker. No offense."

I imagined that Dale Bleeker was used to taking grief from victims and their families whenever they felt the "System" had let them down.

"None taken," he said.

Her eyes were suddenly full of tears when she turned to me. "What do we do?"

We needed to get inside to have a look around, maybe find out something about what Angie and Carlito were up to. "Got a key?" I asked Kimberley.

"No, how should . . . Oh! I know where Mom used to hide one." She led us off the porch and around the side of the garage to a decorative brick wishing well with a wood shake roof to match the house. "I was a little wild as a teen," she said over her shoulder as she reached into the well, tamped her hand around a bit, and pulled out a rusty silver key. "Dad would lock me out if I stayed out past my curfew. I thought he was being ridiculous." A smirk crossed her face. "So did Mom."

"He was probably just concerned for you," Dale said.

Kimberley stopped dusting off the old key. Her nose was pink from the cold. "Oh really," she said, not like it was a question she wanted him to answer.

"I have a beautiful young daughter, too," he said. "You know, having a father who cares about you is not all that bad."

Kimberley's face grew clouded. I took the house key right out of her hand.

"Wait on the porch," I said.

I turned the dead-bolt and stepped inside, leaving the door cracked behind me. The air was pungent and stale, like a pile of dirty laundry. The entryway was done in bone white Formica, a small patch that gave way to wall-to-wall frost green carpeting throughout the living room. To my left was the kitchen. On the right, a hallway that led to the bedrooms. A brand-new big-screen TV set was parked on the tiles in front of the fireplace in the living room. The box it came in was flattened and leaning against the dusty cream-colored draperies, which were drawn across a pair of wide sliding glass doors leading to the backyard. The room was an unholy mess, the glass coffee table littered with fast-food cartons and empty beer bottles. Satin throw pillows were propped against the base of the white leather sofa, an ashtray tilting in the pile carpet a few feet away. I caught an unpleasant whiff of rotting food, looked down, and saw an open bag of cheese puffs swarming with ants.

The kitchen sink was piled with dirty dishes. Cupboard doors hung open. Every glass in the place, from highball glasses to juice tumblers to a fancy German beer mug with a pewter cap, had been pressed into service of late. The pantry looked like bears had raided it. A pile of Cocoa Puffs crunched beneath my shoe as I reached up to grab a checkered dish towel from a hook on the wall.

I smashed a few thousand ants in the dish towel and wrapped the cheese puffs tightly inside the cloth, then opened the door for Kimberley and Dale. Rudy's daughter staggered about from room to room, muttering "Oh God" over and over.

"J., take a look," Dale said from a room down the hall. It was a bedroom converted into a study, with a nice oak desk and custom-made bookshelves fronting plaid wallpaper accented in Kelly green. A black metal filing cabinet stood in the corner beneath a potted bamboo. All four cabinet doors were ajar. Beneath them was a foot-deep pile of manila file folders and loose papers.

"Oh!" Kimberley sputtered from the doorway. Her body began to shake all over. I reached out and caught her just as she collapsed. We stood there, not moving. The only sound was Kimberley's sniffling sobs into my shirt. When at last she lifted her head, I let her stand on her own. "This used to be my room," she whispered.

Dale looked offended by the sight of the woman crying. "Don't worry," he told her. "We'll find him."

The front door creaked. Kimberley caught her breath. Then silence. I put my index finger to my lips and motioned them both to stay still. My feet made no sound on the carpeted hallway as I stepped slowly and lightly, my back hugging the long wall. The front door cracked open and the shadow of a man spilled onto the entryway. Carlito? The nose of a handgun inched inside, stopping me dead.

I glanced about. Holy shit, what now, genius? I was halfway

down the hallway and didn't have time to rush the door to repel
the gunman without getting shot, so forget that. I couldn't retreat
in time to hide either. What brilliant timing.

The gun hovered just above the gold doorknob. Like a helpless
insect, I had simply frozen in place, grateful that the ceiling light
above me wasn't on.

Carlito would shoot me, I was sure. Even if he wasn't a true
killer, I figured he felt murder for revenge was justifiable, even
noble. And by now, revenge had to be on his mind. I'd nearly torn
his arm off that first time we'd met at the savings and loan, right
in front of his woman. Then he and his homies had taken a sound
thumping that day at the pier. And that day at my house, Max had
ventilated the dude's backside with his teeth, another unmanly episode played out in Angie's presence. I'd damaged his pride enough.
He might be a coward and a bully, but I believed he would find
the sack to pull the trigger.

As the door swung farther open, I said a prayer: Dear God, let
him be a terrible shot. I flattened myself against the wall, hoping
he might head into the living room without glancing right, toward
me. But Kimberley gasped somewhere behind me and the gun
swung around.

"Hold it!"

"Don't shoot!" I said from the shadows.

Tamango Perry came out of his shooting stance and relaxed. "I
should have known."

"Jesus. What are you doing here?"

He put the gun in his shoulder holster. He wore a black suit
with a white shirt and a subdued burgundy foulard tie. The confrontation had taken his breath away, but his poise returned as he
straightened his lapels and looked around the place.

"I told you I would keep an eye on the situation." He held up
his cell phone. "A neighbor called and said there was a possible
break-in."

I shook my head. "We used a spare key." Showing him what
Kimberley had extracted from the wishing well.

Tamango looked around. Not a sound came from the study.

"It's okay," I called out. Dale and a pale-faced Kimberley peeked
into the hall. I waved them over. Tamango and Dale said a brief

hello and shook. "This is Rudy Kirkmeyer's daughter, Kimberley," I said. "He's with the Glendale PD."

Tamango bowed slightly. "A pleasure." Then he looked at me. "So, you had a key."

"I used to live here," Kimberley said. "It was in the same old place after all that time." The detective was his usual straight-faced self, which seemed to unnerve her. "It is my dad's house," she added. "I've got a right to be here."

Technically she was wrong, but I let it go.

"I see," the detective said. When I didn't say anything, he said, "And why are you here today?"

He flipped open his notepad, took out a black ballpoint, and listened patiently as Kimberley gave him a short version of Rudy's developing predicament.

"I am sorry," Tamango said, "but I have to ask you to leave. You're trespassing."

Kimberley looked staggered. "What the hell kind of cop are you?"

One who knows the law and plays it refreshingly straight, I thought.

"No, he's right," I said quickly. "We can talk about this more on the street, right, Detective?"

Perry looked amused. He didn't seem to have much of a touch with women, and clearly didn't care. "That is what I had intended."

"Wait," Dale said. In his hand was a framed color photograph. "I should put this back before we go, but you may want to check it out first."

"That's my parents on their forty-fifth wedding anniversary," Kimberley said. "The last year my mom was alive."

In the picture, Rudy stood arm in arm with a beaming gray-haired woman. Rudy's wife had saggy jowls but the same high forehead, fine nose, and creamy skin as Kimberley. They were outdoors in a forested place, posing on a knotty wood porch lined with wooden railings. To their right on a corner of the porch was a handmade birdhouse with a sign over the open door that said "Casa Kirkmeyer." They stood in bright sunlight, but the entire porch was perched among large trees. Behind them a mix of aspens and pines rose from a steep gorge.

"I saw it in the other room," Dale said.

Kimberley held the photo now. "Our cabin in Big Sur."

"Not too shabby," I said. For all the money they'd amassed, the Kirkmeyers certainly didn't throw much of it around. I looked around me again. Beneath the mess, this house was comfortable but very middle-class.

A pad in Big Sur was more like it.

"It's nothing fancy," she said. "They bought it for next to nothing from a friend of my mom's in eighty-three, the year there was all that rain." She held up the photo. "There's a stream way down below. It runs down the canyon. Apparently some idiot whose place was farther up the hill had some flooding during one of those big winter storms."

I remembered the winter of '83 quite well, having never seen the ocean that angry in all my life. The beach at Christianitos endured three months of pounding surf, monsoonlike rain, and high tides that swamped the million-dollar palaces abutting the sand. By February the far end of the pier was so badly battered by thick chocolate-colored storm surf that the lifeguards banned all pedestrians. On Valentine's Day a ten-foot swell hit—along with rain and a thirty-knot wind. Surfing was out of the question. I stood on the Southside beach as a bulldozer chugged back and forth in the sand, rebuilding the berm from the previous night's damage. A dozen or so neighbors and frustrated surfers were there with me, and we gasped as sections of pier fell away like a melting Popsicle. It took two years to rebuild the thing, but the strong crosscurrents coursing through the pier tore up the Southside sandbars, and the surf has never fully regained its pre-'83 form.

"That was a crazy winter," I said.

"Well, somehow the guy managed to divert the flow down his driveway," Kimberley went on. "Right at the cabin. The place had a solid foot of mud in it when my parents got it."

"Big Sur," Tamango said. "It looks like the mountains, not the beach."

"I know, it's amazing," Kimberley said. "It's a few miles straight up this really lush canyon, right off Highway One."

"I don't like it," Dale said slowly. "Looks remote and high up.

That's a bad combination if those two are looking to create an accident for Rudy."

"It's just a picture," I said.

"No," Dale said, "you didn't notice, did you?" He shrugged.

"What about this photo?" Tamango said.

"There was a row of them on a long bookshelf," Dale said. "All knocked flat, like somebody played dominos with them. This was the only one still standing, and it was full of fingerprint smudges."

"Like somebody pawed it before we did," I said.

Kimberley moved closer to the detective. "What can you do to help my dad?" she asked.

He thought about his answer. "Very little right now, I'm afraid. This house may be disheveled, but there's no evidence that a crime occurred."

"But what if they kidnapped him?" she said.

"There's no evidence of that. He hasn't been gone long enough even to be considered a missing person."

"So you're gonna wait for them to kill him before you investigate?"

Another over-the-line crack from Kimberley, but Tamango didn't bite. "I suggest you keep on the lookout around here. They're bound to come back." He nodded toward the fireplace. "They left the new TV." Then he reached into his breast pocket, pulled out a folded piece of letter-size paper, and handed it to me. It was a photocopy of a classified-ad page full of job listings. One of them had been circled:

> ATTORNEY WANTED: A1 Banning Legal Clinic. Head a staff of top paralegals in an office serving the community with first-rate low-cost legal services! Excellent salary! Great working conditions! To interview, fax resume to Mr. Julian at (310) 555-3232. No calls please.

I had heard of Banning but had never been there. It was an agricultural town way inland, east of San Bernardino. "Where did you get this?" I said.

"I drove out to Palm Springs with my wife last Friday night to play a little tennis and escape the weather for the weekend. It wasn't much, though. This freezing wind was blowing across the desert valley. We stayed Saturday, did a little shopping and headed home. On the radio we heard the California lottery jackpot was over eighty million, so we stopped at a 7-Eleven in Banning to buy a few tickets. The line was out to the street. My wife stood and waited while I passed the time at the magazine rack. Eventually I picked up a local paper, saw this. When I did, my first thought was about the law center back in Glendale."

"That's the same guy I interviewed with," Dale said.

"May I keep this?" I asked the detective.

"Certainly. Banning is well out of my jurisdiction."

"Oh boy," Kimberley said under her breath. "News flash: Officer Percy isn't going to do anything."

Tamango's jaw tightened. "It's Perry. Detective Perry. And I have already made a photocopy of it."

"Right." She gave him a tinny smile.

"Madam, the more you talk, the more I begin to see why your father might have done this crazy thing."

Kimberley flipped her hair back over her shoulder and glared at the policeman. "And the more you tell me there's nothing the police can do, the more I see why these two guys"—nodding at Dale and me—"are currently up shit creek."

Dale and I shared a private, mutually sympathetic glance.

The woman could be abrasive, but she had a point.

Twenty-four

"Why are we eating at a dive like this?"

I skipped right by Kimberley's question. "The teriyaki bowl is their specialty, but the BLT is good, too."

The proprietor, a middle-aged Hispanic man with a greasy white apron and a Raiders cap, folded his arms when he heard her crack. We were a block north of the state bar's offices, at Tito's Burger—not burgers plural, just burger, as if they had only one to sell and that was the end of it. The place was tiny but impossible to miss: a flame red log cabin from the 1920s that actually had some kind of architectural significance. A few months earlier I'd seen it pictured in a book on historic L.A. and really hooted at the accompanying historical blurb, a professor at USC quoting Horatio Alger and raving about the frontier ethic exemplified. To me the place is a much better example of your classic L.A. amalgam, in which eating an Asian dish prepared by a Mexican cook in a faux Davy Crockett shack that some academic yahoo has deemed a timeless artifact of American expansionism barely raises an eyebrow.

But it was the perfect place to meet Duke Choi.

"The usual?" Tito said.

"And a large ice water." Ice water in wintertime. Only in California.

"For here?"

"I'll have it in the dining room." My standard line here.

"And for her?" he asked, avoiding eye contact with Kimberley.

She put the back of her hand to her forehead. "I don't feel so hot," she said to me quietly. "May I borrow the keys? Think I'll go close my eyes for a few minutes."

That solved the problem of talking to Duke confidentially. I'd let her tag along with me into Tito's because I had a hard time telling a grown woman to wait in the car, but I was glad I wouldn't have to let her sit in on whatever Duke had to tell me. I handed her the keys.

It was a little after three but the afternoon was unnaturally dark, so it felt even later. The sky was battleship gray, a misty drizzle wetting the pavement. The cars and buses and delivery trucks whizzing by on Eleventh were flicking their lights on for better visibility. I hoped that Carmen had thought to bring Max inside. I should have been hoping just that Carmen would still be there when I got home.

Bar personnel eat at Tito's every day because it's close by, the food is good, and the prices are low. But I felt reasonably certain that nobody from work would stumble in here at this hour. I didn't want Duke to go out of his way, in case someone was watching him closely.

The dining area consisted of four outdoor picnic tables wedged so close together that most heavyset diners usually take one look and order their food to go. Not that a guy my size has an easy time of it; when I eat here, I have to lean my back against the wall and stretch my legs over an entire bench. But space was not a problem, for I was Tito's only customer. He closes at four and was busy refilling condiments and swabbing the stainless-steel appliances in preparation for the next morning's business. I was probably the last order of the day. Perfect.

The screen door flew open and Tito looked up from the shiny metal grill. Duke barely nodded at him and came back to my table, carrying a tattered black briefcase. His face was flushed and the tips of his black hair were glistening. He set down the briefcase and rubbed his hands. "Shit, it's freezing out there."

"Order something," I said.

"I'm not hungry, I had lunch two hours ago." He looked around. "Man, you got interesting taste in food."

"Just order. I'll buy."

He placed his fist to his solar plexus. "I'm still recovering from Tommy's. I can feel that chiliburger fossilizing right about here."

"I'll bring the Rolaids next time."

"Right, next time. Don't think this counts as lunch either, you *still* owe me a nice meal."

"I know. Just order anything, on me. You don't even have to eat it. It'll just be less conspicuous if someone from work should happen by."

His face grew serious. "Oh, okay. Yeah, that makes sense."

I gave Duke a five, then watched him walk over and stare at the menu as if he couldn't read. "Umm . . ." Tito leaned against the counter, suffering in silence. "Lemme see . . ."

This is ridiculous, I thought. "Get the special," I said. "You can't miss." Duke was still holding the five I had given him like a meal ticket. Tito didn't wait for him to change his mind and snatched the bill. A minute later Duke sat down across from me.

"So, what's the special?"

"I have no idea. Probably something without chili."

"I can't wait."

I nodded at the briefcase. "What did you bring me?"

He placed it on the table, spun the combination lock above the latch, and popped it open. Inside was a cardboard file folder full of documents, the kind of folder the bar uses for investigations. But this one was missing the usual label to identify the case name. He opened the file slowly.

"First thing I did was look into those consulting companies Bobby Silver worked for, the ones that did the seminars. Capitol Consolidators and Homeowners Fidelity Trust." He pulled out two thick stacks of documents fastened at the top with metal clips. "They're both limited partnerships. These are all their corporate disclosure docs. Articles of incorporation, bylaws, and statements of domestic stock." He looked over his shoulder. One of Tito's employees was changing a hose on the self-serve soft drink machine, but the place was still bereft of customers. "The statement of domestic stock is particularly useful here," he almost whispered. "It lists the officers. Check it out."

Duke flipped down through the piles of paper until he found the tabs he was looking for. A few of the names I didn't recognize: Raymond Margrave, Edwin Stamy, Arthur Carroll III. The others I did: Nicholas Conforti, Tamango Perry's chief. David Welterstrom, as in State Assemblyman T. David Welterstrom, a rich kid from Oklahoma via Santa Barbara who'd bought the seat three years ago. Willie Clyburn, a former Stanford running back who played five years for the 49ers before he blew out his knee. He was a popular guy who could smile his way through anything, and ESPN had hired him to stalk the sidelines at Pac Ten games, which he followed with an NBC gig. Now he was stalking the halls of the capitol as a state senator. Clyburn had been calling for total abolition of the bar for years. In his view, wronged clients should simply sue their lawyers, a notion that ignored the unfortunate reality that for most little-guy plaintiffs, the litigation process is too expensive and time-consuming to be worth a damn. Even if a client sues a cheating lawyer and wins, collecting is near impossible. Every hard-core legal bad guy I've ever prosecuted has hidden his assets completely, and there isn't a lien or attachment in the land that can tap a judgment-proof lawyer. But to Willie Clyburn, the state bar was useless, a monument to bloated bureaucracy. A month earlier I'd read in the paper that he'd been the one that Governor Webb had chosen to select and approve the bar discipline evaluation panel. I was beginning to appreciate how slick a move it had been. With the probe, Webb had shown the voters he was concerned about governmental accountability, bureaucratic efficiency, and consumer protection. Hell, if the bar was better run, the People of the State of California were the big winners. But by having Clyburn hand-pick the panel, Webb would appease the antibar faction in Sacramento on an even higher level, no doubt gaining political leverage to be wielded later was when a piece of legislation was hanging in the balance and a few extra votes were desperately needed.

I read the last two names again and again.

Stanislav Greuber. Old Skip, always into his investments and talking about retiring early, but not known for having done much with his capital thus far. Word was he was burned out on management, but who wouldn't be after ten years? I wondered whether Skip was a mere silent partner in all of this. Was this just another means to a healthy return on his investment dollars? No, a state bar manager who knows about money matters could spot a financial scam far more readily than most. Skip had to know exactly what was going on—and the rat bastard was using Duke to investigate me.

The last name: Miles Abernathy. Self-righteous ethicist. Clyburn's choice to head the evaluation panel. No wonder Abernathy
had such a hard-on against the bar. With him in charge, the review
panel would be on a seek-and-destroy mission, and I was his first
target.

"Try not to look so excited," Duke said.

"I don't know. The financial scam is pretty complicated, and
these guys are prominent members of the community. Even if it's
a blatant rip-off, people are gonna have a hard time believing this."

"You should see their bottom lines the last couple years. They're
making a shitload of money just from selling annuities and life
insurance policies." He sat back a little. "I always thought that kind
of stuff was a difficult sell."

"Maybe not when you package it right," I said. I told him about
my conversation with Mr. Carpio, the bakery owner.

Duke looked offended. "That's despicable."

"You can see why the Glendale PD didn't go anywhere with
that law center fire."

"Aside from blaming it all on you."

"The cops won't charge me. I didn't start that fire."

His face was pensive. "I've been watching TV and reading the
paper, J. And they already got you suspended."

"Yeah, but with pay."

I didn't want him getting spooked. I had no clue yet as to how
I could use this information to get my job back. I had to let the
right people know about the fraud so it could be investigated and
stopped. With Abernathy leading the discipline review panel, its
credibility would be shot, yet somehow I suspected that the bar
would come out looking lousy anyway. Bunch of corrupt lawyers
who can't even police themselves, the newspaper columnists would
say. That's an angle that will sell papers any day of the week.

I pictured that pair of cowboy boots pointing at a burning ceiling. Bobby Silver, whose original license to practice should have
been issued on used toilet paper to provide fair warning to potential
clients. I couldn't exactly say I missed the guy. But he had been
murdered.

I asked Duke what else he'd learned about the law center.

He went deeper into the file. "I called some realtors in Glendale and asked about commercial rentals on Brand. The second one I called"—he handed me the card of a broker named Mitzi Klinger—"handled the law center listing." He pulled out a title document that looked like a property deed. "The law center was being leased by Capitol Consolidators. I don't have a copy of the lease yet. Mitzi there didn't feel comfortable faxing it, but she promised to mail it."

"What's this?"

"A copy of the deed. I got a title company to pull it."

I scanned the document, recognizing the law center's street address listed below the lot and parcel numbers.

"Alliance Pictures, Inc.," I said. "Who's that?"

"This is where it gets interesting. It's a motion picture production company."

"One that owns office space in Glendale that it rents to people who do UPL and run investment schemes on the elderly? That makes no sense."

Duke smiled. "Till you check their articles. They're incorporated in the Bahamas." Waiting for my response, which didn't come. "You don't produce movies in the Bahamas, J. It's a shell."

Duke showed me the corporate documents on Alliance. "They have no product, never made a movie. You heard of that pornographer from Belgium, Yves Pasqual?"

I had. "He's the guy that sued Steven Seagal for backing out of a handshake deal to do an action flick a couple years ago. It got dismissed. Judge said there was no evidence of a contractual agreement in the first place."

"Pasqual's in trouble with the IRS for back taxes. They've got liens on any income his adult bookstores make for the next ten years. He's cash starved."

"How do you know this?"

Duke leaned forward. "I've got an uncle who works for the IRS. But you can't say where I got this."

"How much is public?"

"The liens that are in place, and there was a prosecution a couple years ago where the government got their judgment." He nodded at the file. "It's in here. Just take credit for it yourself if anybody asks. But that's not even the kicker. You know how that Glendale cop told you he thought the arson was a key to something? Guy was right."

He folded back more documents, revealing a computer printout that listed various search results from a computer-driven inquiry. It was two pages long.

"So what am I looking at?"

"What I got back from the NICB. My search request was for any claims by Alliance for loss due to fire."

I scanned the pages, keeping count in my head of the different addresses I saw. "Six claims in the last twenty-eight months," I said, "all for fire damage."

"Seven," Duke said. "If you count the claim they'll make on the law center."

"How come the insurers haven't put it together?"

He leaned over the table and pointed. "Read it closely. Each policy is with a different carrier. Guess they haven't figured it out yet."

"They will when I send each insurer a copy of this report. So, Duke, how did a movie production company get so many properties all over the state?"

"Pasqual probably had a lot of adult bookstores at one time before videos came in," he said.

"He might have owned some of the buildings the stores were in."

"I think that's likely." Duke's jacket was a deep navy color, but I could see deep water-spots around the collar, and as he hunched to pull it tighter, his shoulders quivered. "Then the IRS starts auditing him, he can see a bunch of liens coming at him down the line, figures out he'd be better off parking them somewhere else a few years beforehand. That's probably how Alliance got created."

I thought of the kick to the balls I'd taken from the Fed last year at tax time. I'd set aside five grand in savings to cover the extra income I made managing the sales of my friend Jackie Pace's surf memorabilia. The tax bill was double my set-aside, close to forty percent of what I'd made. It was enough to make me want to vote Republican. But I'd paid.

"These fucks always find a way to be judgment-proof," I said. Duke started to laugh, but swallowed it when he saw that I wasn't joking. "You've also gotta wonder what kind of tax advice they were passing out at that law center."

"I doubt they gave much advice at all. The place had no lawyer. The best they could do was misuse Dale Bleeker's bar number by slapping it onto pleadings here and there."

Tito brought my teriyaki bowl and set if before me. I thanked him, waited until he retreated again, and pushed it aside. My mind was going too fast to think about eating.

I recalled my original view of the law center as a standard UPL operation, the kind that offers unsophisticated consumers the moon and stars, generating a river of up-front retainer fees for months on end. I thought of what Tamango Perry's detective's instincts had told him, that the arson was the key.

Tito delivered Duke's special. Duke waited for him to walk back behind the counter before he said, "A cheeseburger and fries. What's so special about a cheeseburger and fries? And why are you grinning like that? You look like Jack Nicholson in *The Shining*."

I related my thought about how typical UPL operations work, and how this one was so much smarter. Suddenly I felt starved. I sprinkled soy sauce on my teriyaki bowl and dug in hard.

Duke nibbled a steaming french fry. "What already?"

The beef was chewier than usual, and I took a moment longer with it before I swallowed. That's what you get when you order the last bowl of the day, I suppose.

"For months the place is getting three thousand here, five thousand there to get the job going," I said. "If someone bitches about the nonexistent timetable for completing the job, just feed them a five-dollar legal term or two, preferably in Latin. After that, a long string of phone calls just don't get returned—'So sorry, we're on the other line, can you leave a message?' Any client tenacious enough to stop in for an in-person status update gets the same glib little assessment about how the legal wheel turns slowly, but it does turn."

"I've heard all that before from a hundred victims," Duke said. "So what?"

I gnawed on a broccoli crown, making Duke wait again. "Here's the original part. Just before the inevitable client uprising occurs, an accidental fire breaks out, destroying the unworked files and conveniently providing the confidence men that run the place with the ultimate excuse for nonperformance. 'Hey,' they tell the clients, 'you're bitching about your little files? Look at us! We lost everything, so cut us a break, we'll follow up on your cases in due time.' But the office never reopens."

"Pretty sweet," Duke said. "They keep all the retainers and disappear. Capitol Consolidators and Homeowners Fidelity don't get fingered, 'cause they just came in to do their scam seminars, they don't own the place."

"And the real owner, Alliance Pictures, collects the insurance money." I washed down a big bite of white rice with my ice water. "The few clients lucky enough to have had anything filed for them complain to the bar. The subject of the complaint is this schmuck lawyer they never met, but whose bar number is listed on their pleadings."

"In this case, Dale Bleeker," Duke said.

"Yeah, in this case."

Tito's worker lugged a metal bucket in the front door, a puff of frigid air blowing in with him. Duke rubbed his forearms to keep warm. "Until they open up the next shop in the next building Pasqual owns."

"And do it all over again," I said. "It's a nice source of cash for a guy who can't make any without the IRS grabbing it."

"He probably makes back a hundred grand or more on the building," Duke said.

"And at least that much on the UPL money, plus maybe a percentage on the commissions they're taking from the annuity scam." I pushed what was left of my lunch aside again and studied the corporate documents on Alliance. "Who's helping him?"

"Read the statement of domestic stock." Duke reached into the file and flipped some pages forward and back. "Here it is: Miles A. Abernathy." He sat back triumphantly.

Miles A. Abernathy, what a world-class prick, I thought. "Pasqual is his client, so Abernathy is ringing up the money in more ways than one as well."

"He profits from the annuity scam, and he's probably charging inflated legal fees for funneling the insurance payoffs through Alliance and back to Pasqual." Duke poked a finger at the name and signature on the page. "You've got him, J."

I wasn't so sure of that. "The fact that he prepared corporate documents doesn't by itself mean he's guilty of anything." I scanned the list of officers. "What about these guys, did you investigate them at all?"

"Waste of time," Duke said. "Looked up the CEO's name. He died a few years ago. Ninety-five years old. They probably lifted his name from the obit pages. In the Bahamas, the rules aren't too strict about setting up a company."

"President, Barney E. Malthias," I read aloud. "What kind of a goober name is that?"

"I know. Couldn't find anything on him." Reading the page upside down. "Good old Mr. Barney." He snorted. "It almost sounds made up."

I stared at the page, not following any particular train of thought.

Barney E. Malthias. The letters hung suspended in my mind's eye. Barney E. Malthias. Cutting through my scattered thoughts about Carmen and Albert and Stone Me Stevie, the headstrong redhead napping in my car outside, where Rudy was now and whether Dale was close behind. B-A-R-N-E-Y-E.-M-A-L-T-H-I-A-S. Persisting for some unknown reason.

I ate the rest of my teriyaki bowl.

"J., did you hear me?" I heard Duke say. "This cheeseburger blows and I'm freezing my nuts off." He tapped the face of his watch. "I gotta get back to work."

I realized what the letters were triggering somewhere in my brain: a reshuffling.

"Don't go yet," I said, tugging a napkin free from the dispenser on the table. "Lemme borrow your pen."

Duke paused. In his pocket was what looked like a Waterman, black with gold trim. "Lulu gave me this for Christmas."

I gave him a sideways stare. "Your girlfriend bought you a pen for Christmas. How nice."

"Okay, it was just a stocking stuffer. But you're always bumming pens from me and not returning them."

"Sorry. Sometimes I get distracted."

I held out my hand and he gave me the Waterman. On the napkin I wrote out the name of the president of Alliance Pictures, Inc. Then slowly, beginning with M, I rearranged each letter in the space below, crossing off each letter from the top name as I went. When I was done, the napkin read like this:

B A R N E Y E. M A L T H I A S
M I L E S A. A B E R N A T H Y

Duke slapped his hands together so loudly that Tito stopped scrubbing the grill. "Hot damn, look at that!" Shaking his head over and over. "You'd think he would've been more cautious."

"No," I said. "It was a joke. I'm sure they laughed about it. Bunch of cynical fucks. They don't even care."

I thought of Skip Greuber, looking in on Duke a block away from here, maybe asking the investigator in the next cubicle if he'd been gone awhile. How could I handle that issue diplomatically?

"Look, Duke, we need to talk about something. I know you've been asked to investigate me, and I'll understand if you've got to do what you've got to do." Trying to sound reasonable, but getting the subject out there.

He seemed not the least surprised. "I'm not worried about that. I know you, J. To me, the only dumb thing you did was get too involved in that Bleeker guy's mess. But what am I supposed to do with all this?" He hefted the file. "If I go back in there and lay this on management, Skip'll probably get me suspended too. And it's not like connecting the dots will be easy. Guys like this, they'll put a spin on everything, whitewash the whole thing."

"I know," I said. "But that's why I need you."

He handed the file to me. "Sorry, bud, you're on your own." He got up to leave.

I stood up and grabbed his arm. "Wait a minute." He looked up at me, his round face blank with fear. I hadn't intended to intimidate him, but he was giving up a good eighty pounds. My grip fell away. "Don't go yet."

Duke was straddling the bench awkwardly, but he made no move to extract himself further from the table. "I'm waiting."

"You put all this together," I said. "I'm a trial attorney, I can't act like I'm the investigator, too. I can't wear two hats at once." I sat back down, but Duke remained standing. "Not to mention, I'm still suspended."

"You should've thought about this. I handed you this stuff on a silver platter. Now it's not enough?"

I slowed my breathing. It was time to make my pitch.

"I'll need you to go on the record."

He shook his head. "That's more than we bargained for at Tommy's, J."

I was down to my last card. Duke knew it, too. "I'll do what I have to do, if it comes to that."

He looked trapped—yet defiant. "You would use me like that? Risk my job?" He paused. "Go to hell, bud!"

I didn't much care for his choice of words. "You want to talk about using someone, *bud*?" I said. What, do you think I'm John Wayne or something? I risked my neck to attend a high school dance with an underage kid who was being stalked by a dope-dealing thug and his buddies. And you're offended that *I'm* using *you*?"

Duke hadn't moved. "His buddies were there?" he said after a frozen moment.

"Yeah, man, he had friends. Nice guys, too, probably the same ones who relieved themselves on you that time you were facedown, spitting teeth like Chiclets. Great conversationalists."

He gazed as if picturing a scene. "They hassled you?"

"We had a nice chat in the men's room while I was taking a leak that night."

"A fight?"

I held out my right hand, displaying the bulging knuckle on my middle finger. "Your sis kept the prom pictures from that night. I got this little souvenir."

"I didn't know," Duke said, almost mumbling. "Why didn't you tell me?"

I stepped clear of the table, leaning over to scoop up the file Duke had brought me. "I just did."

I couldn't sleep worth a damn that night. Carmen was in another bed again. I'd made the foolish mistake of mentioning Therese

Rozypal for God knows what reason. Carmen ran with it, said maybe my "obvious" shared attraction with Therese was an indication that I wasn't ready for the commitment of marriage. I defended poorly, using plenty of cold, hard logic and not nearly enough reassurance, which, I realized far too late, was all that she had really wanted. Carmen and I had been together for two years—a relationship record for me. I'd always thought of her as a complete package, always assumed she was The One. But now, for the first time, I seriously questioned whether I possessed the versatility and stamina required to sustain a long-term relationship. Words deserted me with such great frequency these days. My feelings and motivations were even further out of reach.

Was my attraction to other women, however fleeting, merely a manifestation of the most primal urge known to man? What had it meant when I'd looked up and closed my eyes while making love to Carmen the week before and seen Therese, naked, the shadows of shimmying tree branches brushing the ceiling behind her in the dark? Not such an easy image to file away. Over and over, legs twisting in the sheets and blankets, I'm thinking, Hell, so I notice other women, is that a crime? Maybe I could love them under different circumstances, but reality makes that issue moot. The unhealthy impulses are there, I know, but what's the harm if I never act on them? Does my face, with its sun wrinkles and liver spots and thick fighter's nose, the eyes that go dull sensing confrontation, does it betray my secrets that easily? Am I telegraphing my longing with a laugh or a nod or a tip of a drink, and, conversely, confessing my guilt to the woman I love through a poor choice of words or a heated inflection? So I twisted and thrashed and when sometime well past midnight, those thoughts submerged beneath an incoming tide of sleep, I pulled up the heavy quilt, rolled over, and buried my face in the pillow, left with the one question I could not answer: Can I love just one woman?

Eloise Horton likes to come in to work early. I phoned right at seven-thirty, figuring her secretary wouldn't be in to screen the call. I was right.

"We need to meet. Right away. You, me, and the chief."

The line was silent. Then she said, "Forget it, Shepard. I learned my lesson. This thing's going through the proper channels from now on. You can call your union rep if you want, but I'm sure you already know that, don't you."

"I don't want to talk about getting my job back, Eloise. Not yet at least."

"Then what is it?"

It would be a mistake to reveal too much of what I knew about the law center and the various players connected to it, but I had to give her something. "That law office they say I may have burned down in Glendale, I know the people that are behind it. They're running an investment scam targeting the elderly, using offices just like it. They'll run a UPL operation out of the office for several months, have their investment seminars there at night."

She paused. "Go on."

"I've got to know this conversation is confidential."

"And why is that?" Giving me attitude.

"Someone who works with you is involved in it." Shit, I thought, now I'm really out there.

"You're not talking about yourself, Shepard?"

"No, boss, I'm not." I silently cursed her shitty demeanor, then sucked in a deep, calming breath. "I'm very serious. I'll stake my job and my reputation on it."

I could hear her breathing on the other end. "Okay," she said finally, "this conversation is just between us."

"On your word. Say it."

She let out a big sigh. "On my word."

"What happens next is the office catches on fire. This way, the UPL clients have nowhere to go, and nobody gets a refund of the unearned fees. The company that owns the buildings—same company every time—they collect on the insurance policy."

"Interesting. So how did a suspended DTC like you come to know these things?"

I wasn't about to mention Duke.

"I have the documents to prove it. I'll bring them to the meeting."

"Why do you need to talk to the chief?"

"This thing has bigger implications. The people involved are high profile. The chief will have to think about how to handle it."

"Sounds fishy, but I'll mention it to him," she said. "Give me your number."

"Mentioning it is not enough. You have got to get me a meeting with him. Ten, fifteen minutes, that's all I need."

"You've embarrassed me with your irresponsible behavior already," she said. "And that was a lousy thing to do, having that uppity union twerp jump all over me."

Let it ride, I told myself.

"Let me tell you something: I am not inclined to let you embarrass me again," she added.

At that moment, I shut my ego off just long enough to remember whom I was dealing with. Eloise Horton, a litigation manager who didn't know how to litigate, a Peter Principle stretch into the position at any rate, but worse, a woman with a daily opportunity to look damned foolish—and she knew it.

"Boss, here's how it will be," I said a little softer. "If I go in there and make an ass out of myself, you'll be able to wag your finger and say, 'There you go, Chief, the guy's a knucklehead.' You may even have something real to use to get rid of me. If that's what you think of me already, I'll just be proving you right."

"Amen to that," she said, but I sensed that she was troubled.

"But if I show the chief these documents," I went on, "and he sees how serious this really is, and he takes action to stop the people involved . . . Well, you're my manager. You brought me to him. You supported me when I was down. You showed some vision."

"What you're saying is, I'll get a mention."

I shook my head. Fucking Eloise.

"I'll make sure of it." I cringed at what I was about to say. "Who knows, you might even get promoted." Christ, that result would do wonders for morale in the L.A. office. They'd be serving Jonestown Kool-Aid at the promotion party.

Max barked outside. Albert was not downstairs for breakfast yet. He'll be down soon now, thanks to the two hundred-pound rooster out back, I thought. In the kitchen, Carmen pushed down the lever on the toaster. From the dining room where I sat, I could see half the kitchen table, the edges of a section of newspaper turning on it like a paddle wheel. She's going for the crossword puzzle first, I thought. Christ, what had they done with Rudy Kirkmeyer?

I waited a little longer for my manager's decision.

"Okay," Eloise said. "We have a meeting at nine. I'll talk to him after."

"Outstanding." I gave her my home phone number. "When will you call?"

But she had already hung up.

Twenty-five

The sun came out a little after eleven. I was in the front yard in my oldest pair of disintegrating Levi's, pulling weeds from the rose beds while the dirt was chunky and soft and scooping displaced earthworms off the walk. Carmen was inside, getting Albert ready for a few games of bowling. I'd begged off during breakfast, saying I had to wait for Eloise's call, but the phone hadn't rung all morning.

The wet street echoed with the haggard sound of an overtaxed muffler. Wiping the sweat from my eyes, I looked up in time to see a little Nissan pickup with a battered shell and big back tires chug to a halt just beyond my gate. Stone Me Stevie jumped out the driver's side and gave me the howzit nod. I didn't react.

"Finally got it running," he said, closing the gate gingerly behind him. He wore a white tee beneath a wrinkly Pendleton shirt, a faded red Bay Surfboards ball cap on his head. His jeans were low on his hips and wet at the ankles. Despite the weather, he wore only black rubber thongs on his feet. "So, what's the haps, man?"

"You tell me," I said.

"Good fuckin' news, bro, I found 'em." Grinning.

"Watch your language around here."

He glanced about vacantly, as if he were trying to glimpse a winged fairy floating on the breeze. "Sure, cool."

I wiped my hands with an old rag, still gripping the gardening spade I'd been using. "Let's hear it."

"They been hanging down by Warner, the free parking lot behind the Jack in the Box. You know, where the buses turn around."

I knew the place. It was only ten minutes south of town down PCH, a big cul-de-sac where Warner Avenue, a street that originated a good twenty miles inland, came west until it petered out in the sand. Mediocre sand-bottom waves broke there—ridable waves, but the place was not really a surf spot.

"You talk to Leanne?"

"Yup."

"You tell her what I said?"

Stevie rolled his head a bit, searching for those flying fairies again. "Yeah. She's pretty pissed about everything. Her boyfriend's not too stoked that you kicked his ass."

"But you set him straight on that little misunderstanding," I said, not believing Stevie possessed the sack to have done any such thing.

"Um, yeah. Well, kinda." When I glared at him he took his hands from his pocket and extended them like a saint appealing to a higher power. "Fuck, J., gimme a break. There were like, five guys there, a couple of 'em were pretty beefy, too. They would've worked me."

"Gosh, that would've been tragic." I wished those guys would have known the truth about what Stevie had done and taught him a lesson he'd remember forever. Then I had an idea. I set the rag and spade down on the walk. "Wait here," I said.

I went inside and made a quick phone call. Then I went upstairs and asked Carmen and Albert to come down in a few. Five minutes later, Mickey Conlin pulled a black Ford Thunderbird right in behind Stevie's minitruck.

"Mickey, howzit," Stevie said, his face bright.

Mick was in a navy mechanics jumpsuit. His hair was pulled into a tight ponytail and his fingernails were ringed with black. He nodded at Stevie without comment, shooting me the stink-eye. We all looked to the porch as the screen door creaked open.

Carmen and Albert didn't advance more than a few feet onto the porch. "Hello, Mick," Carmen said.

"Carmen."

Albert squinted into the sunlight, his head cocked slightly to the right.

Mick's arms were folded, his sleeves rolled up to the elbows. His forearms were as thick as a menacing genie's.

Stone Me Stevie was so still, you'd have thought he'd stopped breathing.

Carmen eyed me with suspicion. "What's going on, J? We're going bowling."

"This is Stevie," I said. "He's from the neighborhood. He surfs the pier a lot. Couple nights ago we bumped into each other, and he told me a story about how he was out one morning recently, carving a re-form to the beach, and some guy cut him off. After that, he sort of lost his head, because the other guy never even saw him coming and probably had no idea he'd gotten in anybody's way. Right, Steve?"

Stevie hung his head and took a few tentative steps toward the brick porch. "Hey, man," he said to Albert, "what can I say, I'm fuckin' "—stopping himself—"I mean, I'm really sorry I punched you. It was a totally uncool thing to do."

Carmen's face was taut with constricted fury. Her mouth opened, but she withheld comment. Albert looked past Stevie in the distracted way he often does when he carries on conversations, but I was certain he understood what he had just heard.

"O . . . k-k-k-kay," he said. Then he looked at his sister. "H-he s-s-said he's s-sorry."

Carmen came down the porch steps and stood before Mick. "I misjudged you," she said.

"No problem," Mick said.

They stood very still, looking into each other's eyes just a tick too long, and I felt a tingle shoot up my spine. Damn, I thought, I know that look. I should. It's the kind I've shared with Therese Rozypal lately.

Carmen hoisted her black purse on her arm, motioning to Albert. "Let's go, hon." Then she regarded Stevie at close range. "I don't want to know what J. did to get you here, but thank you for coming."

Stevie shrugged. "Okay."

Then she stepped into Stevie's face, startling him. "I don't believe in an eye for an eye, it's too Old Testament. But if you ever touch my brother again, I swear, you'll have hell to pay."

Stevie swallowed. "Yes, ma'am."

Carmen turned and put on an instant loving smile for her brother. She surprised me by leaning over and kissing me on the cheek. "We'll be back in a couple."

Stevie, Mick, and I watched Carmen and Albert clack through the gate and onto Porpoise Way.

"So," I said to Mick. "The night I saw Stevie on the pier, he was telling me he thinks he's becoming something of a tough guy."

Mickey's eyes were unblinking as he surveyed the twitching Stevie. "No shit."

"That being so, I think he should quit bugging guys like us to fight his little battles for him, don't you?"

"Sounds reasonable."

"Seems to me," I said, "if he's gonna be on his own now, maybe it would help him to get a little conditioning. Maybe we could show him a few moves."

Mick played along beautifully, cracking his knuckles as he widened his stance.

Stevie was in full brick-shitting mode, his palms outstretched again. "Whoa, hey, man," he said, his voice cracking. "Like, I really appreciate the offer, but I mean, fuck, it's cool!"

"I guess another possibility might be . . ." I paused, savoring the moment.

"What, man?" Stevie begged.

"Well, you could take a different tack altogether. Share a wave now and then."

"Give the other guy the benefit of the doubt," Mick added.

Stevie puzzled for a moment. "I dunno. I mean, shit, man, *you* try it on a Saturday morning, good day at Northside. It's a fuckin' zoo out there."

He was right, in part. Surfing an overcrowded break will test one's patience in a hurry, and on plenty of occasions, if you're looking for trouble, some inconsiderate bonehead will supply you with enough reason to start something.

Then Stevie tugged down on the bill of his cap, and caught me rather by surprise.

"I'm gonna try, though," he said. "Balls out, all the way."

"You mean it?" I said.

Stevie put his hand over his heart, his breathing still coming too fast. "Swear to God, you guys. Fuckin' swear to God."

• • •

Mick stayed for some reheated pot roast. We talked about his shop, how business had picked up last week with three bearing repacks, a handful of major tune-ups, and a full engine overhaul and tranny replacement on a Winnebago—a six-thousand-dollar job.

The phone on the kitchen wall rang. Eloise Horton. "Tomorrow morning, eight o'clock. You, me, and the chief."

"Eight, you got it, I'll be there. Thanks for—"

"Just don't screw it up," she said, cutting me off. "And try to ignore the impulse to make me look bad." She hung up, the sharp click jolting my eardrum. Awkwardly, I put the receiver back without another word, not quite fathoming what the hell that woman had to be so angry about. It would be my ass in that meeting, not hers.

Mick must have sensed my discomfort. "Trouble at work?"

The phone rang again. "Nah. There you go," I said, "calling back to apologize already. I love this job." I picked up the phone again, feeling like a punching bag. "This is J."

It was a long-distance operator, asking if I'd accept the charges on a call from Dale Bleeker. I said yes.

"J.! Thank God you were home." He sounded half out of breath. "I've been driving for hours. This is the first chance I've had to call you. They came back to the house early this morning, with Rudy."

Dale's little stakeout had paid off. "How did he look?" I asked.

"A little bewildered, but you know him. Otherwise I'd say he was fine." A large roar that sounded like a big truck passing on a highway rose up, then faded away. "They only stayed a couple hours, then they took off again."

"Where are you?"

Another roar, so loud that Dale had to wait for it to subside. "At a truck stop in a little place called King City. Not quite to Salinas."

Salinas is a long way from L.A., a good four- to five-hour drive north, toward San Francisco.

"What are they doing?"

"Eating. Carlito stopped at a hardware store first, carried out what looked like a tool set, stuck it in the trunk of the Lexus. Can't figure that one out, but I'm darn glad they pulled over when they did. I was practically out of gas." More noise from the highway. "J., I think you need to get up here. I think they're headed to that cabin in Big Sur."

So did I. If they went west toward Carmel and Monterey, Big Sur would be easy to access heading south on Highway 1. We waited again for the highway noise to die. "How far you think the cabin is from here?" he asked.

"An hour, more or less."

I looked at my watch: 1 P.M. The sun had been setting at around five-fifteen lately. If I left right now and drove like hell, I'd still pull up in total darkness. I couldn't picture searching for a remote cabin in the coastal mountains at night. Big Sur is a rugged place still mostly preserved in its natural state. No fast-food joint and 7-Eleven on every corner, no minimalls. No streetlamps, either. I would have to drive up tonight, check in somewhere, and set out for the cabin early tomorrow morning.

And I would have to take Kimberley. She would insist.

"I'll watch them till you get here," he said, assuming I'd made the decision to come up. Damn, I thought, Eloise is going to have her panties in a bunch over this one.

"Dale," I said, "don't crash in your car tonight. You're a long way from Glendale. You could freeze."

"No, no. Got a blanket in the trunk. I'll be fine."

"Don't do anything but watch them until I get there."

"Wouldn't dream of it," he shouted over more highway thunder. I couldn't tell if he was being glib.

I hung up, then picked up the phone again, held it, put it down. Just now, I didn't quite feel up to dealing with Eloise Horton's rage. Mick finished off another biscuit, apparently content to mind his own business. Having heard parts of both conversations, he probably knew I'd just put myself in a wicked bind.

"Thanks for coming over," I said.

He grinned. "Think little Stevie had to change his underwear when he got home." He wiped his mouth with his napkin. "But you could've put the scare in him yourself, J."

"Wouldn't have been as much fun, though."

"Fun, my ass," he said. "I know why you invited me over." He was talking about Carmen.

"What can I say? You're my friend, and she was wrong about you."

"Please." He dropped his napkin on his plate. "Don't give me the false loyalty shtick." Then he stood up and looked about the kitchen. White curtains facing the backyard fluttered before an open window. Slowly he crossed the room, stepped into the afternoon sun that streamed in through the window over the sink, then crossed out of it again, leaning against the counter. "She's yours," he said. "That's exactly as it should be."

"How's that?"

Mick's eyes seemed to fix on an unknown point across the room. "You're different from me. Always have been. You remember when we were just learning, and started getting good enough to surf the outside break?" I nodded yes. "Well, I still remember how pissed off I was that you were the first one to paddle outside to give it a go."

I said, "You were good. Right with me, at least."

"Followed you outside the same day, not that I was ready. But even after that, you were always . . . different."

"Oh sure, I had quite the eye-catching style," I said. "Six-two and a hundred and forty pounds of overcooked rubber. They called me the Spastic Tic."

Mick laughed. "That's not what I mean." He waited. "I remember how, when we got good enough to sit with the pack, you always sat the farthest outside."

"Missed a lot of good ones that way."

He was looking right at me. "Yeah, but it always seemed that whenever the biggest deep-water wave of the day rolled through, you were there. I'd scratch over the first wall with the pack, and there it would be, this big, beautiful bluebird rising out the back. More often than not, you'd be the only one in position to catch it." His gaze shifted to somewhere far away again. "That was always your approach. And I envy you, man."

We drove up that night and crashed at a place called the Travel-Inn near Carmel, a desperation move when the punishing rain became too great a hindrance to cruising around and comparing the area's hotels. The Travel-Inn was an unfortunate choice, combining high prices with warped mattresses for a uniquely torturous lodging experience. I'd awakened in the dark several times with the distinct impression that somehow I'd managed to crawl inside a satellite dish to sleep. Kimberley said she'd slept poorly in her room, staring at the ceiling as she second-guessed the way she'd dealt with her father the last two years. We met up again at seven in an ugly little hot-pink lobby full of plastic plants and complimentary breakfast rolls that could break your teeth.

But we were here, and it was time to take back Rudy Kirkmeyer.

Kimberley pointed to the sign that said Rocky Point. "Slow down, this is it."

It was a dull gray, blast-the-car-heater morning, wet fog clouding over the yellow lines like a new storm's heavy breathing. I'd driven this stretch of coast highway several times before and knew the ocean was just below us, but it was completely invisible for now. The cars streaming north on Highway 1 all had their lights on, telling me that the weather they'd encountered to the south was no better. I waited, the Jeep wagon's blinker ticking. The clock on the dash clicked over: 7:57. Damn, I thought, I should be at the state bar right now, settling in at the chief's private conference table up on the top floor. Oh well.

Kimberley was wearing her shades, even with all this gloom. "So, what's the plan?" she said as I finally cut a left and headed up the canyon road.

I didn't have a plan but wasn't about to rattle her. "We're getting your father back," I said.

The road ran steadily uphill and straight inland. To our left a creek full of rushing brown water sliced along the base of the hills. Modest A-frame cabins and vacation homes were set on the near bank among a web of gravel turnoffs and dirt driveways. The trees thickened with our ascent—pines, coastal redwoods, aspens, their trunks mossy and strung with deep green, climbing vegetation. The canyon walls seemed to rise up higher and steeper with every switchback. The stream had now gone out of view, well hidden by the overgrowth. Heavenly rays of sunlight sliced through the high branches. Apparently we'd risen above the marine layer. The road narrowed and I kept the Jeep wagon in low gear; we were still climbing.

"Your ears pop yet?" Kimberley said.

"They just did." I was amazed at the transformation. We'd driven no more than three or four miles, but it was as if we were somewhere high in the Sierras.

"I always know we're close when they pop."

Without warning, a shiny black sedan swung into view just ahead, blasting me onto the dirt shoulder with its horn. I caught a brief glimpse of the driver as the car shot by, strafing my wagon with loose pebbles. Kimberley wheeled around, watching the car disappear through a plume of white dust. We idled there, my wagon half off the road, a fresh coat of dirt settling onto the hood.

"It was them," she said. "I saw her, I saw Angie."

"So did I."

"And that prick with the beret, I saw him too." She took off her tiny sunglasses. "But I didn't see anyone in the backseat." Still studying the last, empty curve in the road behind us. "Did you?"

I wasn't going to lie to her. "No."

She leaned forward, those long white fingers coming up to shield her eyes. "We're too late, aren't we?" Verging on some kind of a breakdown. "This is all my fault."

Twenty-six

The Jeep rattled from side to side as I guided it off the dirt shoulder and up onto the slab of shiny black pavement. Kimberley sniffled, her long eyelashes fluttering.

"What are you doing?" she said, sounding weakened.

"Keep looking for the turnoff," I told her.

She'd fished a tissue from her purse and was dabbing her eyes and nose. "I'm kind of upset here." The car blasted through a soggy chuckhole, rocking us both. "Do you mind?" she half shouted.

I wasn't in the mood for any more talk of regrets. "Look, I can appreciate that you're upset, but this isn't the time. Pull yourself together." That was too strong, and I could feel her recoiling next to me. "Your dad needs you, Kimberley," I added.

Her sniffling died away as we curled higher and higher up the canyon. Then, just as the road briefly straightened itself, she pointed to a mailbox on the left. She had put her shades back on following her little cry.

"We're here," she said, her voice still a pale imitation of the rumbling original.

"Don't be scared," I said. She was shaking when I put my hand on her shoulder to steady her.

She swallowed. "How do I do that?"

"You don't have to deny that you're afraid. You just have to practice putting it out of your mind for the time being."

She stared at the floor mat beneath the dash. "I don't think I can handle this."

"Okay. You can wait in the car."

I opened the car door and walked across the ribbon of gravel and dirt that passed for a road. A steep driveway not much wider than a bike path cut sideways down the hillside for less than a hundred feet, then abruptly changed direction, angling along the side of a one-story wood-paneled cabin without a garage. The surrounding woods were dead calm, but I could hear the shimmering echo of water flowing over rock far below. I got back into the Jeep and slowly navigated the drive, parking it sideways across the hairpin turn. In the event that Angie and Carlito returned, I didn't want to be surprised.

The cabin had a small front porch and awning, with a pair of curtained glass windows in front, both of which were cracked open. I crossed the porch and peeked through the glass.

"That's from the flood I told you about."

I almost jumped. Kimberley was standing not five feet behind me, pointing to the faded brown stripe that lined the bottom of the entire structure. "You can see where the waterline was."

I didn't bother to ask her if she was okay. Perhaps she'd tried my mind-control suggestion. Maybe she just wanted Rudy safe so badly that her own safety didn't matter for now. Either way, I needed her help.

No lights were on inside the cabin. I tried the front door, but it was locked. Kimberley went to a hummingbird feeder that hung from an awning near the porch, sliding her fingers around the base of it. "Shit, they took it."

These Kirkmeyers with their hidden keys.

The front door had a dead bolt, and I didn't want to break it down, as it was the only entrance visible from the edge of the road. If we had to leave it that way, someone could loot the place before it could be repaired.

"Let's try the back," I said.

Kimberley made a funny face. "Got any rope?"

As soon as we made it around the side, I saw what she was talking about. The cabin had been built on a flat ridge that stayed well hidden among the trees, but the pitch of the hillside was precipitous. We held hands, sidestepping along the cabin's south wall. A corner of decking and wooden railing supported by a framework of thick posts jutted right out over the edge, like a defiant chin. I let go of Kimberley's hand and reached for the railing, my feet skidding on a bed of fat brown leaves. I was at eye level with the decking, and through the railing, something about it looked amiss.

I was reminded of that shabby motel bed that had tortured my spine the previous night.

"Lemme find a way in first, and I'll come through and open the front door," I said over my shoulder.

I strained to jerk myself up and over the top rail and heard a sickening crack, followed by a woman's screams.

I slid maybe a dozen feet face first, a two-by-four whacking me just below my right eye as it cascaded past me and down into the gulch in a shower of splintering wood. My head spun from the pain and the view below me: a long, steep drop to a creekbed lined with bluish boulders. Black dirt and dead leaves flew into my face, and I felt the waistband of my jeans tearing into my pelvis. But I'd stopped sliding.

"Don't move, I can barely hold you!" Kimberley shouted. She was flat on the dirt, puffing that red hair out of her eyes. Her downhill arm had a death grip on the bottom of my pant leg, and her uphill arm strangled the base of a sapling that had snapped off cleanly a few feet from its base.

I dug around in the dirt until I felt a wiry root. I yanked it up and hung on. "I'm okay. You can let go."

It took a few long minutes of careful crabbing on all fours to get back up over the ridge. We leaned against the cabin, breathing hard. Then we crept around back and had a closer look.

A few supports remained, but most of the decking and all of the railing had gone straight down the hillside. I remembered the funny look the deck had just before I'd reached to pull myself up, making me think of that warped bed last night, the satellite dish. Shit. The deck I'd been staring at was concave in the middle, a part of its support structure already gone.

I told Kimberley what I'd seen. Then we crouched together, peering down through the trees. She'd lost her sunglasses in the scramble on the hillside and had to shield her eyes with a hand. Half her nails were broken, a few of them bleeding.

"By the way, thank you for saving my butt," I told her.

"You don't have to thank me. This is turning into the biggest fiasco of my life. We find my dad alive, I'm telling you, I'll probably kill him myself."

The tangle of branches below made it hard to see much of the gulch, but I didn't rush myself, studying the shapes one by one. A small, dark, well-rounded boulder at the edge of a line of rushing muddy water stood out. What looked like the branch of an overhead tree just above the well-rounded rock appeared, on closer inspection, shaped more like an arm. A man's body, facedown.

"I think I see him," I said slowly.

Kimberley crowded in closer to align herself with my view. The black ski parka I'd loaned her had a jagged tear just below the heart.

"Is it Dad?"

The body wasn't moving. A sizable hand was twisted palm-up into the sun, a slice of powder blue shirtsleeve encasing the wrist. I felt a pang of sadness shoot through me like a jolt of high voltage.

"No. It's Dale."

I gave Kimberley the car keys and sent her to get help, then slowly, deliberately started working my way down the hillside. A rocky ridge halted my downward progress, forcing me to bear farther right through a dense jumble of brush. For a minute, I thought I might have to go back up and begin my descent all over again. I paused for a blow, resolved to hack maybe ten more feet before turning back, and within two steps, stumbled right onto a trail. The thing was no more than six inches wide and absurdly steep, but I followed it down, sliding a good part of the way on my ass.

Dale's skin wasn't yet cold, but he had no pulse. Both his legs appeared broken, his left foot twisted backward, the shoe missing. I turned him over, cleared his bloody tongue, which he had swallowed, and started CPR. Ten minutes later, I stopped.

Slats of finished wood from the cabin's decking lay all along the creekbed. I wondered what had happened to my friend. The cabin was nothing fancy, but it was nowhere near decrepit. The decking looked solid and well constructed; that's why I hadn't hesitated to reach for it.

There was no way I could move a man Dale's size back up the hillside, but there was also no way I was going to leave him there like that. I didn't care if he was dead. He deserved better.

I held his head in my lap, brushing his loose brown hair straight, waiting. I recalled the glide in his step that first day he'd chosen me as a juror, those big hands working as smoothly as a magician's to emphasize a point, the voice as soothing as it was authoritative. All that was years before the rapid, spectacular decline that had brought him to me, but I didn't care about that anymore. A chill ocean breeze blew up the canyon. My jacket was torn at the armpits, the sleeves soaked with icy runoff from the creek. I held Dale a little tighter. You will be remembered well, I told my secret mentor. Then, with my thumb, I gently closed his silvery eyes to the world.

Nothing stirred uphill, and eventually I stopped looking—hell, either they were coming or they weren't. My right eye smarted to the touch, and my hands were rubbed raw just below both wrists from my slide off the collapsing decking. The worst pain was radiating from my rib cage when I shivered, which was more frequently now that the sun had ducked away. Lucid white clouds drifted up the canyon, the tallest trees scraping their undersides into vanishing swirls of smoke. A voice inside my head did battle with the silence, hushing the creek and the wind through the trees and the nervous tittering of unseen birds. "J.," it called to me, quietly at first, then louder. "J." I tried to quiet the voice with thoughts of home, of Porpoise Way and Carmen and Albert, Max's big sphinx's head patrolling the yard outside the kitchen windows. "J." A wrinkled hand reached out and shook my shoulder. "Hey, J."

Rudy Kirkmeyer stood over me, gazing upon Dale's peaceful visage.

"Where did you come from?" I said.

"I've been hiding."

He sounded coherent. "Hiding?" I asked.

"Up there, around the bend."

"What happened?"

He took his time answering. "Some wood, lotta wood came crashing down a while ago. So I waited."

"You waited."

He nodded, the hillside bearing down on us like a merciless giant. "Didn't hear anything for a long time after, though."

It was the first time he'd ever spoken to me with his faculties this much intact. Resenting the deception, my jaw tightened.

"Where's Kimmy?" he said.

"Up there, getting help."

He couldn't seem to take his eyes off Dale. "How bad?"

"He's dead."

Rudy staggered back. "Dead? No, no, no! He can't be!"

I leveled an icy stink-eye on the old man. "Rest assured, he's not faking anything."

A helicopter came and lowered a bright red basket three times, plucking Rudy first, then Dale, then me. They flew us to a small hospital in Monterey not three blocks from the wretched little motel where Kimberley and I had slept the night before. Rudy was given a general physical and released, his hands wrapped in white gauze. During the chopper ride over, he seemed particularly stimulated, so I asked him to recount what had happened.

"Woke up last night to this strange noise outside, out back. Carlito was out there. Crouched down, by the decking."

"You saw him?"

"Well, no, that was the thing, he was under it. Had a flashlight."

"What was he doing?"

Rudy's face glazed. "You're J., right? How's Dale?"

He was fading again. This time I believed it, for he had no more reason to employ any false pretenses. The chopper glided low over wild meadows and offhand clusters of oaks.

"What was Carlito doing?" I said a few minutes later.

"Lotta grunting and huffing and cursing. Had a flashlight under there. Clanking noises." Then he paused. "Am I in trouble?"

"No, Rudy. You're okay."

It didn't take a genius to figure out their plan: a fall like that could kill even a young man. The last time I spoke by phone with Dale, he said Carlito had stopped at a hardware store to buy tools—tools he'd used to deconstruct that deck just enough for it to give way.

Then Rudy surprised me with another burst of lucidity. "Knew my daughter offered an extra fifty grand for the divorce, but that Angie, she's a spitfire."

"She was looking for your will."

"There wasn't one, either. I was real worried I might tell her, too, you know, in one of my . . . lesser moments." He looked away. "Carlito wouldn't let me out of his sight. I thought, I'm dead. But I woke up this morning with an idea. Like a miracle or something, you know? There it was."

"What was your idea?"

"I'd stage an accident before they got up. Their accident, the one I knew they were planning for me." He went silent for a patch. "Sorry, having a . . . a spell. Like two voices in my head talking at the same time." His hands chattered in his lap.

I told him to take his time.

Just before we landed at the hospital, he told me the rest. "Found some twine in the kitchen utility closet. Then I slid out the sliding glass onto the deck. Whew, that wood was sure creaky. Stayed flush against the house, sidestepped to the edge, then I slipped through the railings. Beneath the deck, one support looked pretty wobbly, bolts were all loose on it. I backed the bolts off by hand the rest of the way, then I tied the twine around and around the post. Trailed the twine behind me and slid on my backside down the hill a way. Hit the trail down below, top of it, but didn't move. I don't know how long it was, I have trouble with time. But I lay there, in the dirt, top of the trail, jerking that twine, jerking, jerking, come on! Nothing happened, that back porch didn't budge. After a while—least I think it was a while—I saw Carlito up there, stomping around, knew he was looking for me. Gave up my idea and figured I'd be safer down in the gulch. Slid the rest of the way down." He closed his eyes. "I get dizzy thinking about it."

"How did you wind up farther upstream?" I asked.

He stared at me. "Was I?"

"Yeah, you came downstream to meet me."

That familiar glaze had returned. "Oh, right. I . . . don't know." Then his eyes sparked. "But there is a neighbor up the canyon a little way past our cabin. I could've . . . was probably trying to get there. Doesn't matter, though. I didn't get fifty feet beyond the next bend there. Fell down on a pile of boulders, I do remember that." He looked at his feet as if they were a new discovery. "My ankles were killing me."

"What about Dale?"

"Don't know. I heard Carlito swearing up there. Then this big crash came a little later." He closed his eyes as if to help clear his mind. "Then another."

"Another what?"

"Another crash." Rudy shrugged. "I think it was a little later. I have trouble with time."

My best estimate—and what I told the police—about what happened to Dale was that he'd moved in quickly when he saw Angie and Carlito split in the Lexus alone, thinking they'd left Rudy behind and this was his chance to grab him back. Finding the front door locked, Dale had most likely done what I did, curling around to the back. Climbing up the railings, he'd gone down—all the way down. The second crash Rudy heard came when I duplicated Dale's failed attempt to get inside the cabin from the rear.

We returned to the cabin with the police and spent another hour telling the same stories before they let us go. It was just before noon when we reached the bottom of Rocky Point Drive. The morning fog was gone and the sunlight dazzled overhead, the ocean wind-whipped and electric blue. We took a vote on whether to go north, then cut inland until we hit the 101 southbound for L.A., or head south on Highway 1 for the slower but ridiculously scenic drive through Big Sur proper. I've seen so much scenic coastline that I didn't really care to see any more that day, so I voted 101. Kimberley had never driven Highway 1 through Big Sur but had heard about it all her life, so she voted to head straight south. In a move that probably signaled a powerful future trend, Rudy instantly sided with his daughter.

We stopped for lunch at a restaurant called Nepenthe, a glassed-in place high on a cliff-top with a good menu and friendly earth-mother waitresses. No one said much. It was the first time I'd eaten since those teeth-cracking rockamuffins at the motel that morning, and my avocado club and side salad tasted wonderful. Kimberley had given her father the business at the hospital, but since then, she'd left him alone. He'd been through plenty, and, contrary to his daughter's cynical assessment, he'd weathered the action with a mind he couldn't trust.

The drive was all any tourist could ask for, but it flashed by like an old rerun I'd seen too many times. For once, the ocean's vast seductive powers held no sway over me. Instead, in every craggy outcrop smashed by pouncing surf, every empty sandbank buffeted by the brisk onshores, every twisted cliff-side tree branch groping for the sky, I saw Dale. I thought of what he'd said a few days ago about learning from me not to sit back, but to act. Christ. He'd ignored my instructions to wait until I arrived to help Rudy, snaking his way around the back of the cabin, just as he probably thought I might have done . . . and just as I eventually did. As I navigated each turn, eyes fixed on little more than the endless yellow stripes ticking by beneath my window, I was struck by the notion that I'd somehow mentored him in his final days, contributing to a short-lived burst of self-confidence, and a pointless, horrible death. The thought unsettled me, and I sat there, gripping the steering wheel, the most beautiful coastline in the state blowing kiss after kiss that, on this day, could only fall short.

With Big Sur behind us, the highway jogged left toward the rolling hills of Cambria and Hearst Castle. A few miles north of town, I spotted a handful of cars and a mammoth tourist bus parked in the dirt along the shoulder. Across a flat meadow just above the beach, people were standing and pointing and taking pictures.

"What's that?" Kimberley said.

"A spot where the elephant seals have established something of a natural rookery," I said. "Last time I checked, there were at least a few hundred of them."

"So, what do they do?"

I smiled a little. "Pretty much whatever they want."

We whizzed past the parked vehicles and I checked the scene in my rearview mirror. Then I hit the brakes.

"Why are we stopping?" Rudy said from the backseat, his first words since we'd left Nepenthe.

"Lock the doors and stay in the car," I said. I patted my hand beneath my car seat until I felt the bill of the New York Yankees ball cap I keep stashed for those bad hair mornings that sometimes follow a surf session. "I'll be right back."

Jogging back up the road, I found an opening in the fence and cut through a flat, muddy meadow pocked with wild grass. The bluffs ringing the beach were sunny but severely windblown.

Twenty feet below, an army of elephant seals lounged and slept and made happy with one another, seemingly oblivious of the spectacle they represented. A smattering of onlookers milled about the scene, tilting into the wind as they snapped picture after picture. A little to the south, a young couple stood alone on a narrow bluff-top. Beneath them, two of the biggest specimens on the beach were locked in battle, slamming chests at the waterline. The young man appeared to be riveted by the action.

I walked up beside them and peered down onto the beach.

"Fuckin' unbelievable!" the guy cried. "You gotta get that on film!" His gal began snapping away, then looked over at the guy in the pulled-down Yankees cap.

"Hey, man," she said. "How 'bout a picture of us together?"

I reached for the camera she was handing me. "Sure."

Angie and Carlito locked arm in arm on the bluff. "Smile," I said, squeezing off a few. I studied the camera, a nice Panasonic reflex that I figured was Rudy's. "This isn't yours," I said, slipping it into my jacket pocket.

"Hey, what the fuck, man?" Angie said.

Then I took off my cap. "Not that I need a reason," I said to Carlito, stepping into him fast, "but this is for Dale." I slapped his ear with an open left hand and caught his fall with a solid right.

Carlito groped on his knees, his mouth drooling blood, and he actually smiled as if he would savor kicking my ass. He swung first, hard and fast, catching a piece of my shoulder but little else. "Come on, man!" he screamed.

I saw the red oozing through my jacket before I felt any pain where I'd been cut. The little shit was clutching a box cutter, wobbling before me like a drunken boxer. Then a blast of dirt hit the side of my head, temporarily blinding me.

Angie's mistake was to jump on my back. That tight little body of hers couldn't have weighed more than a hundred pounds, and with my one good eye on a rushing Carlito, I flipped her over my shoulder and flat across his chest.

Now, when I gave my report to the police in Cambria later that day, I did tell the reporting officer—who at this point in the story was giving me what looked like the official stink-eye—"Hey, please understand, I don't ever hit females." And since technically I'd flung Angie like a sack of potatoes into her charging boyfriend, I felt I hadn't violated this section of my personal code. But that was it for my little editorial with the cop, because I don't have any rule about pushing a girl over a bluff and onto a pile of horny elephant seals. Or the girl's boyfriend.

No violations there, either.

Twenty-seven

Reginald Hewitt liked a table in the southwest corner of the Tower restaurant for lunch, according to the hostess I bribed with a twenty to seat me at the next one over. He apparently ate lunch alone most days, reading a book or simply watching the traffic flow by down below on the Santa Monica Freeway. I got there twenty minutes before his 1 P.M. reservation and settled in with an iced tea, a copy of the *Times,* and the evidence file Duke Choi had put together for me. The view from atop the Transamerica Tower thirty-two floors up was too good to pass up, a stout westerly blowing the usual smog dome farther inland today. I put down the paper, checking my watch every few minutes beneath the white tablecloth, sat back, and through the ceiling-to-floor glass followed an endless procession of big jets floating down like paper gliders as they headed for LAX.

I let the chief settle in and order his meal before making my move.

"Mr. Shepard," he said, recognizing me instantly. He was a thin, well-kept black man with a long face and professorial black-rimmed glasses. Despite his age, which I figured to be around sixty, his short Afro was still shiny black, but he'd lost a large tract of hair behind his forehead.

"Please excuse me for interrupting your lunch."

"I hope you're not here to argue for a raise." He almost smiled.

"I'm sorry about missing the meeting with you and Ms. Horton."

"Okay."

I couldn't think of what to say next. "You're not in trouble with the police?" he asked.

"The fire?" I said. He nodded. "No, sir. I've been working with a detective on the Glendale force regarding the unauthorized-practice-of-law operation that was going on before the place burned down. He says there's no evidence that I did anything but pull a dead man out of the building. Which is the truth."

"Mr. Silver. He was already dead?" I told him yes.

Chief Hewitt sipped from a tall glass of ice water. "So, what is this about?"

"I have a problem," I said, "and it's not what you might think."

He'd brought a book called *Devil in a Blue Dress* with him, and he fiddled with a bookmark before closing it. Then he took his glasses off and rubbed his liver-spotted forehead. A waiter passed by slowly, probably wondering if I was hassling the chief and should be shooed away. But Hewitt gave no such signal.

"You're not here to ask me to get you reinstated?" he said.

My shoulder was stiff where I'd been stabbed and my head was pounding from lack of sleep. Yet this was it, the moment to either close him, or be closed out.

"No, sir," I said. "I mean, not until I've won you over completely."

The chief didn't laugh. I felt like a crash-test dummy strapping in for another run.

"Join me," he said.

I started in with my story as soon as the waitress took our orders and went away. I don't think I looked up once the next twenty minutes. The chief listened carefully, absorbing each layer of detail with a nod and another new question for me. When I finished, he sat back and twirled the straw in his ice water.

The bandage on my shoulder itched like hell beneath my white shirt. I tugged at my tie, which seemed to be strangling me.

"Well, I agree with you," he said after a time. "It's a problem. But it's my problem too, now that you told me."

"Yes, sir."

"On the other hand, that does not mean that I trust you to know what to do here." A waiter with a silver teapot glided by our table. Hewitt waited until the man was gone. "We're going to catch holy hell for this, you know. Lot of successful people involved. They'll fight like tigers, call it a witch-hunt. Use the press on us the way they've done to you already."

"We've got the facts on our side."

Hewitt sighed. "Not all of them." He wiped his mouth and dropped his white linen napkin on the table. "I brought Skip Greuber in myself. He had worked under me at the DA's office in Major Frauds." The chief paused, then tossed off a quiet little gallows laugh. "The board of govs will want my head on a platter."

The board of governors is the elected and appointed panel that directs the agency. The chief spends a good chunk of his time answering to them for everything from day-to-day staff productivity to general policy issues.

He leaned forward, extending a gnarled finger. "We've got to stop that disciplinary evaluation committee in its tracks. I've been on the phone with general counsel in Sacramento. Webb's capitol cronies are using Abernathy's claims to stir up a lot of antibar sentiment, way more than the usual rhetoric. If it keeps up, he thinks it may give Webb the courage to veto our dues budget when it hits his desk later this year. That happens, we'll be shut down completely." He took a drink of water. "Assuming you go back to work tomorrow, how long to file a notice of disciplinary charges against Mr. Abernathy?"

"A case like this will take a little time," I said. "Thirty days, at least."

"That won't do. They'll grind us down in the meantime."

I had an idea. "What about an interim suspension order? Give me an investigator, I could get an interim suspension petition and some declarations together, file the thing by next week, ask for an ex parte hearing within twenty-four hours, we'd be in business."

"An ISO," he said, using the more common abbreviation. "Interesting."

An ISO is what you want the judge to issue against the offending lawyer after you've made your pitch. The Business and Professions Code allows the bar to file a petition asking the court to suspend an accused attorney immediately and until the disciplinary case is filed and decided. To prevail, the bar must demonstrate both that they would be likely to prevail in the underlying case, and that the ongoing harm to the public would be greater if the lawyer was not suspended by an ISO than if he was. Evidence supporting the petition is confined to written witness declarations, which means the damn things take a lot of work to put together. Because of the dual thresholds of proof and the labor-intensive nature of the beast, not many ISO petitions get filed—or granted—but there is no better way to take a dangerous lawyer out of commission in a hurry. Chief Hewitt studied the tablecloth, his chin down. "How are you gonna show there's a likelihood of ongoing harm to the public? The Glendale office is burned down. No more investment seminars, no more UPL with the daily walk-ins either."

I went into the file and located the flyer that Tamango Perry had given me, spreading the wrinkled edges flat with my hand. "This could be the next operation. If we can show they're poised to do it again, then it's ongoing. I called the number this morning. Apparently the attorney position is still open."

"Can you do the interview yourself?"

"No way. They know me."

"Of course they would." Hewitt massaged the bridge of his nose where his glasses had left an indentation. "How about one of our investigators?"

"I don't think it'll work. My guess is they're using Skip Greuber to verify bar numbers, since an active bar number to stick on pleadings is what they need the most. He'd know something's wrong if we used a bogus number. He does, they'll probably fold in no time and move on to another property somewhere else. We might not find out about it for months."

"Until a new batch of complaints rolls in," Hewitt said.

A busboy in a white uniform appeared with coffee, but we waved him off. I remembered Dale's description of his job interview and, rather suddenly, saw the problem in a way I hadn't yet come close to considering. "I've heard this Mr. Julian character is a Hollywood wannabe."

The chief brightened. "Didn't you say Mr. Pasqual's offshore company is in the movie-production business?"

"That's right. So, what if we were to do a two-for-one on Mr. Julian? We get an attorney who looks like she ought to be in pictures to do the interview. She tells him she's a lawyer, but what she really wants to do is act."

"The old L.A. cliché."

"But it's a good fit," I said. "He'd want to know why she's out of the loop professionally anyway. That's exactly what they look for when they hire."

"Someone who'd be happy to stay out of the way, take a check every now and then for doing absolutely nothing."

I pictured the setup. "During the interview, she could voice the usual struggling-actress aspirations. Julian the wannabe ought to warm right up—he gets to be the big know-it-all with a beautiful young woman. He'll be running off at the mouth in no time."

The chief paused. "I like it." Then he frowned. "Where we gonna get a beautiful young lawyer who ought to be in pictures?"

Outside, the sun beat down on bending rows of shining cars streaming every which way. "Mr. Shepard?" I heard the chief say.

"Yes, sir?"

I was still picturing Dick Nixon sweating bullets all those years ago, caught off guard by the visual wonders of a single fawning Girl Scout.

"My feet hurt," Therese Rozypal whispered over her shoulder. We were seated at adjacent booths in a chain steak house just off the San Bernardino Freeway, somewhere about fifty miles inland in the vicinity of Pomona.

"I'm telling you, the shoes are worth it," I whispered back. "They really put a bow on the package, if you know what I mean." I was talking about the shiny black pumps she'd shown me this morning before scrunching into her little Mazda Miata for a noisy drive out here from Newport Beach.

"Yes, J., I know what you mean. Your eyes back in their sockets yet?"

"They haven't quite recovered. That's why I'm over here, facing the other way."

She wore a tight-fitting black dress, sleeveless with a cream-colored front panel. Far too racy for an attorney interview, but her line for Mr. Julian would be that she had an audition later, reading for a postmodern Audrey Hepburn–type role. Cherry red lipstick, a pile of wavy blond locks swimming down her back. When she walked in, half the noontime bar patrons across the room nearly fell off their stools craning for a perve.

The waitress working our section stopped at both of our booths and got blown off twice, muttering as she retreated toward the kitchen.

"Should I order when he gets here?" Therese asked, sounding a tad anxious to get on with matters.

"Only if he asks you to eat with him. Just let him take the lead."

"Don't look now."

I had a perfect view of the hostess's station near the door but could see no one coming.

"Well, hey there, honey," a male voice boomed. "Mind if I join you for a drink? I'm buying."

What I saw from my booth at a one-quarter turn was tan loafers, cuffed gray slacks, a jaw hanging open like a gumball dispenser, and a lot of nervous energy. He must have come over from the bar, because two other young gents in shirts and ties were looking on from their barstools as if they'd already placed bets on the outcome.

"Hi. Sorry, I'm waiting for someone." Therese's tone was terse. "But thank you for asking." Ah, better, I thought. Stay loose for the interview.

"Aw, c'mon, just a teensie-weensie little old drink. Now how can that hurt?"

"No thank you. As I said, I'm waiting—"

"For who?" Busting a gut now. "Hell, why worry about it? Whoever the lucky guy is, he ain't here yet. Waiter?" he barked at a passing busboy, puzzling the guy. "One lousy drink, that's all," he said to Therese. "What'll it be?"

"I'd like you to leave," Therese said, her voice shaky. Suddenly I felt rotten about asking her to get dolled up this way. No wonder she usually downplayed her looks. Who would want to put up with this kind of crap all day?

"Tell you what, lemme just sit down with you a minute and maybe we can just talk, get acquainted."

That was it. I wasn't going to let this goofball blow Therese's calm all to hell before Julian even arrived. But before I could get out of my booth, she took over.

"Listen, pal," she said in a low, even voice, "I tried polite and polite didn't work, so now I'm gonna tell you, if you don't turn around and walk away right now, you'll get a shot of Mace in the eyes, which means you won't be able to see me when I start scratching your face off. And I will."

"Hey, okay, I didn't—"

"Now, I really don't want to do that to you right in front of your buddies," she went on, "so why don't we both just smile a lot while you head on back to the bar, hmm?"

"Hey, well, nice meeting you," he said, stumbling over a chair leg in the midst of a rapid backpedal. "You have yourself a fine afternoon."

"Nice," I whispered to Therese when he had gone. "You're pretty resourceful."

"What did you expect? Just 'cause I'm dressed like a bimbo doesn't mean I am one."

I checked my watch. Five till noon, the interview about to happen. Hoping Therese's shoes weren't hurting her too badly, when I saw the open black shirt and gold chains coming straight my way. He was much as Dale Bleeker had described him, all the way down to the cell phone on his ear.

"Okay babe. Ciao." Chirping a fake kiss over the line, then gliding past my elbow, jaw loosening, apparently not yet believing his good fortune. "Well, hell-low."

They exchanged overly friendly greetings.

"I'm Mr. Julian."

"Charmed. Nico Reed."

The real Nicolette Reed had died of brain cancer at twenty-nine five days earlier. Chief Hewitt had gotten her name from the bar's Membership Records Department, driven to the funeral down in Santa Ana by himself, and asked the parents for permission to use her name this day. They had said fine. Their daughter had just passed the bar exam last summer but was already too sick to go to work. This way, they felt, at least she might be able to leave behind some small legal legacy. Therese, in a gesture of respect for the dead, told me she'd be shortening the name to Nico during her interview. It turned out to be a fortuitous move.

"Nee-co," Julian said, savoring the sound of it. "How enchanting." Therese giggled. In a mirror behind the bar, I caught his reflection as he leaned over and kissed the back of her hand— Christ, what a showman. "So tell me, what is Nee-co short for?"

"I'll give you three guesses."

"Hmm. How about nee-co-tine?" Tossing off a carefree chuckle. "It's addictive. And I've got a feeling you are, too."

I cringed from my lonely station next door.

Therese tittered, playing it to the hilt. "Close enough," she said, "close enough. Now it's your turn. What about Julian, is it a first or a last name?"

"What if I told you it was . . . a middle name?" More light-hearted guffaws.

"Really? You mean it?"

"I'm not lying, I swear. My first name is . . . no, I really don't want to relive any of this."

"Oh, come on, tell me." The lilt in her voice calculated to melt any man's resolve.

"No. I probably shouldn't."

"Please."

I was positioned here to take notes of anything he said that might be . . . well, notable. But with this guy, the prospects seemed as dim as his personality.

"All right," he said. "Are you ready for this?"

Yes, jack-off, I wanted to say. We're ready.

"It's Rene."

Therese giggled. "Ooh. Too bad."

"I know. Believe me."

"That must've been hard for you in school."

"Please. I used to get my head beaten in every day for having a 'fairy' name."

"Rene Julian," Therese said like a royal courtesan introducing a king. "It does have a nice ring to it. What's on the end?"

I could smell the guy's reluctance. "You don't wanna know, Nee-co-tine."

"No, I do," she said. "I'm an actor."

"So you said on the phone. How very intriguing."

"I love good names. They tell me a lot about a character I'm playing . . . or someone in real life, too. A strong name can convey so much."

"All right," he said, sounding it out this way: "what does Ruh-nay Julee-onn Da-veed Pasqual convey to you, Miss Nico?"

He was the son of the pornographer, Yves Pasqual. Had to be. I imagined Therese with her long legs crossed in the booth behind me, displaying some sort of gesture of female domination—say, rolling the tip of her pink tongue over her plump upper lip, or raising her chin like a lioness.

"More than you can know, Rene," she told him.

The ISO petition hearing against Miles Abernathy was nearly concluded but still curiously lacking something. Certainly not outside attention. He'd retained Roger Turnbull—whom I now realized Abernathy had handpicked to represent Bobby Silver in Silver's ill-fated bid for reinstatement. Turnbull is a consummate media masseur, and he'd been stroking the press since the day I filed the four-inch-thick document exposing Abernathy, Alliance Pictures, the investment scams and UPL, and the string of torched former office sites. As a result, the head clerk had moved the hearing down the hall to the largest court department in the state bar court, the one the Review Department uses to hear appellate matters. Reporters from the *Times* and the *Orange County Register* were present, as was Deidre Sharpe, the blond amazon from Channel 6. In preparing my petition, I'd had Duke Choi collect a pile of sworn declarations from Mr. Carpio and a host of senior citizens that frequented his Cuban bakery and had been bilked by the annuity scam. They must have chartered a bus from Glendale, because about forty angry-looking white-haired folks made the trip with Carpio and his scowling wife, throwing daggers with their eyes at Abernathy and his counsel every time they uttered a word.

Duke Choi leaned against the courtroom's back wall, in a shiny navy polyester suit and the same maroon knit tie he always wore, content to blend in with the scenery as much as his cheesy ensemble would permit. The reporters standing near him paid him no notice, but anyone who'd read the petition knew that Duke Choi's declaration was the cornerstone upon which the entire case was built. I still owed him lunch, but Duke didn't owe me a thing in return, not anymore.

Skip Greuber didn't attend. My ISO petition against him would be filed in a few days, but he was already on an administrative leave without pay, courtesy of the chief. About an hour after Julian Pasqual left his interview with Therese Rozypal, aka Nicolette Reed, Greuber used his state bar computer to tap into all the membership-records information he could find on Ms. Reed. The report from the head of the bar's Computer Services Department hit the chief's desk before five that afternoon, confirming that Greuber's involvement with all this carried well beyond that of an unwitting investor.

Hewitt was still so burned that a bar manager he himself had brought in could betray the agency this way that he insisted on sitting with me at counsel table for that day's hearing, something he'd never done before.

Julian Pasqual was a no-show as well. He'd been arrested for arson and second-degree murder by Tamango Perry, the police detective the Glendale City Council had installed as interim chief while it pursued an inquiry into the host of alleged misdeeds perpetrated by newly suspended police chief Nicholas Conforti. Two witnesses had placed Julian Pasqual's mist green Turbo Saab convertible double-parked in the alley just before the law center had burned, and a search warrant executed upon his Century City apartment had turned up a host of interesting incendiary devices. Pasqual's attorney also understandably found it difficult to explain away the unsold screenplay his client had foisted on one Nico Reed, aka Therese Rozypal, over a business lunch recently, angling for the young actor's feedback. The screenplay, entitled "Scorcher," followed the exploits of a suave-but-deadly arsonist known only by the handle Gastogne. Ham-fisted and overly melodramatic, the script was amateur-hour stuff all the way, redeemed only by a handful of riveting scenes in which the mysterious Gastogne displayed a true insider's knowledge of fire-starting techniques.

I'd been hoping that the presence of the chief and the Glendale contingent might make Judge Renaldo take the petition against Abernathy that much more seriously. Hewitt felt that Renaldo's standing as the eldest judicial arbiter on the bench in state bar court presumably made him a decent match for the case as well. But so far I couldn't get much of a read on how the old judge had reacted to the thirty-eight pages of brief and accompanying attachments I'd filed. Having witnessed firsthand the debacle involving Eugene Podette, his wife Trixie, and the rest of the Von Trapp Family

Singers just a few weeks prior, I wasn't at all confident that Renaldo could resist getting sucked in by the gravitational pull of Roger Turnbull's spin. Not that Turnbull was saying anything worth listening to beyond the standard my-client-the-misunderstood-martyr crap he'd been force-feeding the TV and press people for days now. I just sensed that the party that would prevail in this battle would be the party that could strike the right emotional chord with the aging jurist.

"This is a cheap political stunt," Turnbull raved, taking time to turn and level a stare at Chief Hewitt. "And this . . . so-called prosecutor, Your Honor"—pointing a loaded finger at me—"he's clearly using this proceeding, this charade, to attempt to lift the cloud of suspicion off himself for playing a role in the fire in that Glendale office." Looking now at those in the gallery. "A fire that conveniently destroyed files that might have implicated his pal, Mr. Dale Bleeker, a bad-apple lawyer and convict whom the bar had already placed on probation." The prick obviously had no respect for the dead.

When people feed me bullshit in large doses, eventually I do get full and just can't swallow any more. When this happens, my ears close off and my mind wanders elsewhere—as in anywhere else. So I sat there, next to Chief Hewitt, watching Roger Turnbull sing the lead in his own little underwater operetta, thinking about the revival-hall sign that Dale Bleeker and I had stared out the window at that first day he came to my office. PRAYER CHANGES THINGS.

I said a tiny prayer for old Judge Renaldo, offering to God my feeble thoughts on the importance of serving the truth.

Do prayers get answered? I won't know in this lifetime, but I would like to think so, because just then, without warning, the opportunity to turn the whole damn case my way poked its way up out of the chaos and bloomed before my eyes like a rare desert flower. And as so often happens in the practice of law, this brief chance to win it all arose not from any brilliant tactical maneuver on my part, but from a simple mistake committed by the opposition.

"Your Honor," Miles Abernathy said when Turnbull had finished, "I would like to address the court for a moment myself."

"Objection," I said. "That is Mr. Abernathy's counsel's role."

"I agree," said Renaldo. "Mr. Abernathy, these interim-suspension matters are submitted in the form of briefs with attached exhibits and written declarations. Of course, the lawyers for the parties may make oral argument at the hearing, which your counsel, Mr. Turnbull, has ably done."

"But, Your Honor," Abernathy said, not a wrinkle or crease to be found on his tailored black suit, "I implore you to give me the opportunity to defend myself directly against these spurious charges."

At this exact moment I saw my opening.

"No objection."

The judge regarded me with suspicion. "How do you mean?"

"Well, Your Honor," I said, "the code gives you the discretion to hear witness testimony if you choose. And my thought is, if Mr. Abernathy is allowed to testify, then the state bar should have the opportunity to call a single witness as well. It's only fair."

Renaldo ruminated silently, his face a deeper red than usual. "You're certain you want to do this, Mr. Abernathy?"

"Absolutely, Your Honor," Abernathy said, ignoring a subtle ix-nay hand signal from Roger Turnbull. Abernathy was apparently operating purely on ego now, and he didn't wait to be invited to testify; he just walked to the witness stand and raised his right hand.

It's true, I told myself, it's true: The lawyer who represents himself has a fool for a client.

Roger Turnbull was clearly unprepared for this, but he is a gifted lawyer and so he had little trouble muttering a few open-ended questions to get his client rolling. Abernathy's testimony was little more than an extended harangue of me, the chief, and the unspe-cified "cowards" that facilitate the out-of-control agency that is the state bar. The petition to suspend him was nothing more than a Machiavellian plot to undermine the integrity of a vital disciplinary review probe commissioned by none other than the governor of this state, Burton Webb.

Blah, blah, blah.

When Abernathy finished, I might have scored a few points on cross by asking him a series of specific questions about his hands-on involvement with both Capitol Consolidators and Alliance Pictures, Inc. But he refused to answer pretty much down the line, alternately citing the attorney-client privilege and his Fifth Amendment right against self-incrimination. Renaldo took it all in without expression.

As soon as Abernathy left the stand, smiling as if he'd just shredded my ISO, Roger Turnbull shifted gears on the judge. "May we take a five-minute recess before making closing arguments, Your Honor?" he asked, presumptively sidestepping my right to present a witness of my own.

Renaldo caught it. "We're not there yet, Mr. Turnbull."

"But, Your Honor," Turnbull said, "the bar's petition is over three hundred pages long, if you count their attachments and exhibits. Surely they don't deserve to add to this obvious overkill."

Renaldo's face seemed drained. This case had gotten a lot of attention, which meant that he would too, especially if he screwed it up somehow.

"Fair is fair, Counsel." Then the judge turned to me. "Mr. Shepard, you may call one witness."

I suppose anyone in that courtroom with a legal background would have laid odds that I would call Duke Choi to underline the bar's evidence with cool, utilitarian efficiency. But the judge had read my petition, and it was straightforward. Something critical was still missing from this case. I sat at the table, pouring a glass of water to buy a few more seconds. Chief Hewitt didn't squirm or lean closer to inquire with a discreet whisper as to what the hell I was going to do—no, far from it. His spine was straight against his chair back, his eyes fixed on some point behind the bench, unflinching. The message he was sending to Renaldo was simple: I trust my prosecutor, so should you.

Trust—the single element that linked this case from the start. Wasn't trust what the investment seminars were selling more than anything else? Trust us, this will help your children inherit your estate virtually tax-free. Trust us with all the details, we'll handle them. And wasn't trust what the law center fostered in nervous clients when they slapped Dale Bleeker's name and bar number on a pleading? Not to worry, you've forked over a nice retainer and received no results, but look, our in-house attorney is backing the project. You can trust us, the work will get done. The fire? Devastating for us, of course, but trust us, we'll be in touch as soon as we're back on our feet.

"Mr. Shepard?"

"Yes, Your Honor, thank you." I was out of time but ready to make my decision.

The gallery was too full to turn and study each row of faces, looking for my only witness of the day. But he'd called yesterday, promising that he'd be here, saying he felt it was his duty to be present and accounted for in some small way. I hadn't argued.

"The state bar calls Rudolph Kirkmeyer," I said, hoping he was back there somewhere. The chief didn't even turn around, which made me think, if he has the faith that strongly, so should I.

The gallery murmured behind us as the judge flipped through his list of exhibits. "I don't see a declaration from anyone by that name, Counsel."

That's because the day after Big Sur, Kimberley had zipped Rudy back to Seattle with her on the first available flight, making him all but unavailable. Since then I'd sunk back into a miserable losing game of telephone tag, much like the one I had played with Kimberley before she came to reclaim her father. By the time Rudy picked up the phone himself and dialed me, I'd pretty much given up on ever seeing him again.

"Mr. Kirkmeyer is a firsthand, percipient witness to some of the activity at the law center you've read about in the petition," I said. The problem was, I didn't know for certain how much Rudy had actually seen, or how the revelation that he suffered from a degenerative disease would play to Renaldo in terms of his competency. But Dale's death had haunted Rudy during his Seattle stay. It was all he had wanted to talk about when he called. And he sounded okay—most of the time.

Renaldo looked up.

"Good morning, sir," he said. God, was I relieved. As he made his way up front, Rudy Kirkmeyer looked like a tourist stepping off a chartered bus in Vegas: tan leather Top-Siders, checked pants, white golf shirt, and a navy blazer that somehow made the look just formal enough to work in court. Renaldo's clerk stopped him before he sat in the witness stand to take his oath, and when Rudy held up his hand, his impish eyes appeared more alive than they'd ever been. I hoped this wasn't how he looked when he was terrified.

I asked him about his age and former occupation, where he lived, how long ago he had retired. Pausing noticeably at times, he recounted his years of water-and-power service, his Glendale roots going back to post–World War II, his retirement three years ago. His wife's death from cancer less than a year later. At that moment, Judge Renaldo abruptly stopped staring into space and fixed on the witness. Rudy Kirkmeyer noticed the attention shift and sat up a tad straighter. But Rudy could not have known that the old judge had lost his wife under similar circumstances.

"Do you know of a place in Glendale called the law center?" I said.

"Yes, I do. It's burned down now, but I went there with a friend, Lester Gibson, about three, four weeks ago on a weeknight, to check out a seminar on how to set up your estate so your kids—I mean, your heirs—won't get taxed to death when you die and your money goes to them. Lester and I thought it sounded too good to be true, so we wanted to check it out."

"What happened at the seminar the night you attended?"

He shook his head. "It was a strange, strange night I'll probably never forget. The man running the seminar, name of Bobby Silver, he made all sorts of promises about how they'd figured out a way to beat the estate tax with this annuity life insurance scheme."

"We know about how that works already," Renaldo said. "What happened that made it such a strange night for you?"

"Well, Your Honor, quite honestly . . ."

I held my breath for Rudy as he closed his eyes. If you didn't know him, you might think he was fighting off a nasty headache.

"Would you like to take a break?" Renaldo asked him.

"No, thank you. Anyway, I'm not the most emotional guy you'd ever want to meet. But that night, I sat there for two hours, watching other people my age getting so gung ho about a deal that sounded fantastic until you realized that nobody running the seminar could even explain the details of it. Now, I don't know that much about financial matters, but I knew this was one to stay away from."

"Did you leave then?"

"Tried to," he said, "but Lester wanted to stick around. So we stayed. I can't say how long. I'm not so good with time."

That seemed to raise Turnbull's eyebrows a hair, and he leaned over to whisper something to Abernathy.

"All I could do was sit around waiting," Rudy went on. Then he frowned. "It was depressing, sitting there watching other folks get their hopes up like that. I must have looked pretty hopeless. What I didn't realize at the time was how lonely I'd become since my wife had passed on."

"What made you realize how lonely you were?"

Rudy shrugged at the judge as if to say here comes the good stuff. "A young lady I met, right there, at the seminar. Name is Angela Ho. I call her Angie."

"How old is she?"

"Early twenties, I think."

"What happened with Angela Ho?"

"She was attractive, funny. I was nervous." He shut his eyes again.

"She showed interest in you?"

"Objection, relevance," Turnbull moaned.

"Overruled."

"She stayed next to me the whole night, acted like she saw something grand in me. I was . . . acting senile, just to save myself the embarrassment, but the more I did, the more Angie seemed to go after me." He looked at Renaldo. "She asked me a lot of questions. Of course, by then I thought she had to be after my money. I found out later that she talked to Lester. He might have let a few things slip, too."

"Objection, the witness is speculating."

"Overruled," Renaldo said, this time with more authority.

"You mentioned that you thought she was after your money," I said. "What money?"

Rudy paused as if he were contemplating a complex puzzle. Don't lose it, I wanted to say. Hold on a little longer.

"My wife, she spent thirty years building up a portfolio that was worth a bundle now."

"So what did you do?"

He shrugged. "Dumbest thing in my life. I married Angie."

"Mr. Kirkmeyer, are you senile?" I asked. People behind me murmured and gasped.

"Well, no. But sometimes. It's . . . hard. My memory comes and goes now." He looked straight at Judge Renaldo. "I can't always gauge time."

"Objection," Roger Turnbull said, on his feet now. "This witness is clearly not competent to testify."

Renaldo said, "Your objection is noted, but I don't know enough to rule on it."

"But, Your Honor—"

"Sit down, Mr. Turnbull." Then the judge turned to Rudy. "What are you suffering from, Mr. Kirkmeyer?"

Rudy's eyes ticked back and forth like an anxious bird's. "I . . . don't know, Your Honor. I have to go to the doctor. Could be Alzheimer's. My daddy had it."

"Mr. Shepard, how many more questions do you have?" Renaldo said. I couldn't tell if he was set on protecting Rudy, or ticked at me for pulling a stunt on him. I told him I had just a few more. "Proceed."

"What about the law center? Did you go back there?"

"We did. Angie, me, and her boyfriend, Carlito." People in the gallery whispering at that tidbit. "See, I thought my money was safe because the account was in my name. Meantime I let Angie clean out the safe-deposit box at the savings and loan, about forty, fifty thousand worth of cash, bonds, and jewelry."

"Why?"

He shrugged. Then his body shook a little, as if he'd got a chill. "I was so confused. The day after we got married, I woke up, I'd forgotten who she was." When he gazed into the gallery, I knew he was looking at Kimberley. "I was pretty lost. But Angie, she got this idea that she could get at my account if she had a power of attorney. I played along."

"What do you mean by that?"

"Sometimes it would be like two voices fighting in my head, for real. Other times, I'd just act like they were there." He looked at Renaldo. "The two voices." The judge nodded.

"Why play along?"

"I was embarrassed. And scared."

"So they took you back to the law center?"

"They did. We . . . were supposed to meet the guy who did the investment seminar, Bobby Silver. Then go to the bank to get the money."

"Did you hook up with Mr. Silver as planned?"

"Not really. He was late. You and Dale . . . Dale Bleeker, you were both there." He stared at me hard. "Was that the day?"

"Your Honor," Turnbull pleaded. "This witness is not competent. How can we continue to—"

"Overruled," Renaldo said. His lips were tight. "Ask another question, Mr. Shepard."

"What happened next?" I said.

"Mr. Bleeker, he stepped in and tried to help bail me out of the situation. Mr. Silver showed up late," he repeated. Then he regarded Renaldo for a moment. "Good thing, too."

"Did they get your money?"

"No. They tried everything. Mr. Bleeker . . . and you . . . kept 'em away." He looked up at the bench. "They even tried to kill me. Mr. Bleeker died trying to save my neck." Tears came. He was struggling again.

"What about your wife—the Ho woman—and her boyfriend?" Renaldo asked. "What happened to them?"

"They're in jail. I think it's called felony murder." He shrugged. "They tried to kill me," he said redundantly, slipping again. "Dale . . . is dead."

My work with the witness was done. "So then, is it fair to say that what you got from your contact with this law center was, let's see, an investment seminar that you knew was shaky, a young woman looking to cheat you out of your life savings, and an attorney, Mr. Silver, who was in league with Ms. Ho and who tried to bilk you, too?"

Rudy nodded. "Yes."

I had no further questions.

Roger Turnbull wasted no time exploiting Rudy's greatest weakness. "So, Mr. Kirkmeyer, you think you may have Alzheimer's?"

"Yes. I'm seeing the doc again next week." He searched the

gallery, probably for Kimberley. "I think it's next week."

"You said you have trouble remembering things, gauging the passage of time. And when all this was happening to you, you were very confused."

"Yes. I . . . Confused."

"But you had the wherewithal to 'play along,' as you put it, didn't you?"

"Wasn't easy."

"Are you playing along here today?"

"No."

"What parts of your testimony are you really remembering, and what parts did Mr. Shepard tell you to say?"

"Objection, argumentative."

"Sustained."

But Roger Turnbull was unruffled. "Mr. Kirkmeyer, just answer me one more question. You really don't know your own mind anymore, do you?"

Rudy's eyes were red. "It's hard . . . hard to say what."

"Hard to say what you know and don't know, isn't it?" Turnbull said, trying to finish Rudy's thought for him.

Rudy waited, gazing about the courtroom, the close-set blue eyes finally settling on me. Yet, at the same time, the eyes were still searching for something more, marking an inner transition—like a gearbox shifting—a crossing-over to a private place, a place of secrets, the lips following suit as they curled into a splendid, childlike smile.

Twenty-eight

"I know what it's like to feel confused," Judge Renaldo said, leaning into the cushions of his back high-backed chair.

He slowly regarded the faces in the gallery, as if he were taking inventory. I figured he was still missing his wife, whose death had been a powerful source of disorientation for him.

"Those people who came to the so-called Glendale Lo-Cost Law Center?" he went on. "They were confused. And at least one that I heard from directly was scared, too. Losing his faculties while others circled around him like vultures." His voice was haggard but brimming with distaste. As the judge ruffled a few pages before him, apparently searching his notes, I took notice that no one else in the courtroom was moving.

"Before I rule, I will outline my findings. And my analysis must begin with the many incestuous links that Mr. Abernathy had formed between Alliance Pictures, Capitol Consolidators, and Homeowners Fidelity Trust."

"Your Honor," Roger Turnbull said, "I must object to that characterization of—"

"Quiet!"

With a servile nod, Turnbull faded back into his chair.

"Now, as one of a small handful of part owners of the two investment-consulting firms, Mr. Abernathy must be held accountable for profiting from a scam hosted by a dubious nonlawyer, Mr. Silver, among others. His claims that he was unaware of the nature of the businesses were unpersuasive in light of the quite handsome profits that each transaction yielded. Any investor who starts making—or losing—a lot of money is going to study that trend immediately, so I don't believe Mr. Abernathy is credible in saying he didn't know. He knew," the judge said as Abernathy and Turnbull bristled. "Capitol Consolidators was also leasing the law center, an office that engaged in the unauthorized practice of law, according to the declaration of Mr. Shepard and the declarations of five former clients who have filed complaints within the last two weeks. Mr. Abernathy's dual affiliation with Capitol, the lessee, and with Alliance Pictures, the lessor, cannot, as he suggests, be either explained away or overlooked as a mere coincidence."

The old judge hacked into the sleeve of his black robe, and we all waited for him to sip some water from a plastic foam cup. "As the legal counsel for a client's shell company—a company that owned and operated UPL shops, burned them down, then collected the insurance money—Mr. Abernathy may have been less culpable, since it has not been proven yet that he had knowledge of, or directed, those nefarious activities. But he was on hand to help set up an offshore company that, as indicated in the declaration of the IRS investigator pursuing Mr. Yves Pasqual, apparently existed for the sole purpose of circumventing a host of multimillion-dollar government tax liens already in place." The judge eyed me. "At the trial in this matter, the state bar should be prepared to establish that Mr. Abernathy had more direct involvement in the company's ongoing operations. But preliminarily, his assistance to a wealthy client in creating a tax dodge appears to have been tantamount to moral turpitude. He helped Mr. Pasqual subvert the law, even scrambling the letters of his own name to conjure up Barney E. Malthias, a fictitious company president, and listing that fictitious name in an official corporate document of his creation."

The judge paused, his face grim. "Apparently you thought this was something of a lark, Mr. Abernathy."

"I did not," Abernathy said, glaring at the bench.

"Your Honor," Turnbull pleaded, "perhaps an order that my client divest himself of any further contact with the business entities in question might suffice."

"It will not," Renaldo said quickly. "What we're looking at today is a substantial likelihood of future public harm, yes or no." Frowning at his notes. "The answer to that question is yes. The state bar has brought to light a disturbing pattern of activity by Alliance Pictures over the past two years: several offices burned down, a host of disgruntled citizens left in their wakes, these citizens the victims of the unauthorized practice of law, their retainer fees exhausted without any real services having been provided to them. Their only remaining option to file a grievance with the bar." He sighed. "One gigantic mess."

Turnbull was up again. "Your Honor—"

"Sit down, Counsel, you've had your turn." Eyeing the unmoving gallery. "And in the Glendale law office, seminars were run touting what appears, from every indication, to be a scheme that preys on elderly citizens with the promise that they can preserve their financial legacies for their heirs." He shook his head slightly. "Is it likely that this despicable scheme will continue to be carried out, along with more unauthorized practice of law, at yet another location? I believe the declaration of the bar's deputy trial counsel, Therese Rozypal, establishes that such an effort is most definitely ongoing."

Abernathy stood and faced the judge, his eyes narrowed by anger. "Your Honor, as you know, I am part of an *ongoing* effort to evaluate the state bar's current disciplinary operations, which, as you also know, includes a thorough review of the state bar court and its effectiveness."

"Sit down."

"If this ruling is in any way an attempt to dissuade me from that purpose—"

"Sit down!"

"I can assure you, it will not." Abernathy turned to regard those in the gallery when he'd finished.

Renaldo didn't falter, waiting a few seconds more, silently assuring the courtroom that he'd afforded the respondent his due process, even tolerating Abernathy's insult to his integrity. Then he said simply, "Petition granted. I will review and sign the order by this afternoon. Good day."

I wanted no part of the scene that followed, nor did Chief Hewitt. Abernathy and Turnbull went straight for the media as we knew they would, and when I'd packed up, Hewitt nodded to Judge Renaldo's clerk. "This way," he said. We followed the clerk through the lone door exit behind the bench, then took a disorienting series of turns down one short hallway, then another, finishing with a hard right through a set of cherry-wood double doors. The clerk disappeared and we stepped into an elevator, not a soul around, riding to the top floor encased in soothing silence. The elevators doors glided open up top, with no one waiting to climb aboard. The chief didn't move, but instead removed his glasses, inspecting the lenses absently before sliding the frames back over his ears. Then he shook my hand. "Good luck." He said it in a way that politely let me know I wouldn't be following him out of the elevator and back to his office to hash over the ISO hearing or any future strategies. I thanked him and waited for the trip down, reminded of the day I'd dodged Eloise and left the building via this same route with Dale.

I'm a back-door man, I'm a back-door may-annn.

The chief turned to go with that familiar crimped walk of his, like a turtle bearing a too-heavy shell. But before the metal doors clipped shut, our eyes met again, and I thought he might have winked. Or at least I'd like to believe that's how he went out.

It was the last time I would ever see him. That weekend at an emergency meeting of the bar's board of governors, he outlined the ISO and the ongoing related investigations already under way, summarized the known facts relevant to the pending action against Assistant Chief Trial Counsel Stanislav Greuber, dealt with the un-pleasant media fallout that had followed Renaldo's ruling, and ten-dered his resignation.

I surfed alone very early the next morning, riding smallish low-tide lines well down from the pier on Southside. Out to sea a front was rolling in from the northwest, and when the sun came up, the light caromed off the oily surface sheen before me and front-lit a vast bank of purple-and-gray cloud cover, the sky and sea melding seamlessly at the vanishing point. The waves worked quickly across the outer bar, shifting and parrying and offering up an occasional smooth, open face, but it was mostly a tease, like the glimpse you get of a lovely girl on another platform as your train pulls away from the station. I gave chase anyway, not that it mattered. The ocean lets you take only what it will give you.

The coroner's office told me it wouldn't take much for me to pick up Dale's body, just an authorization from next of kin, so I went to see Georgette Bleeker and found her at home on a Tuesday afternoon, glaring at me through a peephole. I hadn't seen a house that messed up since Rudy's place in Glendale. Surfaces were coated with dust, windowpanes glazed with greasy smudges. A trail of ants threatened what looked like an afternoon snack from a week ago: cheese doodles, broken off like brittle fingers in an open jar of peanut butter. In the dining room, a silver tea service was displayed on a long buffet table against the wall, every piece tarnished a bruised blue and yellow. Spiderweb tendrils drifted in a sea of dust motes. I didn't need to check every room to know that every window in the house was closed.

Georgette wore a forest green ankle-length dress embroidered at the neck with creeping white flowers, and red flats in the style of Japanese slippers. On second glance, the dress might have been more of a sporty, if threadbare, nightgown; by the wan light of a single crooked lamp behind her, it was hard to tell. Her mousy brown hair was swallowed up in a tight ponytail in back, like dirty water spinning into a drain. She tamped at the hair obsessively, confessing that I'd caught her tidying up before Leanne got home from school, a pathetic fiction which I let pass without comment. Hands still at work, she creaked down into a sofa the length of Dale's Buick and listened impassively as I recounted Big Sur, then signed the release I'd brought with me as if it were one of those cards you fill out in a mall to win a new car. Before I could get the hell out of there, she disappeared into the kitchen and returned with a folded brown paper grocery sack, handed it to me, and told me Mr. Bleeker had left some things in back, near the pool, and perhaps I could gather them up for him.

"Mr. Bleeker. . . . might want them," she said, tamping her head a final time as she clapped the front door shut just behind my heel.

I curled around the garage and past a row of overgrown rose-bushes to the backyard. The swimming pool was empty but for a small square in the deep end that was backed up with brackish water. Across the yard near the shallow end, a wooden gazebo hid in the shadows of a well-shaped fig tree. Some of the slats in the gazebo's latticed roof had come loose and lay at odd angles. Beneath the broken roof, a lounge chair sat beside a rusting iron table painted white. I walked over.

366 ≋ John DeCure

There was nothing left but a partly folded peach-colored quilt full of dead fig leaves, a stack of brittle mail bearing Dale's name resting on the table beneath a small, smooth rock from the garden, and a newspaper clipping from a local rag called the *Shoreline Gazette*. The story detailed Dale's indecent exposure arrest and subsequent firing, then closed with an arraignment date and a quote from the prosecuting deputy DA that all men were treated the same under the law and this offender would be no exception. I read the brief description of the incident. Bleeker was at the end of Spyglass Circle, which overlooks La Costa Drive, when he flashed the girls walking home from school down La Costa. Christ, I hadn't noticed before that his great downfall had transpired on the edge of Christianitos. I knew those two streets to be in a newly constructed neighborhood with homes built into a steeply pitched hillside. The area had been overlooked for decades because of a lack of level ground, passed on repeatedly until there was simply no more land left in the area to develop.

Folding back the creases in the paper, I kept reading. An open container of alcohol was found in his car, and he appeared to be under the influence, but was not charged with any alcohol-related offenses. I pictured Dale lying out here at night, under his ratty blanket, rereading the account again and again, as if the spectacular collapse of his family, career, and life could not be believed without further verification.

Telling Leanne Bleeker of her father's fate was not an experience I had looked forward to, and when Carmen offered to come along for moral support, I'd quickly said yes. Leanne must have been very close to Dale for a good part of her life, for she seemed to know why I'd come to see her and was shaking her head—no, no, no—before she even heard the news. When I said it, she bent forward, gasping for air. Then she ripped free from her boyfriend Kurt's grasp and scrambled into the back of his battered white van, chucking pots and pans and thrashing around noisily until Carmen went inside and calmed her down.

"She's bleeding," Carmen said a minute later. My first thought was that Leanne had cut herself on a sharp edge during her explosion of grief. But when I looked inside and saw what Carmen was talking about, I knew it would be a very long night.

We took my car, since the van wasn't running. "How far along is she?" Carmen asked Kurt as I looked both ways before running the light at Warner and PCH.

"About seven and a half months, I think."

Leanne Bleeker gave birth to a three-pound ten-ounce baby girl by a cesarean section just after two the next morning. The baby, whom they named Whitney, would fight for her life for five days in the preemie ward, but she gained weight steadily and the fluid in her lungs eventually cleared enough for Leanne and Kurt to take her home on a rain-slicked Sunday afternoon. Home meant Porpoise Way for the time being, until Leanne could heal and regain her strength and Kurt could find a paying job and save enough for a deposit on an apartment.

Kurt wasn't so bad, just a tad unfocused. In a way, his relaxed manner reminded me of myself at a younger age. We talked about what he could do for work, what kind of jobs had a future and which ones looked like dead ends. I bought him a suit for interviews, paid for a haircut, and took him to a job fair at the Long Beach Convention Center. Computers interested him, but he would need training at night school and that seemed like a more long-range goal. New car sales was the highest-paying no-experience gig around, and Toyotas seemed to sell themselves more than any other car. He applied at every dealer in the area, got on a few callback lists. In the meantime he worked around the house, doing chores and small projects that I just didn't have the time to get to myself. Several times I offered to take him for a surf, but he always passed. He never spoke of the time he'd spent in the hospital because of me, nor did I offer any awkward apologies for that day in the parking lot at the pier. What was done was done, and there seemed to be little point in talking about it. As for his friends, it was unlikely that they would ever find acceptance with the pier crew, but they were welcome in my home and they came around frequently during the time he and Leanne were my guests.

Carmen never stopped caring for Leanne and the baby, a timely distraction that temporarily put the brakes on our squabbling and also served to keep Albert and her under my roof a while longer, giving me time to make amends. With Carmen less available, I had more time to look after Albert than ever before. He and I bowled a lot, hit a few G-rated movie matinees, watched our share of *Jeopardy* on the couch together after dinner, and took Max to the vet for his shots and a flea dipping one weekend. But I surfed alone, early mornings, usually before he was even out of bed. It would not be until later that year on a summer trip to a desolate Mexican beach break that Albert would finally screw up the courage to carry a board down to the water and paddle out again.

I didn't see my friend Mickey Conlin in the lineup on any more early mornings at the pier, so when I ran into him one night at the magazine rack in the used-book store on Main, I asked him where he'd been hiding out. He told me he'd always promised himself that if it ever stopped being fun, he'd hang it up. I felt guilty for dragging him back into the surf of late just to have a little company, and for getting him into that scrape with Carlito's bunch. Mick could only laugh at the notion that I was to blame. For him, the thrill had simply died, a long time ago. He'd always hated being an enforcer, but that was the role people saw him in. It was his legacy, and he no longer had the energy, or the interest, to live it down.

Miles Abernathy and Yves Pasqual were named in a lengthy federal indictment for conspiracy to commit tax fraud. Although Abernathy eventually resigned from the practice of law with disciplinary charges still pending, the state bar did not fare well in the PR department. The disciplinary review panel remained loyal to their fallen leader and found enough new faults to proclaim the agency to be structurally unsound. Bar opponents devoured the panel's three-hundred-page report, rejoicing at every nitpicking finding and renewing their cries for abolition. Some things never change.

I can only assume that Rudy Kirkmeyer stayed in Seattle with his daughter, Kimberley. He called a few days after the ISO hearing and said he wanted to help pay for any funeral arrangements I made. I told him to call me in a few more days when I knew more about how they would proceed. I never heard from him or his daughter again.

We buried Dale Bleeker in All Souls Cemetery in Long Beach a few days after Leanne and her new baby left the hospital. It was a pristine late-winter morning, the kind that native Californians take for granted. A feisty local storm had pushed through the night before, shaking the dead leaves from the trees and leaving the sky a screeching blue. The mass was sparsely attended. Mick Conlin made it solo. Georgette was a no-show, as were Dale's coworkers from the DA's office. A retired judge named Yablonski came and said some stirring words about the man he chose to remember, the legal warrior at the height of his powers. (Later, at the cemetery, Yablonski stepped over to me, the sour heat of Scotch on his breath, and admitted that he hadn't seen Dale in going on ten years.) I also spoke of the man as I'd first glimpsed him, but I added that Dale had died a meaningful death in the service of others. That latter part got to Leanne, she later told me. She regretted having pushed her father away for the better part of a year, said she never really understood that he'd lost his marriage by standing up for her in his too passive way, not until it was too late. Now that she wanted to fix things between them, he was gone. It isn't fair, she muttered on the way to the burial site, over and over. It goddamn isn't fair.

When we got home Carmen served coffee all around, but I'm not much on java and was of a mind to spike my cup with something smoother than nondairy creamer. Mick followed me to the liquor cabinet, then Kurt, then Albert, then Father Elden, the priest who'd said the mass. From this an impromptu wake evolved, something of a mocha milk-shake throw-down with Stoli and Kahlúa and Baileys Irish Cream doing all the heavy lifting. We toasted Dale as best we could by laughing and joking and fibbing and beating back the inevitability of death through a showing of sheer indifference until someone looked at his watch and said, Whoa, where did the afternoon go?

Later on, when Kurt and Leanne were holed up with the baby again and Carmen and Albert were crashed on the couch and everyone else had gone home, I put Max on the leash and slid my one-speed bike into the alley. Yesterday's storm had bumped up the surf overnight, and that glorious rumble was everywhere. But instead of the usual wave check down at the end of Porpoise Way, I pedaled west across town toward a tract of new homes I'd never before seen. Ten minutes later, I was walking the bike up the base of Spyglass Circle, cursing a steep pitch of blacktop that was more like San Francisco than westside Christianitos. When I reached the top I followed the street to the end. Big two-story residences ringed three-quarters of the bluff, but a prime lot to the left remained undeveloped. Still walking my bike, I made my way over to the lone open space and took in the view. Below me, the hillside dropped away precipitously. Clusters of ice plant trailed down from the curbside like stalactites, nothing but mud waiting farther down-hill. At the bottom was another street with a sidewalk and a young magnolia climbing out of a concrete planter—La Costa Drive.

I'd read the news clipping about Dale's arrest enough times to know what it said, but I removed it from my shirt pocket, unfolded it, and read it yet again. Max sat on the curb and rested, his big jaws open.

This was the spot where Dale had been when he'd made the colossal mistake of stepping out onto a tricky hillside to relieve himself, a career-ending move of the oddest sort. Observing the setup, one could say it was bad luck the way it all happened, for two schoolgirls to be walking by on La Costa at precisely the same moment that he slipped and fell, his member flapping in the breeze on the way down. But it was not merely chance misfortune that had brought Dale to this high place. He was buzzed, late afternoon on a weekday, not the first time a lawyer has done that but then, why here? He could have got shit-faced at a lot of other spots in town without putting his old Buick through the torture of chug-ging up Spyglass. The man I'd known briefly the past few weeks was more deliberate than that. There had to be a reason.

I sat down next to Max and stroked his awesome black head. The sea breeze was light onshore and flaccid, but it still carried a winter bite. In half an hour the reddening sun would skim the water and drop away. Zipping up my jacket, I admired the wide-angle view to the southwest that lay before me: six blocks of Northside real estate, from Fourth Street down to Main, a row of daunting beach homes along Ocean Avenue, and beyond their jag-ged roofline, a chunk of pier jutting into the blue expanse, big swells thrusting at its underside. And, wait—a sliver of pier parking lot, a few painted white lines, an outer fringe. Perhaps a favored spot for an outsider like Kurt to have parked his dilapidated van. God, it was a good half mile from here, but if Leanne was in that van, to Dale, the draw would be powerful. Yet it was too far to really see much, too removed? . . . .

Perhaps the distance told the story, how a lifetime of forward progress could be halted, undone, then roll in reverse, quite literally beating a retreat to higher, safer ground, a hollow place on the outer margins of being. It shook me to think how easily one could lose everything, and suddenly I wanted to be back on Porpoise Way again, in a narrow little beach house with a bathroom full of loose earrings and face-scrubs and henna conditioners and fancy hairbrushes and an upstairs toilet that didn't flush right because somebody forgot to read the sign and jiggle the handle, and a kitchen with yet another pile of dishes amassing in the sink and an empty box of my favorite cereal piled atop the trash that would need to be taken out before dinner, and a big dog barking and a tiny baby crying and a video no one was watching playing on and on in the living room.

I mounted my bike and guided Max around the handlebars, but before I put my feet to the pedals, I looked back a final time, studying the ocean's movements for a hint of what the morning might bring. White water slapped against the pier like silent shell bursts, but the Northside wave zone with its ubiquitous pack of surfers was hidden behind the big homes in the sand. Farther out, in deeper water, a dark lump of swell rolled through proud and unimpeded, a big bluebird gathering energy for its final push. Tomorrow, swell permitting, I might find an hour to slip out there beyond the others, to sit and rest and sort my thoughts and say a small prayer for the future, and wait, eyes scanning every shift and pulse and undulation, muscles twitching at the sea's first whisper of a new beginning.